Glider
Colin Hooker-Haring
All Rights Reserved.
Copyright © 2025 Colin Hooker-Haring
v3.0

This is a work of fiction. Names, characters, businesses, places, events, locales, and incidents are either the products of the author's imagination or used in a fictitious manner. Any resemblance to actual persons, living or dead, or actual events is purely coincidental.

The opinions expressed in this manuscript are solely the opinions of the author and do not represent the opinions or thoughts of the publisher. The author has represented and warranted full ownership and/or legal right to publish all the materials in this book.

This book may not be reproduced, transmitted, or stored in whole or in part by any means, including graphic, electronic, or mechanical without the express written consent of the publisher except in the case of brief quotations embodied in critical articles and reviews.

Outskirts Press, Inc.
http://www.outskirtspress.com

ISBN: 978-1-9772-7502-8

Cover Photo © 2025 Baris Sehri. All rights reserved - used with permission.

Outskirts Press and the "OP" logo are trademarks belonging to Outskirts Press, Inc.

PRINTED IN THE UNITED STATES OF AMERICA

Sunday

1

Their shins were flecked with mud, like the bikes beside them. A breeze from the valley rolled up the hill and through their hair, a relief from the summer heat.

"Last day of summer, dude," said Greg.

Virg turned to see Greg digging some dirt from his ear.

"Not looking forward to tomorrow," he replied.

"I just wish something would happen."

"I think you have those freezey squeeze pops in your outside fridge," said Virg.

"No, like, something *big*," said Greg. He was looking down the hillside into the creek. Then he scanned past the corn stumps and into the open sky.

"Well, no more gardening for your mom," said Virg. "That's something to look forward to. Maybe she'll take me on for some *hedge trimming*." He lazily hung his tongue out, closed one eye, and pumped his pelvis in the air once—too hot for more effort.

Greg tried to stifle a laugh but relented. He lay back in the dirt with his hands behind his head and closed his eyes. Virg mirrored. The sun shone through their lids and danced an orange blanket of muted psychedelics into their minds.

They fell into a comfortable, brotherly silence. A pair of connected dragonflies buzzed past and stopped on a twig yards away. Curiosity jolted the boys. They wrapped their elbows around their knees and leaned in. The buzzing stopped.

"I must have you in complete silence," said Virg. The dragonflies jumped vertically, resuming their buzzing. "... or like, however you want it."

"That's my man," joked Greg.

The dragonflies stole away down the valley toward the creek. Their buzzing floated away with them. A barren cornfield stretched its arms on both sides of the boys, holding the buzzing close by.

"Dude?" urged Greg.

"I *am* one," said Virg.

"Dude?" Greg looked back and forth around the fields, then down to the creek, growing furtive. "You hear that?"

"Dragonfly sex?" said Virg. "Sure."

"You see 'em?" Greg motioned down to the creek. The dragonflies had moved on. Somewhere up or down the creek. Out of sight. Definitely out of earshot. Yet, the buzzing still whined.

Virg grabbed a handful of dirt beside him and chucked it aimlessly toward the creek, hoping to scare the dragonflies into view. Nothing moved.

"Must've flown away."

"I still hear 'em," said Greg.

Virg stood up and looked behind them, turned, and skipped down the hill to the creek. When he turned back toward Greg, his eyes crept past his friend and into the sky. He smiled.

"Whatchu got?" asked Greg.

"Some little plane. Check it out," said Virg.

Greg loped down and plunged both feet into the creek, gaining slight relief from the heat. He turned to look up the hill and saw something small in the air above the horizon. "How big you think it is?"

"Well, it's not a 747, right?" said Virg.

"It's like a personal plane or something," said Greg.

The image of the plane grew in the sky quickly. As the humming whined on, it was losing its altitude fast. The boys froze as they realized they weren't watching a nifty flight. They were about to witness the crash of a plane. Both boys tracked the craft across the sky as it pitched and plunged into the dirt on the other side of the creek. Rocks and dirt exploded, surrounding the impact as the plane ground a long gash across the field. Greg ducked to cover his head, and his knees plunged into the cold creek. Virg pressed himself into the creek bank and turned his eyes to the dirt cloud hanging in the air, cradling the plane.

Greg looked at Virg for confirmation, his heart pounding. Virg's mouth hung open, his gaze directed at the aircraft.

"Can we . . . ?" said Greg.

"Not yet. Sometimes things explode," warned Virg.

"Let's get my dad," said Greg.

"Naw, man. If someone's in there, we shouldn't leave him," said Virg.

Greg looked at his friend and clocked the fear in his eyes. He turned back to the plane, jumped out of the creek, and took off running toward the crash.

"Wait! Explosions, dude!" yelled Virg, running after him.

They circled the craft, taking in its novelty. It was a brown eggshell color. Smooth and completely intact, save for a bent propeller on its nose. It was about twelve feet long. They peered through the window to see a man waving at them. He smiled and pushed with both hands on the glass, popping it free from the plane's body.

"Hi," said the man. He was tall and broad. He wore wraparound sunglasses, a black, long-sleeved shirt, and jeans with a sweaty blue bandana tied around his neck. His greyish hair was cropped short, and his stubble was fresh.

"You okay?" asked Greg.

"Yeah. I bumped my knees, but nothing bad. You guys here to help?" he asked.

"Yeah, before it explodes!" yelled Virg.

The man laughed and wiped his brow with his sleeve. "It's a glider. Not much that can explode in this thing."

"Why'd you land it here?" asked Virg.

"I got caught in a wind current, and it blew me down here from . . ." he paused and looked back into the sky, "the Boston area," he answered.

Greg's eyes went wide. "You're in Pennsylvania."

"Drifted a bit too far, I'd say," said the man. "This looked like as good a place as any to end my trip."

Virg turned to Greg. "Wanna get your dad or something?"

"I could try to ask him, but he has Pete over to watch the Phillies game," said Greg.

"In a minute," said the man. "We oughta get this off the field, right? How 'bout down there by the creek?" He pointed down the hill toward the small road bridge.

"Yeah, so no one takes it!" said Virg.

When the man moved his shoulders toward the glider, the boys saw just how broad and dense the man's muscles were. He held the propeller end over his shoulder as the boys supported the tail and wings. He naturally held his side much higher than they could. Cautiously, they carried the glider down the creek bank. Their shoes were pleading to plant themselves in the mucky creek's bottom. Each step close to the creek got deeper and muddier. Flies guarding the creek feasted on all three of them as they led their cargo under the bridge.

"Just here will do," said the man.

They set it down on a dry patch of riverbed that stuck its paunch out from the bank, shaded by the road above. "Nice 'n' dark. Doubt anyone'll see it here."

"Creek stole my shoe back there. Doubt anyone will find *that*," muttered Greg.

"It's right here, dude." Virg popped up from the creek's scrub grasses a few yards away with the mucky shoe in his hand.

They scurried back up the bank. Greg's muddy shoe squeaked every step up the brim like a poor fiddler's hornpipe. The man looked up and down the tiny abutments on which the bridge held the road. No glider in sight.

"So, any pay phones around here?" asked the man.

"Well, the post office probably has a phone you can use," offered Virg. "Just down at the corner, maybe a quarter mile away." Virg pointed down the road past a rusted Airstream trailer in a dirt driveway. Beyond that and a rim of bushes, an American flagpole rose next to the post office. The flag was peeking just above the trees next to it.

The man saw the flag that Virg was pointing at.

"Good enough," said the man. He walked down the road without turning back for receipt of any plan. His gait was broad and unapologetic. His eyes were desperate.

2

Virg and Greg stood watching the man walk down the road. They gawked as if an astronaut had enlisted them on his impending voyage. He walked until he turned the corner and walked out of sight. Greg looked at Virg with a sense of wonder.

"To the Batmobile!" yelled Virg as he ran up the road toward their bikes.

"You think he'll let us fly it?" asked Greg as he ran to lift his ride.

"Definitely. We're saving his life," said Virg.

"Sure doesn't look like he needs saving. He's a pretty big dude."

"Maybe he could use a damsel to save. That's where you come in," said Virg. He and Greg both laughed. They rolled their bikes up the hill to a crest near the road.

"Turn left to spy on big man, turn right to get your dad," offered Virg. He was looking down the road toward the post office, hoping to get some action with the new guy.

"If we're helping, let's get my dad," Greg suggested.

"Damn. Knew it," said Virg. They hopped on their saddles and pumped their pedals as they sailed down the hill.

3

The big man turned up the road. As he caught sight of the post office, he quickened his pace. The building looked like an old Nantucket shingled number converted into a mail shack. His pulse quickened as his plan took shape. "Calm down, walk in, just ask for the phone," he muttered to himself as he saw the door and reached for the knob. About seventy-five little combination locks adorned the wall on his right. The little room on the other side of the door was cozy and tidy. The counter ahead had some nice areas of wear. It looked like neighbors had rubbed through the red paint while resting their elbows. Perhaps they'd asked how much it would cost to mail a birthday card to Colorado.

Shuffling up to the counter, he put his elbows in those worn spots and looked around the mailroom. He didn't see anyone but ventured a few inquisitive hellos. He heard a slight echo in the room beyond the counter. It was almost empty.

"Need a stamp?"

The voice caught Hutch off guard. A man, standing about four feet tall, ambled around a shelf. Then he stepped up a low set of stairs to come eye-to-eye with the big man.

"Thought the place was empty. Just came for the phone," blurted the big man.

"Don't recognize you," retorted the mail clerk. "I'm David." He extended his arm across the counter, almost poking the big man in the chest.

"Hutch," said the big man as he backed away to grasp the tiny hand in his own. He shook twice and managed to smile with his mouth closed. His eyes didn't agree. They were wild.

"It's nice to meet you. You just moved here?" said David.

"Had an accident. Won't be here long. I just wanted to call the wife to see how much trouble I'm in," offered Hutch.

"I got a phone but can't let anyone behind the counter. Got regulations to keep," said David.

"Does the cord reach around past the counter?"

"Alas, friend, it does not. Want to open a post office box?" David smiled and pulled out a form.

"Listen, I'm not going home tonight. I'm stuck here. I just need some help," said Hutch.

"I see," he paused. "I'll give her a call if you need to check in. Heck, I'll call a car for you too if you need one . . ."

Hutch reached across the counter and grabbed David by the pocket of his shirt, pulling him up so his feet dangled behind him, his belly pressed into the little wooden wall. He felt Hutch's stale breath on his lips. His eyes steeled, Hutch's brow was knit with salt and little quivers.

"It's urgent. And if you can't help, I'll help myself."

4

Virg opened the front door without knocking and followed the sounds of baseball bats cracking. Reaching the living room, he found Greg's dad, Tim, and his friend Pete frozen under the spell of announcers' voices—each man flanked by empty beer cans.

"Just in time for the seventh-inning stretch." Tim turned to find Virg and Greg looking at the TV. His smile evaporated as he saw their state. "Jesus, you can't remove your shoes before hitting the carpet? Good thing school starts tomorrow."

Greg looked down at his shoe and his bare, muddy foot. "I took off the bad one," he said, pleased with himself.

Virg ignored the dig. "Hey, there's a guy who crashed a glider in the field. Do you think you can swing the truck around to help him?"

"Yeah, he's not hurt, but the glider's not in great shape," added Greg.

"Eh, what do you say, Mr. Beer? Helpey or relaxey?" Pete asked the can in his hand. "We'll give one of your cousins to him, maybe," he said as he stared into the can's empty hole. Pete got up to get another can from the minifridge behind his chair.

"Well, if he's crashed, he'll be stuck for a while, yeah? Pete and I can give him a hand after the Phills blow this one," said Tim as he turned to look at Greg. "Just in the field behind the creek?" He reached up to the corner of his mustache and rolled it between his fingers.

"Yep, we put the glider under the bridge," said Virg.

"Okay, just let us enjoy the Phills snatching defeat from the jaws of victory," said Pete. "Oh, and maybe get another shoe, Gregory. What happened to it?"

"Creek sucked it off me. Ritual sacrifice to the gods of summer. Maybe we won't have to go to school if they accept my offering," said Greg.

Pete chuckled. "I, as their leader, report that we do not accept. Your offering must include a playoff berth for our crappy team."

"We're screwed," said Virg.

They went out the back door to collect their bikes. Greg opened the garage door and grabbed an old pair of replacement sneakers. "Let's go back to the glider. I wanna learn how to fly it." He took the dried, muddy shoe and slapped its sole against the garage door's frame.

"Yeah, right. You'd need more than one day to learn. Let's quit school and become pilots," said Virg.

"I think we have to, like, get extra school for that," said Greg.

"Free, private school. Let's just ask big dude to teach us if we help him," said Virg.

Greg tied his shoes and wiped some dirt off his shins. They mounted their bikes and pointed their bars toward the sun. As they careened down the alley toward the bridge where the glider lay, Virg lifted his arms up like wings and held the bars steady with his knees pinching the stem.

5

They skidded to a stop in the gulley below the bridge and cast their bikes aside. The balmy wind was picking up as the sun was tumbling low. The high grasses beside the creek were dancing. Whitecaps picked the skin of the creek's cold pockets. Making their way down to the creek bed, the boys wanted another look at their salvaged glider. Turning to face the shadows under the bridge, they stood wide-eyed and puzzled.

"So much for your lessons," said Greg. The glider was gone. Wind groaned through the bridge's empty mouth.

"Uh, well, it's close by or something, right? That guy was big, but not big enough to move it by himself." Virg stared through the bridge to the corn stumps in the field beyond. "He *needed* our help, *right?*"

"Maybe not. Did he drag it? There must be ruts in the mud where he pulled." Greg walked further into the shadows beneath the bridge.

"Go check the other side of the bank. I'll stick on this side and see if he dragged it further down."

"Hey, meet back here before sunset, right?" asked Greg. He pinched at an itch on his elbow and drew back blood under his fingernails. "Big sucker never saw it coming." He flicked the smashed mosquito corpse into the grass.

"I'll see you soon. There's only so many places it could be," said Virg.

They walked in different directions. Greg upstream, under the bridge; Virg downstream into the sunset, following the current. Their pulses quickened with the thrill of the chase. Something big was happening, and the boys were hunting for it.

6

He sat behind a veil of tall grass. As he looked from high on the hill, the creek bubbled far beneath him. He was sitting in the same spot where the boys lay and first heard his glider. The two boys were plodding along the creek banks in different directions. They mostly looked down at the banks but would steal glances up into the expanses of fields and the trees surrounding them—checking for tire tracks. Hutch kept still and low.

The boys had turned and began wandering back to the bridge. Virg skipped pebbles into the creek as Greg ran up the bank and stuttered back down to the water like a sandpiper. A hawk screamed from the trees just behind Hutch. Both boys paused to look up at the source of the sound.

Hutch felt their gazes scratch back and forth over him. He exhaled and pressed himself into the grass. Their heads whipped back to the road above the bridge when a truck blared its horn and came to a stop. The boys ran over to meet it and talked to two men inside through the window. Virg raised his arms, palms facing up, shrugging his shoulders.

Hutch heard the driver yell, "You lost, we lost," joking with a smile on his face. "Don't be late! School tomorrow," the man yelled as the truck drove away. The boys sat next to their bikes and looked into the creek, talking, laughing, and stretching the day as far as it could bend. They hugged when the sun was long gone and the sky held a pale blue. The skeletons of their bikes lifted off the dirt, and they held them between their legs as they rued the fate of the next day—the time lines and the order. They rode up to the street and rolled back toward their homes.

Hutch stood up in the half-light and turned to the trees behind him. He paced into the thicker darkness beneath the canopy and searched for broken twigs and dry branches. The air between the trees held the warm smell of sap and the sharpness of pine needles. Hutch took a deep breath and unclenched his jaw. Pressing his fist into his other palm, he snapped the little nitrogen bubbles in his knuckles and sighed.

He turned to find a long, bare blue spruce branch—good and dry. Next to it sat a small fox, staring at him. The fox's dusty grey coat basked in the soft mineral light of the sky. The orange-furred rim on her neck highlighted her focus on Hutch. They stared at each other for a few moments, each searching for the other's scent past the crispy needles blanketing the forest bed. A pointy ear on the fox rotated to tune in the visitor in her little radio.

Hutch squatted down and sniffed. "Just visiting. That okay?"

The little grey tail flicked up once and settled silently behind her. Satisfied, the fox's ears fluttered and turned her around to lurk toward the grasses near the creek. Hutch watched her slip into the grass and whisper away.

He picked up the branch and a few twigs. Carrying them back under the bridge, he made two piles. After several trips, he set the little twigs into an inverted cone. Pulling the lint from his pocket, he twisted it into a wick and wrinkled it between some of the twigs. He pulled out his lighter and lit a cigarette. Best to wait until the sun had left him far behind before he let his kindling burn.

One opening under the bridge held the last murmur of light, and the other held an inky blackness above the grasses. He rose with the cigarette in his mouth and stepped over to where the glider was stowed. His hand rose and softly thumped the hull of his craft.

"Attagirl," he said.

The craft didn't catch any of the light from the ember in his mouth or the sky behind it. It was hidden in the same place they'd left it, out of focus to anyone looking for it. He waved his hand over it twice and dragged his index nail down his thumb into his palm. The glider condensed in the darkness. He sat and pressed his back against a bridge support, pulling on his cigarette and closing his eyes. It was going to be a long night.

7

The bike under Virg peeled down his driveway. He squeezed his brakes hard and leaned into the drift as the bike came to a screeching halt. Pebbles peppered the garage door. "Safe," he muttered to himself and dropped his bike. He opened his front door to the sharp garlic scent of his dad's pesto.

"Hi, Mom!" he said as he scurried past. "Smells great, Dad. How long?"

"Five minutes. Hey, how'd the last day of freedom feel? I made pesto for your death-row meal," said his dad.

"Nice rhyme. You'll never believe what happened. This guy crashed his glider into the cornfield, and we helped him move it, but then he disappeared. Isn't that wild?"

"He disappeared in front of your eyes? Like, evaporated?"

"No, we told him to use the phone at the post office, but he never returned. But get this . . . His glider disappeared too. And it was big enough that he needed our help to move it. We put it under the bridge. Greg's dad and Pete brought the truck, but nothing was there when they showed up. Pretty weird, right?"

"So, you don't know where he is now?" asked Virg's dad.

"No."

"And where's he staying?" asked Virg's mom, Rose.

"I don't know, Mom. Maybe he got the glider working again and flew back home," answered Virg.

"How far away is home? Maybe he got a relative to tow him out," said his dad.

"He said he hit a wind current near Boston and ended up here."

"Think he has relatives here?" said Virg's dad.

"He didn't know where he was. We told him Pennsylvania," said Virg.

"Well, I hope somebody found him," Rose said, rolling her ginger red hair behind her ear. "Maybe Pete came back and helped him out after sunset. I'd hate to see a guy wandering around a crash site in my field after dark," she said.

"Rose, can you set out utensils? Dinner's almost ready," said Virg's dad.

She set her newspaper on the arm of her chair and headed toward the kitchen. Her fingers slid into Virg's hair, and she stopped moving. She looked down at his head and shook some of the dirt and salt out of his mane. Noticing the dirt on his outfit, she leaned down.

Rose whispered, "Hey, grab a sock and scrub some of the dirt off your shins before dinner. Thanks." She kissed his head, turned, and sneezed. "Got some good pollen on you too."

"Be right back," said Virg.

"Ooh, wait. Wanna see a magic trick?" said Rose.

"Yeah!"

She took a small paper airplane from her pocket and displayed it in her left hand. Her hand clasped around it, and she raised her right arm above her head. She slapped her hands together and opened them both. The plane was gone.

"Wow! How'd you do that?" said Virg.

"Not finished," she responded.

She closed her left hand again and peeled her index finger down her thumb into her palm. When she opened her hand, the plane was sitting in her hand.

"Awesome! How'd you do that?" said Virg.

"Magic." She smiled, and a sparkle passed through the corner of her eye.

8

Virg tossed and turned in his bed. The expanse of possibilities the new school year promised, the unsolved mystery of the man and his glider made no room for sleep in his mind. He breathed deeply and exhaled deliberately, trying to calm his nerves. He did this again and again. Inhale, exhale. He was grateful that something had happened on his last day of summer—grateful for the mystery, the adventure. He smiled and drifted off for a time.

He opened his eyes as the moonlight spilled onto his pillow. He pulled the covers off and silently set his feet on the floor. Some feeling drew him to his window in bare feet. He hunched over to look out his window toward the bridge. Through the trees and beyond the field behind his house, a small fire threw waves of orange glow onto the creek banks and the bridge's ribs.

He's there, thought Virg.

The hair on his arms stood straight on its ends. The moonlight was so strong that it would've drowned the orange flickers, but he knew where to look. He had no idea how long he stayed trained on those waves of color under the bridge, hoping for a shadow or a silhouette breaking the crest of the creek banks.

The bridge was mesmerizing. He was drooling at the idea of catching sight of the pilot. In an instant, the fire went out. No waves of orange, no flickers. It didn't die out slowly. It just doused.

Virg examined the field. He peered through the trees, everything visible in perfect blue moonlight. He scanned for movement and found himself crouching lower in the window. His gaze shifted from the creek to his yard and his fence line. He sensed the shadows tickling the moonlight. A small shadow pierced his crystal blue yard.

The fence corner drew his attention. A dark contour snuck along the fence close to the ground. It dipped into the moonlight and revealed itself to be a small fox. She blended into the grey moonlight. An orange rim on its neck caught Virg's eye. Her shoulders softened for a moment, and her eyes relaxed. The fox sniffed a bush and made its way underneath the sprigs. A tree just beyond the fence bent in a gust of wind. Its shadow flickered beneath it as the moon stabbed through its branches.

Another gust pushed the shadows away to reveal a still, pale face. It peered just over the fence. Virg could see the white hair whipping in the wind. The shadows reclaimed the face for a moment. Another strong gust let the moon display a face looking directly into his window. The eyes held Virg. He couldn't make out the face, couldn't see his eyes. Was it looking at him? Was the moonlight too strong to let his gaze through the window? He felt his throat clutch. Suddenly, he jumped away from the window and put his back on the wall beneath it. Virg slowly sucked in a breath and pushed it out. He jumped back up into the window and looked down under the tree.

Nothing. The face had vanished just like the fire under the bridge. Virg adjusted his angle to look sideways at the house next door at the end of the fence. He saw Greg's stricken face in the window turn and stare at him. Greg's mouth was open. His eyes were wide.

MONDAY

9

Virg's morning hadn't arrived yet. Dark blue clouds held the moonbeams through the wind currents. The slow movements in the sky let Virg's mind shuffle through his options. He stared out the window without the ground in view. Virg almost expected the man with the glider to visit his window. That guy was close already.

"Did he move that quick? . . . Is he after me or Greg? . . ." he whispered to himself. Still asking himself questions without speaking, his heart began rapping against his ribs.

He watched the moon shift slowly. "If he didn't visit the window, he could visit my bedroom door . . . that pilot moved so quickly from the creek to my fence. How did he do that?" he let out of his mouth.

No answers appeared. He began to count each of his breaths. They were thick, and he slowed the pace down. After thousands of breaths, he saw the orange hue of the morning sun. When rays burst over the horizon, Virg ran to the bathroom and peed for a long, long time. When he finished, his breathing opened wider. His heart slowed down. He washed his hands and stared at his darkened skin beneath his eye rims in the mirror. *I'm okay*, he thought. *I made it to morning. What about Greg?*

Virg closed his front door and slung his backpack over his shoulder. He hiked up the alleyway for two minutes before he saw Greg standing still at the bus stop. Dirt and stones crunched. No other sounds spread out. As he walked up the alley, Greg hadn't moved at all. He just faced the road with his head down, holding his backpack straps.

"Greg," Virg spoke from about twelve feet behind, "did you see the guy last night?"

Greg said nothing. Virg sped up. He curled around in front of Greg and took in his disposition. Greg looked to be holding some secret.

"You did, right? I saw you with your—" said Virg.

"He saw me," whispered Greg. He didn't move his face to look at Virg. He kept staring at the road. "He looked into my eyes. I can't even explain what I felt."

He paused for a moment and looked up into Virg's eyes. "I know why he's here. I know what he wants. I know why he left," said Greg, ". . . and I don't feel safe."

"Dude! I saw him too! And I saw you! You looked freaked out. I mean, I was too. But why did he disappear? Why does he know where we were?" said Virg. "I didn't even sleep, dude. Did you sleep? You look fine. Just chill." Virg noticed that Greg still didn't move.

"Wait, did he talk to you?" asked Virg. He patted Greg's shoulders and the back of his hair. When he touched Greg's neck, the icy feeling spooked him. "Greg, did you sleep? Your skin is cold!"

"I slept. I'm not tired. I'm just freaked out, dude," said Greg.

"There's a bus coming soon. You wanna go to Learn Zone, or you want to find the dude who's definitely still here?" asked Virg.

"I'm thinking about so much right now, I don't know if I can even take notes."

Virg looked up and down the road. He grabbed Greg's arm and pulled him into the bushes by the alleyway. They crouched underneath the sticky brambles. "OK, dude. Something happened. You talk to me, I'll write it down. We can share that with the school, right? There's got to be some freaking essay we have to write. 'Wha' Happen When Summer Squeeze Out . . .' some crappy review of no-learn time."

"Get more ink, pal. I learned too much last night," said Greg.

"All right, let's hit the hillside to see who's looking for us—pilot or angry parent," said Virg. He turned his head around to look at the nearby forest line. He remembered the path that would lead back around their houses over to the creek and the cornfields. He just hoped no one would find them running away from the bus. He looked at Greg and shook his head toward the trees.

"Let's go," said Virg.

They ran into the forest to block their movement from adult perception, passing through the morning shadows under branch arms full of leaves. They curled around to the hillside that they lay on the day before. Keeping within the trees, they stared at the ground of their walks on that previous day. Greg and Virg sat down within the rows of trees behind the tall grass. The hill, the creek, the bridge—everything looked the same as the previous day. They looked down at where the plane had grounded into the empty cornfield. There was no shape, no grind, and no proof of the aircraft skidding.

Virg and Greg looked at each other.

"He took it. He took that skid," said Greg. "I'll show you that it's not gone."

Greg started to stand up. Virg's hand grabbed the back of Greg's shirt and pulled him back down on his knees.

"Hang on, dude. Everyone will see us in the empty field. Maybe later, but everyone's commuting right now. Just wait," said Virg.

Greg sighed and crossed his legs.

"I have a notebook. I didn't sleep," said Virg. He reached into his backpack to pull out a notebook and pen. "Tell me everything that you dreamed last night."

10

Virg scribbled down each piece of the shared dream from Greg's skull. It felt like the pilot had poured a barrel of visions into Greg's sleep. It didn't even make sense—tiny boy pacing around a campground, making weird, repetitive gestures with his hands. One fact made sense—he can hide. He can hide himself. He can hide objects. That was frightening.

"Did you get any of this when you were awake?" asked Virg. "I mean, I saw you freak out. Your eyes were as wide as your mouth."

"I mean, I don't remember. I just remember the endless dreams. I mean . . . I guess I got a lot of images, *BANG. BANG. BANG.*" Greg made gestures of lights bursting at his face. "But I feel like I fell asleep right away," he said.

"It's wild, dude. I didn't sleep at all. Did you see his face?" asked Virg.

"Yeah, man . . . It didn't look the same. But it was his face," said Greg. "It looked like the moon. I mean, it's normal size, but the moon was so bright. Maybe it was just reflection, but that's all I saw."

Virg slapped his notebook closed and pushed his hands into his hair.

"I don't get it, man," said Virg. "We had completely different nights. Sucking on different flavors!"

"Quiet!" Greg whispered loudly.

He stared over Virg's shoulder toward the road. He pushed him down even farther into the tall grass. A woman paced along the side of the road. She came upon the field and stared into the ground. She stopped and closed her eyes, then took a deep breath. She walked away from the road, down the concrete bridge arms that reached into the creek. She removed her shoes and rolled her pants up to her knees when she set foot near the water. Then she walked straight under the bridge and disappeared.

"You think that's the pilot with a new hairdo?" asked Virg.

"It's a fucking woman, dunce," said Greg. "You think that he's changing?"

"Nah, she walked differently. I mean, my mom walks that way," answered Virg.

"You tell her about the plane we put in there?" asked Greg.

"Duh, I pretty much told them everything. But they know that it disappeared. I told them about the hike back and forth. I don't think she'll find it if we couldn't," said Virg. "Besides," he looked away from the bridge and back at Greg, "... *Why* is she looking for it?"

"If that's your mom, should we go down there and see what she's doing? Maybe she knows something that we don't. Did she see the huge pilot dude last night? I know he was right next to your house," said Greg.

"No idea. Damn," said Virg. "What would she be doing down there?"

Virg shoved his hands through his hair as he bent his gaze down into the grass. He felt trapped already. *Does Mom know that we're not at school? Does she know about the glider?* "I need to see what's going on down there," he whispered to Greg.

"Me too, but you held me back, dirt hole," said Greg.

"I have to see what's going on," said Virg. "It's been a few minutes now, and I didn't see her leave. Is she injured? Or did she fall in some kinda creek suck? I have no idea, dude."

"We can go to the creek cradle part in the forest. Then crouch through the creek close enough to see her from the field. We're low enough that the weeds and Liatris Stars will cover us," said Greg.

"Jesus, you a gardener?" asked Virg.

"I just know what the heck is here," Greg replied.

"Don't let me get stung, Grandpa," said Virg. He got up low, bent over, and jacked his thumb near his butt. "I'll pass by, but don't hit me with a blazing star."

"You know what it is too, dick," retorted Greg.

They hiked about ten feet behind the weeded forest line not to be seen. They could still see the bridge, even as they arrived at the creek between trees. Greg slipped off his shoes and shoved them in his backpack. Virg rolled his pants up around his knees. They slipped down into the creek, hunched over, and kept their eyes fixed on the bridge. The river's current muted the sound of each step. Nothing was moving around the bridge. When they got about thirty feet away, their gazes went straight through the bridge to the sky and field on the other side. There was nothing in there. Virg's mom was missing.

11

A wide angle of shade fell from the bridge's shoulders. The shadow slant spread over the creek and the hillsides leading up to the bridge's ends. It held right over Rose and Hutch. They sat on the grass near the side of the bridge that Virg and Greg hadn't seen—at least not yet.

"It's weird that you're here. How'd you find me?" said Rose.

"I didn't mean to find you. I just meant to get out of there," said Hutch. "Have you seen the camp? . . . I mean, I guess you haven't even thought about it."

Rose said nothing.

"I don't mean to scare you, but the whole feeling has changed there. No one's near the town. Mata moved the camp to Maine. Northern Maine . . . There's no roads," said Hutch.

"What?!" Rose loudly responded. She caught her tone and lowered her voice. "Virg told me you came from Boston."

"Yeah, that was like fifteen years ago. Well, we've been in Maine for about twelve. I think that Mata needed fewer distractions. And his students are more focused. That's turned into an issue. Very alone, a bit focused, but he pushes. There's no one to calm him down. I sucked at it. I mean, it became a fight," said Hutch.

Hutch dropped his forehead into his left hand. His elbows rested on his knees. He knew the danger of giving out all the facts of his turnup. He turned his head to watch Rose's reaction. She stared into the creek as her eyelids twitched a bit. She seemed to be lost in thought.

Hutch took a deep breath. "Maybe you should go. I gotta fix this glider. I'm sorry that I contacted you last night. I saw your kid, but I linked with you. I heard your thoughts. I'm sorry," said Hutch.

Rose didn't react at all. She kept her stare into the creek. A slight breeze opened up the waiting moment.

Hutch broke the silence. "If you saw Mata now . . . I just tried to get out." He stopped for a moment and almost whispered. "When I found you through your son, I just, I thought it was right."

The silence returned. Rose took a slow breath and touched Hutch's broad shoulder. He turned, and her earthly-purple eyes stared deep into him. "How bad is he?" asked Rose. "Anyone injured?"

Hutch kept her gaze. He didn't say anything. Suddenly, he noticed some movement to his right in the corner of his eye. He whipped his head around to see two small boys hiking the creek banks. They passed under the curve of the metal bridge above them and looked up the other side of the hill. Then they turned and looked right into, just above, and right past Hutch and Rose.

"Did you conceal us?" asked Hutch. His voice was as quiet as a silent breath.

"Did you see my hand when you sat down?" said Rose. She repeated a slow hand wave over the boys and dragged her thumbnail into her palm. "I mean, you did that to your glider, right?"

"And my fire last night," said Hutch, in a normal volume. He wiped his brow.

They turned their heads to see Virg hiking up the other side of the creek. Their eyes dropped straight down to see Greg standing beneath them. He stared directly into their area. A confused look crept into his eyes. His brows angled tightly. He opened his mouth and flicked his jaw down to open his ear canals. His eyes flickered back and forth across Hutch and Rose. He appeared to have heard something.

"Virg . . . Did you hear that?" asked Greg. His eyes kept the two adults in stillness. He turned to face Virg. "I heard someone."

Greg ran up the hillside toward the road. He crouched beneath the bridge railing to hide from traffic. The road was empty, as was the field surrounding him.

"He heard us," whispered Hutch in Rose's ear. Greg missed kicking Hutch in the hip by about four inches when hustling past.

Rose slapped her hand over his lips and held his jaw. She pulled his eyes to hers and mouthed the words "Shut up" without making any sounds. Greg paced backward away from the road and walked into the shadows just above Rose and Hutch. He treaded just behind them into the grass, barely a foot from Rose's left shoulder.

"Hey!" yelled Virg. He was in the middle of a tall set of cattails on the far side of the creek. "I found the glider pilot's wood ashes from last night!" Greg's head spun away from the road to hit Virg.

Greg turned away from the road and toward the bridge shadow beneath him. He began to run immediately, just a foot above Rose and Hutch. They had no time to react. His left foot quickly caught Rose's sweatshirt pocket and ripped it away from her torso. Greg tumbled and spun over the hill grass into the creek. He splashed and stood up as quickly as possible.

"What the heck was that? I thought you were a baseball player," said Virg. "You never tripped at first base on a double."

Greg turned from Virg to look at the hillside. "There was something that held my foot for a second. Gripped my toe." Creek water flowed and dripped off of him. He slowly paced toward Rose and Hutch. He felt pulled back into their vibe.

"You gotta trip again?" asked Virg. He walked back into the water, leaving the wood fire scraps and cattails behind him. He watched Greg's attraction to the hillside.

"I heard a little rip sound. You see anything ripped?" Greg asked Virg.

Rose felt that Greg was looking straight into her eyes. She stood up, grabbed Hutch's shirt, and pulled him up onto his legs.

In his ear, she whispered, "He feels us."

She wrapped her hand around his arm. "Follow me."

Holding Hutch's arm, she pulled him up to the road. She looked both ways and quickly pulled him across. Her hand pulled his elbow past the road and back down the hillside toward the creek. She pushed Hutch against the stonewall that held the bridge above them. Her index finger dragged her nail down Hutch's palm and then her own.

"Let's meet them again," said Rose. She walked into the shadows, under the bridge, and toward the kids. Hutch turned and followed slowly behind her.

Hutch took two steps and then held still. "Not me!" he whispered loudly. "They have questions, I'm sure." He dragged his nail down his palm and laid his back against the bridge wall. The moment he touched the bricks, he disappeared.

Rose didn't look at him. She just kept walking under the bridge toward the kids.

"Hey! You guys miss the bus?" she yelled from thirty feet away under the shade.

"Mom!" yelled Virg. "We thought that we saw you, but you disappeared! Where'd you go?"

Greg still stood on the hillside with the sun's rays behind him. "We thought you were here," he said.

"Just checking all the spots where that glider could have been," said Rose. "I heard what you said last night. Just seeing if the story is real or imagined." She looked back and forth at Virg and Greg. "You're pretty good at summer stories." Then she smiled. "Looks like you're still making some."

Greg slowly walked down the hill back to the water bank while she spoke. His glance crawled all over her. "How long have you looked for the glider?" he asked. His view scanned for any little odd quirk. A little breeze flowed under the bridge from behind Rose. The gust grabbed her sweatshirt. Her right pocket flipped a snapped corner against her zipper a few times. Greg made the connection and stepped closer to her.

"You ripped that? I heard a rip just a couple of minutes ago," said Greg as he pointed to her pocket.

Rose looked down at her pocket. "Yikes, that's new," she said. She faked a surprised look and raised her arms. "I can fix this when we get back ... from *school*. Let's head over to our car. You guys are still in the first period. Not a huge deal, but don't tell Dad. He's already at work." She smiled and wrapped her arm around Virg's shoulders.

Greg didn't move. "I heard you rip that. Where were you? I thought

I heard you talking before that." Greg's eyebrows pressed down, and his heart began to pound. "I don't want to go to school. I have enough to think about, and it's only getting weirder!"

"Tell me what you're worried about on the way to school. I'll hang out in the parking lot if you want to talk." She grabbed Greg's shoulder with her other arm. Her light hike up the hill pulled them in a friendly fashion. "Tell me why you stayed back from school. I'll tell you everything I know too."

They headed down the road as Hutch watched them from the bridge. "Don't bring me up," he whispered.

A light sound slid its way into Greg's ear. He turned to look at the bridge and saw nothing . . . but he felt another presence.

12

Greg and Virg both crawled into Rose's station wagon. Greg's eyes lowered to the dirty plastic floor in the car. He was exhausted. It was a long night, and he'd been running and creeping around all morning. He peeked over at Virg and saw him touch his index finger to his lips, gesturing, *Don't say anything*.

"You guys still trying to enjoy summer? I know that it's technically not over yet," said Rose with a smile.

"Eh, the first day is never good at school. It's just an overview of our courses. Never any discussion of existence or involvement in our summer. Sometimes an essay . . ." said Virg.

"Greg, you have any school disappointments?"

"Nah, I'm just tired. Needed another day in the sun." He looked over at Virg.

"Hey, you're lucky you still have weekends," laughed Rose.

"Yeah," Greg looked out the window and watched the emerald evergreen trees shine in the sun. He didn't want to leave the outdoors.

The car spilled out of the farmed and forested area and through a few towns on their way to the school. But Greg and Virg couldn't think about school. They were focused on their nights and the missing glider. And the unexplained moments since yesterday caused them to glide silently through their own experiences. The wagon arrived at the front of their school in what felt like thirty seconds. The boys got out and walked toward the front door of their school.

"Good luck, my loves! Have a good start!" yelled Rose out of her passenger window.

The boys heard nothing. Greg looked into a classroom window on his left. He saw something regular and typical. Students quietly stared at their teacher's introduction. No one looked distracted or confused by a nearby invisible voice.

Virg looked into the office window on his right for tardy forms. No one looked out to see him enter the front door. He grabbed a metal bar and pulled the door open. "I have my notebook. I'll take down the rest of the notes from your night. See you at lunch," said Virg. Turning, he quickly walked down the hallway toward the room for the end of the first period.

Greg wanted to close his eyes and fall into a heavy and dark sleep. He turned the opposite way and walked with a slow, sleepy gait, looking like a zombie.

13

It was just after the fifth period. Virg left his environmental science class and headed to his locker. He threw his books inside and grabbed his notebook. Walking down a brick-walled hallway, he couldn't stop thinking about all the questions he had for Greg. He wasn't finished asking about the pilot man's connection during Greg's dreams, although he'd already asked Greg plenty of questions. Maybe he could give him a break. The guy slept but was more exhausted than Virg. It just doesn't make sense.

Virg reached the end of the hallway that opened into a large, high-ceilinged, circular room. The brick walls spread out to include large windows along the floor and a huge, frosted roof circle in the center. A ton of tables and support beams were between him and the line to buy food. He followed the brick wall past the windows to reach the ordering lines.

He wasn't even hungry. Virg was distracted enough to just grab a wrapped PB&J and a small carton of milk. He headed to an empty table near the entrance, where he came in and waited for Greg's arrival. His fingers rolled his notebook pages and snapped his mechanical pencil's tip out. Virg started to draw a creek, then a hill and a bridge. He drew the glider and the empty cornfield. That missing gouged line in the dirt bothered him. He wrote "check" and drew a line from the word to the gouged line. What about the missing glider? He scratched another arrow pointing under the bridge.

His next thought was, *What about Hutch?* He paused for a minute. His hand stopped drawing, and he looked down the hallway at nothing in particular. His eyes didn't focus. He asked himself, *Why do I know his name?*

He looked back at his drawing. He squeezed the pencil hard and drew the name "Hutch" under the bridge, again on the bankside, repeated up at the top of the hill. A harder pressing from his hand dug that name into the page. *Goddamn it, why do I know his name?* he thought.

"Holy shit."

Virg's focus wrapped around and over his shoulder to see Greg only inches away, staring at his drawing. Greg threw his lunch tray down a few inches to smash right next to Virg's sketch. His cheeseburger and fries bumped up and down and spilled a few fries onto the tray. Virg had forgotten about eating and suddenly felt famished.

He looked into Greg's eyes. Greg stared back at him. "How'd you know his name?" asked Greg. "Hang on . . ." he paused and closed his eyes. "I heard that in my dreams. I just didn't make the connection." He reached for his tray and filled his fist with fries.

"I never learned it. I don't know what's going on," answered Virg. "I mean, he was closer to my house. If he contacted us, was he sharing his name? I have no freaking idea, dude!" Virg was getting upset and raising his voice.

Greg had just stuffed fries into his mouth, but he grabbed Virg's shoulder and whispered with a full, "It'th okuy, mun. Juss cheel. Thtay calm." He quickened his chew and swallowed twice.

They both looked at the drawing again and the locations of the name sank into Greg's mind. He sipped an apple juice and said, "You put his name in these areas. You think that he moved around to those places? I didn't see him, but I thought I felt him."

"I don't really feel like I know where he was. I just kinda had a feeling," said Virg.

"When we biked back after he walked away, I felt him here." Greg pointed to the top of the hill near the trees and tall grass. "Didn't see him. When we came back instead of busing this morning, I felt all kinds of weird connections right here." Greg pointed to the creek bank next to the bridge. "That was so powerful. I felt like there were people there. I just couldn't see 'em. And, duh, below the bridge . . . We followed him there holding the glider."

Virg's hand returned to the page and drew the street connected to the bridge. He drew it down to the bottom of the page and curved it left to meet a side street. Then he drew a small postage house where the streets connect and wrote *Hutch* on top.

"He went here too. We sent him down. Is he still there?" said Virg.

"I don't think so. He went back and forth according to my *feelings.*" Greg quoted tiny little fingers in the air and smiled.

"Why are we feeling this?" asked Virg. "You seem more connected than me. I have no idea what's going on, but you dreamed all kinds of stuff."

Virg paused and pulled the paper from around his PB&J. He shoved half of it into his mouth and chewed quickly. Greg did the same. He grabbed his burger with both hands and took a nice big bite. They stared in the same direction at the wall and munched for a little while. It was nice to have a shared feeling.

Virg swallowed and looked back at his notebook. When his eye crept downward at the local mail house, he turned to Greg and asked, "You think David met him?"

"He visited, right? For a phone call? Who'd he call?" asked Greg.

"We have no idea, man," said Virg. He shook his head and blew out a dramatic sigh. "We don't know shit." Virg's eyes opened wide. He spun them over onto Greg. "But you said that you felt his presence today, right? What if he's still here? Where's his glider?"

"Let's just talk to David and then look for Hutch after we check in at home. It's the first day at school. You got any homework so far?" asked Greg.

14

The school finished its first day at 2:45 p.m. Virg walked past some open classroom doors and some kids waiting for their chorus to meet up. A nearby piano got jammed with half-step mashes by what sounded like the fingers of a football lineman. Didn't sound like a musician. He hustled past and pushed open the fat metal door to step into their parking lot. The midafternoon sun hit Virg's eyebrows and forehead. He closed his eyes and took a deep breath. His tired hands held out his bus number on his first-day memo.

"Thank God that it's still summer," he said.

Greg sat with his back on the school wall near the exit. He noticed Virg soaking in the sunshine. He pushed up off the ground and walked toward him. Greg's eyes crawled down to peek at the bus number on Virg's memo. He looked up, found it, and ran over to enter their assigned bus. Virg heard Greg's hustle over the pebbly pavement. He popped open his eyes and began to run after him. Three tall stairs led them right up into the open-window cabin. Their butts grabbed a pouch in the same beltless seat. Their bodies rested as the sun beamed onto their laps. Various nearby conversations and silly student songs pushed the boys into a daze. They felt separated from their peers.

The bus rolled and bumped through old towns. Those two kids rode it into their fields and neighborhood. A grind into the bus's brakes shoved them forward and back before they got up and quickly exited. They got off the bus one stop before theirs. The bus took a few seconds to ensure they got off the road before it took off. Greg's gaze shifted from the bus to the mail house on the other side of the road. They crossed the street and walked to the mail house from their neighbor's area. Greg hid behind a blue mailbox. He stretched his neck around its right shoulder. His eyes moved up and into an open window on the side of the building. He peered around the box's shoulder and peeked hard through the darkness inside the window.

Virg, three feet behind him, said, "David! You still in there?"

"Yeah, come on in. Bring Greg," bounced David's voice through the screened window.

Greg looked around at Virg, stood over the mailbox, and raised his shoulders. They crossed the lot and upped the stairs leading to the front door. Virg pulled the door, rushed forward, and quickly shoved his head through David's little window. His eyes crossed back and forth as he searched for the mail host. He said nothing. The door smacked the frame as it closed. Greg paced up beside Virg.

"I'm here! What do you need?" David's voice came from behind a shelving unit holding some big brown cardboard boxes.

"Where are you?" asked Virg.

"I'm working," stiffly replied David. "What are you looking for? How you guys doing?"

"Well, I'm looking for this guy," said Virg. No response. "... Hutch," he added.

There was a long moment of silence. "Why can't you see me?" said David.

"Uhh ... You're workin—"

"You said his name. Now, you won't find me," said David.

"I just wanted to ask you a question," said Virg.

David paced slowly into Virg's vision from behind the shelf. "How do you know him?"

"I don't know him. I didn't even know his name. I, well, we," he turned and pointed at Greg, "we saw him crash his glider into the field. But then he disappeared, reappeared, kind of appeared in the disappearance ... We're just curious!" said Virg.

"I saw him. He needed my phone. That's fine, but not allowed. He disagreed and lifted me with one arm to get a different answer. He didn't hurt me, but he stretched the neck of my shirt. He put me back down, and I let him in here to call someone. I didn't hear what he said.

Glider

I just asked him to leave," said David. "And no," he added, "you can't use my phone."

David turned and quickly walked back behind his shelf, holding boxes. A scan noise popped from his instrument. He reached up, grabbed the package, and brought it back to the countertop.

"Here's a box for your mom, Virgil," said David. He flipped his gaze to Greg. "*You* got nothin'."

"You're telling *me*," said Greg. He turned and pulled open the exit door. His footsteps dragged across the concrete stoop in the parking lot. The sun hit his forehead, and he closed his eyes. The door shut behind him.

"Did he tell you about his crash?" asked Virg.

"Car crash? He didn't look injured," said David.

"He bumped his knees a bit, but it was in a plane crash. The glider was pretty sick. Claimed that he wasn't injured," said Virg.

"You saw him crash a glider?"

"Yep. Greg and I were sunbathing in the field, and he crashed into it," said Virg.

"He must not know anyone around here. Came to the post office for the phone." David rolled his eyes.

"I told him to ask for the phone at the post office," Virg quietly responded.

"So, now you know: no phone booth, just mailboxes." David turned and returned to the envelopes piled behind his mailbox shelves.

"Well, I didn't think he knew anyone, but he found Greg and me near our yards after dark." Virg gazed at the floor.

David turned and paced back to the small counter. His little feet quickly brushed across the floor. He turned the low knob on the counter and opened the half-door toward Virg. David stood in the doorway frame and opened his mouth. His eyes met at the same level as Virg.

"Say that again."

15

Greg had sat against the flagpole in the parking lot. His brain was cooking under the delicious sunbeams. A slight breeze flowed past his upper lip. The beads of sweat cooled down; then his nose warmed them back up. "Goddamn, not being in school feels good."

Another slight breeze cast a scent of marshmallows past his nostrils. That caught Greg's attention. He opened his eyes and let them flow around the parking lot. The breeze had come from the street running from the corner behind the post office. Greg drew a deeper breath through his nostrils. He let his eyelids roll down, and his nostrils widen. That scent bloomed widely in his facial canals, growing toward the whiff of a creamy icing. *That scent is getting better*, thought Greg. His mouth watered as he stood up, slowly following his own steps toward the road behind the post office. His nose pulled him through the parking lot, over a grassy, weedy hedge, and next to the road.

He turned his head right, looking up the road past the corner. His eyes pulled left, down the road, and back toward the small bridge where they stashed the glider. Greg's eyes shut again. His neck calmly slid his nose up the road to his right. He almost raised the tip toward the treetops. Calm lungs pulled a slow breath into his nostrils. It washed his scent cells with a damp, stone, concrete fragrance.

A weak gust from his left side grabbed his nostrils and pulled his body back toward the creek. He smelled a wet, smoky hibiscus scent. "Holy shit," he whispered out loud. His eyes stayed closed as if the sun and the smell floated him toward the creek.

He left the post office behind him without a single thought. His legs drew him quietly and directly down the side of the road. He paced closer and closer to the aroma that pulled him. His lungs pulled a deep breath and upped his pace. The smell was growing and getting better. His legs widened their pace, and he began to run. The balls of his feet paced into the grass, combing his shoes with each step. He felt those gusts of flavor going in and out of his nostrils repeatedly. Greg's lungs were filling with this delicious smell.

He caught the crest of the scent and turned to follow that aroma down the hill and under the bridge. Turning hard, he slapped his forehead off an object he didn't even see. His legs whiffed out from under him, and his upper body stopped immediately. He didn't even remain conscious as his body hit the ground. His frame slipped down into the creek's dirt bed. Then Greg lay still and quiet.

16

Virg pushed the door open and stepped out onto the parking lot gravel. Some dry pebbles rolled under his shoes. His thin, queasy legs led him over beside the blue curbside mailbox. A light shade of yellow softly poured into the rims of Virg's vision. It slowly crept from the corners of his eyes and stuck around the rims. A rolling stomach wave splashed low in Virg and removed the strength of his legs. He swiftly sank down onto his butt with the mailbox still in his hand. He slid his fingers down the metal corner and gripped a metal leg. The nausea whisked away as he relaxed for a moment. His eyes finally cleared, and his balance shifted back toward solidity.

Where is Greg? he thought. He stood and looked left over the bushes behind the mail house. Then he turned on the road and swung his eyes to his right. The park and the single-story ranch district were nearby. Virg considered walking past the ball field and into the ranch area. They trick-or-treated all over that neighborhood last year.

He wanted to find Greg. The recollection of sharing those treats and costumed parades pulled Virg back into his memories. There were great spots where they hid and scared each other in this neighborhood. He began walking toward the area he remembered. *I'll check the Halloween route, the park, and the bike jumps in the forest trail*, he thought to himself.

"I need to tell him what happened to David. I don't think Hutch is gone," Virg said out loud.

Virg spent two hours pacing in and around all the spots he thought of. *I'm gonna get yelled at if I miss dinner.* He found nothing that told him that Greg had visited this neighborhood. *Eh, he probably went home. Maybe he's still exhausted*, he thought. Virg turned around, looked toward his place, and began to hike back home.

17

The paint-flaked garage door at Virg's house was still open. He paced around a corner into his driveway. His eyes peered into the garage, and he saw his bike leaning against a shelved tool kit. Did he want to grab that and bike around to find Greg? A rumble and a gurgle reminded him that his tummy needed a visit from what was inside his fridge. He passed the garage and opened his front door. Swinging the door closed, he ripped off his backpack and softly tossed it onto the carpet to his left.

A voice from the staircase above him reached out. "Virgil, is that you?"

Virg recognized his mom's voice. "Yes, I'm back."

"Late to leave, late to return," joked Rose. "Come on up. I have someone to introduce to you."

She walked over to the banister rim at the top of the stairs, smiled, and peered down at Virg. Virg heard another set of footsteps and assumed it was his dad. He took two steps up the stairs . . . and saw Hutch walk behind Rose to the rim of the staircase.

Virg immediately stopped. His mouth opened.

"It's okay, kid!" Hutch raised his hands in an attempt to look calm.

His hands were big. He crouched down, looking relaxed and conscious. His image just appeared even bigger, like a boulder about to roll down the stairs and flatten Virg.

"Dad?!" Virg yelled, searching for help.

"Hi, Virg," his dad responded from the kitchen. "You like mac and cheese, right? I'm using some dry mustard, cayenne . . . uh, and a little nutmeg. Sounded great to me. I'm giving it a shot. You down?"

"I'm downstairs. Do you know this guy . . . Hutch?" responded Virg.

His dad responded as Hutch and Rose looked at each other. "Ah, I just met him. Have you met him? Did Mom introduce you yet?"

"This is Hutch," said Rose. "I've known him a long time. I used to work with him in Massachusetts."

"Yeah, Greg and I already knew your name," said Virg. He took a deep breath and let it out, "But I don't know why. You didn't tell us your name when we sent you to the post office."

He took two slow steps back down the stairs and kept his hand on the banister. "I saw you last night. Greg saw you. We barely slept."

". . . I didn't mean to scare you," said Hutch. "I used the phone you told me about. No one answered when I called. I asked David for help, and he couldn't. I kept walking until I found the nearby town to ask about a pickup of my glider. That took awhile, but they'll show up tomorrow. I camped at the bridge last night. When the sun went down, I noticed someone's voice."

Hutch slowly looked over at Rose and then snapped his focus back to Virgil.

"I thought I heard a voice in this direction. When I moved toward it, I smelled your Mom's garden. She used to grow the same plants back in Massachusetts. Rose always grew rosemary. I didn't know she lived here, but I smelled the same scents, which reminded me of her. I saw you and Greg when I came by, and I didn't mean to scare you," said Hutch. "It was already a little late. I just wanted to see if anyone was still awake."

Virg's eyes scanned from Hutch to his mom. "He heard your voice?" he asked.

"My garden has a voice," she smiled as she replied. She pointed her thumb over to Hutch on her right. "This is the guy you were telling us about yesterday. I didn't realize that I knew him. He's never flown a glider in front of me before."

Virg's eyes turned back to Hutch. "Also, I talked to David at the mail house." He took another step back. "He didn't exactly *enjoy* your visit. Is this visit going to end the same?"

Hutch held up his hands again, surrendering. He sat on the top stair. "My bad. I picked him up because I was desperate, and I didn't have any friends or help. I mean, I *did* camp in the middle of nowhere last night," responded Hutch. He let a smile creep into his face.

"Why are you here . . . in my house?" asked Virg. "Why did I already know your name?"

"Dinner's ready!" yelled Virg's dad from the kitchen. "Take your seats!"

Hutch stood up and turned his head toward the kitchen. "Mr. Murphy, can you come here a second?" asked Hutch.

"Dude, my name is Doug," said Virg's dad as he comfortably stepped out of the kitchen wearing an apron and oven mitts. "I already told you. Come grab a seat."

He held a wide oven pan full of cheesy macaroni as he looked down at Virg. "What's the big deal? Hutch, Mom's friend," he shook his head toward Hutch, "is staying for dinner. I'm not sure he's eaten anything for a while. What's your deal?" Doug asked.

"I'm scared! I've been different since he showed up, and no one knows what's happening to me. It's been . . . *weird!*" responded Virg. His brows were sweating, and he didn't feel safe. It felt like he was changing and maybe unraveling.

Doug cocked his head to the side and looked at Rose and then looked back at Virg. "I mean, can you do magic yet or something? Have you reached that age?"

Rose, now at the bottom of the stairs, grabbed Doug's arm. She looked into his eyes. He looked at her and then looked back at Virg.

"Puberty, my man!" said Virg's dad. He raised his pan and shook his hips in a small celebration. "You're probably changing," he said as he smiled, then raised and lowered his eyebrows like he was sharing entertaining secrets.

"Yeah, your mom used to do magic and stuff as part of her job," said Virg's dad. "Cool, right?" His eyes opened wide as he said it. "She's been doing magic right in front of you for a while. I figured you'd see it at some point." Doug seemed quite comfortable with the idea.

"Hutch can do it too, but his is a little different." Doug winked at Virg.

Hutch and Rose both turned their eyes at Doug and looked as though they had been slapped and gone unconscious. They said nothing.

Doug looked down at Virg and then back and forth at Hutch and Rose. "Okay! Let's eat before this gets cold."

18

They all sat at the table as Doug filled the plates with piles of mac and cheese. Virg had left his shoes on, just in case he had to escape. He sat still, waiting for Hutch to stop staring at him before he chewed a chunk of mac. Hutch noticed and looked down, grabbing a big forkful and jamming it into his mouth.

"Whoa, let's say grace first," responded Doug. He held his index finger up.

Hutch's eyes widened and rolled toward Doug. Their eyes met, and Doug saw Hutch's regret. "Chew it, man. I'm just joking. You're hungry as heck, probably," said Doug. He laughed lightly and turned to Virg.

"You hungry yet?" he asked.

"I'm starving, but my stomach doesn't feel ready for this," Virg blurted.

"I'm rearry shorry," Hutch said with a mouth full of pasta. He stared across the table at Virg. He kept chewing and quickly swallowed. "I didn't know if I'd see you again, and I didn't know that your mom, my friend, had a kid. I'm surprised too."

Virg cut the tone. "You just told me that you scheduled a pickup of your glider. Greg and I went back down there, but the glider wasn't there. Did you move it on your own?"

"Not really," responded Hutch. He fell into silence, not sure how to respond. He turned his gaze to Rose.

"How did you move it?" asked Virg.

"I didn't." Hutch's focus slid down, staring at his plate. "I made it invisible."

"How?" said Virg.

Rose turned her gaze from Hutch to Virg. She backed up her chair and stood up from the table. She walked over to Virg's corner of the table and rested down on her knees. Her hand reached into her pocket, and she placed a folded paper airplane on the corner of the table. Her left hand passed over it once. She raised and opened her right hand a yard from Virg's face so he would look straight at it. She moved the hand down next to the paper plane. Her index finger pinched against her thumb and dragged slowly down to the base where it connected to her hand. The moment her finger met her palm, the plane disappeared.

She looked back at Virg. "I've been showing this to you for a long time," she said.

Her index connected with her palm, and she flipped her finger straight out toward the invisible plane. It immediately came into vision. "It's possible."

She breathed deeply and sat on the floor with her crossed legs. "One never knows if their family will have the skill or not. I found out about my possibilities when I turned twenty-nine. It's different for everyone," she said. "You're twelve." Her eyes turned to meet Virgil's. She added, "You knew Hutch's name. I noticed his confusion when you said it out loud. He didn't tell you his name, did he?"

Virg looked away from his mom and closed his eyes. "Greg and I didn't know him, but I wrote down his name at lunch." He looked back at his mom.

"You're changing," said Rose. She smiled and ran her fingers through Virg's hair above his ear. "Don't be afraid."

The home phone rang on the wall just five feet behind Doug. Their eyes all swung toward the phone for a moment after the first few rings happened. Doug waved his hand down and said, "Keep eating. If it's someone who we need to talk to, I'll pick it up."

It seemed more important to make Virg feel supported and understood.

The voicemail came on and said, "*You've reached the Murphy residence. Please leave your message at the sound of the beep.*" In the recorded message, the family all said "*beeeeep*" simultaneously.

Then the machine popped its own *beep*, "*Hi, Rose, this is Tom. You said you drove Virg and Greg to school after you found them. Did you pick them up today, or did they take the bus home? We're sitting down for dinner, but I haven't seen Greg yet. If you've seen Virg, let me know. If not, maybe they're still running around out there. I saw them back in the field yesterday and drove by to check on 'em. Thanks!" beeeeeep.*

The message ended. Virg turned to Hutch and asked, "Did you make him disappear?"

19

Tim hung up the phone. He hung it up in their kitchen pantry and turned to his wife. "Whelp, there's still some sun in the sky. I'm gonna roll around and hunt for your son. Rose didn't pick up."

He smiled and leaned in to kiss his wife. She smiled and presented her cheek to him. Resting his hand on her far hip, he popped a kiss on her cheek. Sue chuckled and put her hand on his. He let go and meandered toward the door to their driveway.

"Sue, give that pot of chili a kiss from me too," he added.

"Find that boy of mine," Sue said, "and don't give him a whoopin' when you find him." She smiled as Tim put on a light plaid button-down and hoisted his keys into his chest pocket.

"I'll keep the pot warm and waiting for you both. Don't drive too fast," she added.

As she stared at him, she pulled her grey and auburn hair back behind her ear. Then she turned back to the kitchen, rolling a lime in her hand. She picked up a knife and began slicing it on the counter.

Tim's mouth watered as he turned and opened the door. The chili rolled around in his mind. Walking down his driveway, he swallowed and cut the idea out of his mind when he saw his truck. *Where did I see him so far?* he asked himself. Climbing into his vehicle, he started the ignition and shut the door.

He wasn't looking anywhere. His mind just combed through the possible locations where Greg might be lurking. *He and Virg were searching and hopping around in the creek*, he thought. He looked up through his windshield and shifted to Drive. His truck crawled forward about five feet, and he hit the brake.

He shifted his gears to Park and looked at his phone. Thumbing his number buttons and whipping it to his ear, the other line rang.

The call was picked up, and Tim heard, "You know that the Phillies are losing already, right? Why you calling?"

Tim smiled and asked his neighbor, Pete, "Have you seen Greg or Virg yet? Are you watching in your garage? They've told me that you always have Bazooka gum for free," said Tim.

"Hey, I get some good luck when they stop by, and I make 'em chew Bazooka with me."

"I know. Any luck so far?" asked Tim.

"Nawp. I said we're losing . . . and it's early in the game. I haven't made anyone lucky as of yet," said Pete.

"Greg's not home yet. I'm sure he's just running around and enjoying himself. Probably running around to forget about school."

"We stopped by their empty glider spot. Are they still looking around for a prize over there? Diggin' for buried treasure at this point?" Pete said as he scratched his hairline and chewed his gum loudly.

Tim rolled his hand over the back of his neck and scratched his head. "That sounds about right. Thanks, Pete. I'll swing by that creek bridge, the baseball field, and uhhhhh, maybe by your garage—just in case you're keeping them for a win possibility," said Tim.

"I have 'em. I feel the win approaching. Just popped open another Bazooka bucket!" yelled Pete. Silence fell for a moment. "Good luck out there, my man."

Tim finished his chuckle, thanked Pete, and closed his phone. He scratched his mustache for a moment. His hand shifted his gear into Drive, and he rolled up to the street. Looking left and right, he pressed his pedal and pulled onto the road. His confidence was present. He'd find Greg, he thought. Then he shivered, and his stomach turned.

20

"You wanna call Tim back?" asked Rose.

Virg blurted, "I figured Greg just went home."

"When did you leave him?" asked Doug.

Virg looked down and wiped his hands on the napkin over his knee. "Greg and I went to the post office to ask David . . . about Hutch. We told the new guy here," pointing at Hutch, "to go there for help and use a phone."

Virg looked up and met Hutch's eyes. "Who did you need to call?"

"Where did Greg go?" Doug asked Virg, trying to take control of the conversation. "He left before you?"

Grabbing the arms of his chair, Virg pushed back from the table. "I don't know. When I went in, he didn't follow," responded Virg. "That wasn't the plan. I figured he was disinterested."

Virg lowered his head and remembered the night before. "He's known more than me, anyway. Seems like he's following . . . or trying to get away from the images that took over his dreams last night."

The chair across from Virg pushed back. Hutch got up from the table.

"Doug, you want to go try to find Greg?" asked Hutch.

"If Greg's missing, someone's gotta find him. If Tim leaves before Rose calls back, we should add some help while it's still light out," said Doug.

Hutch reached down to grab his plate. He raised the back of it to roll all the contents into his mouth. The acute angle was high and his fork just scooped and pushed all the cheesy elbows into his mouth. He began to chew aggressively, raised his chin, and turned toward Doug.

"Lwets dewit," blurted Hutch.

"Can I come too?" asked Virg.

"You've already looked for him in the other neighborhoods, right?" said Doug. "Can't ask you for more. Please finish that dish. It's darn tootin'."

"Be safe," said Rose. She grabbed Doug's arm and pulled him close for a kiss.

"I'll be tootin' too," laughed Doug. "See you soon." He gave her back a quick kiss and turned to leave.

Doug stopped and turned around toward Rose. "And talk to Virgil about those changes. We didn't know he'd be like you . . . but I'm glad that he is."

Rose smiled and touched Doug's cheek. "Be safe."

Doug and Hutch hit the staircase and went down to open the front door. Doug put on his sneakers, and Hutch tried to chew as best he could. He sat on the stairs and pushed on his boots. Doug rose to grab his car keys and opened the front door.

The shake of the keys made Hutch look up at Doug and say, "We can walk. I think I know where he is."

"How do you know?" asked Doug.

"I definitely connected with them both last night. I didn't expect them to be looking out their windows—feeling my presence outside. I was trying to send a signal, and then I saw their eyes. If their minds just got opened up, I'd assume they'd go back to where they met me. They could be looking for some connection with their change." Hutch shook his head.

"I'll follow you," said Doug, raising his hands.

Pushing off the stair, Hutch stood up and opened the front door. Doug followed him out and down the stairs and onto the lawn.

Hutch turned around and looked toward their backyard. "Over your fence and toward my glider. Let's hit it."

He jogged over and grabbed the top of the fence. He pushed a foot to the wall and swung his other one over. Rolling over the fence was easy and athletic. Doug clicked his tennis shoes together and began climbing that fence.

21

Tim rolled up into the baseball park. His gaze peered through the trees at the edges of the field. Nothing was moving in or around those trees. Slowly spinning his car around the parking lot, he gazed up and over the field to look beyond the street on the other side. He raised his lookout to the forested hills beyond. Unfortunately, he couldn't even get a good look at all the places within his eye scape. He didn't see deer or birds walking around on those hillsides.

"Ain't here," he said to himself.

His car rolled down the road. Seeing the post office on his left, he drove past it and made a left around it. The truck passed by big bushes, and Tim looked behind the post office to see if Greg was hiding somewhere. His wheels rumbled across the back road toward the creek. He passed a few houses, and the empty cornfield opened up into his vision. The sun had set, but warm lines of peach and ruby colors still flooded over one another above the hill.

Tim's stare up into the clouds was so relaxing. He saw the reflection of the colors in the sky popping off the down-flowing creek over to his right. That sparkling water tumble whisked down the hill and under the bridge. His head curled from his right to a straightforward focus. Something moved in the left corner of his eye.

Tim whipped his foot toward the brake and slowly pressed on it. In the corner of his eye, he thought he saw two tops of heads descending the creek bank. Did he see anything at all? *Is my son running away from me right now?* he thought. Pulling over on the right side of the road, he quickly jammed his stick shift to Park. Then he hopped out and looked both ways.

A little sedan began to slow down as it crossed the tiny creek bridge.

The driver lowered his window.

"You okay? Gonna fish or need to fix your car?" asked a wrinkly old man. He smiled, looking as if he would stop and help.

"I'm okay," Tim gently responded. "Just looking for my kid. It's his first day of school, but I haven't seen him since he got out. I've gotta make sure he's not avoiding his homework." He smiled.

The old man smiled back and said, "If I see a kid ripping up notebook pages on the sidewalk, I'll let ya know."

The driver bowed his grey-haired head, raised his window, and rolled away. Tim looked up and down the road. He hustled across the street and quickly paced down to the creek on his right. It was dark under the bridge, but he saw nothing. He looked through the shadow to the open end. The orange reflection spouted a warm beam off the water up to his gaze. The horizontal glimmer highlighted many footprints in the mud around the creek. He leaned down, almost inspecting them. The footprints looked to be about Greg and Virg's size. There were tons from their search the previous day.

"That glider search was a muddy marathon," said Tim.

He stood back up and turned his gaze down the creek current. Those tiny ripples rolled away from him. A slight split of the tall, dried weeds caught his eye on the bank. The parting of those dry yellow weeds went down to the creek for about another twenty feet. Tim crept up onto the bank and moved toward the split. He pressed up on his tiptoes and saw mashed weeds and dirt holding the pressed rims of larger footprints.

He had no idea if this trail meant anything, but his legs pulled him in that direction. The light in the sky was dwindling. Tim turned his head back and saw the sky's rim changing to a deep blue. That shade was slowly being pulled downward. He turned and followed the trail.

"Before I can't see anything . . ." he paused, then took a few more steps and added, "I thought I saw something."

He turned his eyes behind himself for a moment and pulled in a breath. Then he turned back and upped his pace down the trail.

22

After the slam of their front door beneath them, Rose pushed up from the floor and grabbed some plates off the table. She barely turned over her shoulder. "Grab some dishes and bring them into the kitchen."

"I'm still eating," responded Virg.

"That's okay. Bring it in and sit on the kitchen stool. I'm going to start cleaning up."

Virg rolled his eyes and slowly pushed his chair back. He dreaded getting a speech from either of his parents. The subject was probably going to be about something he could improve upon. He grabbed his plate and fork and slowly dragged his feet over the carpet as he walked into the kitchen. The stool was pulled out, facing the person at the sink.

"I'm not going to yell at you. I'm sorry," said Rose.

Virg's stomach turned. "What do you have to be sorry about?"

"I've been sending you signals over the years . . . little ones. But I didn't see any curiosity or uncomfortable reactions from you." She shook her head, looking down at her sponge. "I thought about telling you my little magic tricks weren't just tricks. I wasn't trying to confuse you—"

Virg cut her off. "How could I have known? It looked like magic. I've always thought it was real."

Rose put her sponge into the tiny-bubbled lake in her sink and turned to Virg. "There's no real regularity with this gift. Some people notice their physical or mental adjustments and ask about them. I would assume that some don't. You're lucky if you notice your changes before you're five."

"I'm a bit older than five, Mom."

"You're still a bit lucky." She smiled and turned back to the dishes. "It happens differently for everyone," she said. "I noticed that I could talk without moving my lips at age twenty-two. I was about to graduate with a degree in history . . . not magic."

She snuck a look at Virg to see his reaction. He put another forkful of mac in his mouth and smiled.

"Am I beating you?" he asked.

Rolling her eyes, she said, "Probably. I was maybe a little tipsy when I contacted people with my mouth shut. I thought it was natural. They did too, until some figured it out." She shook her head. "I was lucky."

Virg stacked his plate on the countertop beside him. "What happened?"

"My friend thought about a crush on a guy in the room. I heard it and asked her about it . . . but I didn't say anything. I just silently contacted her. That person started to freak out and silence others in the room. She pushed me away, saying, 'How did you do that?' She saw me asking her about her feelings but didn't see my lips move."

"How'd you get out?" asked Virg.

"A man standing close by heard our room get quiet. When she asked me what I was doing, he stepped close to me and started making jokes about being a ventriloquist," said Rose. "I didn't know him, but when they calmed down and left me alone, he started talking to me without moving his lips."

A shiver hit Virg's shoulders. Rose shut off the water. "He told me that people like us seldom find one another. We're not a usual type of partygoers."

"Did he teach you how to use those . . . powers?"

"Well, eventually," said Rose. "He told me that a professor noticed him. The teacher invited him to come to the chapel on campus."

"It's religion?"

She laughed. "It's not the effect of visiting Jesus or anything like that. The chapel was quite empty, and when the organists would roll in to practice, it almost gave Hutch and the professor an easy sound buffer. No one is watching if you're whispering to the person next to you in church. If anything, it looks like you're sharing ideas about the music or faith. Hutch told me that they'd applaud when the organists finished a piece. Those whispers turned into just looking like they were praying. Quickly, they stopped using their mouths to connect. Really, their 'prayers' were just bouncing thoughts between their minds." She jokingly bounced her fingers around the word *prayers*.

"Hutch must have made you a churchgoing cheerleader," said Virg.

"Come on!" She rolled her eyes. "Some churches are great. Either it gives you a place to share your meditation, or you can join musicians for a melodic exploration."

"That's not even close to what I see when we go." Virg looked at her from under his lowered eyebrows.

Rose went back to scrubbing the dishes in the sink. "Depends on the venue, but you can explore anything you believe in. Don't have to share it."

"Okay, so did you sing in the choir in that place?" joked Virg.

"Nope, but that was just how Hutch met that professor. I was kind of done with church by the age of twenty-two. But when I met him, it was in the church. That's where Hutch introduced me to that professor. I brought some coffee, and I only spent ten minutes there."

"Did you learn all this from the professor?" asked Virg.

"Here, start drying these." Rose flew a dish towel at Virg's shoulder. It flipped and opened as it struck him on the shoulder. He slapped his hand against his chest to catch it before it fell.

"Hutch would walk with me through the park around Moyers Lake. The park surrounded the river and lake beneath the campus. It was a good place to have conversations without people hearing what we discussed."

"So you—"

"That's how I began to learn about this," said Rose, cutting him off.

Virg grabbed a handle on the dish cabinet and opened it. "So, do you just figure it all out over a couple of attempts?"

"It depends on the person. Some concepts are learned quickly, but some of your abilities are gained through potential theories you conceive."

"Um . . . What the heck does that mean?" Virg shook his head and grabbed another dish from the dry rack. "You're saying I have to make stuff up and then learn about it?"

"You have to notice what you are capable of," Rose responded calmly. "If you think about something you want to do, you might be able to do it. But you might not." She shrugged.

"This guessing game sounds awful," he said.

"You should know," Rose looked directly at Virg and shut off the sink again, "Hutch and I helped people learn how to meet their potential. We both started working at a tiny camp in the summertime after we graduated," said Rose.

"What? You've met more people like this?" asked Virg. His stomach turned, and he took a seat on the stool.

"Not a lot of them. But I've helped some."

"Where do you find these types of people?"

"I didn't find any of them," said Rose.

"Well, who did?"

"Hutch's professor. That was one skill he discovered on his own."

"How old is that guy? Is he still around?" asked Virg.

"I don't know how old he is, but I worked for him. He was the one who founded these summer camps."

"Was there anyone like me at these camps?" Virg's heart began to beat harder.

"Not when I was there. There were no kids and no teenagers. It seemed that if Hutch or the professor met someone similar to them, they would invite them." Rose shook her head and sat down on a stool in the kitchen.

She looked back at Virg. "It's hard to find the right person. They found some nice people who had a similar potential. But those new friends were uncomfortable opening up, or they didn't like visiting a campsite for those reasons. The professor seemed to get frustrated if his guests had no interest in experimenting."

Rose peeled her hair up off a touch of sweat on her forehead. "The professor mentioned looking for the potential of younger people. I kept teaching for about three summers."

Her gaze rolled up over Virg's shoulder. He watched his mom as her pupils opened wide. She looked straight through the window behind him. It looked like she lost her thoughts. She held no expression.

"Is he still teaching?" said Virg.

"Why don't you go down to hit the couch? Take a breather."

Virg got up, looking tired, and went down the stairs toward the couch. As he descended the stairs he said aloud, "I can't believe *I'm asking you* about teachers. I'm not in school right now! UGH!"

Rose opened the kitchen cabinet and pulled a pen and notebook out. She made her way out of the kitchen and toward her little antique mail-writing table.

"I may have to ask some questions when your dad and Hutch get back," she said to Virg, even though he was too far away to hear. She opened her notebook and clicked her pen. Rose released a sigh as her body felt a little jumpy. Her mind began to build possible scenarios that led to Hutch's appearance. Her thoughts began to scare her.

23

Greg's hands were folded together as he lay unconscious in the big man's arms. Doug walked behind Hutch and couldn't see Greg on either side of him.

"Thanks for carrying him," whispered Doug.

Hutch cleared his throat as his arms lifted Greg onto his chest momentarily. The kid was still breathing. The small cut above his eyebrow had stopped bleeding. A dried red trail led across his temple to his ear.

Doug turned back, looking toward the sunset ridge on the hill. His gaze lowered to their little trail. The path wasn't obvious, he hoped.

Don't follow us, Tim. I don't think you wanna know what happened, Doug thought.

He turned back up the trail, thinking about Hutch doing his finger-based magic movement while removing their image from Tim's visuals. It would've looked like they had just run down to beat up Greg before Tim arrived. Luckily, that old guy driving by gave them a moment to cover themselves. Doug stopped as they reached the fence.

Hutch turned back toward Doug. "You wanna climb over the fence, and I'll toss him into your arms?" He smiled and winked.

"Gimme just a second," replied Doug. Crouching down, he ran up to the fence and latched one sneaker onto a wide screw in the wood. He pushed up, caught the top of the fence, and rolled himself over onto the ground. It sounded like he crunched some leaves and joints on the ground.

"Ugh. I'll be back in one second," rumbled Doug's tone through the bottom of the fence.

He ran into his little shed, followed by sounds of tools rustling and bumping against the walls. Hutch saw the door reopen and heard Doug pacing back. A creak and a snap came from the other side of the fence. Hutch saw Doug when he reached the top of the fence.

"Hand him to me. I have a ladder. Should've thought about that earlier." He sat on the top rung and reached his arms toward Hutch.

Hutch lifted Greg to the top of the fence. Doug put his arms under Greg's shoulders and legs and slowly pulled him over. He paced down the ladder and brought Greg over to the tiny couch on his porch. He grabbed a towel and placed it underneath Greg's head.

Climbing the fence, Hutch whipped his leg over and caught a stair. He rolled his body over to be rooted on the ladder. Over the fence, Hutch peered just for a moment. The light in the sky was diminishing. It was a beautiful moment after sundown. Barely any lights had come on in nearby houses.

Hutch's gaze wandered up and down the creek. A little movement down by the creek made him freeze in his place for a moment. Tim's shaved head held just a little reflection on the top. Hutch raised his hand and pulled a line from the tip of his thumb down to his palm.

The little reflection that Hutch could barely see moved back and forth momentarily. Reflections off that cranium lowered beneath the weeds, closer to the creek. Hutch stepped down the ladder, closed it, and walked over to the couch, where Doug had begun icing Greg's eyebrow.

Greg opened his eyes and felt a tiny pain in his right eyebrow. His hand shot up to it and felt a little adhesive pad glued down. His light press didn't hurt. It just felt a bit sensitive. He saw Virg sitting next to him at his feet. There was a little porch light just above.

"Dude, did you smell that marshmallow?" said Greg. "I think it knocked me out."

Virg spun his head toward Greg with his mouth open for a second. He smiled. "Um, I didn't smell any marshmallows."

Greg's eyes blinked several times. "I think I ran into something." His fingers softly inspected his eyebrow again.

"Yep, ya did, buddy. That's what I was told when Dad and Hutch found you. You, uh, *found* the glider with your forehead."

"Do you have any marshmallows? I'm freakin starving."

Virg jumped off the couch and slid open the porch door. "Daaaaad, mac and cheese time again!"

24

Rose watched Doug jump up and go toward the fridge. He whipped open the door and grabbed the pan covered in tin foil. Slamming the door of the fridge, he spun around and grabbed a fork out of the utensil cup with the drying dishes. Carefully hustling past Rose and Hutch, he descended the stairs toward the back door.

When Hutch stood up, Rose silently observed his movement toward the kitchen. Grabbing the cabinet, he opened a door and took an empty glass. Flicking on the sink's faucet, he filled his glass and returned to sit at the dining room table.

Quietly, Rose asked, "So you're still working at the summer camp?"

Hutch rested his glass on the table and looked into her eyes. Then he lowered his gaze back to his glass. "It's not a summer camp now."

"When did Mata extend the teachings?"

"He retired from school right after he found an old Boy Scout hall in the middle of the woods near the Appalachian Trail in Maine."

"He lives there now?" Rose lowered her chin, seeming concerned. "Did he move the summer camp?"

"He changed the temporary camp into a way of life. This camp had restrooms. It had a fireplace. It was near to the river." He raised his shoulder and crossed his arms. "It gave us real time to reflect and work on our gifts and lifestyles."

". . . if you were living there for years . . ." Rose shook her head.

Hutch jumped in. "It was beautiful. We helped each other and ended up helping many people." Hutch's eyes lowered, and he quickly let go of his breath through his nostrils.

"But something went wrong?" Rose added.

Hutch looked up at her and held his breath. "I have skills. Your son looks like he's gonna need some help."

"Yeah, I just noticed that too. Duh!" said Rose. She shook her head. "Do you have more experience helping people his age?"

"Not a lot." His eyes met hers and then shifted back to his glass.

The downstairs door slid open, and they heard Doug yell, "The mac is working! He's feeling better!" The door swiftly slammed shut.

25

Sitting up on the porch and snacking on the mac pan, Greg looked into a mirror at the cut on his forehead. Doug sat on the floor in front of him, holding the tiny mirror. Rose slid the glass door open as Hutch followed her.

Virg turned to see the adults and said, "He was smelling marshmallows and felt like he needed to hunt them down."

"It was a freaking strong smell. That's one of my favorite smells," said Greg.

"What's your favorite memory?" asked Hutch.

Greg's eyes opened wider as he looked past Rose to see Hutch. "Dude! You're the monster. How ya been?"

"I've been better." He wiped his hand across his mustache and flicked salt crumbs from his finger.

"Virg told me you're a Boy Scout counselor," said Greg. He happily grabbed another forkful and shoved it into his mouth. "You know how to help us out with the crazy dreams you gave to us?"

"Kind of," said Hutch, "What's a memory you were thinking about before you went missing?"

"I was just enjoying the sun's rays earlier today. Reminded me of yesterday, just hiking and helping you down by the creek. Hiding that glider. Except, we didn't hide it. How did you hide it?" He looked back at Hutch. The smile on Hutch's face confused him.

Greg added, "Am I gonna be slammin' my head against things that I enjoy from now on?"

"No," Hutch laughed and cleared his throat. "It looks like you got too excited and followed an enjoyable memory."

Hutch walked toward Greg and sat down, crossing his legs. "I removed the visuals on the glider. You didn't know that. It looks like you remembered it was there, but you didn't notice it until you rammed your head into it."

Hutch raised his hand toward the fork Greg was holding. His finger peeled down on his hand, and the fork disappeared. He ripped his finger back up and out at the fork, making it immediately visible.

"Sick," said Greg. "So, you don't actually remove them; you just make them disappear."

"So far," said Hutch.

"Teach me that!" spouted Greg. He refilled his mouth with another forkful.

"You should probably get a good night's sleep. Maybe I'll meet with you two tomorrow after your *real* school." Hutch turned from the kids to look at Doug.

Doug smiled and passed his gaze toward Rose.

"You can come back after school tomorrow," said Rose. Greg and Virg looked at each other. "But now that you're feeling better, I've gotta take you home. Tell your dad we ate on the porch . . . which you *did* do, Greg."

"What should I tell him about my forehead?"

"That you were running around our neighborhood with Virg after school. You two split up, and you ran into something," said Rose.

"Copy that," said Greg. "Do you have any marshmallows? I can still kinda smell 'em."

26

Sue heard her doorbell ring. She was sitting in a recliner, watching *Jeopardy!* Rolling her recliner lever, she lowered her feet to the ground. Pushing off her chair, she stepped toward her door. When she opened the door, she saw Greg with a little patch over his eyebrow.

"Jesus! What happened to you?" Sue yelled.

Rose put her hand on Greg's shoulder. "He's fine. Our two little ones were running around after school, and after they split up, Greg hit his head on a sign. When Doug found him, he asked Greg to just sit and relax. We patched him up and gave him something to eat. Just wanted to make sure he was okay before we brought him back. Sorry about that." She patted Greg's shoulder and lightly pushed him toward the doorway.

Greg turned from Rose to his mom and said, "Yeah, I didn't mean to come home too late or worry you. We had Mr. Murphy's mac and cheese out on their porch. Rose told me that she had found a phone message from Dad when she came back inside. Is he still looking for me?"

"Yes," said Greg's mom. She pressed her hand on his back and brought him toward her for half a hug. Her gaze shifted to Rose. "Thank you so much, Rose." Turning back down to Greg, she said, "Please, grab the phone and give your dad a holler. He's probably pretty worried right now. It's dark out there."

She patted Greg on his lower back as he went past her toward their phone.

"Thank you so much for bringing him back *and* for feeding him. He gets so pushy when he's hungry." She shook her head and then smiled at Rose.

"No problem at all," Rose responded. "No jogging for a little while," she said, raising her voice for Greg to hear.

"Have a good one," Sue said as she closed her door.

Greg punched the number into the router phone. It rang once, then was picked up. "Sue?" Tim answered.

"It's me," said Greg.

"Oh my gosh, I'm glad it's you," shouted Tim into the phone. "Are you okay?"

"Yeah. We were biking, but I ran into a sign when we split up."

"Well, ask your mom for an ice pack and lie down. You ate?"

"Yep. Virg's Dad's mac and cheese," said Greg. "I'm ready for a little nap."

"Good to hear. I'll be home soon," said Tim, "Hey, just hand me to your mom before you head to the couch."

Greg extended the spiraled cord and handed the phone to Sue. He popped open their tiny fridge in their laundry room and grabbed an ice pack, making his way to their couch. Sue watched him pass by.

"Looks like he'll be fine," said Sue as she raised the phone to her ear.

"Was there blood on him?"

She took one quick breath, almost like she smelled the air, and said, "I didn't see any, but they patched him up pretty well. Did you already know he was hurt?"

"I found some big footsteps and blood drops in the grass by the creek. I have no idea what that means, but I guess it's not from our son," said Tim.

"Jeez," said Sue, "you think there's someone else out there with an injury?"

"I have no idea. Could have been a deer . . . or a dog . . . or something. Anyway, I'll see you soon. Make sure that tyke has an ice pack on his bruise."

"He's got one," said Sue as she looked back into the living room. Greg was lying flat on the couch with the ice pack covering his forehead and eyes. It looked like he was fast asleep.

27

Doug sat in his easy chair with a ginger seltzer in his hand. He took a sip and turned toward Hutch. "You think they can fix your propeller? You're obviously staying here tonight, right?" he smiled.

Sitting down heavily on the couch, Hutch let out a sigh. "I can sleep right here on the couch if you don't mind." He spun, pulling his feet up onto the couch as he lowered his head onto a little woven pillow.

He closed his eyes and said, "I haven't been sleeping on something this nice in a while."

"You mentioned that camp you're staying at. You sleep on a cot?"

With his eyes still closed, Hutch grumbled, "Yyyyep."

"I have one in my garage if you want to re-create your free and forested snooze." Doug took another sip from his bottle and smiled.

"I'd probably rather sleep just in the grass on your lawn," said Hutch with his eyes closed.

"Tiny forest, lots of squirrel droppings," said Doug.

"We have an extra bedroom, you nerds," added Rose. She descended the stairs from Virg's bedroom, having just tucked him in. Rose plopped herself in a corduroy chair beside Doug.

"It'll feel like a hotel. Thanks, you two," said Hutch. "That propeller on my glider is scheduled for a tune-up, but they're waiting for the blades to arrive. Nothing's super wrong with the glider, but I do need a new blade before I can fly back."

"You can stay here until it's fixed," said Doug.

Hutch nodded and said, "I'll cook dinner tomorrow. You got a farmer's market around here?"

"How long is this gonna take?" Virg's voice came from outside the living room.

Doug, Rose, and Hutch turned their heads into the hallway nearby to see Virg standing there in his pajamas. "You got time?" Virg said straight to Hutch.

"For what?" asked Hutch.

"Teaching me something I should actually learn before I fall asleep tonight. I barely slept last night, and I don't know what's gonna ebb and flow before I lose consciousness."

"You're gonna be fine," said Hutch. He looked over at Rose and turned his gaze back to Virg. "But I'll help you understand your gift after you learn some necessary information at school tomorrow."

Virg stood looking at Hutch with his hands on his hips. He turned his eyes toward Rose. "Do I have to go to school if I'm registered in *this* school?" He pointed at Hutch.

"Real school? Yes," said Rose. "And Hutch's help? You can probably use that these days . . . also, I just tucked you in."

"Hear that?" said Doug to Virg. "Two schools for you now. Cheers!" He raised his ginger seltzer.

Virg's hair fell in front of his eyes as he let his forehead fall downward to show his disappointment. Turning slowly and hiking back up the stairs toward his bedroom, he said, "Don't teach me during my dreams. And stay away from Greg too."

"I'll see you tomorrow," said Hutch as he closed his eyes.

In his head, but not out loud, Virg heard, *I will teach you how to do this tomorrow.*

He didn't feel it in his ears; he felt it roll up his throat and into his mind. The sound was deep and almost echoed. He put his hands over his ears and quickly jumped under his bed sheet. His hand reached out to his lamp and flipped off the switch. Was Greg sleeping or just lying there with his eyes open? That thought rolled in his mind for a few seconds. *This is a stinkin' marathon*, he thought to himself. Once he closed his eyes, he fell asleep.

TUESDAY

28

The next school day went fast. Greg felt rested after getting through the night without any dreams. He felt that he could focus.

Virg thought about reading through the notes he took from Greg's dream. When Greg woke up on the porch, Virg asked him about what he had seen. Greg described his dream when he became unconscious after ramming his head into the propeller.

But Virg stopped. He didn't even want to think about it. The notes were confusing and nonspecific. They talked about the new assignments and teachers through their lunch but didn't bring up the day before. After finishing their school day, they sat together in the same bus seat.

The driver pushed a lever to close the door, and they started to roll home. Greg shifted his eyes from his backpack toward Virg when the bus moved. His idea of going home had altered as he remembered his last few days. Was Hutch still going to be there?

"So you're getting lessons when you get home, right? Like tonight?" said Greg.

"Well, I don't know what we're doing. But I know that Hutch can do all kinds of weird stuff," said Virg. "Last night, when I went to bed, he contacted me. But I didn't *hear* it. There was no sound. I just knew the message that he was sending. Wait, no, he said something about teaching."

"I want to learn how to do that with ice cream truck vendors." Greg looked out the window as they passed a park with people in line at an ice cream truck. His fingers touched his temples. "Toss me a cone through the fifth window on the bus," he said with just one repetitive tone and his eyes closed. It looked like he was focusing his statement on the old, mustached guy. The old man was handing cones to a woman carrying a tiny child on her waist.

"I'm not sure that's how it works or what this is for." Virg opened his backpack and looked at the thick batch of notebooks and folders he held. "I've gotta do an essay about summer." His elbow bumped into Greg's ribs. "I should write about your dreamin' and forehead slammin'."

"Great, Turd-gil," Greg turned toward Virgil with a fake frown on his face. "Tell your two dads I'm gonna write about their new lovely relationship as my summer essay." He opened his hands above his head, imagining a poster. "My Neighbor's Dad and His Heart Pilot."

They both jokingly slapped each other's hands and wrists, getting each other to finish their comedic jests. Calming down, they peered out the bus window at the neighborhoods passing by. Classmates slowly returned to their homes as they left the bus.

"I'll let you know how the first lesson goes," said Virg, sounding serious.

"Be careful," said Greg. "We don't really know this guy yet. You said he lifted our post officer off the ground, right?"

"David's not an officer, but yeah. He said that Hutch asked for his phone. And he mentioned calling his wife."

"Weird. Has he called his wife from your house?" asked Greg.

"Well, no. Not that I know of. Also, David said he didn't hear what Hutch said. But the tone was dark. Didn't sound like he was talking to his wife or his mom . . . or anyone nice to him."

Greg kept looking at Virg, trying to see if he was serious. "You wanna go back to the post office?"

"Not really. My mom told me that she and Hutch used to work at a camp together."

"I thought your mom was an antique fixer," Greg said.

"She's a freelance antique architectural salvager. Like, a wizard who can make dead stuff look alive." Virg turned toward Greg.

Their eyes met.

"Can I learn how to do that? Can I come to the lessons?" said Greg.

"She went to school for that. Or maybe she went to summer camp for that. Well, not for making stuff alive again, just for designing." Virg lightly elbowed Greg to remove his begging expression. "Really, I have no freaking idea about anything anymore."

Greg was still staring at him. His gaze was just sending a pleading vibe through Virg's backbone.

"Okay, dude. I'll ask Hutch if he can teach you. But I have no idea what I'm going to learn. And it's probably gonna suck." Virg threw his hands up and flapped them down on his thighs.

He let out a tired breath. "I'll call you after my *freakin' lesson* . . . After my *freaking day full of classes*." Virg's eyes rolled up as he lowered his eyebrows, knowing there would be no relaxing or chilling after dinner. "Ugh," he added.

"I think I'm gonna need some help with this, dude." Greg's hand wrapped around Virg's arm. "I've gotta know how to stop thinking about everything I dreamed on Sunday night. When I relax and let my mind wander, it keeps returning to what I saw in my sleep. I don't know what that was."

Virg looked down and then out the window.

"I just want to know why I got that . . . or how I can manage it," added Greg.

"For sure," Virg turned with a smile. "There's so much we don't know yet."

29

Virg and Greg got off the bus and waved goodbye to each other. As Virg walked across his front lawn, he saw that his dad's car was gone. He grabbed the front doorknob and began to kick off his shoes.

"Hey, kid," he heard from down the stairs in his living room.

"Hutch guy?"

"Your parents went out for dinner," Virg heard from downstairs as the volume of a TV news channel lowered.

Frozen in place, Virg stopped pulling his left heel from his shoe.

"Umm, why?" Virg said as he stared down the stairs, looking at no one. All he could see was the light pouring through the back door window, meeting the steps at the bottom. No shadows were moving through it.

"They wanted me to help you," Hutch said from around the corner, past Virg's view. "I'm not gonna run after you or anything. If you don't wanna learn, that's fine with me."

The sounds from the television rose. Virg thought about running out, but his foot kept pushing on his heel. He took off his socks and began to sneak down the stairs silently. When he turned the corner, he heard Hutch opening a Pop-Tart package. The wrinkling noise made his mouth water.

"Want a Pop-Tart?" said Hutch. He didn't turn.

Virg sauntered past the chair that his guest sat in. Sitting on the couch nearby, he reached out to snatch the Pop-Tart. He reclined and bit the corner off the tart.

"Is there dinner?" asked Virg.

"Yeah, your dad said there's leftovers in the fridge. I told him I'd cook, but they've still got stuff. I'll cook tomorrow night."

Looking back at the Pop-Tart in Hutch's hand, he asked, "You like the frosted strawberry one?"

"I haven't eaten anything like this in, uh, over a decade," responded Hutch.

"Where'd you find it?"

"The box was in a closed plastic chest in the garage," said Hutch.

"That's, like, really old," Virg said as he slowed down his chewing.

"It's a Pop-Tart. It would still be edible if I bought this back in 1995." Hutch's eyes didn't shift from the TV set. He looked like he was genuinely relaxing.

Virg stared at Hutch's relaxed face and decided to make it less comfortable. "So, what did your wife say when you called her a few days ago?"

Hutch turned his head to look at Virg. "That wasn't my wife that I called. I was trying to be nice and show my need for that phone. David was pretty unhelpful."

"So, who'd you call?"

"I had to call my boss to let him know I won't be working until I can return. He seemed pretty comfortable with that."

"Who's your boss?" asked Virg.

"He's a scoutmaster. He runs the camp. We cook, clean, and teach at that campsite."

"So you're a Boy Scout? I've already been one of those."

"I'm everything that he is. Chef, maid, and teacher, except I'm not an owner." Hutch happily bit into the tart.

"Is he a pilot?" asked Virg.

"No. He just doesn't have any experience with planes. If he wanted to learn, I'm sure he would pretty fast."

Virg looked at the floor and sighed. "What if I don't want to be taught this weird stuff? I don't even know what I can do."

Hutch turned off the TV and turned in his chair to face Virg. "Neither do I. But you're young. It could be an advantage because people your age think everything is possible."

Hutch reached out to touch Virg's shoulder. Virg looked up and straight into Hutch's eyes. The old eyebrows were lowered, and the greyish hair on his head made him look like he was becoming a polar bear. He was generally about the same size as one.

"I'm sorry," said Hutch. "I didn't mean to begin your process. It's my mistake. I just want to help you have control of it."

Hutch lightly gripped Virg's shoulders with his giant hands. He let go and leaned back in his chair. His other giant hand slowly brought the piece of Pop-Tart back up to his mouth when Virg didn't respond.

Virg smiled. He snapped his Pop-Tart into a few pieces and started eating them one by one. He stood up and chewed as he walked quickly toward the staircase.

"I'm heading over to the garage. I'm popping open that camping chest for some more tarts. See you in the backyard in five." He turned toward the steps.

Hutch stood up and waved a hand in the air. "Please do not get any more of these. You're gonna have to kind of meditate or something."

"See ya in the backyard," said Virg as he nodded. His serious tone made him look like he was the boss. He raised one hand to show him his fingers. "Five minutes. You want a soda? There's a little fridge in the garage too."

"Uh," Hutch lowered his head and lightly shook it, "no, just water. Can I ask you not to drink any soda? Please?"

Popping a thumbs-up, Virg said very seriously, "Confirmed. No water for me, just a cup o' urine for you." He smiled and shut the door. Then he crossed by the porch window toward the garage.

Hutch took a deep breath and flushed it through his lips. His eyebrows tightened as he predicted the upcoming experiment.

He sat back in the chair until he saw Virg heading into the backyard through the glass door. Standing up and crushing the tart wrapper in his hand, he stepped toward the sliding door and tossed his wrapper into a nearby garbage bin. Opening the sliding glass door, he stepped out and found Virg sitting in the grass with a pile of Pop-Tart packages and two soda bottles.

"Listen, I don't know if you're ready for this," said Hutch. "I feel like

I may have stunted you."

"I'm frickin' fine. If anything, learning how to control this is gonna make me feel better." Virg pushed his hands together and cracked his knuckles. "I've been getting thoughts and feelings I'm not used to. Like, I knew your name before you said it. Teach me how to forget some stuff at least or avoid the direct reception."

"Okay, okay." Hutch opened his hands and sighed.

He sat down on the grass and wiped his forehead. Looking back up, he saw Virg just staring at him. "You're not gonna like this."

"Yep. Haven't liked any of this so far," said Virg.

"Sit. Cross your legs."

Virg sat down directly about ten feet from Hutch.

"It's different for everyone," said Hutch. "You might hear me, or you might not."

Virg closed his eyes and took a deep breath. "Don't kill me."

"That's not even close to what I'm doing."

Virg pulled in a deep breath to fill his lungs. A light breeze passed a grassy scent under his nose, followed by a dandelion aroma. He let out a breath.

Are you chill yet? passed through his ears on the breeze.

"I'm chillin'," he whispered.

So, you can hear me, can't you? he heard in his head. Virg popped his eyes open and looked into Hutch's eyes. *Close those, please.* Virg didn't see any movements on Hutch's face. He closed his eyes again.

OK. So I don't have to teach you how to listen. Did your mom teach you that? softly rolled into Virg's mind. He shook his head as a response.

"How are you doing this?" he said out loud.

Don't speak out loud. You'll get the hang of it. It's like an extra muscle that needs some reps. Virg smiled and almost laughed. An excited breath rumbled out of his lungs. He lowered his shoulders and tried not to make any sounds. Pulling in another breath, he imagined that he leaned forward onto his hands, crawled toward Hutch, and whispered in his ear.

Nothing happened. The silence continued.

Virg took a breath and let the chirp of birds in the trees ripple past him. A soft breeze let his breath exit softly.

What are you thinking? rolled into Virg's mind.

"I'm creeping over toward you and whispering in your ear," Virg whispered quietly.

Directly into his head rolled, *Weird. Please don't imagine that. The creation of sound provides a vibration into the surrounding objects. Grass, trees, humidity in the air—your sound wave will hit anything and bounce off it into my ears, right?*

Virg nodded his head.

Imagine that you have that. Imagine that you aimed and loaded a wave of sound. Think that it'll bounce in the same way.

As he thought hard, Virg's shoulders slightly raised as he pushed. His body tightened. He pushed out a big rumbling fart.

He opened his eyes, and Hutch was staring at him.

"Yeah, I heard that," said Hutch. "Not exactly the perfect practice."

He stood up and walked toward Virg's living room. Sliding the door open, he went in. There were a few sounds of clinks and grumbles while Hutch looked around. He came back out with a silver triangle and a bar attached. Bending down onto his knees, Hutch put the triangle in Virg's hand.

"It's got a wire at the top. Hold that." He showed Virg how to hold the wire on the triangle and the little bar.

"The mental sound is actually a vibration. That's what you hear when I send it to you."

He pointed at the triangle. "Practice on this, and you'll hear your voice when your thought is transferring correctly."

"Jeez. This practice sounds horrible," said Virg.

Hutch raised his fist toward Virg and said, "This is what you've asked for, right?"

Virg raised his hand to bump Hutch's fist. "OK, I'll work on my homework. I promise."

Hutch got up off the grass. As he turned back to the house, the corners of his eyes wrinkled, and a smile crept into his face.

30

Returning from their date, Doug touched the brake before the alleyway and turned toward his driveway. When they stopped, Rose opened her passenger door and stood on the gravel. Her shoulders shivered, and she grabbed her hair. She pulled up her hair for a moment and then let go. It spilled back onto her shoulders. As Doug stood up, he saw her shiver again.

"Are you okay? Getting sick?"

"I'm fine, but I'm feeling a difference." She touched the back of her neck under her hair and gave it a quick massage. "I think that our boy is learning quickly."

"The po'boy you ate or the boy you raised?"

"I haven't felt this in a while. And I'm starting to hear cusses about Hutch." She moved down to one knee. It looked like a heavyweight tugged her down to the ground.

"Whoa, you okay?" Doug ran toward her and swiftly threw his arms under Rose's arms for support. "You can toss here if you need to. Could be the Brandy Milk Punch."

"I'm not going to throw up. He's just really strong. Hang on." She raised her arms to her head and closed her eyes.

Virg sat on his rear porch with his eyes closed. As he was concentrating on the triangle in his hand, a quiet vibration of it was almost visible. It was almost silent. It had been loud before, but he figured out how to lower the volume and keep it vibrating consistently. He was aiming his thoughts directly at that instrument. Virg couldn't stop practicing that method. It almost became therapeutic. That sound hummed continuously. His focus remained, even as his mind wandered.

All of a sudden, he heard *STOP. PLEASE.*

His eyes popped open, and he dropped the triangle on the porch deck.

I just got home. See you soon.

Virg turned and ran into the house, up the lower staircase, and toward the garage.

When he whipped past Hutch, he heard the guy ask, "Hey, you okay? How's the practice? I started resisting your sound current, but you were really improving."

Virg whipped around a corner. Quickly opening the door, he jumped onto his front lawn and turned his head toward the car. Both his parents were kneeling next to the vehicle. He ran to Rose and hugged her. She squeezed him while kneeling and began to smile. Virg and Doug held her while helping her stand.

"You have strength, little one," Rose said as she began pacing toward their front door. "But you have no aim."

Virg raised an eyebrow and turned his head. Looking a little confused, he said, "I did—"

"You weren't focused. Your mind was wandering. Your voice was pretty loud. I didn't know that you have that strength."

Doug put his hand on her shoulder. "She had to kneel."

Hutch, standing in the open front doorway, said, "I began to resist his current, but I didn't know you were on your way home ... or how strong it had gotten."

"It was strong enough that she looked like she was about to vomit. You can only get Brandy-Milk-*Punched* so much on a weeknight," Doug responded, raising his arms and smiling.

Rose asked Virg if he had any homework as they made their way indoors. She offered to help when he nodded and followed him into his room. Virg sat and pulled the books from his backpack. Rose grabbed a beanbag chair, set it beside her son, and collapsed into it. She faced Virg and saw the exhausted look in his eyes.

"No homework," Rose said as Virg turned around to look at her. He raised his palm, and she slapped it. "Just work in the morning."

"Thank God," Virg said as he rolled back into a relaxed position, looking like an elbow pasta noodle.

"What did Hutch help you with? You're already passing your thoughts pretty well."

Virg turned to her, looking surprised.

"But more importantly, what have you learned about Hutch? I got some of your thoughts directly when you were out back."

"Well, I didn't practice that long. I just kept trying to make that bell ring. When it worked, I just kept doing it until it seemed easy. I thought about other stuff once I got the hang of it."

Rose shook her head. "What has Hutch told you about? Just the silent connection?"

"Well, that's all he told me about the skill. But I asked him about lifting David off the floor in the post office. And the intense phone call he had with his boss."

Rose's heartbeat pumped a bit faster. "He lifted the postman off his feet?"

"That's what David said. Told me that Hutch needed to make an *urgent* phone call." His fingers pumped air quotes on the word. Virg rolled his eyes. "The scoutmaster, camp-owner guy, needed to know if Hutch wasn't returning."

"Any answers?" Rose asked as she folded her arms.

"David told me that Hutch didn't find who he was looking for, but he'll get back to him about his glider shortly."

"Jesus," said Rose. She leaned back and sighed. "Anything else?"

"Yeah. David said that he heard their conversation quickly in the beginning. But then they stopped talking. He said Hutch closed his eyes and kept the phone at his heart for a little while. There was no goodbye before he hung up."

"When I heard your thoughts in the driveway, you said Hutch told David he needed to call his wife."

"Yeah, but the voice David heard was low."

"Okay, I'll talk to him about it. Thanks for all your help, sweetie." Rose leaned toward Virg and kissed him on top of his head.

"Thanks. So, I don't have to do my homework?"

Rose reached down to snag a large, rectangular paperback next to Virg's desk. She flapped it into her son's lap. "*Calvin and Hobbes* is a great homework. Start cartooning and improve that vocabulary. No homework. I'll help you tomorrow before we leave for school."

"Done," said Virg as he got up from his desk. He calmly tossed the book on his carpeted bedroom floor. Lying down on his stomach, he opened it up to the first page of cartoons. Only needing one moment, Rose saw her son imagining himself within the sketch's world. His feet were stacked behind him, and he looked calm. Leaning on his elbows, he crossed his legs behind himself.

Rose smiled, pushed off the beanbag chair, and rolled forward to stand up. As she turned away from Virg, her smile vanished. She grabbed the doorknob and closed the door behind her as she left. Rose turned back for a moment, but she stopped. Turning back around, she made her way down the stairs.

31

Tim was sitting at his dinner table stirring a bowl of whiskey ginger carrots. Those button-sized slices drew his eye momentarily as Sue described her workday just ahead. His eyes rolled away from the bowl toward Greg's forehead. In the morning, they'd removed one side of his bandage to see if it was still needed. It wasn't bleeding any more. The kid just had a touch of black and blue above the scab line. The scab itself was like a wide letter U. It wasn't too serious. He'd heal. But the cut itself didn't look like it was received from a fence collision.

"So, I'll be heading over around 9:30 p.m. Just check in with Greg to see if that homework is done," said Sue. Tim didn't respond. The direction of his gaze made Sue repeat herself.

"Tim, make sure that he does his homework."

He and Greg both looked directly at her. "I will," said Tim. "Do you have a couple of essays or anything for tonight?"

"I don't have any homework due tomorrow, but Virg said that Hutch will be his tutor. I might head over to Virg's place tomorrow for some tutoring." He looked down at his plate.

Tim dropped his fork on his napkin and raised his hands. "What? You already need a tutor? What for? Pretty sure you haven't taken a single test yet."

"Everyone gets a tutor these days. It just helps you get better at studying and using your skills."

"I'm pretty sure that you know how to read. Also, your grade in German last year was an A+. Is he a tutor for college résumés?" Tim's pressured gaze shifted toward Sue.

She responded quickly. "Yes, your son is doing great." Her wink made Tim relax. "But I support you being interested in your own studying methods. If you want some help and are comfortable telling us that, we support that choice." Her eyes met Tim's. She smiled and shoved a stabbed spinach leaf into her proud jaw.

Tim kept quiet. His wife and son discussed the teachers Greg had met and the upcoming basketball season. While sharing his plan to try out for a travel basketball squad, Greg's tone was lively and calming. Full from his meal and tired from his workday, Tim floated toward relaxation.

Then his eyes crawled back to Greg's wound. An open curve and a sharp slice just confused him. The possibility of getting a cut like that from a fence just returned him to his question.

He held his tongue and waited until after he loaded the dishwasher, watched the news, and heard Greg brushing his teeth upstairs. His son was posing in the bathroom mirror, acting like Arnold Schwarzenegger, making his tiny biceps flex. Tim calmly leaned against the door frame.

Greg turned to see his dad smiling. "Oh, hey, Dad. I'm not supposed to be lifting yet, but these puppies are becoming warhorses on their own. Think that'll give me a role as a power forward on that travel squad?" His tongue shot out and curled as he pumped a flex of his bicep.

Tim chuckled. "As long as you still have a clean forehead when you try out. And, hey, with that cut, did you actually hit something like a lantern . . . or I don't know. I'm not calling you out, but I just wanted to know if you hit something other than a fence and didn't want it to be weird when you told us. Looks like you hit something sharp."

His son lightly touched his scab as Tim watched his eyes scan back and forth in the mirror. "Um, if I remember correctly, there was a piece of metal that they put on their fence, like for designs and stuff. Virg's mom is like an antique person. I don't remember what it was. An oar or, umm, like a plane or something?"

"So there *was* metal on their fence?"

"Yeah, but—"

"No worries. I just wanted to see if you needed a tetanus jab or anything. I'm sure you're fine." Tim turned and walked back around the banister and down the stairs. As he lowered from step to step, he decided that tomorrow, *he might sit in on the tutor session.*

WEDNESDAY

32

Greg sat in his chemistry class, and the lights went down as a slide show began. His pupils dilated, and then his exhaustion led him into a shallow nap. He couldn't forget his dreams the night before, and a few images passed by in his memories.

With his elbows on his desk and his chin in his hands, he tried to keep his eyes open, staring at the projection screen. While the lights were off, the projection beam was warm and golden. Images on the screen showed a vertically split desert. All the levels, deep into the ground, accented the size and distance of the land. Pointed arrows connected to a list of items, identifying each level of the desert grounds. A water hole was surrounded by sand with a geothermal pool beneath it. Greg was almost falling asleep again. The warm colors and the low lights were meeting him in the final period of his school day.

He almost saw himself within the images on the screen. *I wanna flow down into my geo pool*, he thought. He shook his head as some memories cropped back into his consciousness. His dreams on the night Hutch arrived cropped back into his mind and opened wide as he fell into a snooze. Did he just dream that all over again? The moonlight on Hutch's face drew Greg's mind back into his dreams.

His heavy eyelids closed comfortably. The image of the moon brought him back into his mind to see Hutch. The man held the hand of a small child. The tiny hand in Hutch's mitt looked like a seed in a bucket. Through a vast forest, two individuals paced comfortably past rows of trees. Hutch rested his other hand on the kid's chest to stop her momentarily.

Greg didn't hear any talking but saw their mouths move. Then Hutch pointed at the tall white pine tree in front of them. They stood looking at it, and the kid raised her other hand as a fist. The grand pine tree they stared at disappeared. Hutch's mouth hatched into a tiny smile. He turned his head to look at the kid.

The little girl opened her hand, and the tree came back into view. She began to raise her hand, and the tree rose completely out of the ground. Dirt, moss, and pebbles were slipping off the base of the root wreath. Hutch's mouth opened with fear as he saw the tree torn from the ground. It floated effortlessly in its natural position.

As the kid clenched her fist back together, squeezing hard, the entire tree exploded and shot splinters in every direction. It looked almost as if every single cell was split apart. Hutch's eyes blinked and opened wide. His hand raised swiftly with his pinkie pointed toward the tree. He shut his eyes quickly and squeezed the child's hand in his. All the chips and shards flew past, around, and through the two hand holders. The splinters lodged into the dirt, roots, and trunks surrounding them.

A shivered breath poured out from Hutch's lungs. He turned his head down to see the person next to him. The girl smiled and stared straight back at Hutch. She reached down, ripped a splinter from the ground, and shoved it into Hutch's thigh.

The kid's laugh and Hutch's scream jolted Greg back into reality. His eyes flew open in the dark room. He peered around, and no one was paying any attention to him. They were staring at the screen ahead or sleeping with their heads on their desks. The classroom lights flicked back on and startled Greg. A moment later, the dismissal bell rang. He pushed his chair back and packed his folders into his backpack.

Virg saw Greg enter the bus. He waved his hands and pulled his backpack off the seat next to him.

"Good day, huh? Not much homework yet."

"Yeah, not much." Greg sat beside Virg and laid his backpack between his legs. "I'm seeing my dreams again. They're from that first night we saw Hutch outside."

"I was gonna ask you about that. I still have those notes, but I don't really know the story, and I haven't asked Hutch about them yet."

"Don't say anything," Greg replied softly.

"I don't have to. I mean, you know more about those images than I do."

"The dreams came back. I fell asleep during my science class, and they just popped back up."

Virg lowered his brow, looking curious. He kept silent, just waiting for Greg to go further.

"OK, so I told you I saw him with kids at a camp or something." He put his palms over his eyes, shutting out any light. "This time, I saw him leading a small kid through a forest. He was holding the guy's hand. The kid didn't touch a tree, but he lifted his hand, and a tall one ripped itself outta the ground and just floated. It was gigantic. He gripped the air, and that thing exploded into itty-bitty pieces that flew and sank into everything around it."

Virg's mouth dropped open as his eyes widened. "A kid? Did he die? Did the splinters stab them?"

Greg kept his hands over his eyes. "No. Hutch made them into water or clouds or . . . uhh . . . something that doesn't hold anything physically. Those shot right through them."

"I wanna learn how to do that."

"The kid was a child. She picked up a splinter and stabbed Hutch in the leg."

"Jesus. This was a dream?"

"I wasn't inventing it. It feels like a memory, but it's not mine."

"Is that possible?"

Greg took his hand off his eyes and looked Virg in the eyes. "I have no idea, but I want to find out."

"Hutch told me that he's planning to make dinner tonight. Think you can come over for din din and a tutoring session?"

Greg smiled as he let his head lean back against the bus seat. "I'd like to do that before I fall asleep again." His stomach rumbled, and he turned toward Virg. "Any idea what he's cookin'?"

33

Greg opened his front door and saw his dad. Waving, he said, "We're all invited to dinner at the Murphys."

Sue paced toward their living room, holding a plastic bin with dozens of pairs of underwear within. "That sounds pretty nice. What are they making?"

"Their tutor guest is gonna cook for them tonight. I have no idea what he's making, but he's using the grille. I think he went shopping today."

"Ooooh yeah. Let's do that. They like to eat on their porch in their backyard? Sounds like a party." Sue turned toward Tim as she put the hamper near a folding table. "Dad, look into the garage and see if we have any Pinot. It's Wednesday, but if they're sharing their dinner, we can gift them a sip of relaxation. Also, that tutor sounds great. Cooker and teacher? Sign me up." She winked at Greg.

"Sounds good to me," said Tim. He rose from his chair and thought about his plan to ask Hutch about his glider. Tim was curious about Hutch, but he also loved to examine and improve vehicles. It would be good to get the opportunity to talk to his son's new tutor. He smiled a bit as he opened his back door and approached the fridge in his garage.

"How's your head feeling?" asked Sue.

"It's feeling pretty good. I fell asleep at the end of my last class today."

"Oh, come on. Did anyone yell at you?"

Greg shook his head. "Nah. When I woke, I saw others asleep too. It was a projection screen. The lights were off, and it was the end of the day. I bet that the teacher was asleep too." He smiled and saw his mom shaking her head.

"Just keep learning and try to pay attention," she said. She pulled clean pairs of underwear from the hamper and tossed them onto the table next to her. As she began folding, she said to herself, "I'm not surprised that you're looking for a tutor."

Greg heard her and snickered. "Gotta learn my lesson."

Tim slammed the door behind him with his foot. He was holding a bottle in each hand.

"You okay with Pinot Grease-io and Pinot Noir? It's like light and dark of a similar-sounding flavor." He lifted his shoulders.

Sue kept folding. "Sounds great. Just pop the *Grigio* into the fridge and nest that Noir in the long bottle bag."

"You've got a lesson this evening?" Tim asked Greg.

"He'll meet the tutor tonight," answered Sue. "Perhaps he can stay after for a lesson if he wants to." She raised her eyebrows, looking at her son.

"Umm, my current lesson is 'How to eat correctly without staying hungry.' Can you teach me?" He stood up, hunched over, and limped with one rigid leg toward his dad. It looked like he became Igor from Frankenstein. He lowered one eyebrow and crunched his lips and nose together, creating a hideous impression center.

Tim chuckled and said, "You look a-teach-able, my assistant." He tapped his index finger on Greg's head, wrapped his arms around him, and hugged him. "Head up and start working on your homework. Gotta finish that before we head over."

Greg's head lowered. "All right. I have almost nothing. First week in school."

He went back through his living room to grab his backpack. Sue and Tim looked at each other and smiled. Greg quickly hiked up the stairs, and they heard him toss his bag next to his desk.

Tim went upstairs into their kitchen and put a Pinot Grigio into their fridge. As he closed the fridge door, he didn't move for a moment and just listened to a little voice coming out of Greg's room.

"OK, number one: splinter explosion. Number two: what is the deal with your camp? Number three: can I make things disappear? Number four: does slamming my head against something help or hurt my learning abilities?"

Tim barely heard what Greg was saying as he approached his bedroom door. Greg walked toward the door and pulled it open.

"Hey, what's up?" Greg saw his dad and was holding a notebook and a pen.

"What's your assignment? Are you supposed to ask questions?" Tim looked confused.

"No, it's just a little list I wanted to make. I've been having dreams, and I'm just writing down things I want to figure out."

"Like, to use in your art or something?" asked Tim.

"Uh, for sanity. I don't wanna go crazy." Greg smiled and raised his fist toward his dad.

"Respect." Tim raised his fist and bumped. "P.S. homework completion leads to meal consumption."

"I'm hitting the bathroom," said Greg as he stepped past his dad.

Tim looked into Greg's bedroom for a moment, then turned back and leaned against the wall in the hallway.

34

Hutch had fired up the grill in the Murphy's backyard. The coals got warm as the venison's hindquarter lay seeping in a plastic bucket. Juniper berries, sage, bay leaves, and mashed blueberries surrounded the meat. Hutch had also splashed a pour of local Chambourcin wine into the bucket, and six shorn sweet potatoes sat on the grill.

A car door slammed closed in the driveway. Rose slid open the porch door and waved at Hutch to meet her on the stones. She introduced him to Sue and Tim. Doug popped out and gave Tim a high five, followed by a hug. Greg stood holding the two bottles of wine for the Murphys. He handed them to Doug in one bag.

Tim's perspective shifted into the Murphys' backyard. He got excited seeing the grill and the rope that was tied from the fence to the wooden pillar of their laundry drying rack. His eyes popped wide when he saw the entire hide of a deer hanging on the rope. It looked like it was separated from the animal, just like a complete set of pajamas. It was just hanging and drying.

"Whoa, dude." Tim looked back at Hutch. "*Very* nice to meet you, man." He extended his hand toward Hutch's paw. As Hutch's big hand engulfed Tim's, he turned back toward the deer hide. "Did you salt that thing?"

"Sure did. The only things I bought today were this bottle of wine and that bag of salt." She pointed toward the open Chambourcin bottle sitting next to the grill and the bag lying against the outdoor laundry line post.

"Dude . . . Welcome to PA! You're gonna teach my son how to get one of those on his own?" Tim said, pointing at the hide. "He might be learning things that people really need to learn." Tim opened his arms and hugged Hutch.

Hutch rolled his eyes as Tim's head contacted his chest. Tim squeezed Hutch's core until he chuckled. Lightly tapping Tim's shoulder, he said, "I'll try to do my best. I don't know exactly what he needs to learn yet. But after dinner, I was going to sit with him and Virgil. Just for some introduction and tryouts."

"I'm okay with that." Tim backed off, and his eyes lowered to the bucket next to the grill. He saw the stack of blueberries and leaned over to sniff it.

"All local," said Hutch.

"Wow, it's sweet and . . ." he paused to pull a few small sniffs from the bucket, "clean smelling." Tim rose with his brows pushed into his nasal bridge. He looked a bit confused.

"That's the rosemary. Kinda scrubs your nostrils with that sweet, grassy scent."

"Where'd you get these?" Tim turned his head onto the grill, pointing at the sweet potatoes. "And these?"

"Well, local stuff, but Rose got those blueberries from the farmer's market. I always just rip them off bushes in Maine when I can. The sage, juniper berries, and bay leaves were on the hills I passed by. Clipped 'em and tossed 'em in that bucket." Hutch pointed down to the venison container.

He turned his head back up toward the mountain ridges. "When I went onto the hill this morning, I brought a sack and a bow with me. That's how I got the deer."

"Wow," said Sue. She looked at Rose and lightly pressed her elbow into her ribs. "Guy knows what he's doin'."

"You got those sweet potatoes from that market?" asked Tim.

"Well, when I returned with the deer, I saw some yellow vines in the sandy spot next to the river at the top of the hill. I recognized them and pulled a few. That ridge faces south and gets a ton of the sun's rays. I pulled out some wild sweet potatoes at just the right time. It's probably been a while since they got planted or fell out of someone's pack." Hutch smiled.

"How do you notice something like that?" asked Sue. "We've been here for years. I've never seen a ripe sweet potato vine."

"Well, I've farmed a lot lately. Some of the farming is finding wild, ripened plants. There are tons of mushrooms up in Maine from June to Thanksgiving. I figured I'd go with Rose to your local farmers market, but I found a bunch of tasty-looking wild ones this morning." He pointed toward their surrounding Appalachian Mountain ridges miles away. "Those tall rims have tons of stuff. Different on every level."

"You must know those mountains really well," said Tim.

"Well, not those." He tossed his open hand back toward the nearby peaks. "I know some of Maine's mountains, but these are sort of similar. Just more bugs where I'm from."

"I thought you said that you flew here from Boston . . . Did you fly from Maine?" Virgil was staring at him with a confused look on his face.

Hutch turned fast and looked at him, but he didn't respond quickly.

"I, uh . . . I live in Maine these days." He paused again. ". . . but I got that glider in Boston. Sold an old one in Maine and found a better one in Boston."

Virg saw a bead of sweat roll down Hutch's forehead. He said, "I'm glad that the wind steered you down to us and not back up to Maine."

Hutch caught his composure and smiled at Virg. "Me too."

Tim smiled and threw his arm around Hutch as they clinked their glasses together. "My son's right. We're glad to have you."

They shuffled onto the porch where Doug showed them open chairs to rest in. They sat and talked about scouting and camping for a while. When the coals were covered with white-grey ash, Hutch dropped the dripping venison onto the grill and closed the hatch around the meat and potatoes. The three men sat together in the porch chairs and waited for the meal to cook.

Rose and Sue sat on the nearby porch couch, sipping and gossiping. The men sat nearby, sharing stories about their childhood and boy scouting. Greg and Virg listened for a while but then jumped off the porch and ran into the grass for a game of cornhole. Hutch got up and made his way back to check on the grill. When he did, Tim took another sip from his glass and got up—following Hutch.

"Hey, thanks so much for helping out Greg. I'm looking forward to your skill-sharing bizzness," he said.

"No problem. It's great to meet you too. So glad that you have all that experience."

"Let me know if you ever need help fixing that glider. I grew up with my grandpa, who was a mechanic, and I've got some skills in that regard."

"Sounds great. I dropped that off at a local guy, and he's just waiting for the blades to get delivered."

Tim took another sip and swallowed. "Greg told me he helped get that glider under the bridge. It wasn't there when Pete and I drove by to help out."

Hutch said nothing. He grabbed the tongs and flipped the hindquarter on the hot, black bars. A slight lather crept out of his forehead as he considered his response. His eyes stuck to the meat, avoiding Tim's gaze. Wiping his hairline with his wrist, he reached back down to turn the sweet potatoes.

"I made a call down at the post office. Rose helped me out and got that over to the mechanic."

"That was quick," said Tim. The wineglass in his hand wiggled slightly as he moved it to his mouth. He took another sip. "So you knew she was here?"

Hutch grabbed the grill handle and lowered it down to contain the heat. As he did, he turned his large frame toward Tim.

Tim's vision looked at the enormous shoulders before him and shifted up into Hutch's eyes. They looked nervous and impatient. Above his eyes, Tim saw a pool of sweat lifting out of his skin. "Doug told me you camped next to your glider that first night."

Hutch took a small step forward. Tim's neck craned upward.

Doug's voice broke in over Tim's shoulder, "Yo, Hutch, come over here and hear about Sue's brother who lives in Maine. He's got an oyster farm up there. You ever want to try some of those when you get back? C'mere!"

Hutch's gaze shifted from Doug back down to Tim. Then he raised his eyes back to Doug. "Rose helped me that first day, but I didn't feel comfortable staying at her place if I would get the fix in just one day. I'm used to living outdoors. After that first day, the mechanic told me the update would take a few days. That made me more comfortable to accept her offer. Sleeping in a bed for the first time in a long time? C'mon." He smiled, grabbed Tim's shoulder, softly turned him around, and brought him back to the families.

As Hutch and Tim returned to the group, they both thought, *Gosh, that was a close one.*

After gobbling the tasty berry-sauced venison and potatoes, Greg and Virg still had some high energy. They popped off the porch and ran into the backyard to spend some of it. When their parents left the table and went inside, Doug dropped a stack of cards on the living room table.

"Anyone ready for some poker?" He reached behind to the bookcase and grabbed a tiny green see-through visor. He turned around and slapped it on his head.

"I haven't played in a long time," Hutch responded, pushing himself forward in the chair to see the cards.

Sue laughed. "I'm down. Anyone want another round?" She stood up and made her way toward the fridge in the garage.

Tim and Rose raised their hands. Doug turned and winked at her. She smiled and made her way to grab another round.

Doug got down on his knees and shuffled the deck on their coffee table. "I'll walk you through for a sec." He met eyes with Tim and Rose. "Wanna do a little fake round for him?"

"Heck, yeah. It's been a while since I played too," said Tim.

"Always happy for a refresher," added Rose. They all wiggled their butts into their seats and smiled as they got comfy.

In the backyard, the boys were wandering along the fence. They found a spot far enough away to sit down with some privacy. Sipping their ginger ales as Virg rested his back on the fence and extended his legs out on the grass, Greg watched him and did the same. They stared through the fence toward the alley that met the main road.

Looking in the same direction, Virg said, "You have that list of questions?"

Greg popped his little four-question piece of paper out of his back pocket. He opened it up and handed it across his lap onto Virg's.

"Hmm," he said as he read through them quickly.

"I mean, I'm gonna ask 'em," said Greg.

"That's totally fine. But maybe wait until after he tries to give you some skills."

"I can do that," Greg nodded and pointed at the paper in Virg's hand, "but I'll probably be thinking about these the whole time."

Virg looked down the alleyway toward the road. A soft, warm light from the streetlamp splashed over the road at the end of the alley. The road was visible, but anything from the end of the alley to their backyard was dark and calming.

"I think it'll be easier to open your mind in the darkness. Less stimulations," said Virg.

Greg raised his gaze down the alley toward the streetlamp. They both saw a small shadow crawl onto the alley with the soft light behind it. It looked like a small fox pacing around and lifting its nose.

The two boys sat up just a bit, still leaning against the fence. "Is it smelling that grill?" said Greg.

"Probably. But don't they eat small things like frogs?"

"Didn't we see that fox around the creek?"

"No idea, dude," said Virg.

Whipping its nose around a few times, the fox followed the scents across the alley and away from the house. The boys relaxed. A touch of cool air swept past them. After sundown, the idea of letting their minds wander in the dark felt a little relaxing.

Greg turned to Virg and said, "Yeah, I'll wait to ask him. I wanna follow what he says in our lesson. Seems like the right time of day to learn."

Greg lifted his bottle toward Virg. They clinked their ginger ale bottles together. Lying back and taking a sip, they enjoyed the little bubbles in their mouths.

After their game, Hutch was maneuvering through questions from Tim and Sue. They loved hearing about what Hutch and his boss, Mata, did in Maine. The idea of working at a healing adult scout camp sounded blissful.

"You just teach people how to live independently?" asked Sue.

"Well, yes, but we try to help them notice and enjoy the real world around them. It's almost therapy." Hutch was sweating down the back of his neck. He'd been trying to avoid the truth of his connection to Mata and their actual occupation.

"That's great. You said that Mata was your professor. What'd he teach at college?"

"He taught psychology, but he taught gardening too. *That* one was quite popular."

Rose started getting uncomfortable thinking about Mata. She thought about the moment she found Hutch down at the creek. He had mentioned his boss's changes. Rose hadn't asked him what the issue had bloomed into. Why was Hutch's tone totally positive when answering Sue? He hadn't mentioned any magic or issues with his boss to Greg's parents. He hadn't attempted to explain this camp's mystical nature.

Rose didn't hear it, but her name was being spoken repeatedly while she was lost in thought.

"Rose, Rose?" Doug reached out and softly put his hand on the back of her arm. Her attention shifted from inner monologue to the people at the table looking at her.

"Sue had a question about you knowing Mata." Doug pointed toward Sue.

"Oh, I'm sorry. What did you ask?" Rose rolled her hair behind her ears.

"So you'd met this guy too?" asked Sue.

Hutch turned his gaze toward Rose. She looked back at him, seeing a slight plead for agreement.

Rose turned back toward Sue and said, "Yeah, I worked for him for a few summers, but I didn't want to spend my entire year at a campsite. I was drawn to old towns that held strong, beautifully made buildings. That's kind of what I majored in."

She lifted her shoulders, then turned her focus to Hutch. "Is Mata your wife nowadays?" She smiled and saw Hutch's face flush red.

"No, I haven't proposed yet." He patted the back of his neck with his napkin and smiled. "Why? Did someone suggest that I sound like I'm in love?"

"David, the clerk down at the post office said that you wanted to call your wife from his phone when you arrived." She stared directly into Hutch's eyes, waiting for a sign.

Hutch looked down at his plate. "I said that so I could use the phone. I'm sorry I did. Just thought I'd sound more needy if I brought up calling my wife." He looked back at Rose and said, "If I just asked to call my boss, I figured I wouldn't get any help."

Rose kept her eyes on him. He lightly raised the bandana on his neck to remove the sweat below his hairline.

Tim broke the rising tension. "I'd call my boss too if I were about to miss working shifts." Everyone chuckled. "Ya know, one time, I was hired to help weigh the concrete pieces of an in-ground pool. These people were living on a cliffside, and if you want to hack into that ground, you need people who can tell if it's safe."

Everyone began to relax as Tim's topic took their focus. Rose kept her eyes on Hutch for a moment. Then she turned toward Virg and saw him give her a little smile. He looked comfortable. A little dish of Rose's leftovers sat next to her. Grabbing the plate and her fork, she returned to stabbing the venison.

35

The families had finished their dinner and games. Slowly, they made their way back onto the porch. They looked up as the stars burgeoned from the vast darkness above. After Tim and Sue helped move the dishes into the kitchen sink, the adults finished their glasses and went to the front door. Before they left, Greg's parents hugged the Murphys.

Tim shook Hutch's hand. "Thanks, and let me know how it goes. Not too late now." He pointed toward the backyard, where Greg was still gnawing on a Popsicle stick. "He's got a different school to visit tomorrow." Tim winked.

"I'll do my best," said Hutch.

"Backyard lessons tonight?" asked Tim.

"Yeah, a lesson in the backyard should be nice and easy tonight. I may take them to the forest near the baseball park tomorrow. Seems nice and quiet there too."

Tim nodded and reached out to Hutch's hand. He squeezed lightly. "Thanks for doing this." Tim and Sue made their way outside, held hands, and began to pace back to their home.

As Rose and Doug made their way up the stairs and back to the kitchen, she turned to face Hutch. "Give them a nice and easy session." She took another step up on the flight. Then stopped and turned around. Descending and walking straight over to Hutch, she hugged him and said, "Thank you for dinner. That was wonderful."

Her eyes moved up to his. "Be careful. Please don't push them. Just a little help is all they need." She smiled and turned to go back up to the kitchen.

Hutch turned toward the porch door. He took a deep breath and felt his gut working hard to digest his dinner. Moving through the sliding glass door, he shut it behind him.

"You guys wanna just relax in the grass for a minute? My tummy is still working."

Greg opened his eyes. He lay flat on the porch's couch with a Popsicle stick protruding from his mouth. "I'm relaxin' already, Scoutmaster." He closed his eyes again.

"Okay, good." Hutch wiped his forehead with his bandana. "Let's just lie down in the grass." He walked across the porch and into the open space in their backyard. Hutch wandered on the lawn until he felt comfortable and not distracted. There were almost no beams of light brightening their grass. A soft glaze from the moon just calmly warmed their perspective. Hutch's eyes adjusted. Natural trees and bushes surrounding their grounds hid the lights of houses nearby. He sat down cross-legged. Then, because his stomach was protruding over his pants, he lay back and spread out on the grass. He felt massaged by the lawn as the cool blades of grass cupped his neck.

"This is a good spot," he said out loud.

Greg and Virg spotted him and walked in his direction.

Seeing the big man lie down, Greg said, "Perfect. He'll teach us how to relax. I've been waiting for this my entire life."

"As long as he's not lying on tons of rabbit turds. That might help me lose my focus." Virg turned to Greg, and they both giggled.

Both boys sat down and lay back, spreading their legs.

"So, how are you feeling?" Hutch asked.

"Umm, I'm fine," responded Virg.

"Greg, how's your head?"

"Feels fine." He reached up to touch the spot he rammed against the glider.

"Good." Hutch let it get quiet for a moment. "Do you remember smelling that marshmallow before you whacked your head into the glider blade?"

"Yep," said Greg. "I smelled a marshmallow. But I didn't smell your glider."

"Yes, your mind creates associations early on," responded Hutch. "Your brain will find options, and your mind will push you in different directions. You're using old associations to decide what could be good or bad."

"So, you're saying that I have no idea if my feelings are real or suggested . . . in my brain?" asked Greg.

"You're changing," said Hutch. "Good luck."

"He helped me," Virg said to Greg. With his eyes closed and his head in the grass, it seemed like he trusted Hutch's lessons.

"So what should I do?" asked Greg.

Hutch answered, "Just quiet down. I'll reach out to you. When you receive my message, allow yourself to relax and control where your thoughts are flowing. It's almost as if your breaths will be aimed at me. They'll hold your thoughts. At least use that as an example. It's not really the full reality."

"Okay," said Greg. He took a deep breath and released it calmly.

"Don't fart," said Virg. "You get a D on this test if you do."

They both laughed and lightly rolled back and forth in the grass. Suddenly, they both heard *No farts needed. You both stink already.*

"Holy . . ." Greg stopped and opened his eyes. He looked straight up into the sky. Looking at the sheet of bright stars, he felt like he was floating for a moment.

You don't need to speak out loud. You and Virgil both heard my thoughts on the first try. That's wild. Congrats, gifted student.

Greg said quietly, "Virg, you hear this?"

"Yep, I did last time too. You can aim your message by thinking about the person you want to connect with."

That's right, they both heard.

Greg closed his eyes and imagined floating up toward the stars. Hovering above, he imagined that he rolled back around, looking down. He imagined his voice shooting down at Hutch lying in the grass. *You reached out to me on the first night I met you. I got tons of weird information this way.*

Those thoughts poured quickly out of Greg before he even imagined what he was doing.

You're really good at this. Creeping into Greg's mind, Hutch's words made his heart beat quickly.

Still imagining himself above and staring down at Hutch, he said, *Why did you do this to me before I even knew you?*

I didn't know that anyone except Rose could receive this. I didn't know you were here, Hutch responded. *It's kind of amazing that you're this far already. I'm hearing your thoughts. Not everyone hears these. You have to work on connecting with people who can receive your thoughts. It's a skill on its own.*

Before Greg could control his message, he let out his thoughts. *Number one: splinter explosion. Number two: what is the deal with your camp? Number three: can I make things disappear? Number four: does slamming my head against something help or hurt my learning abilities?*

Shut up, Greg heard. Virg extended his leg and slapped his heel against Greg's shin.

Hutch's voice seemed calm. *I don't know what you're asking, but I can help you with other things. You've already got the hang of this. How to make things disappear? I'll work with you and Virg tomorrow on that.*

Greg felt a bit more comfortable from that response. *How do I limit my voice?*

You have to create a small vibration and aim it directly at the people you want to hear it.

Still floating above the lawn in his imagination, Greg turned his head directly at Virg. *I hope he didn't hear everything I said.*

Virg responded directly to Greg. *I did.*

Let's finish this lesson for tonight, breathed Hutch into their minds. *I've got a full belly, and I might have to walk around to help digest this. You guys can practice this with each other if you want. That's probably helpful.*

Hutch rolled forward, raising his back off the ground. Sticking a hand behind himself in the grass, he pushed up to stand. Virg and Greg looked exhausted. They kept lying down but opened their eyes to see Hutch standing above them. His broad silhouette removed tons of stars from their vision. He extended a hand to each of them.

"Nice job tonight, my students."

They couldn't see his face but noticed his smile in the widening of his skull. His jawline rounded and extended as his smile puffed his cheeks outward. They both rose to reach his hand. He grabbed them both lightly and lifted them to their feet effortlessly.

"Head to bed and get a good night's sleep."

They shook their heads, and Greg looked at Virg. "Marshmallow moment?"

"Dude, you had a popsicle," said Virg.

They opened the sliding porch door and shuffled inside. Lightly arguing over their additional desserts, they didn't turn around to thank their teacher.

Hutch watched them go inside. He stood still for a moment. Slowly pacing backward, Hutch turned and began walking up the alley toward the streetlamp. When he reached the end, he made a left and began pacing down the road. Lightly rubbing his hand on his stomach, he thought about his day. He enjoyed his morning hunt and thought about the hide hanging in the backyard.

Hutch slowed down his pace when the post office came into view. Moving past the inbox, he rested his hand on the doorknob. He gave it a tiny wiggle and felt the lock. He closed his eyes and put his fingertips on the brass bolt. Focusing his energy on the fixture, he turned his hand. The bolt slid out of the rim of the door frame. The door opened easily. He stepped into the pitch-black entranceway. Grasping the tiny mailroom doorknob within, he opened it and stepped into the storage room.

Hutch lifted the phone off its hook. He left the dial wheel untouched. As he closed his eyes, the shell of the phone vibrated lightly in his hand. No ringing happened. The phone rested completely still in his hand. A light scent of smoke rose out of the old earpiece. A quiet buzz rolled into Hutch's ear. He spun around to ensure no one was in the office. The message from the phone silently hummed into his skull.

He answered in silence, floating his thoughts through the receiver. *They're further along than we thought. Let me just open them up before I come back. They don't even know what they're capable of.*

Another small buzz came through the phone into Hutch's ear.

They can view memories already. One of them had a vision. It showed some of the others we've had, sent Hutch.

Another buzz.

No, I won't tell them. They know enough.

Thursday

36

Greg woke up in his bed with an empty stomach. He immediately got up to explore the kitchen but peeked out his window toward the Murphys' backyard. Looking at the spot he lay on last night, he took a deep breath. His focus crawled upward toward Virg's bedroom window. Virg seemed to be on his knees with his eyes and nose just above the base of his window.

You're up. Greg heard in his mind. He backed away from the window and almost tripped. Holding himself upright, he slowly paced back to see Virg.

Can we, like, have another alarm set for the mental contact? Greg sent it to Virg.

No response came. When Greg got back to his window, he didn't see Virg. Greg threw on his shorts and buttoned up a short-sleeve shirt. On his way downstairs, he rolled his fist in his eye to release some wax and flakes.

"Morning, student," Tim said as Greg entered the kitchen.

Greg popped on a fake-looking smile.

"You feeling more prepared to explore this weekend?"

"I'm gonna explore a midday nap this weekend," said Greg as he scratched his scalp. His mane felt ironed into a spike during last night's sleep. He opened the door to the fridge and pulled out a bottle of orange juice.

"There's bread toasting right now. You want an egg or something?"

"That'd be swell," Greg said as he yawned. He poured the juice into a coffee mug.

Tim got up and buttered a pan on the stove. Cracking eggs into a tiny bowl, he asked, "When do you think he'll take you on a hunt?"

Greg rolled his eyes. "I dunno. Seems complicated. I mean, I just learned how *not* to talk while hunting. Just sending signals and stuff." Greg reeled his hands around in the air and faked some signals.

"Wild!" Tim looked totally pumped as he whipped the eggs with a fork. As he poured the eggs into the pan, he turned to look at Greg. He noticed his son massaging the bump on his forehead. Tim's gaze was a little worried, and Greg saw the message.

"I feel fine, Dad. I'm still waking up a bit." Greg took a big sip from his mug.

As the kid removed his hand from his forehead, Tim saw that the cut had improved. No bruise, just a very dry scab that would probably fall off soon. He felt a bit calmer.

"Just don't pick your scab," he said as he flipped the eggs in the pan and lowered the heat. He tossed a shred of cheddar on top and covered the pan. "You'll have a scar if you tear that thing off."

Are you ready yet? Greg heard loudly in his head. He backed away from the table and almost flipped the chair. He flapped his hands over his ears, letting go of the mug and seeing it crash to the floor. A small pool of orange juice splattered around his naked feet.

"Whoa, are you okay?" Tim turned to see Greg holding his head.

Closing his eyes and imagining Virg sitting in his bedroom at the foot of his bed, he thought, *Shut up. No alarm yet. Wait until you see me walking toward the bus stop.*

Tim stared at Greg, focusing his thoughts. His son had his eyes scrunched closed while holding his ears. "Do you have a headache? I thought that your head got better. Should I take you to the doctor?"

"I'm okay," said Greg as he opened his eyes. He stood up and grabbed a paper towel. Crouching down to clean up the juice on the floor, he said, "I just thought I heard something. My hearing is still so good 'cause I'm, like, still young. Sometimes, I hear really high pitches and weird stuff. Spooky sometimes." He shook his head as he scrubbed the juice off the floor.

"Are you sure you're okay?" Tim didn't look convinced.

"Well, I'm pretty hungry. My stomach is turning over too. When are those eggs ready?"

"Almost," Tim said. He turned as the bread shot up and out of the toaster. Tim grabbed both pieces and began to butter them. As the eggs also seemed ready, he picked them up with a spatula and tossed them onto the buttered toast.

"Eat, my man. I'll grab you some more orange juice too." Tim saw Greg toss the paper towels into the garbage. He met his son at the table with the plates and poured some more OJ into a new mug.

"You sure your head is okay?" said Tim calmly.

"Yeah. I just had two schools and not enough extra credit treats yesterday." Greg smiled and made Tim chuckle for a moment. "I'm sure I'll get better with the rhythms pretty soon."

Tim put his hand on Greg's shoulder. "You're in good hands. This guy seems pretty skilled. How was he last night?"

Greg didn't know what to say. "Umm, well, we meditated. To find a deer, umm, ya gotta be silent and good at listening. He helped us with spending all our energy just listening and focusing on the sounds around us." Greg spun his hands around in the air as if there were a lot of floating stimuli that he had to process.

"Hmm, gotta start at the beginning, I guess." Tim scratched his chin as he leaned back in his chair. He went silent and took a bite of his toast. "Maybe I'll take up some meditation. I've heard it helps with your heart too." Tim raised his eyebrows as he took a sip of his coffee.

"Sounds good to me," said Greg, feeling like he just lucked out. "I'm gonna head up the alley and wait for the bus. It's nice and silent up there. Just gonna wait early and read a touch of . . . this," he reached over onto a tiny kitchen sideboard and grabbed a copy of *Animal Farm*.

"Geez, you want to start that first thing in the morning? These lessons must be good for you," said Tim as he shook his head. "Enjoy the fairy story."

Greg got up and shoved the book into his backpack. Then he grabbed another paper towel and wiped his feet, getting the sticky juice off. He smiled at his dad and swiftly hopped downstairs to exit and make his way up the alley.

"Be safe," shouted Sue from their basement.

"You betcha," shouted Greg as he shoved his feet into his shoes and closed the door behind him.

Greg was quickly hiking up the alley. He stopped about halfway up and closed his eyes. Imagining Virg, he sent, *I'm in the alley. What do you want?*

I wanted to see how you're doing, Greg felt pass into his mind.

I live with parents who have no idea about this crap! You don't, threw Greg into the mental canal as his eyelids pressed down hard on his face. Complete silence passed into his mind as he waited.

I'm sorry, sent Virg into Greg's head. *I'll see you in just a bit.*

Silence again. *Mom said I could bring you another bag of marshmallows. I just asked her.*

Greg smiled as he continued his walk toward the bus stop.

Sitting next to each other on the bus, Virg handed him a bag of mallows. Greg took them and shoved them into his bag. Virg raised his hand as if to begin an arm wrestle. Greg slapped his palm on Virg's. Pulling Greg in for a hug, Virg squeezed him with one hand pretty hard as their hands were still connected between their chests.

"I'm sorry. I'll try to do better. My mom is now just blasting me with comments." Virg changed his tone to match Rose's. *"Did you brush your teeth? The garbage can is still at our end of the alley. Can you take that up to the road?"* He changed his tone back to his own. "I just have a radio in my mind, and I can't alter the station."

"Maybe you can learn about a shield tonight or something . . ."

"Sweet Jesus, I hope so." Virg stuffed his forehead into his hands on his knees.

"So, can we learn more stuff tonight?" asked Greg.

"Well, yeah. But last night, you shared thoughts you planned to ask him about. It seemed like he heard you." Virg looked at Greg with a touch of attitude. His brow was lowered. "I don't know if he understood everything you said. But, hey, we're good at this crap. We're certainly learning quickly, right? It could mean that you and I qualify as 'gifted.' Kind of unlike the place we're headed to right now."

Virg backed off and leaned into his seat. He took a deep breath. "OK, you're right. It kinda seems like it's easy to learn his stuff so far. Has he taught us anything? I feel like it's been easy so far."

Greg was looking through the bus window. "Let's ask for his opinion on what it is we've seen . . . well, kind of seen."

"Do you think he knows that you're reading his mind? Or are you? You're just seeing his memories, right? Is that a skill?" Virg asked. He turned his eyes. Greg was looking far out into space while picking his nose. Virg was still looking at him.

"You disgust me," said Virg as he stared at Greg, digging into his gifted mind.

Greg took his finger out of his nose and turned toward Virg. He looked serious. "I've been wondering this entire week. And I haven't wanted to. Let's get our questions answered tonight."

Virg nodded his head and looked out the window. He thought about his creations and suggestions and their activities over the years. It's been fun. Was Greg in control now? Did he just need his questions answered? It seemed like he needed something more than Virg did.

Virg turned back to Greg. He put his hand on Greg's knee.

"Let's see how he can help us. I want to bounce off some of my mom's communication. She's firing thoughts at me like a machine gun. That, and I'll ask about the dreams you've been having," shared Virg.

"Thanks. I'll shovel my dinner down and come find you after the day is done." He smiled and patted Virg's hand on his knee.

"Can you say, 'Can we end early?' in French?"

Greg shook his shoulders. "I'm takin' German. And I suck at it. I'll try to scan my teacher's mind and see if he's one of us."

"Probs won't work. Only works for the other rare weirdoes who have superpowers."

"How is hearing our thoughts a skill?"

Virg responded, "Probably good for everyone else. They don't even want to hear what you have to say. You sound like an ogre in his childhood; immediate needs and not much vocab."

Greg reached into his backpack and tore open his bag of marshmallows. He shoved two into his mouth at once. "This ogre is hungry and needs some answers." He turned his head back toward Virg. "And that Hutch dude kinda looks like an ogre, right?"

Virg chuckled lightly. "Yeah, he's big. Hopefully, he'll be a big help."

They both smiled as their bus got closer to the school. They were quiet, and they imagined their days ahead. After a few moments, they rested their heads on their seats and fell into a deep sleep.

It felt like a moment later when the bus driver slapped the seat in front of them pretty hard. The heavy sound in front of them shot them into present awareness.

"Let's go," he said. He waved toward himself as if they should follow him. Wearing a Phillies T-shirt, their driver's outfit drew their minds back to the first day Hutch showed up. Tim and Pete were watching the Phillies.

"We don't know why he's here," said Virg.

Greg remembered what Virg was referencing. "He told us that he didn't mean to be here. He got lost in the wind current. Also, I don't care. He's been helping . . . especially after his deluge into my dreams on Sunday."

"I hope you're right," answered Virg as they got up and followed the driver off the bus.

37

When the school day ended, Virg and Greg left the building together. Rose sat in a parked car. It was waiting in the lot on the side of the school building. She honked her horn twice. They both switched their gazes over to meet her waving at them through the windshield. They looked confused and made their way over to her.

"Hey, boys," said Rose through her open window. "Want a ride?"

"Sure!" said Virg.

"Yeah, that sounds good," added Greg.

"Is anything wrong?" asked Virg.

"No, but, Greg, your dad asked me to pick you up and just make sure that you're okay," said Rose. "He's still working, and I finished my project on the Bethlehem barn a few weeks ago. I'm free. I told him I'd pick you up and check in."

"I'm pretty good . . . kinda," answered Greg slowly.

"How's your head feeling? He was still worried about that. You dropped a glass of juice this morning," said Rose.

Virg looked embarrassed as he sat down in the backseat of the car. "That's my fault."

"How so?"

Virg turned his eyes up to look at his mom in the rearview mirror. "I was contacting him early on in the day."

"Oh, Virgil," she responded. "He's in a house with people who don't have the same ability that you do. You can't freak them out."

"You did that to me!" quickly responded Virg. "And Dad doesn't have it either. I'm getting all the messages, and there's no time off."

"Okay, okay," Rose raised her hands, showing her openness to Virg's point. "I was just trying to help and give you practice. I'll stop." She turned her head to look at Virg. "And you stop too." She shook her head toward Greg and then gave him a loving look.

Greg slowly pulled a marshmallow out of his backpack, then popped it into his mouth. Rose saw it happen in the rearview mirror.

"I'm glad you like those. You're preparing for your lesson tonight?" she asked as she started the car and shifted into reverse.

"Gotta keep my energy up," said Greg.

Rose took them back through the towns between their school and their homes. She left her window open, and the boys behind her also opened theirs. The silence and warm wind current gave them all a conscious moment of relaxation. None of them thought about their day. They just enjoyed the descending sun and the warmth that increased as they continuously absorbed its direct rays.

As the car slowed down, Rose pulled into Greg's driveway.

"I approve. You can tell your dad that," she said as Greg got out of the seat behind her. "You're lookin' good, tyke." She extended her hand, and Greg lightly high-fived it.

Then Greg paced toward his front door and turned to look at Virg in the backseat. "I'll see you after dinner."

"I'll save you a piece of dessert," yelled Virg through the open window. He turned his head toward Rose. "Do we have dessert tonight?"

"Your dad said he's making a lime tart with blueberries and blackberries after dinner."

"Oh, man, don't save any for Greg. Just give him more marshmallows."

"Same as I was thinkin'." She winked at Virg in the rearview mirror and pulled out of the driveway.

On the turn to get back to the road, Virg turned his head to peer at Greg entering his home. He reminded himself not to contact him.

38

Virg and Hutch were licking their dessert plates at the same time. Their tongues prickled with the sweet, sour pairing of the lime with the sweet berries and buttery piecrust. Virg sent a thought to Hutch as their eyes met. *I thought I was the only one young enough to do this kind of thing.*

I'm still young in the home-eating world. Let me have my piece, responded Hutch into Virg's mind. They both smiled at each other.

"No secrets," said Rose. "Tell Dad if you're enjoying your meals." She smiled.

"I think it's pretty obvious," said Virg.

Hutch put down his plate. "The lemon-crème-chicken pasta was great. Also, this lime pie is so stinkin' good. I don't think I've had any fresh citrus in years. Thank you so much, Doug."

"'Tiz my finest art form," said Doug as he raised his arms up toward the sky. He looked like he was playing Zeus or some godlike character.

"Bravo," said Hutch. "After I take a therapeutic nap," he turned his gaze from Doug to Virgil, "do you wanna contact Greg? I can take you guys out and see how to help."

Virg turned his head toward his mom. "Can I contact him?"

"Just go knock on his door. He's right around the corner. Tim will appreciate that." She shook her head and made the tactic seem so obvious.

"I just learned this skill and can't even use it." Virg shook his head as he stood up and began grabbing dishes. He entered the kitchen and placed three plates and some silverware into the sink. "I'll see you guys after I collect Greg."

He waved above his head, lazily saluting, and went down to the door to throw on his shoes.

Hutch lay back in his chair and shut his eyes.

"Tough to digest a treasure chest like that, huh?" asked Doug.

"I'm so glad that I'm here. And thank you so much." He looked at them both. "Both of you."

Doug and Rose both noticed his calm grin and a strange flash in his eye. It almost seemed as if he contained and pressed down a fierce thought.

"Hit up a couch. You've got a lesson coming up." Doug extended his hand to Hutch. Doug's fist was fully covered as Hutch grasped him to get up. Hutch seemed okay as he reached out for some dishes at the table. He grabbed the remaining plates and began to take them into the kitchen.

"Leave 'em, kid," said Doug. "You've still gotta teach some little brutes this evening." He shook his head, seeing Hutch put all the dishes in the sink and turn on the water. "Chill, take a rest." Doug lightly patted him on the shoulder.

Hutch turned back and made his way down the stairs. As he left, Doug and Rose met each other's gaze. They couldn't communicate in their minds, but they both knew that the other one saw something weird in Hutch's eye.

Virg took his time walking across his lawn, lightly crushing a long grass patch. He enjoyed the soft pressing sound as his thoughts wandered to Greg sitting in his kitchen, not worrying about anyone interrupting his thought process. He got a real rest, thought Virg. During a five-minute crawl between houses, he listened to the soft breezes and the sounds that he imagined.

Stepping onto the crushed pebbles in the alley, the sounds of owls wakening at sundown let his mind wander. He thought of the summer that just passed by and their days spent on the forested hillsides and the weeded creek. The thought calmed him as he closed his eyes for a few steps.

Before Virg's mind latched onto past events, he reached the Fishers' front door as his mind cleared. He raised his hand to knock, and Sue opened the door with a trash bag in her hand.

"Oh, good evening, Virgil!" Sue smiled and walked just past him into their driveway. "Do you want me to find Greg?" She popped the cover of the trash bin and tossed her bag into it.

"Sure, thanks. We're gonna head back to get another lesson." He pointed behind himself toward his home.

"Oh, that's right." She turned her head up toward the second floor. Shouting, she said, "Ey, Greg! Virgil's down here!"

Greg popped into his screened window and pressed his nose against the grid. Looking down, he saw his mom and Virg. "I'll be there in one second," he said as he vanished into his bedroom.

Virg and Sue stared at each other momentarily when they heard some crashing and zipping noises from Greg's open window. The following sounds of him slamming his door and running down the stairs happened in moments right after. They both smiled at each other. Greg quickly met them at the front door, wearing his button-down shirt and shorts.

"Quick, huh? Can you get ready this fast for your *normal* school?" Sue chuckled a bit. "No notebooks? How do you learn this stuff from your camp master?"

Virg jumped in. "Reflexes and noticing natural skills. That's the idea, anyway. It's been pretty helpful so far."

Sue looked satisfied with that answer. "I'm gonna grab the recycling and fill this can. Hang on a second. Can you guys take these up to the road?" She walked past them to the front door and dropped a trash bag.

"I don't mind," said Virg.

"Ugh, this is *home* homework!" added Greg.

"Keeping yourself healthy and informed is a homework that's due every day," said Sue. She turned and went back upstairs for a moment.

Virg and Greg turned toward each other and shot their eyeballs up into their descended eyebrows. It looked as if they smelled a true stench. Sue returned with a paper bag full of cans and containers.

"Thanks, excellent students. You both get an A-plus." She kissed Greg on his forehead and lightly squeezed Virg's shoulder.

The boys grabbed the rolling garbage bin and the recycle bin. Greg picked it up with both hands and kept it on his hipbone. Virg pulled the trash bin behind him.

"Ya know, my dad is usually the trashman. He has a stinkin' truck. He just loads these and rides them up there in thirty seconds," said Greg.

"Yeah, well, he's not home yet, right? I didn't see his truck."

"Naw, he's not home yet. He called Mom and asked her to wish me luck with my evening lesson. I guess he's still working."

They made their way up the alley toward the road. Making a few stops, Greg rested his bin on the alleyway to rest his shoulders. Virg planted his can vertically a few times. When they reached the road, they staked their bins and approached Virg's house. The sun was going down as they strolled toward it. As it lowered further below the bouquet of trees, they noticed Hutch lying on the Murphys' front porch. His head pointed to their door, and his legs rested on the three stairs beneath.

They made their way closer and saw his eyes were closed. As they arrived near Hutch's feet, Virg asked. "Hey, can you teach *us* how to sleep?"

Hutch slowly opened his eyes. They saw his pupils take a moment to adjust. "Whoa, how you doin', kids?" he yawned. "It got a bit dark, huh?"

"A bit, but we're ready for a lesson," answered Virg.

Hutch stretched his arms over his head and yawned. "Dude, your dad can really cook. I haven't had those flavors and tastes in a while. Really good stuff."

Greg jumped in. "*You* are a good cook too. Last night's was delish."

"I haven't made dessert in a long time." Hutch let his mind wander as he closed his eyes. "Mmmmmm, that lime and berry . . . good God." He stood up and stretched his back for a second. "Lemme just head back inside for a minute. I've gotta take a leak."

Greg turned toward Virg. "He's getting pretty freaking comfortable

Glider

on his vacation, huh? Where's my sample of his dream? I want that. I don't wanna dream any more memories and just talk about dessert."

Virg smiled and said, "Okay, come on inside. I've gotta pee too."

They made their way into the house. Hutch went to the upstairs bathroom, and Virg went to the downstairs one. In the meantime, Greg asked for and wolfed down a tart slice. As the three of them opened the porch door and put their shoes back on, the sun had set beneath the hillside. Only a few warm colors spread low across the sky.

Hutch pointed toward the forest. "Let's head to the forest for this lesson. I need to get in a little hike before we get back to work. It's pretty nice and a bit quiet over there. If you need to do more than pee, the baseball park is right next to it." He raised his shoulders and let them fall.

"We're following you, dude," said Greg. "And yes, I'd better heighten my heart rate before the lesson. I'm about to take a tart nap."

They walked down onto the road and hiked in the grass beside it until they reached the forest's glade. The opening in the set of bushes made Greg turn around and scout to see if anyone was following him. A thought about getting lost after dark made him shiver for a moment. He felt a presence for a second. But when he turned, he didn't see anything behind him. Calmly, he turned back to the forest and followed the other two.

They hiked only about a half mile up into the trees. Close by on their right was the forest's end beside the creek's northern rivulet. That small stream section and the rim of trees just separated them from the empty park by about 300 feet.

Hutch sat on a fat tree root and said, "You guys can sit for a moment and let your minds get comfortable. Go through whatever you need to and open your eyes when you're ready."

Virg and Greg looked at each other and back at Hutch. Their leader had already closed his eyes and looked like he had quickly met a meditational rhythm. His breath looked nice and focused. It was a good example, thought Virg.

After about one minute of conscious breathing, Greg opened his eyes again. The darkness surrounding them had opened his pupils even further. Above the tree rim in the sky, there were no clouds. The pure and blazing light from the stars allowed him to see everything before himself.

Greg began to feel a bit nervous and blurted, "So, how do I make something disappear? Or how do I protect myself from junk flying at me?"

Hutch turned toward him and smiled. "Grab a leaf or a stone or something. Whatever's near your hand."

Greg and Virg didn't stand up. They just looked about a foot away from themselves and reached down to grab sticks.

"You can make it disappear," said Hutch. "Think about a breeze making smoke disappear."

"Yeah . . . I don't get it," said Greg.

Virg looked across the forest and then at the ground just in front of him. ". . . like pee disappearing when I flush it?"

"Use whatever thought works for you," Hutch responded tiredly.

"Is there a way to imagine a practicing process where this works?" asked Virg.

"People can usually develop a hand signal that helps them project their thoughts. Then it becomes a regular rhythm. Some people don't need a motion. Everyone's different." Hutch shrugged his shoulders.

"What do *you* do?" said Greg.

"I look at something and decrease the visuals by creating a scale that I lower on my hand. It's a concept."

He opened his hand, showing them a small stone he was holding. With his other hand, he extended his thumb, clasped his index finger to the tip, and ran it down to his palm. The stone in his other hand vanished.

"Oh, wow." Virg remembered the exact same motion he'd seen his mom use. "I didn't realize that there was a dictionary for the signals."

"There's not," said Hutch. "I saw your mom use this motion too. She learned it at the same time as I did. It's different for everyone. Sometimes, people show up and already know how to command the skill." Hutch turned his head from Virg to Greg. "Like you." Hutch raised his hand with the invisible stone in it. He whipped it straight at Greg's head.

Greg shot his pinky finger out and made a fist just beneath his belt. An invisible shell warped around the front half of his body. The stone slapped straight into the shell, two inches above Greg's forehead scab. It flew straight to the back of his head as it became visible. It landed just behind Greg's back. He didn't feel a thing. It was almost like he turned himself into air. A moment after his jaw flopped wide open, he closed his hand into a fist, and the warping shell in front of him disappeared.

"Whoa," said Greg. He looked down at his hand, and his perspective shifted. Then his eyes went back up to Hutch.

The man spoke into Greg's surprised look. "Splinter explosion. I heard you think about that last night. You've learned from my memories . . . Am I wrong? Reading my mind, that's a skill I haven't taught you how to do yet."

"Why not?" said Greg.

"Because I don't know how to do that. You two are more skilled than many people I've tried to help."

"What about that kid I saw?"

"Usually, the people who come to the camp are your mom's age or older."

"I saw a kid," Greg punched the ground beside himself.

"You saw my memories. It could've been a kid. It could've been a person you imagined to be a kid." Hutch shook his head.

"What happened to that one?" asked Greg.

"Don't you want to learn about what you can do?"

Virg jumped into the conversation. "Yes, how do I do what he just did?" pointing at Greg.

Focusing on his memory, Greg pushed, "You got stabbed in the thigh. Show me your scar. If it wasn't a kid, you'd have a scar a bit higher."

Hutch looked at Virg. Then he slowly paced toward a log of a fallen tree near Greg. He sat on it and pulled and rolled his pant leg up just above his kneecap.

"Take a look," he said to Greg.

Nervously pacing closer to a big man staring at him, Greg focused on Hutch's thigh. There was no scar.

"Okay, I'm sorry. But I don't know how this works." Greg tapped his temple with his finger. "I guess I'm seeing things in my sleep. But I got the most images on that night you showed up."

"You did?" responded Hutch calmly. "I was trying to contact Mrs. Murphy, but I guess you received my passage opening."

"Yeah, like, lots of stories I don't understand." Greg shook his head. "Can I, like, see your journal or something?"

"You want me just to open my mind and invite you in?" Hutch smiled. "That's a skill I'm not quite happy to share just yet."

Virg broke in. "Okay, so, can you teach me the shield skill?" He waved his hand in the air as if he were in a classroom, hoping to be included.

Greg grabbed a wood chip and chucked it straight against Virg's skull.

"Nope, not reacting in the right way," said Greg.

Hutch grabbed Greg's shoulder. "Calm down. Just breathe for a minute or two. Close your eyes." He stood up and walked toward Virg. He lowered himself into a squat just in front of him. "What would you do to avoid something coming at you?"

"I'd close my eyes and imagine I could block it, right?" Virg said as he shut his eyes. "Keep talking," he told Hutch.

Brilliant sent Hutch through a connected thought. *I'll keep describing how much I loved that tart. It was sour, but not too sour. The berries were . . .*

Virg raised his fist and slowly pushed his pinky forward. He imagined a shell around his head and body, just as he had seen Greg do. As he did, he heard the voice disappear from his mind . . . *a touch sweet, but—*

Hutch kept speaking, but Virg kept his eyes closed. The silence around him was comfortable and not scary. He heard his own blood flow and his heartbeat. Even the sounds of the owls and the light breeze disappeared. He opened his eyes and saw an incredibly thin layer of something that looked like water between himself and Hutch. The man in front of him was still moving his lips. Virg's smile surprised him, and he let out a laugh. Greg and Hutch didn't even respond to the sound he made. It seemed that they couldn't hear him.

Virg opened his fist and rested his pinky finger.

. . . I could literally eat that almost every day for the next week, and I don't think I'd get sick. I'd be pretty happy just napping all day. Hutch kept spooning his thoughts into Virg's head.

"It's amazing," said Virg. "Can I alter the shell to absorb thoughts? Like, I dunno, things that aren't shared with me directly?"

"I have no idea," said Hutch. "Right now, it seems like you guys can do anything. Hasn't been hard to teach you so far."

Greg and Virg spent twenty minutes happily tossing objects at each other. As they kept blocking direct contact, the enjoyment of their ability just made them laugh again and again. Hutch sat watching them and felt pleased with their training results. It was almost as if his real gift was just showing up. Ever since he crashed his glider, most of their adjustments had come from his initial mistaken contact. For a moment, he regretted his actions.

Out of the corner of his eye, he saw something just through the trees. Turning his head, he looked toward the tiny light reflection that drew his attention. Nothing. It disappeared. He could see everything across the creek.

"Okay, guys, let's get you back before your parents come looking for us. Follow me." Hutch rose off the log and made his way through the dense forest.

They smiled and nodded their heads so Hutch could see their agreement. Virg and Greg looked at each other and saw the tired looks on each other's faces. They grabbed a tiny stick or two as they made their way to follow Hutch. Some extra ammunition wouldn't hurt.

The moonlight had brightened, and they saw where they were headed. The opening of the trail was lit with the sky's reflections. Hutch looked around the forest line before he led them out onto the opening. For some reason, he made sure that no one would see them leaving this area. He realized that he was used to being alone out in the woods. He shook his head and waved over his shoulder for the boys to follow him.

Tim was staring straight into the woods. He had been sitting in his truck, parked far away from the forested area. The vehicle was parked behind a big baseball park trash can that was picked up weekly. He lowered a pair of binoculars. Stretching out his back and almost touching the windshield with his plastic rims, he kept the eyepieces down and exhaled slowly. What did he just see?

It looked like they were meditating for a while. For a moment, he thought he saw a light reflection just in front of the kids. It was too dark, and they were too far away for him to see what was happening. Was that a moisturizer that Hutch was sharing? After that, they threw things at each other. What kind of lessons were these? They didn't seem to be learning contact symbols through hunting sign language, as Greg had described this morning. Were they learning the concept of how to aim a projectile? Maybe this was prebow and arrow, he thought to himself. Those two boys were just throwing things at each other and barely missing—as if they were missing at all. Tim was just confused.

Suddenly, as the boys were moving around, he saw them at an angle between the trees and clearly saw the back of Greg's head. He saw Virg throw a little stone pretty hard at his son. The twirled stone was pitched straight through Greg's head and exited from the back of it into a patch of dirt. That seemed impossible.

Was this how Greg got that scab on his forehead? If they were just getting stone-throwing lessons, Tim felt like he'd have to keep his son from Hutch's grasp. That scab was wide.

He sat pondering for a while, but his gaze was not focused. The stars above grabbed his attention as bright blue rings wisped around each orb.

Suddenly, a movement at the end of the forest caught his side glance. Hutch's steps past the glade were followed by his turn, making a small wave back into the trees. Tim raised his binoculars back up to his eyes. The boys exited the tree line behind their teacher. Seeing them pace comfortably across the grassy meadow comforted him. Seeing Greg's smile through the binoculars relieved his worry for a moment.

He kept his lenses on that group until they passed the opening and into a rim of bushes. *I've got to wait here until they're back in their homes*, he thought to himself. *Not time for headlights quite yet.* His gaze swept back up into the sky. It was so clear. With his windows open, he took a deep breath and closed his eyes.

FRIDAY

39

Warm breezes bounced off of the sandy baseball field. A few grains rattled across Tim's windshield, shaking him out of his comfortable snooze. He woke up in his truck in the baseball parking lot. Turning his head, he saw clouds above with a warm orange crack in the eastern horizon. It was just about dawn. *Crap,* he thought. *I'm gonna have to tell everyone that I worked late and got a motel room or something.*

He rubbed his eyes and yawned. Opening his car door, he bounced out and jogged to a spot behind the garbage bin. He unzipped and peed right next to it. Shaking his head and zipping back up, he snorted his stuffy nose canals and spat on the ground. Hopping back into his seat, he turned the key left in the ignition. The car responded with a cough. It grumbled but didn't start.

"Oh no," said Tim to his car. "You gotta get outta here." He tried again, then pulled his key out, breathed on it warmly, and stuck it back in. The engine rumbled for a split second but didn't start.

"I left the key in when I fell asleep. Did I leave you with the electronics on?" He just turned the key to *On* and pressed his radio button. No response.

Tim sighed heavily. He opened his door and popped his hood. When he raised the hood with his hand, he got a swift rotten-egg smell from the engine. In response, his lips rolled into a fat frown. He reached in and unplugged his engine battery. As he squatted and lifted it out, the forty-pound vessel almost broke his back. Setting it on the ground, he knew he couldn't carry it.

OK, he thought, *I'll run over to Pete's and get a ride home. I can't just walk back.* "They are probably thinking that I was kidnapped," he said out loud.

He looked at his reflected image on the windshield and saw his hair sticking up in the back. "I look like a barn owl, anyway. I'll say that I stayed at Pete's. He picked me up, and my battery is dead."

What a stupid excuse, he thought to himself. He closed the truck's hood and lifted the battery off the ground. The weight of it made his back and knees feel the pressure. Quickening his pace, he rested it on his back bumper and shoved it into his trunk. The moving of that heavy junk made his knees feel ground up. Resting his hands on his thighs and taking a deep breath, Tim thought about what to tell his family. He began to hike out of the park, rolling around some excuses in his head. When he couldn't find a fake story to tell his family, he raised his gaze and began to jog toward the road.

He looked both ways when he reached the pavement, turned right, and headed toward Pete's neighborhood.

Hutch had woken just before sunrise. He rose to begin a hike and grab some wild spices nearby in the forest. He didn't plan to carry his bow and arrow. There were plenty of deer pieces left in the garage's fridge. A swap of spices would allow them to enjoy the meat he had collected. He didn't pack up; he just dressed and went out into the morning air.

Beginning his route, he felt interested in his teaching spot from the night before. He thought he should see if their tracks were heavy or if there were any signs of them slinging rocks. Hutch wandered out of the Murphys' yard to relax and to get a daytime perspective of last night's lessons.

As he reached the end of the alley, he saw the clouds in the sky and a tiny slit on the horizon. He stood still for a minute. Suddenly, he saw a man run down the baseball parking lot to meet the main road. Hutch backed behind a bush. He saw the man roll his eyes up and down the road. He stopped and rubbed his knees. Then the man began speed walking away from where Hutch stood.

Was that Tim? Is he an early-morning runner? Hutch's mind slid back to the prior evening. As Tim got further down the road and kept hustling around the corner, Hutch began a quick pace toward the park.

When he reached the open parking lot, he saw the forest and glade just beyond the northern connection of the creek. He slowly made his way closer and closer toward the brook. He didn't see any pacing marks or broken tree barks from this position. The view looked pretty clean. He felt a bit safe and content with last night.

Hutch turned his gaze just beyond the baseball field. Looking past, he saw a dumpster and a truck sitting in the lot. He began to walk toward it. Pacing past the batting cage, he recognized the vehicle that met Virg and Greg at the creek. That reminded him of the day he had arrived.

He thought, *That is the one I saw from the hillside when the boys searched for the glider. Did he park here last night?* Hutch kept walking toward it. When he reached it, he peered in the direction it faced toward. It aimed right at the dumpster. Placing a foot on the driver step into the truck, he lifted himself by grabbing the rack on top. He turned toward the woods and saw the view from just the top of the windshield. It peered just over the bin's top level and into the woods.

"He watched us last night."

Hutch remembered that he and the boys were about a quarter mile within the woods. Could he even see us in there? A memory shot back into his mind . . . that tiny reflection that disappeared. Was that from a telescope in Tim's car?

Hutch turned around and began to hike back toward the Murphys' house.

Tim knocked on Pete's door pretty hard. No sounds returned from the entryway. Something pulled Tim's glance to a side window. The curtain was lightly lifted from the corner and slapped back down. A few moments later, Pete opened his front door.

"Oh, Happy Stinkin' Friday, you fish-eyed fool," said Pete.

He turned around in his robe and walked toward his kitchen. Pete waved his arm, inviting Tim to sit with him for a moment. He stepped toward his water kettle. His feet were in slippers that looked like puffy lobsters. After grabbing his kettle and filling it with sink water, he turned back toward Tim.

"Whatch'a need? Want some of my coffee?"

Tim sat politely on a padded kitchen chair. "I have to tell my family that I stayed at a motel last night."

Pete filled the teapot with water and rested the kettle on his stove. When he turned, he saw the anxious expression on Tim's face. "Okay. Did you get a good night's sleep, or was the motel bed full of bugs or something?"

"It's not that," said Tim. "This guy was teaching my son lessons last night, but he did it in the woods next to the park. I wanted to see what it was like, so I hid behind the park's garbage can. Then I fell asleep."

"Okay. Was it a lesson or a freakin' ceremony? What happened?"

"I don't know, but I don't want them to know I'm spying on them. The teacher is a Boy Scout hunter."

"Jesus, he kills Boy Scouts?" Pete rubbed his eyes and pressed his hands on the sides of his face. He didn't seem awake enough to process the concept. He lightly shook his head and blinked.

"No, no. He's both. He's a Boy Scout camping teacher, and he's also a hunter . . . of, like, edible animals. He lives in the woods and was going to teach them skills."

"So you wanted to spy on a guy who wants to teach kids how to be more independent?"

Tim grew a little weary and cut it short. "Ugh, I just need a ride home. I'll tell them that my truck broke, someone gave me a ride, and *their* car broke, too. We just had to stay near the work site. You picked me up, okay?"

"Yep, sounds like a perfect alibi, my man." Pete let out a little chuckle as he turned to open his cabinet and pull out a jar of coffee beans. "Can we take a nice thought-provoking sip first?"

"Yeah, maybe I need another moment to consider my alibi." Tim placed his elbows on his knees and let his head sink down and fall into his hands.

After a quick sip of coffee and Pete changed out of his lobsters, they hopped into Pete's car. He backed out of the driveway and rolled down toward the Fisher's home. As they slowed down near the alleyway, they saw Hutch step onto the road and wave at the car.

"Oh my God . . ." whispered Tim. Pete didn't even hear him as he lowered the passenger window, exposing Tim to Hutch.

"Hey, fresh neighbor, happy early mornin'! You're the teacher, right?" asked Pete.

Hutch smiled and seemed relaxed. "You betcha. Hi, I'm Hutch." Hutch extended his thick arm right past Tim's chest. For some reason, Tim felt like his soul was being lightly choked.

Pete and Hutch had a tiny shake. "You got a nice hand for huntin', don't cha? Tim told me about your venison. Wowee, it sounded like it was better than all the other backyard cookouts in Pennsylvania."

"I'm from Maine. We gotta carry those deer just a bit further than you PA toddlers."

Pete laughed hard and said to Tim, "See? *This* is the kinda 'tude teacher your kid needs. Heck, maybe *I* need him." He lightly poked his elbow into Tim's ribs.

Tim almost peed in his pants when the elbow squeezed his innards. He turned his head toward Hutch and said nothing.

"I'm Pete. I live not too far away. Just givin' Timmy a ride back. Looks like some cars broke down last night. Whatcha gonna do?" added Pete.

"Tim, can you give me a ride to the mechanic today? I think my propeller is gonna show up." Hutch let a small grin flow into his face.

"I think so. Just make sure you call to see if they got it. There's no reason to head over until it's confirmed. Besides, I could fix it if they can't," Tim quickly responded.

"Sounds good. I'll call you later on today. Just come by the Murphys." Hutch backed away from the window slightly.

"Oh, wait," blurted Tim. "My truck has a dead battery. I've just gotta get a new one today. I've been worried that it was gonna happen. Also, I got a ride last night. It really stunk because the guy who picked me up had an issue with his car too." He let out a fake-sounding laugh.

"He brought you back early, huh?" asked Hutch.

"No, Pete picked me up and brought me back. We got a motel room last night. It was within walking distance from the work site," Tim quickly added.

"Well, I've been helping your kids recognize plants and spices. I always use the horizontal rays of early sunlight to find them. When I began a spice forage this morning, I saw you leaving the baseball park."

Tim looked back at Pete. "Yeah, he dropped me off so I could make sure that no one had broken into the car. I forgot that I left my sunglasses in his car when I got out. I just ran back to grab them, and he offered to drive me home. I told him I was a bit sore in my calves from the run to his place."

"I'm a big helper," added Pete with a goofy grin.

"Your neighborhood is full of nice people," said Hutch. "Get home safe."

"Nice to meet you," said Pete.

"Likewise." Hutch waved his hand at them.

Pete took his foot off the brake and rolled toward Tim's house. They both shot a look into their rearview mirrors and caught Hutch turning away from them and walking toward the mountain behind them. About five seconds away, they both said, "Nice job," to each other. Pete let out a giggle at the irony.

40

Pulling into the Fishers' driveway, Pete saw Sue open the front door and make her way into the driveway. When Pete stopped the car, he put a hand on Tim's chest.

Pete pushed his head past Tim and spoke to Sue. "He's safe. The place he stayed at didn't have a working phone. It all kinda broke." Pete let out an embarrassed laugh. "Truck broke, phone broke, another truck broke." He raised his hands at his sides. "Them's the breaks."

Sue shook her head. "Are you both okay?"

As Pete and Tim exited the car, Tim said, "We're fine. I have today off, but I need a new engine battery." He made his way over to give Sue a hug and a kiss on her forehead.

"Yeah, I'll take him to the mechanic. That guy has some truck batteries. Hutch has gotta go today too, I think. They might get his propeller today or something," added Pete.

"Okay, thanks, Pete," said Sue. "Do you want to come in for some breakfast or anything?"

He smiled and approached their door. "Oh, why not? Only had time for a sip o' java so far. Whatcha got up there?"

Sue smiled and held the door open for Pete. "I've got some muffins and oranges. Pick anything that looks good to you." Her gaze rolled over toward her husband. "You okay?" she asked Tim.

"I'm just tired. Had to get through a bunch of breakdowns last night. I'm okay, though."

Sue clapped his butt with her hand as he passed her. "There, there. Go give your son a hug. He might have been worried last night."

"Will do," said Tim as he made his way past. He felt lucky that he got away with spying on his son, falling asleep, and ruining his own truck. Taking the stairs, he went up to his son's bedroom.

Pete paced into their kitchen and grabbed a muffin and a napkin. He sat happily in a living room chair and took a bite off the top of the muffin. "Oooh, blackberry muffins. Wow, that's good. Did you buy these?"

"Naw, the bushes in our backyard exploded in June, but now they're a bit weak. Perfect for baking," Sue smiled proudly.

"I'll say." Pete took a bigger bite. "Mmmmmhh."

As he made his way past them, Tim said, "Get another cup of coffee too. I'll be right back down." He climbed the stairs and opened Greg's bedroom door. It was still early. He saw Greg lying in his bed, his eyes open, staring at the ceiling.

Tim approached Greg and sat on his bed next to him, "Hey, bud, how you doin'? Sorry I couldn't get home last night. How'd ya sleep?"

Greg rolled to face his dad. "I'm good." He looked back toward the ceiling and added, "Do you know about the lessons?"

Tim attempted to look confused and asked, "Um, which ones?"

"My lessons with Hutch." Greg looked straight into his dad's eyes.

"Uh, are you learning about camping and finding mushrooms or something?"

"I'm asking because I saw Hutch's thoughts this morning."

"What do you mean?" Tim looked confused.

"I've been learning how to teach myself. I think I'm better than Hutch thinks I am. We've been learning to imagine possibilities and pull them into reality."

"I don't know what that means. You can do anything you want to?"

Greg sat up and let the covers fall away from his chest. "I can read Hutch's mind. But he doesn't think I can. I figured that out last night."

Tim just shook his head. The concept seemed impossible.

His son went on. "I woke up early when he did. I felt him come to consciousness. I read his thoughts until you walked in to see me. He knows that you saw us at our lessons last night. He saw you leave your truck. He knows what you did, and it seems like he's worried about it."

Tim didn't reply. He kept his eyes open, trying to see if Greg was serious or making up a wild story. His son didn't even blink. He was staring right into Tim's eyes.

"Okay, so you can read minds. That's what you're saying. What am I thinking right now?"

Greg shook his head but didn't close his eyes. "No. You don't have the gift. I can open my mind and affect other things. Yours hasn't opened. I can't get into yours, even if I want to."

"Well, *that's* nice to hear." Tim let out a breath and thought this was all a story his son was inventing.

In Tim's head, he heard, *I can contact you. I just can't read your mind, Dad. You're safe.*

Tim wasn't freaked out, but he turned his eyes and met Greg's. His son smiled briefly and then looked serious again.

"Stand by the door," Greg said. He laid his hand on his dad's shoulder.

Tim tapped his son's hand lovingly and squeezed it.

"I'm asking you to stand and throw something at me. I'll show you what I mean." Greg gave Tim's shoulder a tiny push.

His dad rose up and walked back a few steps.

"Here," Greg pulled a novel off his bedside table and horizontally tossed it at his dad. When Tim caught it, Greg raised his fist next to his torso. "Throw it at me," Greg added.

"I thought you were reading this. Don't you like climbing? *Eiger Dreams* is one of the best outdoor activity books!" He raised it to his face and began to read the appendix.

"THROW IT," yelled Greg.

Tim was shaken by the yell and lightly tossed the book toward his son. It spun and lofted toward Greg. Tim kept his eyes on Greg as the book flew at him. Suddenly, his son closed his eyes and popped his pinky out. The book softly came down on his head, passed right through, and landed on his pillow behind him. Greg opened his eyes and stared at his dad.

"Hey, is everything okay up there?" yelled Sue from downstairs in the kitchen.

Tim turned toward the door and shouted through the small opening, "It's okay, I accidentally woke him up. Sorry. He's fine." He turned his eyes back at his son and began to sit on the floor.

Whispering, Tim said, "So you have some kind of gift or something?"

"You saw this happen last night." Greg looked completely serious.

Tim shook his head, stopped, and took a deep breath. "I did see something like that. Virgil can do it too?"

"He can do that, but I don't know what else he can do. Hutch had mentioned that we're pretty young to get training. That's kind of a benefit."

"So he doesn't train Boy Scouts?"

"It's hard to find people like us, especially at our age. He's done it before, but not often." Greg let his eyes sink down and shook his head. Then he looked back up at his dad. "Don't take him to the mechanic. I don't know what he's going to do to you. He didn't say, but I felt the tone."

"Okay, I'll just—"

Greg cut him off. "Don't tell me. I don't know if he can read my thoughts. I don't think he can, but don't tell me what you will do."

Tim let out a breath. He leaned back against the bookshelf on the wall. "So, you want some breakfast?"

"I do. What we got?" Greg smiled and ripped the blanket off his legs.

"Mom made some blackberry muffins and Pete's down there. Put on some pants and put that book back on your bedside table. Get it off your pillowcase." Tim stood up and took some steps toward Greg. He opened his arms, and Greg came over and wrapped his arms around him. Tim squeezed him hard. When he let go, he turned to make his way back downstairs. Before leaving, he turned back and looked at his son. How was this kid so much more careful and thoughtful than he expected? He felt proud and unprepared at the same time. Closing the door, he turned and made his way toward the staircase.

After having breakfast, Greg said goodbye to his parents and Pete. As he walked up the alley toward his bus stop, the adults waved goodbye from the driveway. Sue saw another muffin, wrapped in a paper towel, puffing out of his water bottle net on the side of his backpack.

"He ate that first one pretty fast," said Sue as she waved.

"So did I. I can't blame him," responded Pete.

She smiled and laid her palm on Tim's cheek for a moment. Then she turned her eyes to Pete and let go. "Have a good one, Pete. I've got more muffins if you want a backpacked one—same as Greg." She smiled as she went back inside.

Pete smiled and said, "Thanks, but I'm pleased." He tapped his belly with both hands.

She smiled and looked at Tim. "Not too much noise. I'm heading back to bed for a little while." She closed the door behind them as Tim smiled at her.

"You ready to hit up that mechanic?" Pete said to Tim.

"Yeah. Let's pick up the battery in my truck before we head over," he nodded.

The eyes in Pete's head rolled as he nodded back. They both opened the doors and hopped back into Pete's car.

Turning toward Tim, he said, "So, do you want a new battery or me to jump-start it?"

"Well, I think it can be jump-started, but I still have to visit that mechanic. We gotta spend the time. I told Hutch that the battery was busted last night. Besides, I want to check on that propeller for his glider. Let's not pick him up. I'll pay for it or whatever."

"Okay, boss." Pete shook his head. "Your chauffeur is ready." He pulled back in reverse and turned the wheel toward the alley. "Where to?"

"My truck is in the park. Let's head to the ball field, Captain." Tim started making baseball coach signs at Pete. They both chuckled.

Riding up the road, they turned into the parking lot. Tim pointed up, just past the field. Pete saw Tim's truck and parked next to it. They got out and set up the jump-start cables. Tim's truck began to charge, and he had a thought.

"Okay, it's working. You wanna unplug and put this back in my bonnet?" Tim asked Pete.

"Yeah, that's fine," Pete nodded and pulled off the cables. Then he held one side of the battery.

They both lifted and replaced it in the engine. Pete pushed his fingers into his lower back, relieving some tightness.

"Hey, Pete, will you stick around while this recharges?" Tim asked.

"No prob. One of us has to do it. Where ya headed?" Pete smiled and walked toward the grass behind the fence on the first-base line.

"I just want to ask Doug a question and maybe use his phone."

Pete lay down in the lightly dewed grass and pulled his cap over his eyes. "Best of luck, reliever."

Tim made his way down the parking lot toward the main road. The sun had risen and was behind the clouds, over the horizon break. As it reached up into the sky, the rolling clouds covered it completely. It was nice not to feel the heat, but it felt a little spooky. He found the end of the Murphys' driveway and walked to their door. After a single knock, the door opened. Hutch looked straight into Tim's eyes.

"Good morning, again," said Hutch. "You ready to take me to the mechanic?"

"Oh, hi!" Tim shouted. Surprised, he lowered his tone, "No, I've got to wait just a minute. Pete is just taking a nap in the park. He always loves that relaxing smell of fresh grass. He woke up early." Tim looked behind Hutch toward the kitchen. "I was actually just gonna use their phone so I could call the mechanic to make sure he's open. I had some time to check in before visiting."

Tim saw a strange light blue ripple across the whites of Hutch's eyes. He looked past him and saw Doug holding a cereal bowl and spoon.

"Hey, Dad!" Tim turned to see Greg yelling at him down the road. "I've been waiting for the bus, but it hasn't arrived yet. Do you think I still have to wait, or can you give us a ride?" Greg waved his hands in the air.

"You need to use the phone?" asked Doug from the kitchen.

"Umm, no, I'm good. I have a priority to get these kids up to their school. Greg's yelling at me that the bus didn't show up. Whoops!" He shrugged his shoulders and turned around toward his son. His feet drew him away from Hutch, and he added, "I will, uh, I'll come back when it's time to contact the mechanic . . . or maybe I'll already have called them." He took a few more steps down the porch. "Talk to ya later," he said to Hutch.

He turned and jogged down the street toward Greg's bus stop. He saw that his son had turned and was also walking back to the stop. *Did he know that I was right here?* It took him a couple of minutes to reach Greg. Virg was sitting next to him at the bus stop.

"So you know about Greg's skill, right?" Virg pointed at Tim.

"I just found out." Tim turned back toward his son. "Hutch's eyes made a weird shift while I saw him."

"I don't know if he knows I'm entering his mind. I wonder if he physically changes when I listen to his thoughts. I connected when he went on a hike for some spice, and I felt him turn around. I heard those thoughts," Greg said as he sat beside Virg.

"You think he *does* know that you have access? Does he feel it?" asked Virg.

"It seems like he doesn't. Or he's not doing anything about it," said Greg.

"Okay, is your bus coming or not?" said Tim. "I'm recharging my truck battery, and I can take you." He looked at his watch. "It's just a little early."

"Yeah, um, Dad," Virg interjected, "your son just had the opportunity to steal you from the big magic gorilla. That's why he ran and told you the bus left us behind."

"Oh, right. Thanks, Greg." Tim looked down at his feet. "Okay, so you can get to school? I've gotta go back to get Pete. He was lying down when I left him."

The boys nodded. Greg spoke softly, "We're just waiting for the bus. Don't go back to the Murphys'."

"Okay. I'll hit the trail and just jump over the creek on my way back. Thanks, boys." Tim hugged Greg and waved at Virg. He made his way across the road toward the trail entrance.

As Tim passed over the road and into the bushes, Virg tapped Greg on the shoulder. "So, can we teach ourselves anything else? What if we have to protect ourselves from *him*." He pointed back toward his house.

"Yeah, in my dream, I saw him and his small student in the forest." Greg sat down and closed his eyes. "The kid had telekinesis or something. They lifted a tree out of the ground. It didn't look too hard to do." He turned his head to Virg and opened his eyes. They both laughed.

"It didn't look like it was going to be *impossible*? You would have said that to me five days ago." Virg lay down to rest on the grass behind him. "I mean, if a tiny kid can teach herself, we can too, right?"

"Well, we've been teaching ourselves so far. At least, that's what it feels like." He leaned down next to Virg. "But we can't skip school."

"Let's teach ourselves now. We're waiting for a bus."

Greg stood up, and Virg followed him. Looking across the street, Greg found and pointed at a cardinal flower next to the bushes. It had small triple-leafed stems that bounced their color off the green bush behind it. A hummingbird flew straight toward it, jamming its beak within the purple opening.

Greg closed his eyes and thought about his memory of Hutch with that little kid. "He said something to her before she could lift it. I don't know what he said."

"What did you see?"

"I saw him whisper to her after she pointed a fist at that tree in front of her." Greg raised his open hand at the flower across the street. With his other hand, he reached out to hold Virg's, just as the girl had done with Hutch. Clasping it, he re-created the memory. Greg imagined the flower disappearing, just as the tree had. In his mind, he saw his closed fist gripping the image. Just as he imagined, he rolled his fingers into a fist. If he had a cracker in his hand, softly crushed crumbs would tumble out the bottom. As he pinched, the image of the cardinal flower disappeared in Virg's view.

The hummingbird backed away in the air. Then the smell of the nectar drew it back. It looked as though it was sipping from nothing at all.

"Oh my God..." Virg whispered. He lightly squeezed Greg's hand.

Greg popped open one eye and almost laughed. He let out one surprised breath and closed his eye again. As he slowly opened his hand, the red color of the flower bled back into their view. It almost made Virg shut his eyes after seeing the vibrant shade of colors. The hummingbird had been sipping inside the tubular flower. The plant's image wrapped its red petal shell around the bird's beak as it reappeared.

"This is what you dreamed?" Virg kept his hand wrapped around Greg's but moved his other hand to poke Greg's skull lightly. He held his finger just before it touched, keeping it a few inches away. He just pointed. "What else is in there?"

Greg was following his dream to see if it was real. He slowly raised his pointing hand only an inch. The cardinal flower rose slightly and tugged at its roots, which were stuck in the dirt. Greg felt it in his hand. Not heavy, he only felt the separation of the ground and the roots tugging at one another in his hand. He raised it another inch and felt a slight pop from the object before him.

Virg swung his focus back to the flower. The dirt crumbled off the roots and the bird happily raised itself to match the level of the sweet nectar. Greg heard Virg push out a surprised breath and then lightly squeezed his hand.

With his eyes still closed, Greg whispered, "This happened as well."

He rolled his fingers into a fist and held it out in front of himself. As he did, Virg saw the flower explode in every direction. It became red powder, green shards, and tiny drops of nectar flying in every direction. Almost immediately, Virg clasped his hand into a fist and shot out his pinky finger. Only a few shards and puffed dust clouds came by and through their conjured defense.

Greg opened his eyes and saw colors and dirt spread over the road in a half circle. The rest of the red powder was rolling off the bush behind it. It looked like they had hit a dirty, paint-filled balloon with a BB gun.

The hummingbird shot away, then came back a bit, hovering. It looked like it had been covered in filth. The boys watched it fly straight to a tiny white birdbath in the nearby backyard. It landed and shook its head. Then it shoved its beak into the bath and rolled its head back and forth across its belly. It preened itself and beaked oil near its tail gland. It oiled its wings and shot itself up and away in a flash.

"You did what he did in my dream," Greg said.

Virg let go of Greg's hand to pull his hair up on his head. His eyes were wide.

"I just learned how to do that—and practiced the crap out of it last night. Tossed some pinecones up and blocked their return. This wasn't as bad as that, but I didn't know it was just gonna be powder. I felt like a stone was gonna slap me." He reached down to grab his shirt and pulled it away from his belly to inspect it. Recognizing that nothing had hit him, Virg turned to look behind himself. "The flakes missed us. You're welcome. No changing before school today."

"You were holding my hand." Greg looked down at his own shirt. "I didn't get hit either. Thanks for not letting go." He smiled.

Virg stepped toward him and hugged him. "Thank you." He stepped back. "Can I try what you did at lunch?"

Greg shook his head as if to say no. But he laughed and said, "Yes, but let's eat lunch next to the garden."

Virg crinkled his nose, not knowing where the garden was.

"You know the one. It's out back. They let us go in there and check on the plants. There's like wooden beams and bushes to keep the deer out. That'll protect us a bit, I think."

They heard a low buzz and some stones crunching up the road. As they turned to look at the noise, they saw the bus rolling toward them. They stepped away from the road and grabbed their backpacks off the grass behind them. Both boys saw some red flakes on them and beat the tiny pieces off.

Greg turned back to look at Virg. "Don't tell Hutch that you know how to do this."

Virg shrugged. "I guess I'll just learn it quickly, like the last two times." He smiled and stepped back from the road as the bus approached. "Can you explain how you did that? You saw it in your dream, but I just want to be able to practice it at lunchtime."

"Taking notes of this on the bus? What if other people see us doing it?" Greg looked a little spooked.

"I've been taking notes about this stuff every day so far, and no one has given a crap. It's kinda what *no one* wants to do on the bus. Unless you have to finish your homework or something."

Greg laughed. "Okay, but don't bring those to our lesson with Hutch tonight."

"Duh..." Virg made a dumb-looking face, frowning and raising his eyebrows. "I don't bring notes almost anywhere."

The bus door squeaked open, and they hopped up the stairs and headed toward their seats. As the door closed, the bus driver looked out her window. She saw a big, freckled circle on the road and bushes: the red and purple leaf pieces and the green and yellow stem innards splattered around each other. Bright flakes sparkled while being back-dropped by the grey road and green bush behind them—one white side-of-the-road line cut under the circle at its bottom.

"Now dat iz better than graffiti." She smiled and shook her head, "Damn. That makes my day." A tiny tear met her eye as she turned to look into the review mirror. She saw the boys sit down and fixed her vision out the front window as she merrily pressed the gas pedal.

41

Rose was walking down the road and turned into the baseball field's parking lot. She had filled a tiny canteen with coffee and had put it in a canvas tote bag hanging on her shoulder. Continuing her walk into the parking lot, she saw a car with a truck parked next to it. As she walked through open parking spots, she saw a man lying in the grass in front of the two vehicles. It looked like Pete. She recognized his little tummy and his greasy red hat. Getting closer, she noticed him lying on his back with his cap over his eyes. A little growling snore rolled out from his mouth.

"Top o' the morning, Captain Snooze." She chuckled as she said it. It looked to her like he was living in his car and just spending his nights sleeping behind baseball fields.

Pete snorted and grabbed his cap off his face. Slipping his cap on his head, he rolled over and looked up at Rose. "Oh, hey! Whatchu doin' here?"

"I was up in our office on my computer, just looking at emails. Something caught my attention through the window. I saw Tim running down toward the bus stop. Virg waits there every morning. Then he talked to Greg and Virg and went up the trail that leads to the park." She handed her coffee canteen to Pete.

He grabbed it, rubbed his eye, and sat up. "What's in this?" He popped open the cap.

"It's coffee. I didn't know if Tim needed something. He looked a little frightened." Rose looked up above Pete and scanned the other parts of the park that Tim may have snuck into.

Pete took it and gave it a sniff. "Ooooh, I dunno. I've already had two cups so far. I just woke up again, and I don't know if this ballfield's

Glider

bathroom is still locked." He closed the lid and handed it back toward Rose. Then he looked at his watch.

"I spoke with Sue on the phone just a minute ago," said Rose. She looked back down at Pete. "She called to make plans with me this weekend, but she said you guys are going to get a new battery for Tim's truck. This one's okay now?" She pointed at the wire connecting the two together. "Looks like you're charging that battery."

Turning back to Pete, she continued, "Sue said that Tim didn't get to come home last night."

Pete looked embarrassed. "I didn't do anything. But I don't know if I can tell you what happened. I'm just a good friend." He raised his shoulders. "I'm helping."

Squatting down to meet Pete's eye level, Rose looked like she was about to flirt with him. "If you don't tell me what happened, I'll grab your belt buckle, lift you over my shoulder, and connect you to the battery's open current."

Pete's eyes opened wide, and he quickly stood up. "Okay, he was spying on the lesson Hutch was doing last night. He just fell asleep. Also, I think he didn't see nothin'." He stepped toward his car and added, "I have no idea what happened. The only thing I know is that a guy teaches your kids, and that's what he did yesterday." Shaking his open hands in the air, it looked like he was ready for his arrest.

Smiling and popping open the cap of her canteen, Rose took a tiny sip and said, "I was just joking, Pete. But thanks for all the info. A mom's gotta know what's going on."

Pete sat down in the grass again. "OK, can I have a sip now?" He rubbed his palm against one of his eyes. It looked like he had barely woken up.

Rose extended her canteen toward him as she kept her eyes up, scanning back and forth. She spotted Tim reaching the glade on the other side of the creek. Although she barely saw him with the clouds above, she recognized him. Turning toward the truck, she noticed a pair of binoculars just behind the windshield. Plucking them off the dashboard, Rose raised them to her eyes. A moment later, she found Tim's face. He was looking downward at his own gait. It looked like he was processing a memory of his own. He had rolled his lips into his mouth and was twitching his mustache back and forth.

"I wonder what was so interesting last night," she said as she lowered the binoculars. She knew that Hutch was teaching lessons, but Pete and Tim were unaware of the real concept. She stepped on the driver-side truck step and put Tim's binoculars back on the dashboard. "I don't want to spook him." She looked at Pete and added, "Can I sit in your driver's seat until he gets back?"

"Yep," he said as he lay back down momentarily. He popped back up. "One sip . . ." he whispered. Turning toward Rose, he said, "Can you just sit there and keep an eye on these? I've gotta run over to the john and take care of my bizznest. One sip was all I needed." He broke into a quick, flat-footed walk, keeping his pelvis at the same level the whole time. Grabbing the public bathroom door, he swiftly opened it and stepped inside.

"Whew!" Rose heard from the park's public restroom.

She turned her head back toward the forest. Just squinting a bit, she could still make out Tim's body. He lifted his head, just looking toward the field. Still keeping his slow pace, he turned and didn't keep walking toward the field. It looked, to her, that he had turned toward the forest. His head went back downward. She saw him squat and stay in one spot, then rise and speed up. Was he seeing a footpath? Was he looking for where they went last night? Rose felt there was nothing he could find if he went in there. Or was there?

He left the glade and entered the forest with a purpose. Rose stood up and began walking toward the forest for a moment. She stopped herself. Then she heard a big *FLUSH* sound. Turning to look at Pete, she saw him wiping his hands on his pants and returning to the cars.

"Pete, I'll be right back," she said, walking down the small hill and hiking across the baseball field toward the creek.

"Hokeydoke. Want me to hang onto the coffee?" Pete stopped in front of the cars.

Rose turned around and tossed her canteen over the bench fence from the first-base line. It soared quickly at Pete as he took off his hat and caught it while holding the brim.

"Yyyyou're outta here!" Pete yelled. Rose smiled, then rolled up her tote bag and shoved it in her belt as she crossed the field. She got to the creek, backed up a few feet, and ran straight to jump over it. Landing across the brook, she hiked up to the glade and looked into the woods. Turning her head back to Pete, Rose saw him lying down again. His hat was placed on his eyes, like before. She turned back and began to enter into the forest.

Doug finished his cereal, gave Hutch a handshake and a shoulder bump, and then headed to work. Hutch sat down on the living room chair as he heard the car engine start up. Reaching up to rub his eye, Hutch had just felt a slight itch. Hearing Doug's car rolling over the stones in the driveway, Hutch closed his eyes again. The accounting office that Doug worked at wasn't very far away, probably a ten-minute drive. As he heard the car rumble down the road, he rose from the chair and entered the bathroom. He flicked on the lights and stared at himself in the mirror. For a moment, he saw a slight blue shade roll over the white rim of his eye. He blinked, and it disappeared.

He didn't know what was happening, but he had a touch of fear roll up his spine. Backing away from the mirror, he flicked off the lights. Thinking about Rose, he closed his eyes and began a connection. Orchestrating the light vibration of the search, he felt the opening meet her, but he didn't send any messages. He stopped.

Hutch sat briefly until he thought about using the post office phone again. David still had an old rotary phone. The signal was so direct. Hutch walked into the kitchen and saw the cordless phone in their pantry. Turning toward their basement, he opened the door and flicked on the lights below. Making his way down the stairs, he saw some tools. He noticed a washer, a dryer, and a dusty wooden door. The grungy-warded lock looked usable. He turned the knob and felt the hold of the lock.

He let go and turned to see a small towel hanging on the workbench. Reaching to grab the towel, he pulled and wiped the door frame and the knob with it. Pressing the towel around the lock as well, he drew off most of the dust.

Knowing how to unlock doors, his fingers met the warded lock. Then he imagined a typical beam on the inside pulling back. He heard a short click, but the door didn't move. *Old lock? Maybe I can't picture the mechanics*, he thought. He took a step back and looked at the door. Grabbing the towel again, he raised it to dust off the top frame of the door. Holding his hand beneath the top corner to catch the patch of dust, a small key tumbled down into his palm. It was covered in soot.

He rolled the towel back up and rested it on a workbench. The key slid into the lock, and the door opened easily. As he slowly stepped into the room, he saw a few bed sheets resting on piles of stored items. Looking to his left, he saw an old rotary phone on the wall with a cord wrapped around it.

Turning back toward the stairs he came down, he paced back toward them and bent down to take a look underneath. He saw an outlet on the wall and an open telephone wall jack right beneath it. He went back to grab the towel and wiped the phone before removing it from the wall. Turning the cord over in his hand, he dusted that too. He plugged it in, placed the phone on the basement floor, sat down, and lifted it to his ear. A small open line had a touch of electrical interference, but it sounded connected. He held it to his ear, and it lightly vibrated in his hand.

Hutch held the phone close to his face and spoke. "They're moving through my lessons. I think they're moving faster than I expected. You come to me. I don't think I can get them there in time."

Rose passed into the trees but didn't see Tim anywhere. The shadows of the tall trees made the view a bit dull. She stopped pacing and just held her spot to observe. Suddenly, she saw Tim rise up from the ground about a hundred yards away. It looked like he was inspecting something on the ground. He faced away from her, but his hand was full, and he was staring into it.

She didn't want to scare him by shouting at him from far away. Looking back over her shoulder, she could see the ballpark through the trees. She didn't see Pete staring into the forest. He was just pretending to pitch on the baseball field. Facing away from her toward the cars, Pete was pretending to play a game.

At that moment, before she turned around, her index finger and her thumb snapped together, and she quickly pulled her index down to her palm. She turned around and saw Tim staring directly at her, but she was completely invisible.

"Hello?" Tim painfully spouted toward Rose. He sounded like he had just lost his mind. "Is that someone I know?" He took a few steps in her direction. Then he stepped onto a fat log and looked around where she disappeared.

"Shit," whispered Rose.

"I was kinda thinkin' this could be a ghost lair, but I hope I'm just imagining it," Tim added a jokey, singing tone to his response. "When I'm in a forest, where I know magic has happened, I'm a bit frickin' scared, but Pete will tip his cap *and* . . ." he didn't finish his line. He just began to run. He opened his hands as a bunch of stones and sticks fell from his grip onto the dirt. He jumped over logs like hurdles, but his head remained at the same level as he popped his feet up over his blockage.

Before Rose could think straight, she just saw him exit the layer of trees and throw himself from the top of the creek basin. He landed on his stomach on the other side. Popping up quickly, he ran straight toward the baseball field.

Pete was standing on the pitching mound. He had his arm wrapped behind, resting on his tailbone. As if holding a ball, he turned his gaze from the plate to look at the imaginary first-base runner. As Pete finished a fake pitch motion, he turned and imagined a home run flying past him. He turned his body toward the outfield and saw the horrific expression on Tim's face. Pete raised his shoulders and stuck his palms out in front of him as if Tim would run straight through him. Tim reached him and tapped him on the shoulder as he ran past him toward his truck.

"Time to unplug. Let's get outta here," he yelled while running past Pete and through the fence toward his car. Tim reached to pinch the cables. He unclasped them and pulled them off, tossing them into his truck bed as a tangled pile.

Pete saw his terror and heard Tim yell at him again, "C'mon!" Did Rose spook him somehow?

"Tim, Tim!" Pete waved his hands over his head as he saw Tim's face as white as a sheet. Climbing up the small hill back to his car, Pete grabbed Tim's shoulders and looked into his eyes. "Rose gave me a sip of coffee. She said she saw you run to the bus stop and then enter the glade. She just went over to the trees. And look, this is her coffee canteen." He reached down and snagged it off the sidewalk in front of his car.

"I didn't see who it was. Whoever it was, they were looking at you, and then they disappeared." Tim's mustache shook a bit as he backed away from Pete momentarily.

"Jesus, maybe it wasn't Rose. You didn't see her? Did someone just kidnap her?" Pete turned his eyes back toward the forest. "Let's save your neighbor."

"You think that Rose got taken by that ghost?" Tim turned his head back to the forest and said, "I can't fight a ghost . . ." He swallowed the extra saliva in his mouth, "but let's go back and try to save her. There's two of us now." He nodded as Pete raised his fist. Tim thumped his knuckles against Pete's. They began walking quickly back toward the trees.

"We're coming to save you!" shouted Pete.

Rose thought she was crouched in the spot where Virg and Greg had lessons the night before. She was inspecting the piles of stones and sticks. She concluded that it looked like the kids had been flinging pebbles at each other. There were small footprints pressed in the shape of a small oval. Hearing Pete's savior impression, she turned her head back and saw them quickly making their way toward her.

Not knowing what the piles of stones meant, she rose and decided to flee. She thought about what Tim was searching for. *What did he see?* she asked herself. Rose held herself in place before she began her escape. Beginning to take a few quiet steps away from the lesson clearing, she kept trying to keep her feet on exposed roots and logs to avoid making footprints.

"You go to the left. I'll head back to the spot I saw before," Tim said to Pete.

They began to split their paths but kept moving in the same direction. Pete didn't know where to go. He just kept hiking and keeping his eyes open. He constantly rotated his head back and forth while looking for Rose. Pete dropped his gaze down to see if he could see a small footprint trail or anything like it. He reached a point about ten feet from Rose. She just froze.

Pete turned his head up from the small foot trail toward Tim. "Hey, I might see something."

"You probably will." Tim turned his head toward Pete but then looked down at the piles of tossed fragments. "C'mere for a sec."

Pete looked back down to remember the trail he found. He turned and walked toward Tim. When he reached the paced oval on the ground, he said, "Tim, I saw Rose's footprints back there." He pointed toward where he just was.

Tim ignored him for a moment. "I just saw this last night. They were throwing stuff at each other. This is the spot they were running around. See?" What Pete had said finally hit his consciousness. "Wait, you saw footprints over where?"

Pete pointed backward, and Rose felt that finger point directly at her. She turned away from them and began almost running for a moment. Then she stopped. When she turned, she saw they hadn't come searching for her yet. She held her position and opened her eardrum to their conversation.

Tim was holding Pete's shoulder. "We'll look for her. But I don't hear her. I'm sure we'd hear if ghosts possess her at this moment. I feel a bit safer with you here with me."

"So, you saw the kids chuck stuff at each other last night?" Pete scratched his chin.

"I think so. But the stones and sticks didn't hit them. I saw them just fly right through the kids. And look, there are piles of them. What do you think that means?"

"I don't know. Your kid's a ghost too?" Pete raised his arms.

When Rose heard that, she took one step toward them.

Tim turned to look directly into his friend's eyes. "Pete, when we returned to the house, and I went into Greg's room, he was already awake." He shook his head and looked down. "He told me that he can read minds and let things fly right through his body."

"Cool. So, did he read your mind?" Pete responded.

"Well, no," Tim said. His gaze went back down, and he turned to look at the dirt. "He said that he could only read the minds of some people." He took a step toward a pile of sticks. "But there was one thing he said that I definitely believe in."

"He can fly?" joked Pete.

"Last night, I was looking through my binoculars, and they were throwing things at each other. See these piles?" He pointed down. "They practiced this for a while, right before my eyes."

Pete flung his hands up in the air. "And then you *fell asleep*. That's not what you dreamed?"

"Pete, when we went to my place, and I went up to see Greg, he gave me another example." Tim touched Pete's shoulder to push him lightly into a sitting position on a log. He re-created the positions that he and his son were in when he tossed the book. "You're Greg. Just imagine that. He asked me to throw a book at him."

Tim picked up a tiny pebble. "He shouted, and I accidentally let it fly right at his head." Tim lightly tossed the stone into the air, and it bounced off Pete's cap and landed behind him. "But it didn't hit him. He squeezed his fist, and the book flew *straight through his head*. No contact, no scar. He knew exactly what he was doing."

Rose thought about Virg, wondering what he had already learned. It seemed that the boys were learning far faster than she had. Once she began lessons, it took her a few weeks to get past the concept of anything beyond sending and receiving mental messages. How much had Hutch taught them already? It seemed like he planned to just get them interested and give them a few skills. This was a far more advanced skill.

Tim's eyes opened wide. "Pete, my son is gifted."

"Maybe in *one* school," muttered Pete. He shook his head and looked confused. "Was this a private forest classroom lesson? That's kinda like a gifted class, I guess."

"I wonder what it's like." Tim turned his head, looking into the woods.

"Well, I'm freaked out," said Pete with a very neutral look. He stood up, adding, "I'm not worried, but I might need to get out of ghost land before I hear the rest." He began walking back toward the cars.

"What about Rose?" asked Tim.

"Well, maybe she didn't find you and just went home. That's what I'm gonna do."

"Still want to go to the mechanic?"

Pete stopped, bent over, and set his hands on his knees. "Ugh, do I have to?" He turned to see Tim's face and said, "Okay, okay. Let's go, chief."

When they both began to walk away back toward their vehicles, Rose turned and ran through the trees and across the glade. Upon entering the bushes beyond, she squeezed her fist and reappeared. Immediately, she turned back toward the two men, and at a quick pace, she waved her hands above her head. Tim and Pete had just passed the baseball diamond. Rose's waving caught Tim's eye. He turned and elbowed Pete.

"Hey, she was over in the bushes, not the forest," said Tim.

"Oh, huh." Pete scratched his head when he saw the spot she was hiking from. They both walked down around the diamond.

"Oh, there you are, Tim!" Rose shouted from across the creek. She jogged down and hopped across it.

"You didn't check on Tim in the woods?" asked Pete.

"Oh, you said the *woods*. Maybe my mind got the best of me. I thought you pointed at the open trail through those bushes. I went through those for a while and couldn't find where I was. Feels lucky to have found you both." She turned to Tim. "How were the woods?"

"I'm not sure." Tim took a pause. "How's your son doing?" He squinted a bit.

Rose felt like Tim hoped she knew something about their sons' new skills. "He's a bit tired," she responded. "I don't think he's got a problem yet . . . first week of school." Rose shrugged her shoulders.

Tim squatted down and sat in the grass. "Okay, I have to bring your attention to something."

Pete sat right down on the grass next to him. He rubbed his hands back and forth, almost warming up for the same conversation he had with Tim in the woods.

"Take a seat. I don't want you to fall over." Tim extended his hand and waved it down—sending a suggestion to Rose.

I know, Tim heard deep in his skull. Rose didn't sit down. She held her ground. The two men didn't respond. The wild tone in Tim's head made him happy that he was sitting.

I know what your son can do, Tim heard in his head. Rose was looking right into his eyes and not waning her expression.

"Wait, you can do it too? I heard him do it this morning," Tim said straight to Rose.

Don't respond, he heard. *I'll talk to you when you get back from your trip. Be safe going to the mechanic.*

"Okay," said Tim out loud. He turned his head toward Pete. "Okay, Pete, let's go to that mechanic and pick up that glider blade for Hutch."

"Is that okay with you, Rose? Are you firing a laser gaze into his eyes or something?" said Pete.

"I didn't say anything," said Rose. "I understand if he's got to grab that propeller. You seem okay to me."

"Well, you're not driving, pal," Pete said to Tim. "Seems to me like you didn't sleep last night. Take a ride, my cowpoke." He extended his hand to raise Tim off the ground.

Tim grabbed Pete's hand and agreed to the proposal. He turned toward Rose. Not knowing how to confirm or respond, he just saluted Rose as he made his way into Pete's passenger seat.

Pete saw it, shook his head, and blinked several times. Turning toward Rose, he said, "Well, I'll take care of this hungover poppet." He pointed at Tim, then waved and got into his car. He fired the ignition and backed out. They rolled down and met the road. As they left, Rose turned back toward her house.

She asked herself if she should ask Hutch questions or if he was hiding things from her. Perhaps she'd pick up the boys again today, she thought. She took a slow walk down the parking lot and toward the road. She stopped and closed her eyes.

It's your mom. I'm gonna pick you up today after school, Virg heard as he sat in his bus seat. He opened his mouth and held in a breath that he almost blew out. He did a quiet cough to clear his throat.

Then he closed his eyes and responded, *See you then.*

Rose proudly broke into a smile and kept walking toward her house.

42

Virg turned to Greg and said, "My mom's gonna pick us up at the end of the day."

"She's still just hitting you up in there, huh?" asked Greg. He tapped Virg's head.

"She's a mom," responded Virg. "Plus, I'd rather get picked up than ride another trip on this stinkin' bus. It's Friday."

When they arrived at school, Greg and Virg went to the office and asked to use their study period to groom the school's garden.

"Do you have experience doing garden work?" asked the office secretary.

"Yeah, my mom has a garden out back, and a farmer has been living at our house for almost a week. He's been teaching us for two nights in a row, and I'm almost addicted at this point," said Virg.

"Wow, how wonderful," she responded.

The secretary looked down into her desk drawer and pulled up a file. "It's about done with the fresh greens and fruit, but there's some almost rotten items too. If you can check it and remove those, that would be great. Anything you remove, if it's good enough, eat whatever matches your fancy . . . or compost it."

"Great!" said Greg. "Thanks!"

"Just sign here and print your names so I can keep a record." She slipped a board onto the counter between them. They swiftly scribbled their names down and signed.

"Thanks again," said Virg.

"No, thank *you*," responded the secretary.

They walked through the opening entrance lobby into the first hallway. Virg turned left as Greg turned right. Spinning back around, they caught each other's eyes.

"Pretend to learn," said Virg.

"Keep your mind on what you saw me do this morning," said Greg. "I'll try to get you up to my level."

"Oh, you little turd," said Virg, as he ran toward Greg.

They both broke into light laughter as they began jokingly pushing each other back and forth. Greg grabbed Virg into a playful headlock as they spun around.

A hall monitor wrapped his hands around his mouth and said, "Okay, okay. Make your way to your homerooms for attendance and the pledge." He made his way closer to them. "I'm talking to you, Greg," he added louder.

The boys stopped and kept chuckling. "I'll see you later," said Greg.

"I'll talk with you in about thirty seconds," responded Virg as he closed his eyes and held the sides of his head.

They made their way toward their classrooms and spent time apart until lunchtime.

43

Pete pulled into the mechanic's parking area. There were no spaces, just a dirt-rimmed half-circle of gravel next to an old Amish red barn. The barn's window shutters held old paint. Flaky, white splinters sheared. There were quirky collections of hexes with fused turkeys, flowers, and shamrocks painted inside. A rusted gas pump was lodged in the ground just in front of the barn's tall doors. A tiny sign that read "*Welcom*" was glued to the tip of its meter. The last letter of the word had been snapped off.

The man in the barn wore black jeans with boots, a sleeveless T-shirt, and a dark leather vest. He turned as Pete shifted his car into Park. As the man stepped past the barn door and into the sun, Tim saw his longhaired ponytail and a horseshoe mustache growing down the sides of his chin.

The mechanic had left his barn doors wide open. Looking into the building, Tim told Pete, "The Amish mechanic looks like he's in Motorhead."

"I bet he likes Jägermeister more than me," said Pete as they opened their car doors.

"You think he and Hutch could beat up Hulk Hogan and The Undertaker?" asked Tim.

"I would *so* pay to see that," whispered Pete.

As the mechanic approached them, he said, "You guys need a tune-up? What can I help you with?"

"Hi," said Tim as he extended his hand toward the mechanic. The man lifted his hands to his shoulders to show Tim the grease all over them. Tim pulled his hand back in agreement. "My friend said he was waiting for you to fix his glider."

Turning his head away from Tim, the mechanic said, "I don't work on gliders." Then he spit a large circle of brown moisture into the dirt.

Pete and Tim looked straight down at the tobacco pool. Looking back at the mechanic, Tim said, "This guy, Hutch, told me that he came here on Sunday and asked you to order a propeller for his damaged glider." Tim could see that the mechanic had no idea who he was talking about.

Tim puffed up his shoulders and stood on his toes. He squeezed his biceps around his torso as if he were squeezing ice-block tongs on a frozen cube.

"Oh, the big guy." The mechanic smiled and added, "Yeah, I asked him if he wanted to come to one of my fights."

Pete jumped in. "You fight?"

"For money." He spat in the dirt again. "He could make *me* some dollars."

"I'd bet on him too," said Tim. "So, you *did* order a propeller replacement for him?"

"I have one. I said I'd give it to him for free if he came to a fight."

"Wow, can I come too?" said Pete. His eyes were wide open.

"If you can bring your propeller friend," the mechanic lifted his welding goggles off his eyes and let them fall around his neck, "you're both welcome."

"So, I can pay you for his propeller now if that works." Tim reached into his pocket.

The mechanic held up an open hand. "Tell him he gets it for free *if* he wins. If he shows up, he'll make me a bunch of money. Heck, I'd win too if he came." He wiped his sweaty eyebrow on a leather lapel.

Pete turned to Tim. "Cool, so we'll find Hutch and watch him fight tonight. I'll bring some beer."

"Sounds good," said the mechanic. He lifted his goggles back up onto his face and walked back into his barn.

They watched him go and then turned back toward Pete's car. Tim took a few steps and asked Pete, "So, when was the last time you saw someone fight for a propeller?"

"I don't know, but just the suggestion sounds fun. How many cans you want me to bring for you tonight?" Pete opened his car door and slumped down into the driver's seat.

"You really are something else." Tim pulled his seat belt and clicked it in. Then his thoughts grabbed him as he peered back into the barn. He removed his seat belt and exited the car, walking back toward the barn's open door. Tim turned back for a moment and held up his index finger to Pete, mouthing, "One minute."

As Tim entered through the vast wooden doorway, he turned to see several cars parked very close to one another. There were old two-seated corvettes and some other antiques. He saw a bent and flat-tired Toyota, as well. Just as he expected, he didn't see a glider.

The mechanic turned around and made his way over next to Tim. He stopped just behind him.

When Tim turned back, he was surprised to see the mechanic so close to him. "Ah, oh, sorry. I just wanted to see if you had that glider. Hutch said that he brought it by."

The greaser kept his eye on what Tim was looking at. "I've worked on a bunch of these. Some took a while to fix, but I ain't been brought a glider to fix." Tim relaxed as the man's gaze floated past him and onto his barn contents. "Let me know if Hutch wants to come get his propeller tonight. I'm outta here by six."

"I'll let him know. Hey, can I have your name and number?" asked Tim.

"Yep. I ain't got no business card."

"I'll take a piece of paper if you have one."

The mechanic waltzed to his worktable and pulled out a drawer. He slapped a blank-lined postcard down and scratched a pen over it. Extending his arm and standing still, he waited for Tim to come to collect.

Tim paced over and plucked it. "Thanks a lot," he looked down and read, "Stinky?" He raised a confused look at the mechanic.

"What did you call me?" he responded.

Tim let his jaw drop, and his head got sucked in toward his shoulders like a scared turtle.

"I'm just kiddin'." The mechanic smiled and began to laugh. "That's my nickname. Use it when you show up at the party. People know me as that."

"Okay, thanks, Stinky."

"It's Thurgood if you want to recommend my business to any of your neighbors."

"Okay, great." Tim turned his tone back to normal. "Where's the party?"

"Two doors down," Stinky pointed down the street. "It's in Audelle's backyard. You'll find it."

"Well, thank you for your help, Stinky Thurgood." Tim turned around and walked back to the car as quickly as he could.

Opening the door, Pete turned to look at him. Tim shoved himself down into the passenger seat and shut the door.

"Everything all right?" asked Pete after seeing the look on Tim's face. He still looked a bit scared.

"Everything is getting a little stinky," said Tim as he smiled, turning toward Pete.

"What happened?"

"Well, we're invited to a party, but I don't know what's gonna happen, really." Tim popped open the dashboard drawer and grabbed a pen. He clicked it and wrote "Thurgood" beneath Stinky's handwriting.

"So, no propeller?" said Pete.

"He's got a propeller but no glider at all." Tim squinted his eyes as he rolled through some prospective thoughts. "Can you take me toward the creek behind the post office?"

With a flippant tone, Pete said, "Oh, your chauffeur would love to. You have a punching bag down there?"

"No, but I might have an answer." Tim put his palms behind his head as Pete turned onto the road.

"All right, but we're giving you your car back after that."

44

Rose opened her front door and took off her shoes. She set the coffee canister beside herself on a wooden key sill. "Hutch?" she said, pushing into every room in her house. There was no response. She listened and heard a smack downstairs. Following the noise, she saw Hutch through the porch windows in her backyard. He was standing over a clothed plastic table. Holding and whacking down a small square hammer, she noticed him softening a large sirloin from his venison batch.

She opened the door as his hammer slapped down again. He heard her close the door and looked up at her. "Oh, hey, Rose. Ribs and sirloin tonight," he said. "That venison's still prime. Salted it that first day. We'll get some battered slices on the grill tonight."

"Sounds great," she said. Crossing the porch and stepping down two stairs to reach the yard, she asked, "Need any help?"

"Well, what sides do you want? It's still early," he said.

"I'll go down to the farm stand and grab some corn and leeks."

"Sounds good."

"You soaking those in anything?" she pointed at two big rib sections resting on Hutch's table.

"Yeah, I saw you had onions all over the other side of the fence."

She squinted, "Those are tiny, right?"

"Yeah, but they're sweet. I saw a bunch as Doug and I were picking up Greg."

Rose thought back about them carrying Greg after he hit his head. "Oh yeah."

"You have tomatoes in your garden, right?"

"Obviously." She turned to look at the vines in the garden just six feet away. She walked over and touched a few orange bulbs. "We're kinda lucky so far. No frosty mornings."

"Then shake those vines and let 'em fall." Hutch smiled when he turned to face her.

"Cherry tomatoes and sweet onions. Not a bad flavor for ribs." She returned to her porch and collected a wicker basket and shears. Putting the basket below, she began snipping the stems just above the tomatoes. As she did, sweet bulbs fell into her shallow container.

She brought a stack back to the table and saw a drum beneath it. "You've chosen a batch bucket for the ribs?"

"Yep," he said. He briefly nodded his head toward what she was looking at.

"I'm just gonna smash these in the bucket. You salted these ribs. They'll need to absorb some of this."

"Then we'll grab some onions, cool?"

"Yep." Rose unloaded her basket of tomatoes into a strainer. After washing them, she shook them around with her hands and switched them into the bucket before slathering the ribs. She smashed them into chunky liquid with her fist. When she finished, she found the hose beside their house and opened the spout to clean her hands.

She turned and saw Hutch holding his hands in the air. "I'll get the door for you," said Rose. She walked over and pulled the porch door open. "Just wash those hands in the bathroom sink. Plenty of soap."

"Thanks," said Hutch as he kept his hands pointed up, containing the salt and meat shards.

Rose imagined the calm walk of plucking onions. Back to the porch, she lifted two sewn satchels off a beam hook. Hiking through the fields should make asking Hutch about the lessons easier. She walked over to their tiny shed to collect the ladder that Doug had used when he and Hutch found Greg. She opened the ladder and placed it to meet the top of her fence.

Her head turned when she heard Hutch closing the porch door. Seeing her waiting, he said, "Thanks for the ladder. I think we'll be okay, but let me go first. I'll catch ya."

"After you," she bowed as he climbed up the ladder. When he reached the top, he turned back to Rose. "The wild ones just look like waxy spearlike grass. You'll find 'em. They're usually just on their own." He jumped over and landed on the field beyond the fence.

Rose tossed the two satchels over, and they landed on Hutch's head. She climbed up and looked over the fence. "I'm good. Outta my way." She waved her backhand.

Hutch stepped back, and she jumped right over the fence and rolled once as she landed. She stood up comfortably and said, "Ta-da."

They walked into the field toward the creek. Peering to the corners of the cut-down cornfield, she saw the bridge where she had found Hutch. They moved toward the rim of the field, where the waxy tips were popping all over. Rose began pulling them and slapping the dirt off on her jeans before she tossed them in her bag.

As they both seemed comfortable, just meandering, Rose asked, "So, how are the lessons going?"

"Pretty easy, so far."

"They're doing well?"

"For sure."

"They can talk without using their voices, right?"

"Oh yeah. I'm sure you know. Virg said that you couldn't stop." Hutch let out a little laugh as he reached down to pull on a bunch of tall grass.

"Yeah, I wanted to help him learn a bit. He's good at it, though. I see that. What about Greg?"

"He's just as good as your son."

Rose wanted more. "So, three meetings so far for Virgil. Since he's already good at communication, have you taught them anything else?"

"Well, it seems like they're teaching themselves," responded Hutch softly.

"I'm sorry?" said Rose. She only half-heard his answer.

He raised his voice. "They're making their own connections. If I bring up an idea, they get it pretty quickly. In fact, Greg brought up an idea last night, and I didn't even have to teach him." Hutch raised his torso and turned toward Rose. "Are you teaching them too?"

She felt her pulse quicken, and her face flushed. "Oh, I told Virg about how I've been giving him examples with the paper airplane. But I hadn't silently contacted either of them before you showed up."

"It almost seems like someone else is contacting them and giving them ideas."

Rose stood still. "Are *you* giving them extra ideas?"

"At their age, giving them what we call a 'tiny example' could be like them jumping into a Salvador Dalí painting. If you're this young, the wider your mind opens up possibilities."

Rose's eyesight faded as she imagined the boys crawling into a painting.

"But what if they're finding very specific examples, not just ideas? Where would they find them?" she asked, moving her focus back to the onion patches.

"I guess we'll find out." Hutch raised his head from another patch of grass and looked into Rose's eyes.

She felt a shiver for a moment. He continued, "They can make a sieve shield. I didn't bring it up. Greg reacted accurately when I tossed a pebble at him."

"You threw a stone at Greg?"

"He asked how to protect himself. I had to give him an example. When I chucked it, it went right through him but didn't touch."

Rose stopped looking for onion patches. She stood up straight. "Did you bring up a ton of concepts for them? Too many?"

"I contacted you mentally on Sunday to let you know I was here. When I did, I knew they heard it too. But at that time, I didn't know anyone else had this skill. Greg seems to have latched onto a past opening. His memories sound pretty strong." Hutch lifted his bandana to wipe his brow.

Rose forced herself to sound calm, "Okay, so it's just concepts. Do they have an endless amount of those?"

"I've asked them to bring up what they're thinking about."

"Well, *that* actually sounds good for kids." Rose squatted down and pulled a waxy patch from the field.

"Maybe taking tonight off would be good for the teachers." Hutch looked at Rose and raised his eyebrows.

She laughed. "Yes, of course. Take tonight off. You're making dinner, for Pete's sake. That's more than enough."

"Thanks."

They both kept silent for a moment. Hutch also squatted down and put his hand on a patch of onion tips. As he did, he looked up toward the bridge. A car made its way down the road and pulled over. Two passengers got out and began to hike away from their vehicle. When they turned to hike down the hillside toward the creek, Hutch stood up and started pacing toward the bridge.

Rose looked in the direction Hutch was heading and saw the empty car. The driver's side still had a door open. She thought, *Drag your finger down your thumb. I'll do the same.*

Hutch silently responded to Rose, *Thank you.* He immediately disappeared in front of her.

Rose did the same and stood up to walk in Hutch's direction. He raised his arm with a closed fist. Right next to his eye, he looked down his arm at his pinkie's aim. His pinky finger pointed directly at the spot where his glider hid. Rolling his pinky around the frame he predicted, he saw the men reach the dirt rim of the creek and make their way into the shadows under the bridge.

Just in time, thought Hutch.

Good thing you taught his son how to do that. Remove it visually and open it up physically, responded Rose through her mind.

I didn't do that last time. That's how Greg got that scar. They'll walk through it, but they won't find it. Let's pay them a visit. Wanna hike down into the grasses by the creek? Hutch asked as they kept walking toward the men.

Nah, the driver door is open. Let's hang out in their car, sent Rose. She didn't hear Hutch chuckle, but she knew he was giggling.

They passed over the hill above the creek and made their way up to the road. Rose sat in the driver's seat and left Pete's door open. Hutch looked both ways, walked around to open the passenger door, and sat in Tim's seat. They both dragged their index fingers up their thumbs to reappear.

Tim reached the top of the creek's bank and scratched his mustache. "I didn't see it either, but I know it's around here somewhere."

Walking behind Tim, Pete shouted when he saw Rose sitting in his driver's seat. "Augh! Sweet meat, it's not cool." Horrified by seeing someone he didn't expect, Pete backed away just to catch his breath.

Tim reached the tip of the hill and said, "It was weirder in the forest, but yeah, people are appearing left and right today." He patted Pete on the shoulder as he met eyes with Rose. "How's your day going so far? Want a ride? Pete's pretty helpful."

With his hands on his knees and catching his breath, Pete waved above his head to agree.

"Sorry, we didn't want to scare you," said Rose. "We were just picking onions for tonight's dinner. There's a lot more venison if you're still hungry."

Tim turned his eyes from Rose to Hutch. "Well, I can't come over tonight, but I might want to invite Hutch to a little party after dinner."

"Oh, like a bowling alley?" asked Rose.

"No, it's for adults only. The Stinky mechanic thinks that Hutch should be his special guest. I think he fell in love." Tim smiled and waited for Hutch's reaction.

"The propeller blades are delivered?" asked Hutch.

"Stinky told us that he's fixing them. But you impressed him so much, he wants you to come to spend time at his party before collecting them."

"Wait, his name is Stinky?" asked Rose. She turned to look at Hutch.

Hutch rolled his eyes. "Um, yeah, Thurgood is known as Stinky. I don't know why. Maybe he doesn't shower." He backed his head into the seat, showing his exhaustion at the idea. "I'll walk over there tonight. I'll get the propeller and sip a beer with him."

"Well, we're invited too. And Pete just can't think about doing anything else tonight. So we'll give you a ride." Tim broke into a devilishly wide smile.

"Aww, you guys are really acting like long-time neighbors." Rose smiled and turned her head back and forth between them. To Hutch, she said, "Yeah, take tonight off and go have a little cheer with that stinky guy."

Hutch bent toward the open driver door. "What time?"

"Whenever you're done with dinner, just give us a call," said Tim.

"Okay. I'll finish dinner, clean up, and walk over to ring your doorbell."

"Sounds good," said Tim.

"Well, we'll give you back your car," Rose said to Pete. He was leaned over, clutching his knees and trying to slow his breath.

Hutch looked into the rearview mirror. Then he opened the passenger door and exited, facing away from Tim. Walking back toward the slashed cornfield, Hutch said, "Drive safe. Thanks for checkin' on the propeller." He didn't look at Tim or Pete at all.

Rose began to follow him. "Happy Friday. Have fun tonight!" She turned away from them and climbed down the hill to follow Hutch.

Pete and Tim got back into the car and watched the other two keep walking away into the open field. "I didn't see them at all," said Tim.

"Me neither. Frickin' freaked me out," answered Pete.

"But they're walking away into the field. When we parked, I didn't see them in the field."

"Me neither. But more and more, I feel like I'm going blind around here."

"You think he's gonna show up for a ride?" Pete looked across the field at Hutch.

"I don't know, Pete. But I'll call ya either way. We're going tonight."

45

After lunchtime, the two boys were sitting in the school's garden. Their fingers were caked with fresh dirt bound in dried watermelon juice. After finding two slightly soft and viciously ripe watermelons, the boys forgot about their plan, naturally. The dirt was all over their clothes and hands as they had opened the melons by cracking them open on their knees. After the snap of the rinds, they shoved their heads into the melon's pink flesh.

This place wasn't actively attended. It felt nice being surrounded by rising greens and plants. The garden hid them from the windows and hallways during the lunch periods. Greg and Virg got through several bites before remembering why they agreed to meet in the garden.

As they cleaned their hands on their pant legs, they sat down and let the sugar dry on their skin. By midday, the sun had escaped the thick clouds, and a bright blue tone covered the sky.

Greg pulled his eyes from the sky and said, "OK, set your melon rind over at the end of this little row." He pointed to a barrier at the end of a row of plant beds.

Virg popped up with a watermelon rind in his hands. He put it down about ten feet away from them. Standing up, Greg raised his hand and waited for Virg to do the same.

Raising his hand to match Greg's, Virg said, "Ya know, I kind of know what to do. When I held your hand at the bus stop, I think I felt how to do it. Lemme try."

Greg turned his head and looked at Virg. He raised his eyebrows. "Uh, I don't know about that. Can I explain what I saw?"

"I think I'm good," Virg blurted. He faced the melon and raised his open hand. Upon squeezing his fist in the air, the melon exploded on the ground. Virg saw the explosion, immediately opened his hand, and raised it. The rind exploded into an almost pure liquid with tiny green shell pieces. The burst whipped straight up in the air, following Virg's hand as he raised it quickly.

Then, as the intense burst reached its vertical peak, it dropped straight down and sloshed its contents on the boys' heads and shoulders.

"I should have just popped my pinky out when it reached its peak," Virg grumbled in a low tone. He seemed frustrated.

"O . . . kay," Greg responded slowly. "I'll repeat what I saw in my dream." He reached down to grab the base of his shirt and wiped it over his eyes and forehead. Quickly walking back to his watermelon husk, he picked it up and placed it in the same spot as Virg had. "You have to raise your hand and keep it open." He looked at Virg's hand. Virg popped up his hand to match Greg's.

"Okay, make a note. I saw that kid raise her hand while it was already open," said Greg. Virg matched him. Greg let his hand go down and kept his gaze on Virg. "Now, grab that rind in your mind, but don't close your hand."

Virg looked at the melon rind and closed his eyes. "I see it."

"Now, raise your hand and pull it off the ground."

Virg raised his palm slightly, but the watermelon rose far above the branches of the garden.

"Open your eyes," said Greg.

Virg popped open his eyes and quickly lowered the angle of his hand. The rind shot down. He just lightly moved the angle of his hand at his wrist, and the movement matched.

"Yes. That's how it works. Hell yes," said Greg as he saw the progression.

"Okay, so if I squeeze my hand in, it will burst?" asked Virg.

"You already did that. What else can we do?"

Virg slowly pressed one finger at a time down onto his palm. As he did, the floating melon broke apart and swirled in a circle—reflecting Virg's intention.

"Holy effing eff. It's following what I'm imagining," Virg whispered.

Greg heard him and smiled. "Hold onto it; don't drop your hand or squeeze."

Virg brought up his other hand, matching the position of his right one. He shut his fingers on his thumbs and spread his hands away from each other. The shards and molecules of liquid separated equally into two flat, floating pads of moisture. Virg drew his hands away from each other to aim them over the boxes of soil and plants surrounding them. He faced his hands down slightly. The pieces of melon and juice rested on the plant beds and seeped in.

"Wow, that's a much-better method than I would've used," exclaimed Greg as he saw his pal composting and watering the garden.

"You hadn't seen that yet, but neither had I. I just did what I thought *should* happen . . ." said Virg, ". . . and then it did."

"I haven't really had that opportunity yet."

"Let's freaking practice," added Virg.

"After school, don't go home. Let me know when you're out."

"Dude, my mom is picking us up today."

"Great. Just tell your mom what we've taught ourselves so far. Maybe she'll be impressed."

"*I* am!" shouted Virg with a smile on his face.

A moment passed by as they began to feel the watermelon juice dry on their skin in the sun's rays. They felt their sticky, sugar-covered skin snap and pop with every movement.

"How is this all possible?" asked Greg while looking up at the open sky.

"In my first lesson, Hutch said, 'You're young. It could be an advantage if you don't think everything is impossible.'"

"So, we can do all this because we haven't closed the gap of possibilities?"

"Let's ask my mom about all her skills when we see her. She told me she began contacting people at age twenty-two. We're like a decade younger than those peeps were."

"That sounds like a lot of time to invent skills." Greg grabbed his backpack and felt the weight of it.

"It feels to me like we are touching just the beginning of our abilities. I think that we got the idea after Hutch contacted us on Sunday . . . like by mistake."

They looked at each other.

"You're sure it was a mistake?" said Greg.

Virg asked, "Did he know about us?"

"We didn't know about ourselves." Greg shook his shoulders. "How did he know?"

"He said that he crashed after catching a wind current. I mean, flying a glider isn't easy. You just float on gusts of wind, right? It's like flying a kite."

"I really wanted to fly that thing after he showed up," responded Greg.

"Me too." Virg looked down at the ground. "But I'm glad you and I are really getting better at this. Thanks, my man. You're a good teacher."

Greg reached over to Virg and wiped his hand across the crest of bangs. The juice rolled down Virg's forehead. They both chuckled.

Greg stood up. "Let's go get some *real* lunch."

"Yeah, and clean ourselves for real." Virg wiped his brows and followed Greg back out of the garden and into the cafeteria. As they came in, a group of classmates stared at the wet, pink boys returning from the garden.

"Your garden is fresh and healthy," said Virg to the crowd.

"You're welcome," added Greg.

Rose parked in the middle school lot. She left her windows open and relaxed in the sun. The rays flew through her window and landed on her chest and lap. The heavy clouds from that morning had passed over her town and into another valley.

On her way to school, she imagined the kids' previous lessons. Glad that Hutch had asked for a break tonight, she considered taking this opportunity to see what the kids understood and were still curious about. Perhaps she could help them more than he could, she thought, although teaching and helping others had been his job for a while. She wondered if anything he could teach them would be better than any skills she could offer.

Calming herself down, she closed her eyes and rolled her head straight into the rays from above. A memory popped into her mind. Hutch had said that it feels like they're teaching themselves. Suddenly, she perked up and thought she would just ask them about their needs. She could turn the kids into teachers. They were at the perfect age.

She looked in her backseat at the corn and leeks she had picked up from the local farmer's market. The paper bags sat in the seat behind her. Next to the corn, the second bag held some fresh salad ingredients. She could still smell a hint of the jalapeños and Meyer lemons nested close to each other.

As she turned back, she saw the school's door burst open, and many tykes ran out as fast as they could. The older students took their time. Most didn't even look at her in the parking lot on their way to the buses. She could tell they weren't thinking about anything but freedom on a Friday.

Virg pushed open a door and looked at the line of buses. He stood waiting for a moment and lightly leaned on a bike rack. His shirt had a light pink tone that almost looked like a tie-dye. Greg left the building, and Rose let out a little chuckle when she saw that the two boys matched. Virg flipped his head toward his mom's car, showing Greg where to go. They came over and opened the car doors. Virg got in the passenger seat, and Greg got in just behind him.

"You guys look great," Rose said. She broke into a smile. "Also, you smell like watermelon."

"Yeah, it didn't feel great. But it definitely got better. You should have seen what we did today!" said Virg.

"Hey," loudly whispered Greg as he kicked the back of the seat.

"Oh, come on. My mom knows about our weirdness." Virg turned toward Greg.

"Well, you should not use your skills enough to freak out your classmates. What happened? Did you make something explode? Did anyone see you?" pushed Rose.

"No," said Greg. "We volunteered to work on the garden."

"Oh, I've seen it. Doug and I had the parent tour a couple of years ago. You guys have pretty broad garden grounds. Lots of different plants, right? Oh, and, Greg, be careful of those bags. We've got some veggies for tonight."

Virg clicked his seat belt and said, "Yeah, the garden's pretty big. I don't think anyone saw us. But they definitely saw us after." Virg reached down and stretched his stained shirt.

Greg did the same, "Yeah, I think yours is a bit brighter than mine."

"Well, try to just practice in our backyard or somewhere nearby. I don't want your principal to give you detention for blowing his mind." Rose smiled. "What did you guys do out there?"

Virg began. "Greg taught me how to move something off the ground. At a certain point, I split it open into tiny pieces and used it as compost in the beds."

"Wow. When did you learn that?" Rose asked.

Greg broke in. "I mean, we basically taught ourselves."

"But Hutch has been teaching you guys for days now." Rose looked confused.

Greg looked embarrassed. "Yeah, at the beginning, he gave us the idea of contacting each other without talking. After that, ideas have cropped up in my head. When he showed up, I had a dream that just kept going and going. When I remember what I saw . . . It's almost like I'm getting examples. I can't help it. I just want to learn about the things that I'm seeing."

Rose turned back and met eyes with Greg. "He contacted me when he showed up. I only heard him asking if I was close by. I think he sensed me, but not you."

Greg looked like he didn't understand.

Rose continued. "What did you learn on that first night?"

"Too much. It was like I was watching his life flow by. It was too fast to read the whole story and recognize people. I don't remember it all, but some of the images crop back up when I take a nap. I still see some when I wake up."

"I've been taking notes," said Virg.

"Okay, don't say anything to Hutch. P.S., You don't have a lesson tonight," said Rose.

"But we want to keep learning," responded Virg.

"Yeah, and it's obvious you don't need him," said Rose.

"But he began teaching us, and it's helped a lot so far," said Virg.

Rose turned to Greg. "He didn't teach you how to read minds, did he? Come on over after dinner. I'll help you learn anything you bring up."

Greg nodded. "Okay, I'll come over after dinner with my fam. Can you just save some of Mr. Murphy's sweets for me?" He looked serious.

Rose looked at Greg through the rearview mirror and turned the car on. "Of course."

Rose dropped off Greg and waved to Sue in the Fishers' driveway. She saw Sue point at Greg's shirt and heard him respond, "Well, I frickin' love watermelon. They had big slices today, and it's hot outside!"

Sue shook her head at Greg and waved goodbye to Rose. She mouthed "Happy Friday" at the car. Rose waved goodbye and backed her car out of the driveway. While the vehicle met the road and sped up, Virg stuck his head out the window to whip his dried-out, sugared hair off his forehead.

As he did, Rose said to him, "Remember, you're not telling Hutch about our lesson tonight. Just enjoy his cooking. There's venison left to enjoy. Oh, and can you help us prep tonight's dinner? I'm helping too. Also, please take a shower before you get to the kitchen."

Virg pushed his sugar dreads back on his head and said, "Yep, no prob. You said corn earlier. Want me to be little husk master?"

Rose smiled. "If you don't mind. Just grab a plate to toss the naked cobs onto."

A quiet moment passed as Virg pushed down on his hair, which felt like it had glued together on his scalp.

He let go of his hair and turned to look at Rose. "When can we start testing you?"

"I don't think I'm going to be tested. Have you had tests yet?"

"I guess not. I just want to see what you know." He smiled. "Oh, there was a kind of a test when Hutch threw a stone at Greg. It didn't hit him, so I guess he passed."

"That's a bit of a test. How about we experiment?" Rose put her hand on Virg's hair and felt the density of the dried sugar. "Geez, you really have to shower."

Virg reached down onto his shirt and pulled it away from his chest. "Yeah, I'm beginning to itch."

Rose laughed and kept her eyes on the road. Virg calmed down for a moment. His window in the car was still open. He closed his eyes and angled his head to catch the wind.

Soon, they pulled into their driveway. They picked up paper bags off the backseat, went in the front door, and then into their kitchen. Rose looked over their sink and saw Hutch lying in a folding chair in their backyard. His eyes were closed, and his mouth was wide open. *A real Friday*, she thought.

Virg saw her staring as he put down the bag of corncobs on their table. He walked next to her and looked out the window in the same direction.

"Shouldn't he be cooking?" said Virg.

"Your dad gets home after five. We've got time. It's what?" She turned to look at the clock above their stove, ". . . about four fifteen."

"Just start husking out back. Oh, and here's a tray." She reached into the cabinet and pulled out a plastic-rimmed tray. Shoving it in the bag of husks, she added, "He'll probably hear that, but he's got time. Well, maybe it's time to activate the charcoal. I'm gonna cut up some of these leeks and garlic. I'll bring some aluminum foil down too. See you in a bit." She lifted the bag of corn back off the table and rested it in Virg's arms.

He made his way downstairs and opened the porch door. Sitting on the porch in a chair, he removed all the cobs and put them on the table beside him. He put the paper bag between his legs next to the chair and husked them, placing the clean cobs onto the tray.

After he husked a few cobs, he noticed that Hutch wasn't hearing or responding to his rips of leaf and silk. For a moment, Virg thought, *What is he dreaming about?* Hutch's open mouth and closed eyes made Virg consider the entrance into his teacher's mind. Virg shut his eyes and imagined he was floating over the porch railing. He saw his body hovering above the open mouth of the sleeping giant. As he slithered down into Hutch's mouth, Rose opened the sliding door and took two steps onto the porch.

Virg heard his mom's entrance. He balked and lightly shook his head to remove the concept. Rose turned from looking at Hutch to inspecting her son's tray and seeing his surprised look.

"You're just stripping those, right?" She kept her voice down so as not to awaken their sleeping guest.

Virg quietly responded, "Yeah, yeah." He grabbed the top of another cob and slowly broke open the top.

Rose kept her eyes on him, then looked back toward Hutch. Slowly, she pulled her eyes back to Virg.

"Can you?" she quietly asked.

Virg popped his eyes back at her. "I don't know. I didn't do it."

"Did you try?"

"Almost, but I don't have any experience."

"I've never tried before, either. Just wait until it's us. I'll let you *try* it later on. Now's not the time." Rose sat on the other side of the table where Virg sat. She lowered her cutting board quickly and lightly tossed it down an inch from the table. Hutch heard it and slowly opened his eyes and stretched his arms up over the back of his chair. He took a deep, relaxing breath and turned toward the porch.

"Oh, hi, there." He leaned forward and rose from the chair. Seeing Virg and Rose working on dinner, he asked, "Is it time to start?"

"We're not in a rush. It's like, just after four," said Rose as she began to roll garlic cloves in a folded paper towel.

"Gotcha, gotcha." Hutch stretched again and said, "Charcoal time?" He reached down to grab an ashcan.

"Yeah, go for it."

Virg watched the man reach down for the bag of charcoal stones. As Hutch began setting up the grill, Virg felt like an opportunity was stolen. Thinking about what Greg had seen, he wondered what Hutch had been dreaming. Virg saw the cook raise his glance and look into his eyes.

For a moment, Hutched flicked his head a bit sideways and asked, "Are you okay?"

"Oh, sorry, I'm okay," Virg shook his head and pulled on a cornhusk to look busy. "I was just thinking about my homework. They asked us to write a story about our summers."

"Gonna write about me?" Hutch kept staring.

"I dunno. Most of what I'm thinking about happened this past week." Virg shrugged his shoulders.

Hutch let out a laugh. "Well, you can certainly tell them about meeting a great hunter and cooker. Want me to teach you about how we're spicing and cooking these ribs? You can write about learning these things."

"Well, yeah, definitely." He put down his ear of corn.

Hutch moved his hand. "Come 'ere," he said, inviting Virg toward him as he opened up the bucket holding the ribs. He explained the best way to attach the flavor and how long they would cook them.

Rose smiled, watching Hutch teach her son and make him a bit more comfortable.

As Hutch and Virg prepped the grill, they got into their rhythms. Doug arrived a bit after the corn had been prepared. They were buttered, rolled through the diced leeks and garlic, and wrapped in foil. The ribs sat above the hot coals and dripped tomato paste back down. Virg's dad skipped heading indoors and just paced around in his backyard, following the scent.

"This smells awesome, you guys!" burst out of Doug.

"Want a beer?" asked Hutch. Doug closed the fence gate as Hutch added, "Oh, c'mon, it's Friday. Take off that jacket."

Doug removed his suit jacket like he was a model—whipping it around above his head. His family laughed, and Virg ran over to hug him. They sat in the backyard while the meal cooked and savored the aromas.

After they had eaten, Doug and Virg took some dishes inside. They separated ways. Doug went to his bedroom to change into a T-shirt and shorts. Virg went to his bedroom to take out the notebook that held his notes on Greg's dreams. He put it on his desk, leaving it in his room, and returned to the porch. Rose asked Hutch to relax and digest. He sat down in the same spot they found him in. She went back inside to help Doug with the dishes.

When Virg came back outside, he sat on the grass in front of Hutch.

"So, you're going to a party tonight. Is that right?" Virg smiled and got a bit excited.

"Yeah, I'm sorry, but I can't give you a lesson tonight. Does Greg know? I mean, his dad is kind of making me go."

"I think he knows. Mom told us when we got picked up from school. We were on her way back from the farm stand. He seemed fine with it. Friday is for chillin'." Virg raised his hand for a high five.

Hutch reached down to slap his hand, and Virg asked, "But *your* Friday is for partyin'. What kind of party is it?"

Rolling his eyes a bit, Hutch answered, "Um, it's kind of an 'Essence of Technology' party."

"Just you and the inventors?"

"Ah, well, me and mechanics . . . and Greg's dad . . . and his friend, Pete." Hutch wobbled his head up and down while mentioning each person he would see.

"Where's the party?"

"It's a couple doors down from the propeller mechanic."

Virg chuckled. "Oh, Stinky's party?"

"You know Stinky?"

"Yeah, that's like everyone's favorite name. Some of my classmates have parents who have used him. They said he's really nice. He's a good fixer. My one friend, Pat, said that his dad got a part replacement for free. He didn't give any specifics, but he said the trade reminded him of some Chuck Palahniuk book."

"*Fight Club?*"

"I don't know. I haven't been allowed to read his books yet."

Hutch stood up and looked at the horizon. A touch of blue tones still hung on the horizon.

"Well, it's about time to get a bit stinky." Hutch made his way onto the porch. He slipped the door open and broadly called upstairs, "I'm heading out for a beer and a propeller. I'll see you guys later."

"Okay, have fun!" he heard from the kitchen beyond the stairs. Hutch turned back around and told Virg, "Stay safe and relax. Enjoy your Friday." He went through their back door and took a few steps into their driveway. For a moment, he turned back to Virg, "Oh, and if your dad is making any dessert, save me a piece."

Hutch stood to watch Virg close the door. The kid smiled, waved, and shut the door behind him. Hutch waited a moment. He saw Virg move back toward the living room through a tiny window on the door.

The big guy turned back and made his way toward the garage. He opened the door and grabbed one of the small camping tents hanging on the wall. Exiting the garage, he silently closed the door, turned around, and walked toward the alley. As he walked toward the road, he looked to his right, thinking about heading to the Fisher's house. Instead, he turned left and kept his walking pace. Soon, he looked both ways and entered the bushes across the street.

Tim sat in a leather reclining chair with his feet up. When his family finished dinner, he wiped his mustache and turned on the Phillies game to check in on their streak. Sitting while digesting his dinner, he picked up his phone and gave Pete a call.

"Are you still watching the Phillies? Looks like they're up right now," Tim said.

Pete answered, "I'm watching. But if I turn it off now, they'll keep their lead. They always fall off the edge and take me with 'em when I watch them after they get ahead."

"Okay, you ready to c'mon over? I'll call the Murphys to see what Hutch is up to."

"Sounds good. See ya soon," Pete said and hung up.

Tim called the Murphys' house and switched the phone to his other ear.

Rose picked up. "Hi, Murphys. Who is this?"

"Rose, it's Tim. Has Hutch had enough of a postdinner nap?"

Rose sounded confused. "Well, he took a nice nap this afternoon, but he already left. Have you seen him yet? Maybe he'll knock on your door in, like, thirty seconds."

"Oh, okay. I asked Pete to come over. We were gonna pick him up, but we'll wait for him here."

"OK, let me know if you don't see him." Rose hung up.

Tim kept the game on and leaned back. When he heard his doorbell, he walked to see if it was Hutch. Opening the door, he saw Pete with a little cooler case in his hand.

"Lemme just see how the Phills are doing. You still watching?"

Tim turned and waved Pete in. "Oh, sure. C'mon. Hutch isn't here yet. Rose said that he just left."

"Want a beer yet?" Pete opened his little cooler in front of Tim.

"I'm good. I think I'm the driver tonight."

"Whoo-hoo!" Pete found a seat and cracked open a can.

"Thanks for driving," said Pete to Tim.

"You got it."

Tim thought about wanting to see why Hutch agreed to a fight. Without saying a word, he asked himself, *Is it common for most people to go to a fight party? Is Hutch that good of a warrior? Can Greg feel something if Hutch gets bruises or cuts on his face?* That last thought gave him a little shiver.

Sue came down the stairs to find Tim and Pete in the living room.

"Timmy, your son's going over to the Murphys' tonight. Virg invited him for a sleepover. I agreed, but he's gotta get a bit of his homework done before he goes over." Sue gave Tim a serious look.

Pete interjected, "Oh, c'mon. It's his first Friday so far in school. Give him a little time to enjoy himself." He sucked down a mouthful of beer with his eyes still locked on the screen.

Sue met eyes with Tim and raised her eyebrows.

"I'm not drinkin', and neither is he," He pointed above at Greg's room upstairs. "He can take tonight off and just go hang with his pal. He's already having double lessons so far, and Hutch is takin' tonight off. Also, he said he worked on a garden in school today. Let him finish this week in peace."

"All right, all right." Sue smiled and went back on the stairs. "First week of school, I'll back off. But next week begins the 'do-at-least-one-assignment-on-Friday' routine. Then he can actually enjoy his weekend and not start freaking out about his assignments on Sunday nights."

"Good point. Next week, he begins the routine. For now, let him enjoy his memories of summertime." Tim grinned at Sue.

She smiled at him and neutralized her expression as she turned toward Pete. Sue went upstairs, and Pete turned toward Tim.

Tim said to him, "Yep, I'm drivin'."

As the Phillies played on, they cracked some doubles and gained a lead. Tim and Pete stood up to stretch by the end of the sixth inning. As Pete rolled backward, he saw the clock.

"Hey, Chauffeur, I've been here a while. Is Hutch still coming?" Pete scratched his nose.

"Y'know, I think we've been conned." Tim made his way toward the stairs. "Hey, Greggy, you're free to go to the Murphys. We're heading out. You ready?"

Tim heard a little scurry from upstairs and saw Greg come down quickly with his packed bag on his shoulder.

"I thought you'd never ask. Thanks, Dad." Greg pointed past them. "To the Batmobile." He ran past Pete, through the door, and kept running past the car..

"Your boy's really ready." Pete crushed a can and stood up.

Tim leaned back toward the staircase and mimicked Greg's voice. "Love you, Mom! I'll be back safe!"

Tim heard a little laugh from upstairs and then, "Love you too! Be safe and have fun!"

The two men entered the driveway and hopped into the car. Tim looked out the car's window at Greg. The kid rang the doorbell just down the street, and Tim saw Virg run down the stairs through a window and pop open the front door. Greg and Tim waved goodbye to each other. Turning his head to the road, Tim took a deep breath and pressed down on the pedal.

"I think we're late to this party," Tim said. "Can we just walk into someone's backyard? We have no invite, right?"

"Well, if there's a fight, I'd expect it to begin once people are hammered. Just having a nice dinner and then punching each other isn't really how this works. You ever been to one before?"

"*You* have?"

Pete looked smug as he heaved a warm breath on his fingernails and wiped them against his shirt. He said, "Only the best of us have seen good backyard fights. Always bet on the slightly older-looking people. They have experience."

Reacting to Pete, who looked so confident, Tim said, "Jeez, is this a regular event?"

"Well, The Undertaker became a legend, but ya gotta start somewhere."

"I rarely hear athletes reference their 'backyard beginnings.'" Tim rolled his eyes.

"Gotta start somewhere," said Pete.

They pulled up past the old red barn where they had met Stinky. Some lights shimmered in the backyard just two doors down. As the car crawled down the road, they saw vehicles parked in long lines on either side of a driveway. The campfire light beamed on the house's back roof and shimmered off a few cars near the backyard. Tim parked behind a line of cars at the end of the driveway. He and Pete got out and began to walk up the paved driveway. Looking past the side of the house, they saw some people in the backyard. An orange glow from the nearby fire pit lighted up the guests.

As they reached the backyard, a few heads turned to look at the two new partiers. There were more people than Tim expected. If he counted, he would've guessed thirty people were hanging out in the backyard. Pete lifted his cooler toward a few glances he was getting from partygoers—vaguely suggesting that he was sharing. One couple made a hang loose sign, popping their thumb and pinky out.

Behind Pete, Tim saw a few quarter-barrel kegs shoved into a big ice-filled cooler. He reached to tap Pete on the shoulder and turned his gaze toward the keg. "You've got some extra gifts in your cooler, but look at the size of *those* things." He pointed his finger toward the kegs.

"Find Hutch first, or grab a sippy gift first?" Pete smiled and jokingly popped up his eyebrows.

"Grab a sip. I'll start looking for him. Let me know if you find Stinky."

"Well, I smell him right now," said Pete.

Tim let out a chuckle. "You know who I'm talking about." He looked past Pete at the crowd. "Enjoy yourself and keep your eyes open."

Tim walked away from the house and into the crowd in the backyard. Guests were playing horseshoes, sitting on a few fallen tree trunks as benches, and making out near the forest rim surrounding the yard. Slowly pacing, enjoying the light of the fire, Tim sat for a moment on a log and stared ahead.

"Hey, propeller friend," Tim heard from behind.

A cigarette was extended from a hand beside him. Tim turned his head to look up and saw a man smiling down at him.

"Stinky!" Tim rose right up and opened his arms. Stinky gave him a half hug and brought the smoke up again.

"Good to see you again, my man," Stinky said.

Tim politely collected the cig offered to him.

Stinky added, "Where's your pal?" He lit his cig in his mouth and extended the lighter toward Tim.

"Oh, Pete's right over there. Let's go say hello. He's good at taking a puff." Tim just held the cigarette and looked around by the keg, avoiding Stinky's lighter. He saw Pete with a red plastic cup in his hand, leaning against the house with his extended arm. It looked like he was flirting with a red-haired woman in a leather dress and boots.

Stinky followed Tim's eyesight right to Pete. "Oh, your other friend is talking to Audelle. I thought you were gonna bring the big guy."

"Yeah, Hutch will be here. We were supposed to give him a ride, but he left before we could pick him up."

"Your friend might not wanna talk to Audelle. She's a bit of a loose cannon."

"I dunno. Kinda looks like *she's* hitting on *him*."

They both saw the woman extend her cup toward Pete's and clink for a cheer. Her lips opened into a broad smile, and she grabbed Pete's hand and pulled him to sit down with her on her house's stoop. Pete sat beside her and opened his cooler to show her his offerings. Audelle slapped his chest lightly with a broad smile and shut the cooler while tickling his chin.

"Well, I think he's doing just fine," said Tim.

"I guess he's a gunner. She doesn't like just anyone."

Tim nested the cigarette on his ear, pinned to his skull. He looked away from Pete and back at Stinky. "I might just take some more time looking for Hutch. Wanna look with me?"

"No need. He's got time. Maybe he's prepping for the fight." Stinky elbowed Tim lightly in his ribs as he shoved his lighter into his pocket. "Not late enough yet, anyway. Gotta see who's gonna win the ol' horseshoe fight." Stinky turned back toward the stakes and began to walk away from Tim.

Tim held still and said quietly, "Where is that guy?"

Hutch closed the post office door behind him. He pushed through the bushes and paced over the dark glade. Making his way into the forest, he turned to look behind himself before entering the darkness beneath the branches. There was no one following him. No flashlights for campers or hikers bounced off the bark or bushes.

Turning back and through the trees, he slowly crept over the logs and around the roots. He hiked until he reached the spot where he gave lessons to those boys. For a moment, he crouched down and picked up one small stone from the soil. Following a rise in the landscape, Hutch hiked up onto a hillside rim that seemed heavily forested and far from paths or roads. Closing his eyes, he began to turn slowly in a circle. As he listened to his surroundings, he heard an owl chirp and an acorn falling onto some roots. There were no sounds of cars, roads, or neighborhoods. He opened his eyes and did the same slow turn. No backyard fires and no porch lights caught his eye.

Hutch sat down in a skilled lotus position. Both shins were crossed, and his feet rested on his thighs. His back was straight, and he rested the pebble in front of himself. His arms were extended and rested on his knees. Closing his eyes, he sucked in a deep breath and opened his mouth wide. Without touching the pebble, he let out a deep groan on one low pitch. He kept the grinding of his vocals channeling at the stone. As his heart rate began to speed up, he didn't stop pushing out his breath.

Suddenly, the pebble began to vibrate. As the earth started to shiver, Hutch raised his arms just a centimeter above his knees. The pebble floated up about an inch and spun viciously. As it did, the stone looked like its temperature was elevating. The dark grey of the stone lit into a light red and quickly became a full yellow.

Hutch stopped groaning and took in another breath. As he did, the stone stopped spinning and was held flat. The pebble shifted from a hot yellow down to a light blue. The color poured into the air surrounding the stone as if steam were expanding from the pebble. Hutch raised his hands another inch, and the steam swung around, forming an open cone above the stone.

The light blue, swinging like a tiny tornado, held its place at the top of the stone. Hutch opened his eyes, lowered his hands, and let the stone rest on the hillside. The pebble looked cool and calm.

Hutch rose from his cross-legged patch, looked around again, and walked down the hill. With a few miles to hike, Hutch smiled at the thought of meeting with Stinky. As he reached the base of the hill, he dropped the borrowed camp tent. Raising his head, he looked forward to getting back his propeller blade. Seeing a squirrel staring at the bluish stone behind him, he said, "Time to begin our party hike."

46

Rose watched the boys hang out with her husband in the living room. They all kept their eyes on the final innings of a late-season Phillies game. Snacking popcorn spiced with butter and pepper, those kids looked happy munching her husband's treats. *My boys needed a rest*, she thought.

Doug fell asleep in his chair as the closing pitcher came out to finish the last inning. Rose approached the kids and waved for them to follow her. She picked up some knit blankets and made her way into the backyard. Throwing open the blankets, she laid them down on the grass in a small circle.

The boys grabbed Virg's notebook and slid the porch door open. When they touched the grass, they looked a little sheepish.

"What's up?" Rose asked. "You guys want to tell me some stories?" She stared right at the notebook in her son's hands.

Greg appeared disappointed. "Well, what Virg wrote down doesn't really make a ton of sense. It's just images and small stuff that I remembered. I don't know how to tell stories for all of these. They're just notes."

"That's fine. Have you tried connecting with images?"

"What do you mean?" Greg sat down on a blanket next to Rose.

"Well, so far, we've contacted each other. Silently, but with full sentences."

"Yeah, that's what you've been doing a lot of," said Virg, sitting down across from Greg.

Rose crossed her legs and closed her eyes. Laying her arms out on her knees, Virg followed the action and copied her. Then he closed his eyes. Greg watched him follow his mom's actions and did the same.

"This lesson is sharing what you see . . . or what you have seen in the past," Rose whispered. "Keep your eyes closed."

They all sat with their eyes closed for a few moments. Rose breathed in. She raised two fingers on both hands and met her temples. The two boys felt a slight opening of light within their eyelids as Rose opened her eyes slowly. As she did, Virg and Greg took in a quick breath. They could both see through her eyes. Turning her eyes toward her son, she saw him awkwardly smile and let out a laugh.

With his eyes still closed, he said, "Whoa, mirror zone."

"You can do that on purpose? You're sending what you see," said Greg.

She closed her eyes again, and the two boys saw pure darkness. She lowered her hands away from her head, and the images were removed from the boys' vision.

"That's one way to do it. You try it first, Greg."

"How do I do it?"

Rose spoke slowly, "First, keep your eyes closed. I raise my hands and lightly press my index and middle fingers onto my temples. Imagine your vision opening, and when you feel something, open your eyes. You're making your vision available and also sharing it with us. Just think it through. Do it slowly."

Sitting and taking a deep breath, Greg thought about Rose's instructions. He kept his eyes closed and reached up to his temples. As he felt his heartbeat pumping through his temples, a slight beat that didn't come from his heart echoed through his eardrums. It almost sounded like he reflected the sound of a heartbeat through a canyon. He popped his eyes open and felt the transfer of his vision. What he heard sounded like a wind current in a jar. The soft noise swept through his skull. Then he looked toward Virg.

Virg saw himself through Greg's eyes. "Is everyone in love with me? I'm looking great." With his eyes closed, he smiled when he saw his own open mouth whipping back and forth.

"Beautiful job," said Rose. "You guys learn really fast. That took me . . . a long time to learn."

"Okay, my turn," said Virg.

"Greg, close your eyes." Rose added, "If you remove your fingers from your temples, you'll cut the connection."

Greg did just that. Lowering his fingers and resting his hands on his lap, the sound inside his head disappeared. He heard and felt the end of the connection.

"That's pretty easy. But, dude, you'll feel like your head is huge on the inside." He opened his eyes and turned toward Virg. "Enjoy."

"Okay, can I try, Mom?"

"Your turn. Stay calm. Just breathe and touch your temples. Close your eyes," responded Rose.

"Okay. What if I talk when I'm sending what I see?"

"You'll be fine. It might sound like you're shouting into a cave or something. I wouldn't recommend it," said Rose.

"Thanks," Virg said as he closed his eyes.

He took a nervous breath and touched his head. As he did, he heard his mind open up. He raised his head up and opened his eyes to the stars. Rose and Greg both let out quiet laughs.

"Love those stars. Almost no clouds tonight," Rose whispered.

"This is amazing," said Virg.

"You *both* are. First try? This is not typical." She smiled with her eyes shut.

Virg closed his eyes and lowered his hands from his temples. The three of them opened their eyes and met each other's looks.

"So, more?" asked Rose.

"Please," said Greg.

"Kowabunga." Virg whipped his hand around in a circle as if he were swinging a nunchaku.

"Okay, if you are sharing images . . . well, memories, and not active current perspectives, you have to open yourself fully."

"Okay, how do we do that?" said Greg.

"Well, this one is a bit more complicated." Rose took a deep breath. She didn't want to look uncomfortable, but for a moment, she assumed these kids would use this skill without fully understanding it. "You shouldn't just jump into someone and search everything. Minds are personal." She looked at both boys.

"What if I didn't want this to happen to me?" said Virg.

"Then it won't. You can agree to it or just tell someone not to explore," said Rose.

"But how can we make sure?" asked Greg.

Rose could tell that Greg was frightened about the idea. Had this happened to him already?

"If you know someone wanting to get in, and it scares you, think about your skull and its solid shell."

Greg popped his pinky finger out and pushed his fist for a moment. A light shell flung around him. "I know how to do this."

Rose shook her head. "I'm impressed. But it's even simpler. You can control a connection to your memory. Just think about the range of your skull. It's very simple. The basic concept of a shell around your mind closes the pathway."

She clicked against her palm with one finger snap.

"That sounds too simple," said Virg.

"Yep, doesn't really need any practice." She shrugged her shoulders. "Moments ago, you shared what you saw by using a physical action. The cutoff of sharing a memory is easier."

Greg looked down at the blankets. His mind rolled back to his memories of Sunday evening. He was fully asleep and woke up when he heard the voice inside himself.

"What about if I'm sleeping? Can someone look at my memories when I'm asleep?"

"I don't know. I haven't heard about anyone trying that." Rose felt a chill go down her spine. She broke back in. "You can contact people if they're sleeping, but typically, you can't wake them up. It might just feel like a dream." She put her hand on Greg's shoulder.

She continued. "Hutch tried to contact me on Sunday, but I was asleep. When I woke up on Monday, the sound of his voice cropped back up into my mind. I was happy to see him the next day and invited him over until he could fix his glider."

"Well, if he's at a party, can I look through his eyes?" Greg asked.

Rose shook her head. "You can't. I doubt he'll open his vision." She knew it was possible, but she felt a bit relieved as she watched Greg lose his interest. To help raise his spirit, she added, "But lie down, and I'll show you how to find memories."

Rose turned her eyes toward her son and then dropped her gaze toward the notebook beside him.

"Are you sure you don't want to show me your notes?" she asked Virg.

"They're just notes. The full story is in here," said Greg, pointing at his head.

"Do you want to share?" she asked Greg. "You don't have to if you don't want to." Rose waited for his reaction.

"Teach him how to do it. I'll open up or whatever you call it." Virg lay down across his blanket and peered up into the stars.

Greg pretended to draw a sword from his back. He whipped his hand around and fake-stabbed Virg's tummy. He lightly crashed his fists on his friend. They both let out a laugh that comforted Rose. She was beginning to get worried. The concept of introducing children to highly skilled theories felt wild. This didn't seem difficult for them and wasn't what she expected.

Their enjoyment calmed Rose for a moment, but she thought, *Perhaps showing them this skill would give them too much power.* Her mind wandered . . . *but I need to see what Greg learned from Hutch.*

"Do you want me to show you how to do it?" Rose asked. "I can help you out if I see what you saw."

"Yeah, I think you'd want to see what I saw," said Greg.

She felt a chill rumble across her shoulders. "Okay, lie down."

Greg lay flat on his blanket and closed his eyes. Rose clasped her hands together and looked like she was about to pray. Her hands met her chest, and she slowly opened her palms toward her chest. It almost looked like she was opening a book and keeping it connected to her.

Greg heard the sound of an hourglass turned over. It was like a soft echo of a pouring sand stream touched his eardrums. It wasn't frightening. As he thought about what he saw when Hutch arrived, he felt like those memories were pulled back in a slingshot. In a slight flash, he saw all of his visions from Hutch swiftly flash through his eyelids.

He heard Rose take a deep breath and blow it back out. She floated her hands back onto her knees. Opening her eyes, she looked at the notebook next to her son. Her arm shot over and grabbed it. She whipped through two pages and inspected the notes.

"Can I learn how to do that?" Greg asked while still lying down.

Calmly, she responded, "Okay, Greg, you've got to sit and cross your legs. Virgil, you can stay lying down." Rose helped get them back into position.

"Do you have a pen?" she asked her son.

Virg nodded and pulled one out of his pocket. Rose quickly scratched beside his notes. He saw her write question marks right beside them. It looked like her eyes were going up and down all over the page. He saw her slap it closed and put it behind her.

Then she turned back to Virg. "So, Virgil, opening and closing your mind is easy. You can hear a light suction sound if someone enters your memories." She pushed out her lips, almost like a kiss, and sucked in a breath. "That's kind of what it sounds like, but it isn't intense. It's almost calming. Sort of like a backward waterfall."

"Oh, that sounds cool. I wish I could see a real waterfall like that," said Virg.

"You will," responded Rose. "Memories shared, you will see. Keep your eyes closed."

"Whoa." Virg turned toward Greg and asked, "Please don't look for when I peed my pants in kindergarten."

"If you don't, I won't," said Greg.

"*You* don't. Oh, wait, okay. I won't."

Both boys laughed. Virg fully spread out on his blanket and closed his eyes. He said, "I'm ready, Doc."

Sitting in front of Greg, Rose put her hands into a praying position. "It'll look like this," she said. Nearing her hands to her sternum, Greg matched the movement. "When you do it, close your eyes and focus on Virg's mind." She turned toward her son. "And, Virgil, think about what you *want* to share. That's what will be transferred."

"Okay," he said.

Greg closed his eyes and clasped his hands together. Drawing his hands onto his chest, he slightly pulled his thumbs away from each other. Then he took a breath and let it go.

Seeing nothing, he opened his eyes.

Rose, keeping her eyes on him, asked, "Not working?"

He shook his head.

"I heard you clap, dude. I just kept thinking about my skull," said Virg, still lying down with his eyes closed.

"Well, that's a good example. It *does* work," said Rose. "Y'know, I think I have to look at these notes again. Can I borrow this?" She raised the notebook behind her. "I think it might help if I focus on this briefly."

She saw the two boys looked confused. "I'm sure you're tired anyway. Just relax. I'll grab you a book really quick. I'll be right back." Rose stood up and walked over to the porch and through the glass door. Moments later, she came back out holding a book and a flashlight.

"Here." She handed a picture book about constellations to Greg and a flashlight to her son. "Let me know what you see up there. I'll let you know what I figured out."

"Okay, thanks," said Greg.

"Thanks, Mom," added Virg.

As she walked away, Greg said, "Do you have any ice cream sandwiches?"

Rose turned and said, "Yeah, I'll ask Dad to bring some out."

As she entered the house, she ran up the stairs, slapped the notebook down on her desk, and opened it swiftly. She had immediately forgotten to wake up Doug for the ice cream sandwich delivery to the boys.

Flipping the pages a few times, Rose was peddling back and forth over her own experiences. What she remembered looked far different from the images she had seen in Greg's mind. The notes in front of her matched some of the visions she remembered. The man she saw in Greg's mind had long hair and a beard. He looked almost similar to the man who taught her at the summer campgrounds.

In the notebook, a description of a small girl and her shattering of a tall tree made Rose feel sick to her stomach. In her mind, she saw Hutch leading a small child deep into the woods. Why?

Greg's memory of Hutch being stabbed in the thigh came back up. Her mind flowed from that memory into Greg's demand to see Hutch's leg at his lesson. Hutch showed that spot to the kids.

She remembered Greg's vision. As Hutch grabbed his pant leg, his index finger connected with his thumb and then dragged down to his palm as he exposed his leg. Greg didn't recognize the motion, but she did. Hutch made something disappear.

She rose from the desk and turned back toward the stairs. Stopping in her tracks, she thought to herself, *Should they know?* Maybe her son was right to be afraid when he first met Hutch. What is Hutch trying to keep from them?

Then she closed her eyes and took in a deep breath. When she opened her eyes again, she felt the fear leave her mind. Walking down the stairs and passing by her snoozing husband, she opened the freezer and grabbed three ice cream sandwiches. She opened the porch door and walked straight to her gifted students. She saw them standing and pointing into the sky. Greg held the flashlight and pointed it at the open book Virg held. Rose sat down on her blanket and handed ice cream sandwiches to the boys.

"Oh, awesome. Thanks so much," said Greg.

"Thank *you*," said Rose. "By the way, he *is* at a party. And you *can* look through his eyes. Sit down." She peeled the paper wrap off her ice cream slider and took a bite.

47

Tim was sitting in his driver's seat with the car door wide open. The party was still rumbling lightly behind the building. He could still see the dancing light beams from the fire pit on the trees behind that house. Some old hippie songs were lightly playing from just one speaker out back. He heard that "Fire On a Mountain" tune buzzing by.

Pete, Tim's flirty ally, was still enjoying the host and singing along with radio tunes that he recognized. Tim had almost quit the whole party and left without grabbing Pete and shoving him into the car. He decided to keep his eyes open and let his friend enjoy himself. The guy had just driven him around all day. Plus, Pete had helped cover his story about the truck's battery. Tim felt it was time to let his friend have some fun.

Getting up and out of the car, Tim looked up at the stars. The moon drew his eyes. Then he let his stare flow through the open sky and into the sprinkling of stars. He recognized the constellation of Scorpius. Just a little curved collection of stars made the scorpion's body, and tiny little claws reached out at its peak.

"There you are," said Tim as he saw the scorpion above him. "Just keepin' Orion away, huh? Thanks, bub."

As he said that, he lowered his look down toward the road. He saw a movement and held still. Someone was hiking with his head down. Tim crouched behind his backseat door. He hadn't closed his driver-side door but kept his gaze on the person walking into the driveway. There were no lights on in his car.

The man kept walking up the driveway. He quickly passed Tim's car, pacing toward the house. Tim knew it was Hutch. What took him so long? Tim had been expecting to see this guy hours ago.

Hutch climbed up the driveway, following the campfire light into the backyard. Tim heard sounds from behind the house rise a bit. Did all these people expect to see Hutch? Tim recognized Stinky's voice over the crowd. The low-grinding sound of Stinky's voice began to silence other party attendees. It was like a cigar-smoking boxing announcer was presenting to the crowd.

As Tim followed the voice walking toward the backyard, a shine caught his eye. Passing a truck with an open cargo bed, he saw a propeller blade laid flat in it. The moonlight rays cradled the blade with a sheer reflection. He stopped and kept his eyes on it. *Well*, Tim thought, *I have no idea what that glider looks like, but I see a propeller blade. Although maybe this could be a blade for a boat*, he thought. He mentally noted the truck and how far back it was, just in case he had to snag this on his way out. *If Stinky's party is some kind of scheme*, Tim thought, *maybe Hutch is gonna need some help.*

He left the truck alone and went up the driveway and around the house. Keeping himself in the dark, he leaned against a corner of the house. Looking around, Tim noticed a new keg. The last one had a big yellow lightning sticker on it. This one had a big green turtle sticker on it.

"I guess it's about time," Tim whispered to himself.

Two partiers were tying little thin ropes between the two horseshoe beds. A square ring was placed between the four bars beaten into the ground. The guests stood around it with plastic cups in their hands. Stinky was holding a metal stand and flicked on a garage spotlight. On the other side of the ring, behind the partiers, another man flicked on the other spotlight. It looked like they had practiced making a stage.

Stinky pulled a little notebook out of a pocket in his leather vest. He ripped a pen out of his pants and clicked the tip out. As he waved at two people in the crowd, Tim saw them nod and step toward Stinky. Both of those people hopped over the ropes in the grass.

"So, we've got Daryl and John." Stinky pointed at each as he explained. "They fought last time, but John wanted another round." Aiming his pen at John, the man slugged the rest of his beer from his cup and tossed it down. Then he grabbed his mane and pushed it back into a ponytail. He clasped it together with a light metal bag tie.

"This is Daryl." Stinky aimed his pen at the five-foot monster. Daryl wore grey jeans and had biceps that stretched his shirt sleeves. "Yep, he's small, but he won last time." Stinky looked around at the guests. "Let me know who you're betting for."

Some people in the crowd raised their hands, but most just looked back and forth at the fighters and kept sipping their cups. Stinky walked slowly around the square. He wrote down the names of the bettors and how much they put down.

With Stinky on his trip around the ring, Tim stepped up onto a plastic chair near the garage. He looked into the crowd and found Hutch sitting on a big log. Tim rubbed his eyes and noticed that Pete was sitting right next to Hutch. It looked like they were enjoying a conversation. Tim immediately jumped off the chair and began walking toward them.

Pete raised his gaze from his beer can and noticed Tim walking toward them. He smiled and said, "He meditated for a while." Pete's thumb pointed at Hutch.

"What?" said Tim.

Hutch heard Tim's voice and raised his hands on his sides. "Sorry I missed you. I didn't know if you were actually going to offer me a ride. I was just meditating in the woods."

"That was a pretty long meditation. Are you worried?" Tim turned toward the ring and looked at the first two fighters stretching their muscles.

". . . I'd be," said Tim, turning back.

Pete chimed in, "I asked him, and he told me that he usually meditates before a fight."

"*Usually?* So you're *used* to fighting?" Tim raised his hands above his head in disgust.

"I'm not, but I have before." Hutch looked calm.

"When I saw you coming up the driveway, I found your propeller blade in the open bed of Stinky's truck." Tim shook his head. "You don't *need* to fight if you don't want to."

"He told me that I get it whether I win or lose. I don't want to steal it." Hutch closed his eyes and took a deep breath as he straightened his back.

"I think he's just the kind of fighter to win some dough!" Pete looked excited. He rubbed his hand on Hutch's back.

"Still meditating?" Tim shook his head and looked over at the fight square. "They're starting now."

Stinky stood in the center of the square and put out his hand. The two men put their hands on top of his. When Stinky shot his hand down and backed away, the men held their arms up and began pacing around the ring.

Tim turned back to Pete and Hutch. "I don't even want to watch this. Can I just go back and grab that propeller? You can fight if you want to. I don't want any part of this." He paced a few steps away, and Hutch's hand rested on his shoulder.

"Don't take the propeller. I'll be fine. I think you know that."

Tim turned back and looked him in the eyes. Hutch gave a little wink and smiled for a moment. Then he turned around and sat back down on the log beside Pete. He closed his eyes again and took another deep breath.

Surprised by the calm reaction, Tim just stood staring at Hutch. *This guy is going to use magic? Does he know that I know about that?* Tim was slightly confused for a moment. He didn't look back at the fight. The sound of a skin getting slapped burst from the stage and was followed by a little surprised-sounding laugh from the audience. Tim couldn't turn to look at them.

Hutch suggested that he knew what he was doing. What does he think I know? This is my kid's teacher, he thought. *Greg's come a long way.* Tim smiled as he was looking nowhere. His thoughts had gripped his consciousness.

Pete stood up and looked over the party crowd. The crowd began to chant a name. "I think Daryl owns the Hall and Oates harmony," said Pete.

John's ponytail had come undone, and blood was dripping out of his mouth. He smiled, then looked right at tiny Daryl. "I didn't win last time, and damn," he spit on the grass, "I ain't gonna win this time."

Tim turned to look and saw that the little guy, Daryl, had no marks on his grey jeans. No grass, no blood, no beer. Those pants looked clean and untouched. John, the other fighter, seemed weary and stained but as happy as he could be.

John took a deep breath and looked woozy. He sat down on the grass smiling and said, "Winner." He pointed right at Daryl. "Thanks for another round, my man."

"Anytime," said Daryl. He clapped his hands and then extended his hand toward John. The little guy easily pulled John's frame right off the ground.

Stinky entered the ring and stated, "Okay, just as I thought. Everybody gets their money back . . . great." He rolled his eyes. "Daryl won again."

Laughing and clapping, the surrounding crowd sounded pleased and rewarded.

"Just let me know if you want to keep the same amount for the next round. You'll probably stick with Daryl, am I right?"

Applause and cheers confirmed Stinky's suggestion. "Great!" he said. "Let's give Daryl a few minutes and a sip of something relaxing. John got a bop or two on him."

A few guests made their way toward the keg as if intermission had begun. Daryl opened a small cooler and poured a shot into a tiny glass. After he sat and enjoyed a quick swallow, he shoved the bottle and glass back into his cooler.

Pete shook his head. "I wonder what he's drinking."

"It's probably just ginseng. Doesn't seem like that match slowed him down at all. Probably just a confidence boost," responded Tim.

"I think he's too small to use liquid courage. Gin just makes me sleepy." Pete turned and smiled at Tim, blinking his eyes quickly.

Tim let out a small chuckle at the dumb look on Pete's face. "Okay, you have to fight him next."

"Great, I'll bet on him too." Pete took a sip from his cup. "Actually, I think I'm gonna bet on Hutch."

"He's next?"

"Yeah, he's right there." Pete pointed across the crowd at Stinky.

Hutch was standing behind him, speaking just behind his ear. It looked like he said, "Yep, I'm ready," then nodded.

Stinky nodded, turned, and entered the ring again. He raised his hands and began the introduction of the next round. "Well, if you're keeping your bet on Daryl, great. But here's a guy named Hutch."

Hutch took a step over the rope and stood behind Stinky. It looked as if the crowd hadn't noticed him at the party. Looking at one another, it seemed everyone was comparing their body size to his. Hutch looked big—especially when regular people surrounded him. Tim thought about professional basketball players coaching sports camps for kids.

Daryl stepped into the ring. The difference in size between Daryl and Hutch looked utterly uncanny.

John spoke up. "I'm keeping my money on Daryl." He pressed a napkin on his lip.

"Me too!" yelled another person beside him.

The gamblers and bidders looked comfy with their choices, but maybe it was just the beer that kept them confident. Most of them had won their first bid. It seemed obvious. Daryl had won matches many-a-time.

Stinky turned around and smiled at Hutch. "I'm bettin' on you."

Hutch shook his head and said, "And if I win, I can take the propeller."

"I gotcha a new one, same size. And yes, it's yours . . . either way." He winked at Hutch. "Thanks for comin'," added Stinky. "I'm looking forward to this."

Stinky laid his hand into an open space between Daryl and Hutch. The two fighters put their hands on top of his. Stinky quickly pulled his hand down and ran past the rope barrier to watch the match.

Daryl raised his hands in a boxing motion and backed away. Hutch stood sideways and looked at the little man over his shoulder. Then he slowly crouched to be almost at the same level as Daryl.

Tim kept his eyes on Hutch's hands. Those fists looked like cantaloupes growing on the end of his arms. Tim remembered his son's hand position techniques. Would Hutch do the same?

Daryl hopped up in the air once and landed. Then he faked a left and right punch for a warm-up and ran straight at the big man across the ring. Hutch let the little man throw a punch right at his thigh. Watching Daryl's fist fly toward his knee, Hutch caught it, clasped his hand around it, and held it firmly. The little guy shot another jab toward Hutch's chin. The big man watched it fly and quickly caught it with his other hand. Hutch held Daryl's fists, swinging them down beneath the man's core. He held tight, squatted lower, flew his fists up above his head, and raised his stance. When his hands rose above his shoulders, he released his grip.

Daryl's body was flung straight up into the air as Hutch released. The little guy flew five feet above the head level of the crowd. His butt led his way down and connected with the grass. Rolling and tumbling a bit, the rope on the horseshoe poles stopped him.

The crowd went silent. The little man got up and brushed off some dirty patches on his pants. No injuries were announced, but it looked like the whole crowd was watching now. Daryl looked okay as he shook his arms and brought them back up into a boxing position. The crowd of bettors let out a slightly encouraging cheer.

Pete elbowed Tim in the ribs and made a jubilant expression. Tim looked at Pete and realized he felt the same way—this big guy looked pretty prepared. *Maybe this guy wasn't going to do any magic*, Tim thought. Hutch looked ready to protect himself in a real fight.

The little man ran straight at Hutch. He jumped low, gliding across the grass underneath him and through his legs like he was stealing a base. He struck up with his front foot, and Hutch grabbed it with both hands and threw the man twirling through the air like an Olympic discus. The crowd let out a low, surprised sound, "*Oooooooh*," as the little guy turned around twice before he came down onto the ground. This time, he connected to the ground on his belly and ribs. He let out a breath that sounded difficult to release.

Pete grabbed Tim's arm and squeezed it as he pushed it against his chest.

"Jeez," Tim slapped Pete's hands. "This is a fight. Are you scared?"

"Sorry," said Pete. He opened his grip and whispered to Tim, "I mean, it's a *real* fight. I'm not used to seeing it quite like this."

"Me neither," agreed Tim.

Daryl hopped up quickly. He took another breath in and began to scream. He ran toward Hutch and started kicking at his nearest ankle. Daryl connected with two swift kicks until Hutch quickly leaned backward and fired his heel into Daryl's chest. It happened so quickly that no one understood why Daryl flew about ten feet away. Hutch's finished position left his foot up near his shoulder. He pulled it back down to re-create his sideways position.

It looked like Hutch connected his heel to Daryl's chest and lifted him off the ground before pushing him away. He began to pace around Daryl, who was lying on the grass. As Hutch walked in a circle around him, Daryl shook his shoulders while lying on his back and then got up slowly. Stepping around the stage, Hutch reached a point where Tim stared directly into his eyes.

When Daryl got up, Tim kept his eyes on Hutch. He saw the big man roll his pinky out and blink quickly for a moment. Hutch lightly shook his head and then held it directly forward. His eyes were open, and he didn't seem to be looking at Daryl. Hutch's perspective looked a bit relaxed.

Tim saw a light blue ribbon of color scroll over the whites of Hutch's eyes for a moment. Then the color stuck, and it looked almost like his full eye whites were going dark. *What the heck is that?* Tim thought. *Does he want people to see this?*

Daryl turned and stared at Hutch. He backed away, stretched his arms behind his head, and leaned forward to stretch out his back. He rolled his head around his shoulders once and put his hands back up. Then he began to run back toward Hutch.

Not moving a single muscle, Hutch didn't seem to see Daryl

running at him. Pouncing up, Daryl twirled in a circle as he raised his leg. He extended it after a spin and whipped his heel right *through* Hutch's nose. It flew through so fast it looked as if it didn't touch. There was no visible reaction from Hutch.

Daryl's leg kept flying in a spin, which he didn't expect. It looked to everyone like the little guy had *definitely* connected to Hutch's face. However, there was no pressure for Daryl to react to, and Hutch's face didn't move at all. The kick spin kept Daryl twirling, and he landed on the ground and rolled away for a moment. He was totally bewildered.

"I just kicked your face," he shouted.

There was no reaction from Hutch.

Tim watched Hutch close his eyes and shake his head a few times. Hutch grabbed the back of his neck and dragged his hand over his head and down past his chin. The big man's eyes focused on Daryl. Then they whipped back up into his head. They looked purely white for a moment. Tim saw Hutch's eyes spindle the darkness. They became blue again and then naturally white. The color almost disappeared in an instant.

Hutch stood up straight and walked toward Daryl. He grabbed the tight shirt at Daryl's chest. Then his left hand came down and grabbed Daryl's belt buckle. He turned his head away and hurled the little man over the crowd and into the grass behind them.

As Daryl was still floating, Hutch turned toward Stinky. "You've got to stay in the ring, right?"

Stinky was still looking at Daryl as he almost floated through the air. He then hit the grass and rolled a few times before he stopped. Slowly raising his head off the ground, he shook it back and forth.

Stinky turned back to Hutch. "I don't know, but I think you've won either way."

Daryl looked fine, but many people in the crowd began to groan. Stinky looked at the crowd and said, "Hey, if ya lost, no biggie. I'll give you back half of what you just bet. Put that on the next round." He turned toward Hutch and said, "You stickin' around? There's some others ready, but the stage is yours."

"I'm done," said Hutch. "Where's the propeller?"

"I can fix it for you…" Stinky stopped when he saw Hutch's reaction.

Hutch shook his head and said, "I've got tools. I'll do it. Thanks for what you did."

"It's all yours." Stinky shook his head and pointed down the driveway. "I put it in the cargo bed behind my truck. You know what it looks like?"

Hutch shook his head.

"I'll take you there," responded Stinky. He turned back toward the partiers. "All right, all right, one little break. Go ahead and relax for a moment," Stinky said to the crowd. "Audelle, you hooked up another keg, right?"

"Sure did," she said as she sat on her porch with a little Chihuahua in her lap. Her hand ran over its little head and down its back. Then she grabbed a plastic cup and made a cheers motion toward Stinky. "Still got plenty."

Stinky nodded and then put his hand behind Hutch's arm—beginning to walk him toward his truck.

Tim and Pete figured that Hutch would leave once he got that blade. They looked at each other and didn't say anything. Pete grabbed his cooler, and then both of them turned and followed Stinky and Hutch away from the party.

Greg's eyes popped open, and he turned toward Rose. "He knows."

"How do you know? Did he stop playing a poker game or something?"

Greg was silent for a moment. He turned to look at Virg.

"He was in the middle of a fight," said Greg.

"Whoa. Who was he fighting?" asked Virg.

"There was a guy who reminded me of David at the post office. Not the same guy, but he was small. But this guy was pretty jacked." Greg pumped his own bicep. "And his clothing was tight."

Greg closed his eyes, focusing on what he had just seen. "The little guy ran at Hutch and karate kicked him right across his face."

"Oh my God, did it knock him down?" Rose asked.

"No, it went right through him. He must've made a shell . . ." Greg stopped for a moment.

He opened his eyes and looked at Rose. "Tim and Pete were in a crowd surrounding him. He looked right at my dad when the foot swished through him."

"A crowd? In the house?" said Rose.

"No, in a backyard. There was a rope near the ground that everyone stood outside of. The ground was empty near him, and some big lightbulbs up high lit them up." Greg shook his head.

"So it is a fight party?" asked Virg.

"My dad was looking right into my eyes. He looked frightened. Do eyes change when someone else looks through them?"

"They can, but it doesn't happen for everyone. Hang on, though. Your dad would never go to a party just for fighting, would he? Has he ever been to something like that?" Rose put her hand on Greg's knee.

Greg turned to Rose and looked frightened. "Hutch knew it was me."

"How?"

"He felt me inside. Can he tell what I'm looking at? He waited and let me see what he was looking at. Then I saw his hand reach back to touch his neck, and he closed his skull. How did he know?"

Rose shook her head. "I thought he wouldn't know what it felt like. Maybe he's let someone look through his eyes before."

"He heard it. I heard his ears rise when I entered. The sounds changed for a second. He felt something he recognized."

"Maybe he has experience. Well, I'm sorry, Greg."

"What should I do?"

"I'll handle it. We didn't know that he was going to fight someone tonight." Rose shrugged her shoulders and let them fall. "Besides, I have questions for him after reading those notes and . . ." she paused for a moment. "Wait, Greg, did you see any memories?"

"Yeah, they came while I was looking at my dad, and they came in quickly. And I didn't even think about them. It's almost like it just lodged into *my* memory." Greg lowered his forehead into his hands.

Rose put her hand on Greg's shoulder and rubbed it a bit. "Take your time."

"I don't think he knew that I was in his memories. He only noticed me looking through his eyes. You taught me how to do both . . . at the same time." He raised his head and looked into Rose's eyes. She smiled.

Greg spun his head to Virg. "Thanks for letting me practice on you."

"My pleasure. I only have like five memories that don't include you." Virg shook his shoulders. "Thanks for letting me look into yours."

"Take your time," she repeated. Rose kept her hand on his back and lightly scratched the lowest rim of his hairline. "What memories did you see?"

Greg relaxed and closed his eyes. "I think I saw what he did right before he reached the party. He took a tent from the garage and left it in the woods. It looks like he prayed in the woods too. Then he just hiked toward the party."

Rose raised her eyes to the sky. She saw a little X-shape of bright stars. Recognizing the constellation as she followed the curved tail, she thought, *We have the scorpion.* She looked at Greg. "Stay away from the hunter," she said out loud.

"Isn't Hutch a fighter?" asked Virg.

"He brought us a deer pretty easily. And you said that it looks like he can fight. He has more skills than we knew about." She turned her head to the two kids. "But *you* have more skills and potential than he notices."

"But you didn't know he can fight?" asked Virg.

"I mean, he's *big*, but when we worked together at summer camps, I never saw him fight anything. We were still getting groceries and cooking on campfires and grills." Rose looked back up at the stars.

"When I saw him on Monday, he mentioned that the guy we knew had changed," Rose added.

"What guy?" asked Virg.

Looking at Virg, Rose said, "I told you about that camp. Hutch mentioned that the leader, whose name is Mata, has changed." She shook her head. "I thought he left the camp for a little vacation. Maybe he left for another reason."

She looked at Greg and turned her head to look at Virg. "Maybe he knew you two were here . . . I think Mata knew."

48

Hutch lifted the propeller from Stinky's cargo bed and wrapped a thick cloth around it.

Tim immediately asked, "Where's your glider these days?"

Hutch shook his head and said, "I hid it."

"Yeah, but where?"

"It's in the forest," said Hutch.

"I haven't seen it."

"Maybe you didn't look in the right forest."

"Take me there," pushed Tim.

"It's late. I think I'm gonna fix it tomorrow and head out."

"How are you gonna 'head out'?" Tim quoted that phrase with his fingers in the air.

Hutch turned back toward Tim. "I have to put the wings back on and roll down the hill into the cornfield. Long enough to lift."

"Oh," Tim cocked his head. "It's that simple?"

"I have to reattach the blade and the wings. My tools are in the cabin."

"Didn't you leave it under the bridge?"

"That's where your Greg helped me put it. But Stinky helped me move it."

Tim turned toward Stinky. "You helped him move it?"

"Sure," said Stinky while shutting his driver-side door. He turned and began to walk back up the driveway without a goodbye.

Hutch raised his eyebrows as if saying, "Whelp," and kept walking toward Pete's car. It looked to Tim that Hutch was lying. Also, Stinky was only interested in heading back to his party to keep winning bets.

Tim stopped him by putting his hand on Hutch's arm. "Greg and

Virg looked for your glider on Sunday night. You didn't get into contact with the Murphys until Monday. That's when you met Stinky. You took your propeller blade there on Monday, right?"

"You must've missed it." Hutch turned to Tim and looked right into his eyes.

"They looked for it for a long time." Tim let go and looked down at the gravel. He felt like it didn't make any sense. The timing was off.

He lifted his head, seeing Hutch walk away. "Did you make it invisible?"

Hutch turned back to Tim and smiled. "I did. Thanks for asking."

"But . . ." Tim stopped.

"You didn't ask. Not everyone wants to believe it's possible." Hutch shrugged his shoulders. "Greg told you?"

"He told me about his lessons."

"What'd he tell you?" Hutch sounded calm.

"He just said he's learning faster than what you're giving them lessons on."

"What's he learning about?"

Suddenly, Tim felt frightened. He asked himself in his head, *Why am I bringing this up?* He turned to see Pete standing there with his eyes wide open, looking back and forth between Hutch and Tim.

"Pete, you can go down and start the car," Tim calmly suggested.

Pete began following his orders, and then he looked back at Tim. "But I can't drive. I already had too much to drink, right?"

"Just start the ignition and sit down." Tim handed Pete the key.

Pete turned and tipsily waddled down the driveway toward his car. He got into the driver's seat and relaxed on the headrest. The headlights popped on.

"Well, do you need help tomorrow with the propeller or the wings?" Tim changed the subject to avoid Hutch's question.

Hutch was still looking at him. "Sure," he turned to look at the blade. He wrapped the blade in a thick cloth and lifted it in his arm. "So, Greg was telling you about his progress outside my lessons? What'd he say?"

"Oh, he told me about the . . . umm, I don't know what it's called.

Invisible shield thingy? I mean, you kinda used it tonight in your fight, right?" Tim's heart rate began to increase.

Hutch grinned. "You noticed?"

"I kinda think everyone did."

Hutch turned toward Pete's car and began walking down the driveway. "It happened pretty fast, and the move right after was more action-packed." He waved his arm once. "Let's hit the car. I'm tired, and Doug's got a slice of pie for me."

Tim felt his heart rate descend as he followed Hutch. As they reached the car, Tim tapped on Pete's shoulder. It looked like Pete had fallen asleep with his left foot still out on the driveway. Tim shook his shoulder, and he woke.

He looked surprised to be sitting in the driver's seat with the engine on. "Oh, I ain't driving," confirmed Pete.

"I know. Can you get into the passenger seat?" asked Tim.

He extended his hand, and Pete grabbed it. Tim crouched a bit and pulled Pete out of the seat. As he helped Pete walk around the car to get into the passenger side, Hutch punched a button above the backseat and let half of the backseat fall forward. He reached past the opening into the trunk and pulled a little lever. A click happened near the trunk, and Hutch walked behind the car to open it. He shoved the blade into the trunk and nested the upper half on the lowered backseat. Slamming the trunk shut, he hopped in the backseat and put his seat belt on.

Tim looked at Hutch in his rearview mirror. "You want to go back to the Murphys'? I can give you an extra bed tonight if you want. I don't know if they're all already asleep. It's a little late."

"It's not Saturday quite yet." Hutch looked at the clock on the dashboard and noticed it was 11:50 p.m. "I can go back there. I think they're sleeping in tomorrow."

Pete turned to Tim. "Wanna stay at my place? This is my car. You can leave it in my driveway." He chuckled as Tim and Hutch looked at each other in the rearview mirror. They both smiled and let out a little laugh.

Tim looked at Pete. "I didn't go home last night, and you saved my butt. I'll take you back and return the car. I can walk."

"I can walk too. Just take Pete home," Hutch said quietly from the backseat.

Tim trembled for a moment and put the car in reverse.

SATURDAY

49

Just after midnight, Rose led Virgil to his bunk bed and asked him to get some sleep. He hopped into the bottom bed, and Greg climbed onto the top shelf. Then she went back downstairs, kissed Doug, and put him to bed. Taking a beanbag chair from the basement, she opened her front door and laid it down on her porch. She came back inside and grabbed a glass of water. The moment before she closed the front door, she saw Virgil walking toward the bathroom upstairs.

"You okay?" she asked him.

"I'm good," Virg smiled. "Thanks for all the lessons tonight. Those were awesome." He smiled and walked into the bathroom.

Rose smiled and said, "You're welcome, my love."

She closed the door behind herself and sat on the beanbag chair. Her eyes scanned through the darkness continuously. Perhaps Hutch would walk by, perhaps not. She didn't know if Hutch was planning something. *He didn't tell us he was going to a fight. Well, neither did Tim*, she thought.

"Why did you come here?" she said out loud. It was almost like she practiced asking Hutch a question. "Did you mean to come here?" She let it silence in the air.

"How did you find us?" she let out. Then she shivered at her own question. *He did find us*, she thought.

She kept staring down the alleyway. Under the streetlamp's rays at the road, two shadows slowly paced through it and into the alleyway. It looked like the big shadow was holding an ironing board or something.

She got a little nervous. Sitting in the darkness with no porch light on, Rose almost extended her pinky to hide herself. But after a few moments, the men walked past the shade of the trees beside the alleyway. The moon lit them a bit, and Rose recognized Tim and Hutch. She hopped out of her seat and began to march toward them.

Before they reached the Murphys' driveway, the two men saw Rose tramping through her yard. They both stopped and took half a step backward. She was stomping right toward them.

"So, fighting is your relaxing Friday event, huh?" Rose blurted at Hutch. She turned toward Tim. "And you knew all about this, huh? You gave him a ride for this?"

Tim backed up and raised his open hands in front of his chest. "Hey, I thought this would be just sipping beer in a backyard."

"I went on my own. I didn't wait for a ride. Had to trade a fight for my propeller. I've got no money." Hutch raised the carpeted blade under his arm.

"He did win," whispered Tim.

"I don't care if he won or lost." She turned her eyes to Hutch. "You lied."

"What did I lie about?"

"You went into the forest and showed up late to the party. You didn't want Tim to follow you, did you?" Rose was getting more vicious.

"I didn't try to arrive late, but I had to message Mata. I haven't seen him for a week. I told him I could fix my glider tomorrow," Hutch responded calmly.

"How did you contact him?" Rose asked. "He's in Maine."

"I opened a stone." Hutch waited a moment and noticed Rose didn't know what he meant.

"What does that mean?" said Tim beside him.

"I sent him a signal to confirm where I am. Then I sent a message. Told him that I had taught some people out here."

"So you're telling him about our kids?" Rose shot back.

Hutch swallowed and put his blade down on the ground. "It's a little heavy," he said. Then he raised his hands just like Tim beside him. "I'm not telling anyone about anything. I'm just letting Mata know why he hasn't heard from me in about a week. I've been busy."

"Yeah, I'm noticing that you've been busy. But I'm not sure why you've been hiding stuff," she said.

Tim turned his head toward Hutch. "You haven't been working for a week, but you're just telling him now? My boss would fire me."

"I don't work for money. I try to help people. It's a team, not a job. I'm part of a community." Hutch let his hands drop down to his sides and looked at Rose. "Mata and I know there aren't many people like us."

Rose kept silent for a moment.

Tim looked at her and back at Hutch. "Hey, I'm sorry, you two, but my wife was a little worried about me last night. Tonight, I've got to kiss her before she goes to bed. Don't wanna hold her up." Tim backed away and began to wave goodbye.

Rose and Hutch both waved at him. "Get home safe," said Hutch.

Tim took a few steps away and turned to leave. He returned to the alley and walked past the brush hedge.

Rose looked into Hutch's eyes. "You told me you were trying to get out of that camp. You said that you were afraid of him. Why are you telling him where you are?"

"I trust him. He's the reason I have a place to live."

"Hutch, you told me on Monday that you wanted to find a way to leave. I let you relax for a week and teach my kids. What was I thinking?" Rose threw her hands into the air.

"Your kids are more skilled than they've ever been. They really are progressing faster than anyone I've ever known."

"That's your fault," she said as she poked him in his chest. "They never even knew that this was possible. This is what they're going to think about for the rest of their lives. Do I have to hide them from you?" Rose poked Hutch again, "*And* that guy you just contacted?"

She shook her head. "... their lives are completely changed forever, aren't they?" Rose looked down at the grass between them. A tear collected at the bottom of her eye. "I left the last campsite and didn't think I'd ever see you again." She let a moment pass, then looked straight into Hutch's eyes. "I wish I hadn't." She blinked, and a tear ran down her cheek.

Hutch didn't say anything. He leaned down and picked up his

carpet-covered blade.

Turning toward the alleyway, he stopped but didn't turn to face Rose. "I'm sorry," he whispered.

"Hutch, is Mata coming here?"

He let a few moments pass by. It seemed like Hutch didn't want to tell her.

"I don't know." He stepped back and began to walk out of Rose's yard.

She shook her head and looked up at him. "Thanks for your help." Rose smiled and let another tear roll down her cheek, "They wouldn't have known themselves if you didn't show up."

She kept staring at Hutch as he walked away. Rose couldn't move. For a moment, she almost called to him and asked him to come back. Instead, he kept walking, and she didn't get the chance. A cool breeze hugged the back of her neck. Rose shivered and sat down in the grass.

Tim had followed the alley back to his house and entered through his back door. He visited Sue and saw that she was sound asleep. Softly, he touched her shoulder and kissed her on her forehead.

"I'm back," he whispered.

"... oh, hi, honey ..." Sue barely woke as she responded.

Tim let her sleep and visited the upstairs bathroom to keep it quiet. As he washed his hands and left the bathroom, he saw Greg's bedroom door cracked open. Remembering that his son was staying at the Murphys' house, he was drawn down the hallway just to check his son's room. He pushed the door and looked into Greg's bedroom. His eyes peered around and looked into his son's bed. The memory of watching a book fly through Greg's head held him still for a moment.

They can hide things, he thought. *And they are. They* all *are.* He thought about Hutch again.

Backing out of Greg's room, he turned and silently crept down the stairs. Reaching the back door, he opened it and walked back into his yard. He turned and closed it behind himself in silence. Standing and staring at the field, he felt drawn to the open moonlit path. Tim turned and grabbed an outdoor blanket from his porch.

The moonlight in front of him drew his focus back to the bridge. Tim inspected the bridge from far away. His eyes then crawled to the forest above. Hutch had told him that he had hidden his glider in the trees. Why would Hutch do that? The glider wasn't ready for a run.

Tim began walking back to the road without even deciding where he would search. "I'm gonna find that glider," he whispered.

Hutch climbed down the rim of the creek and turned under the bridge. He set up a small pile of weeds and a few dry sticks over the ashes of his last fire. Finding one small dry log, he smacked it against the bridge foundation until it split. Then he pulled it open with his hands. The wood was rested together by leaning them on one another. Sparking the fire at the bottom, he waited until it gave him a touch of light.

Taking a few steps back from the fire, Hutch turned toward the bridge, pointed at his glider, and brought it out of its camouflage. Opening the cabin, he took out wrenches and gloves. He took his time to replace the propeller. When he finished, the little fire had gotten a bit low. He stepped back and looked at his contraption. There was still mud on the bottom of the vehicle. The wings were still tied to the roof but weren't attached back on. *I'll work on that tomorrow*, he thought to himself.

A familiar feeling tickled the hair on the back of Hutch's neck.

He's on his way, thought Hutch.

The light of the fire drew his eyes. Turning and bending down at the creek, he cupped his hands around the water and splashed his fire out. He looked back at his glider and drew his index finger down on his palm. The plane disintegrated from the visual field. Hutch turned and walked out from under the bridge, then up the hillside. He felt like he had to follow the road back toward the forest.

    Hutch's hike began slowly. As he was placing steps on the side of the road, he felt the need to speed up. His hand reached back to his neck and grabbed the roots at the base of his hairline. The slight vibration continued. Hutch didn't jog, but he extended his gait. He had to get back to the entrance he had opened in the forest . . . fast.

50

A tiny current of wind kept spinning on the crown of the stone. Hours before, after Hutch hiked away, the stone had stayed as he left it. No one walked by. No scents were drawing any animals near to it. Hours passed as the forest let the quiet sounds of insects comb its thick silence.

All of a sudden, the wind whirled louder. As it rose and expanded, the breeze got stronger. When it reached the branches above, the sound grew. The creaking of bark and branches almost sounded like a tornado was beginning. Then the sounds and gales disappeared.

Suddenly, an old man appeared in the woods. He reached up to rub his grey locks and pulled his hands down onto his lengthy beard. It looked like he was just waking his face in this fresh space. No sounds came out of him. Standing still, he glanced around at the surroundings.

His eyes found a squirrel jumping onto a tree next to him. He whipped his open hand toward it and held the squirrel in its jump just before it reached the tree. It froze midair and let out a squeak. He turned his hand from facing the tree to just in front of him. The squirrel quickly swung right in front of the old man's face. He raised his left hand to mirror the fingertips of his right. As he did, he closed his eyes. The squirrel vibrated swiftly, and the man pulled his hands two inches away from each other. As he did, the carcass of the squirrel ripped apart. The organs floated away from the fur. The bones snapped off of the muscles. All the blood was contained within the separated veins of the animal.

He opened his wrinkled eyes and raised the tip of his middle finger. The bones rattled above the sphere of containment and then fell onto the wood chips at his feet. Moist bones lay still on the tree shreds. He removed the skin and organs with another motion, letting them fall. Holding the meat and veins with one hand, he looked at a wood stump and snapped two fingers on his left hand. A flame burst from the root rims. It breached right up through the open ceiling of the stump.

Closing his eyes, he pulled the blood from the carcass without touching it. Then he pulled his hands toward the fire. Lowering his left hand and raising his right hand, the squirrel's blood pool floated close to the fire, and the muscles were held just above. The fire on the stump slowly boiled away the moisture of the blood. Vapors hovered up into the trees. The remaining powder floated up and fastened around the heated muscles.

The old man held the meat in the air until the pieces were shrunken and covered in ironed blood sugar. He whipped his left hand across the fire when the muscles looked solid. It immediately left the stump. Smoky clouds bloomed softly up into the leaves above. No light came from the log. He slowly drew his right hand back toward himself. Resting one small piece of squirrel in his mouth, he chewed slowly. After enjoying his first bite, he began to close his fingertips toward his palm. It looked as if he was grabbing an invisible baseball bat. The pieces of roasted meat twirled around in a circle, cooling them down in the air.

When he finished his patient consumption of the pieces, he slowly stood and looked toward the glade past the tree line. He sniffed the air and began to look for his camp's wing commander. He closed his eyes and thought, *Where are you, Hutch?* After that, he began to pace down the hill. He smelled the scent of a family: laundry detergent, cut grass, and banana peels. He followed those scents to a rolled-up camp tent. Grabbing the bottom of the bag, he let the tent fall out. It slightly opened itself as it hit the dirt.

Mata crouched and began to frame the tent.

I'm close by, Mata heard deep inside. He raised his head and looked back at the glade. The moon's ray on Hutch disappeared as he entered the forest. His silhouette kept lurching and slowly growing. Mata smiled and reached back down to the tent.

Tim climbed the hill just past the bridge and walked into the trees. He circled around and couldn't find a spot that would fit the glider. The thick trunks were close together. Between them, bushes had puffed and grown. Tim turned back and hiked to the rim of the trees. When he reached the tall grasses at the tip of the hill, he looked down and saw a rippling firelight on the creek's bank. The root of the shimmer was on the far side of the bridge, but the rays let some light peer out of the side close to him.

Tim saw a long shadow of something big. For a moment, he saw shadows that rolled in a circular spin. It looked just like propeller blades. Tim wrapped his blanket over his shoulders and crouched in the tall grass. He waited a few moments and then felt drawn down the hill toward the light.

Tim went down to the bridge but stopped a few times and kept still. Who was down there? Was it Hutch, or did Stinky come down to work on the glider? How did the glider get back into that spot? He took another step down the hill upon each question he asked himself.

Tim heard snaps and pops from the fire as he advanced. In moments between each hill tumble, he heard metal clasping echoing off the bridge walls. When he reached the base of the hill, he hugged his body against the bridge's foundation. Right around the corner was the thing he was looking for, that thing making the shadow on the bridge's wall. Hutch's glider was nested on the creek's bank under the bridge. He wanted to jump out into the water and show his face. He wanted to yell, *I caught you red-handed*, but he was too afraid. He pressed his body against the wall and turned away, looking at the light from Hutch's fire rolling down the creek.

Suddenly, the light immediately went out. When that happened, Tim turned his head away from the creek and stared into the darkness in the field. His pupils widened. He then crouched down on his knees and turned his head around to see the glider. Tim saw nothing but the creek and its banks. Far on the opposite corner, someone kept climbing the hill. The person passed by the guardrail and stepped onto the little rocks beside the road. Tim didn't see who it was, but it had to be Hutch.

He stood up, ran, and jumped across the creek. Tim pedaled fast to get close to the road and kept very low. Peeking up over the bridge's fence, Tim saw a gait he recognized.

"I see you, Hutch," he said quietly to himself.

He turned and ran back down to the creek. Tim raised his hands out in front of his face. Slowly, he paced toward the base of the shadow he saw. His hands pushed on something he couldn't see. It was cold and solid.

"I knew it. It ain't invisible to my hands," he said.

Flipping back around, he ran out from under the bridge and climbed up to the road. Then he turned and looked down the road. He saw Hutch walking back toward the baseball field. Suddenly, Tim could see that man appearing under streetlamps and disappearing under branches covering the streets.

"Thank goodness it's after dark," Tim said to himself.

Raising the blanket up and over his head, Tim began to follow him. He ran toward the shadowed yards while staying away from any streetlamp. While following Hutch, he tried to keep himself invisible. Tim couldn't tell if that guy looked backward when he entered the shadowed patches.

Hutch passed by the post office, looked both ways, then crossed the road. He looked back and forth again and then entered into the bushes. Tim sat down behind the post office. He remembered following that trail in the morning. Did he want to follow? He thought he knew where Hutch was heading.

Tim thought about his son. "My kid wants to know," he said quietly.

He stood up and rested his spine against the back door to the post office. Slowly sliding his way to the corner, he took little steps. Reaching the edge of the wall, he pushed his eyes just around the corner.

Straight across the road, just above the bushes, a pair of eyes was slowly scanning back and forth. Tim pulled back behind the corner. His heart rate flashed into a panicked pace. He breathed deeply, trying to meditate until his heart reached a regular rhythm.

"He didn't see me," Tim whispered.

Keeping a slow pattern of deep breaths, Tim waited for a few minutes. When he felt calm, he turned his face around the corner. He pulled down the blanket on his head to cover his ear. With only one side of his face and one eye, he barely looked around the corner. No eyes, no movement. It looked like Hutch kept hiking back toward the glade.

Tim walked past the post office and toward the bushes. As he reached the road, he saw a difference in the bushes across the street. The streetlamp lightly warmed the road, and Tim saw a splashed red circle. For some reason, he wondered if the kids had made the pretty graffiti tag. He grinned for a moment and walked through it.

Hutch left the glade and stood in place for a few moments. Standing under the trees, he let his pupils widen. He saw no lights at all under the branches. Walking toward the voice he had heard, he shivered once. Peering around the trunks, Hutch saw movement.

Mata raised his head and met Hutch's eyes. The captain's long, grey hair on his shoulders brightened momentarily. A beam of moonlight breaking through the trees made it glow. His beard was a warm golden-white shade. Hutch didn't smile. He raised his hand and kept walking toward his chief. When he got close, they met eyes again.

"Rose is still awake," said Mata.

"Yes, she's protecting her house," responded Hutch.

Mata shook his head. "She knows I'm here." He closed his eyes and took a breath. "And the boys are asleep," he added.

"They don't know about you," said Hutch.

"They will."

"I know."

"How's your glider?"

Hutch looked at the tent. It had been assembled and zipped up.

"The glider's fixed. I just have to attach the wings again. That's easy," he responded.

"Are they both apprentices or beginners?"

Hutch smiled. "They are exceptional. Also, they're highly interested and practicing on their own. They've been asking for a new skill every day. I only coached one skill. They have taught themselves the rest . . . so far."

Mata took a deep breath. He sat on a fallen tree trunk and closed his eyes. His fingers reached into his beard and scratched his chin. The scratching made him look satisfied. Then his grin exposed his ripe, yellow teeth.

"Wait until tomorrow," said Mata. "Do you have somewhere to sleep? Are you welcome in this town?"

"I did, and I was, but not tonight."

"Sleep in the tent. There's space." Mata looked at Hutch and saw his exhaustion. "Did you eat?"

Mata snapped his fingers. A stump in front of him burst into a small flame. It looked exactly like Hutch's fire under the bridge. Both of their faces warmed, and they looked at each other. Mata noticed Hutch's expression and waved his hand over the fire to end the light.

"We'll visit them tomorrow. You'll be welcome." Mata reached out and rested his hand on Hutch's shoulder. "Don't fear. You've done well."

Hutch didn't say a word, but he looked like he disagreed. He opened the seam of the tent and crawled inside. Lying on his side, he closed his eyes and fell asleep almost immediately.

Mata raised his hand and pulled the zipper closed without touching it. There was a small screen opening at the peak of the summer tent. He looked up toward the moonlight that was warming his forehead. Closing his eyes, he put his hands together to pray. Pressing his hands against his torso, he opened his palms as if they were a little journal on his core.

He drew in a deep breath and sent, *Hello.*

Glider

Greg shot up off the floor, and Virg ripped away his layers of sheets. They almost shouted at each other. For a moment, they both thought their bedroom friend was making some kind of prank. A small nightlight highlighted the crazed look on each other's faces.

They didn't say a word, but they both knew: someone far different just looked into them.

"You felt that?" said Greg.

"I heard it," Virg responded. "I felt him in there . . . Who was that?"

"It's the new guy."

They heard their front door close, and someone hastily climbed their stairs. They both quickly opened the closet doors and jumped inside of it. Quietly closing the closet, they pushed dress shirts and pants on hangers out of the way and moved back in front of them to hide. The closet had wooden angled openings. Virg and Greg looked through into the room. The door flew open, and the light was flicked on. Rose stood looking back and forth.

"We're in here, Mom," said Virg. "We thought you were a psycho or something."

He pushed open the closet door. Rose saw them surrounded by dress clothes.

"Did you hear that too? You're awake," Rose said as she saw them.

Virg nodded. "We heard someone."

"It sounded familiar," she said. Rose didn't want to bring up the person who contacted them. She wrapped her hands on her arms and stepped away.

"Are you okay?" asked Greg.

"I think that Mata *does* know that you're both here." She hit the light switch to make it dark again. Moving quickly, she looked out the window toward the park.

"You think that was *him*?" asked Virg.

Rose shook her head. "I don't know. Maybe it's him. I think I know that voice."

"Are we just gonna wait to find out?" asked Virg.

Rose looked around the room and saw Greg's backpack. She crouched down and began rolling up the blanket Greg was lying in. Turning back to the boys, she met their eyes.

"Want to go for a hike? You said you saw Hutch place a tent in the woods, right? I remember you said that."

"Umm, yeah," said Greg.

"You guys still tired? We can sleep somewhere relaxing . . . not exactly where Hutch thinks we are." She looked toward the dresser in Virg's room. "See what you two can fit into. Just pack one backpack. I'll grab a tent. Let's camp tonight."

Rose grabbed the back of her neck, shot her hand over her skull, and let go at her chin. The boys looked at each other and grabbed their back necks. They slid their hands over their skulls and did the same. They seemed to understand what Rose was suggesting.

"Protect yourself from the hunters," she said.

They packed sheets, underwear, and an extra shirt into their backpacks. Reaching the kitchen downstairs, Greg snagged some pudding cups and bananas. Virg watched him stuff those into his backpack. Virg took a few water bottles from the pantry.

Rose stopped at the cabinet and took out a pen and pad. She scribbled a little note on a piece of paper, folded it, kissed it, and set it on the kitchen table. Putting her hand on her lips, she kissed her hand and pretended to throw it up and through the ceiling. Doug was sleeping in the room just above.

Turning toward the boys, she saw them both packed and looking at her. She raised her hand and waved it toward the back door. The boys followed her. Sliding it closed and locking it up, they began their hike past the bridge and up into the mountains.

51

Doug woke up on Saturday morning. He could hear a few bluebird squeals in his backyard. It felt nice to leave his eyes closed and experience warm sunbeams spreading over his eyelids. *Breakfast time*, he thought.

He rolled his blanket off and looked out the window to see the birds in his backyard. A few were sitting on his tray feeders. *Got to drop some more seeds in there*, he thought.

"Breakfast for us both," he whispered to the birds.

He turned to look at his bed. Rose wasn't there, and her side of the sheets were tossed down. Doug walked toward the stairs and saw the light shining through Virg's bedroom doorway. He turned and walked to his son's room. The door was open, but Virg and Greg were not in there. The sheets weren't tucked. Doug listened for a moment but heard no sounds in the house. Everyone was up, but was anyone still here?

Doug thought about early fall festivals and weekend parties the kids had attended in previous years. *Maybe I forgot about a party*, he thought. He paced slowly down the stairs and opened the kitchen cabinet. Grabbing a coffee mug and resting it on the table, a bent card sat beside it. He picked it up and read it.

Dear Hubby,
You're safe. I think that Hutch and his boss will show up today. Don't worry. They will be looking for the kids and me. You can tell them that we're 'going fishing.' I'm keeping the kids safe.
Love,
Your Queen
xoxo

Doug put the card down on the table. He returned to the cabinet and took out a mason jar of coffee beans. Pulling the grinder from the cupboard, he plugged it in and stood still momentarily. His eyes turned toward his front door. He walked back to the cabinet and took two more mugs out. Doug placed them on the table next to the note. He picked up the note, folded it a few times, and put it in the drawer containing pens and notecards. After closing the drawer, he added spoonfuls of coffee beans to his grinder. He decided to brew enough coffee for himself and the two men he expected to show up.

Sitting in the chair on his back porch, Doug sipped on his cup of java and read his local newspaper. He was genuinely enjoying his quiet weekend and the melodies of nature. The sliding door was open, but the screen was closed. He expected to hear his doorbell at some point.

A few moments passed by as Doug fell asleep in his comfy chair. The sun was spreading its warmth over his chest. Then he woke up feeling warm. Nesting his newspaper beside himself, he got up and walked toward his garden.

As he stepped between the raised garden beds, he heard the opening and closing of the screen door on his porch. He turned and saw Hutch standing under the porch's canopy.

"Good morning, Hutch. What can I do for ya?" said Doug.

"I left my handkerchief here last night," said Hutch. He held it in his left hand. "I found it on the coatrack and just got it back."

"You just get back from the party? I didn't see you last night ... or this morning. Figured that you just went camping or something," Doug turned back toward the garden.

"Yeah, I camped out last night. Also, I just knocked on your front door, but no one answered. It wasn't locked." Hutch took a few steps forward.

"That's fine. Want any coffee?"

Hutch took another step forward and into the sun. "Can I introduce you to someone?"

Behind Hutch, a face appeared on the other side of the screen door within the darkness of the interior. Doug took one step back.

"Hi, person I don't know!" Doug waved his hand to the old man. "Want a cup of coffee?"

The screen door slid open. It didn't look like the man moved at all.

"Yes, thank you. It's lovely to meet you, Mr. Murphy."

The man walked out the screen door and down the steps, past Hutch, and extended his hand. Doug noticed the man's grizzly white mane. He grabbed Mata's hand and felt calluses on his thick palm.

"Nice to meet you too. What are ya doin' in PA today?"

Doug walked past Mata onto the porch and waved his hand for them to follow him.

Mata walked behind Doug and began, "I am a camp administrator. Hutch works with me to help people learn about themselves. I'm writing a book about the types of people we've met and helped. He also told me that two children in this area have incredible potential."

Doug climbed up the stairs toward his kitchen. "Sounds like fun." The two men followed behind him.

Grabbing his French press and ground coffee, Doug said, "So, you know who's in PA, but do you have plans? How'd you find out about who's in PA?" He poured some grounds into the press and lit the stove to heat the kettle.

Hutch jumped in. "Well, I contacted Mata to let him know about the character and skills of both kids. It's quite different from those we've tried to help."

"Ah, his name is Mata," said Doug. He pointed at the grey-haired man and kept his eyes on Hutch.

Hutch looked embarrassed. "Oh, I'm sorry, Doug. I thought that Rose told you about Mata."

"She has. But I've never seen him before." Doug smiled at Mata. "Again, nice to meet ya." He winked.

Mata looked into Doug's eyes. "And where is Rose? I don't see any plates in your sink. Are the children with her, as well?"

"She's fishing this morning. I think she took the kids." Doug's focus shifted back to Hutch. "So your boss is here today. I guess you don't have to fly back so soon. Did you get your propeller last night?"

"Yes, I got it back and fixed it last night." Hutch looked back at Mata. "But I suppose that I don't have to leave today."

"Do you both need beds? I think I have a couch as well," said Doug.

Mata held up an open hand. "That's all right. Thank you for the offer. I'm used to sleeping in a forest. Soft soil, natural sounds. They help me to fall into a deep sleep."

Mata leaned toward Doug as he smiled. A morning sunbeam ripped through the kitchen window and lit Mata's face from the side. The yellow spots on his teeth and his light blue eyes bloomed in the rays as he grinned. His grey and translucent hair sparkled and almost rippled in the ray. The sharp colors almost made Doug remember Salvador Dali's *American Dream* painting. He felt those eyes look deep inside of him.

Suddenly, Doug heard a light bubbling on the stove. He rolled the dial back before the boil got fierce and poured the hot water into the French press. Next, he placed the plunger on top and let the grounds steep. A few moments passed by as no one said anything. Doug pulled the two extra mugs he left out and placed a few spoons beside them.

Hutch noticed the two mugs had been put on the counter before they arrived. He said, "Did you expect us?"

Usually, Doug enjoyed making people feel welcome but didn't want to let them know he knew they were coming.

"Well, I didn't expect *you* two. But sometimes Tim or some other friend will stop by on the weekends. I like to be prepared." He smiled at Hutch.

"You're always a good host," said Hutch. He broke into a smile, reached out, and patted Doug's arm.

Doug smiled and stepped back to the French press. He slowly pressed the plunger down and filtered through the broken coffee beans. It made the silence return. When Doug began to pour, Mata closed his eyes and raised his chin. He almost looked like he was falling asleep.

"So how long are you guys gonna stay, um . . . in the woods?" Doug asked.

Mata whipped his eyes back open. They were pure white. After a moment, the pupils rolled down from being pointed back in his head. Doug barely let a gasp out, then turned and opened the fridge.

"You guys like Half and Half?" Doug stared deep into the fridge.

"They're fishing, you said," Mata began. "Do they fish in a lake . . . in a river?"

Doug turned with the carton in his hand. He rested it on the countertop.

"Well, I wasn't told. On my weekends, I just let them wander around and go wherever they want to . . . kinda like what you guys are doing."

Doug then added the milk to their mugs and stirred. The two men beside him kept their silence.

Mata stood up and collected his coffee mug. He took a sip. "Thank you."

"You're welcome," responded Doug.

"I just want to meet those boys. I don't want anything from them, but they could help me in my research. Anything I learn, I could use to help other people that I meet. I want to help." Mata put his mug back down.

"I understand," said Doug, "but I don't know exactly where they went."

Doug looked at Hutch to inspect his mood. Just past him, Doug saw a black carpet pass along the bottom of the window. He didn't say anything, but Hutch's head whipped around to find what Doug was looking at.

"Sorry," Doug let out a few giggles and stretched his arms way up above his head as he squatted down and stretched. "I had just woken from a nap when you showed up. My mind is, um, relaying some of my dreams. I'm just staring into space." Doug let out a calm chuckle and shook his head.

Mata stood up. "Well, thank you for the coffee. We'll go fishing today, and if you want, we'll bring you what we caught." He smiled and left his mug full.

Hutch gulped from his mug to finish off his brew. Walking past Doug, he placed his empty mug in the sink.

"Thank you," said Hutch. He rested his hand on Doug's shoulder and looked him in the eyes. Hutch looked tired, and his eyebrows were pressed down a bit.

"You can stay here if you want to." Doug put his hand on top of Hutch's.

"The deer hide is still in your shed. I didn't wet it yet today. I'm sure it's stiff as a board, but it's ready." Hutch patted Doug's shoulder. "Just buff it over the edges of a boulder or something. That'll loosen it up. Enjoy a fresh carpet."

Hutch turned toward the stairs. Mata followed him. Doug stayed in the kitchen as the two guests walked down the stairs and out his front door. When he heard the door close, he looked back out his window. He moved closer to it and looked down through the glass. All he saw were some vines and bushes down under the window. Doug turned back and walked down his stairs and into his backyard. He picked up the newspapers he left and saw something move in the corner of his eye. Then Doug saw Tim looking at him with a dark brown blanket over his head.

Shooting up and backing away, Doug let out, "Jesus!"

Tim whipped his index finger up to his lips.

". . . is just signin' in the rain!" sang Doug, to make his reaction sound regular to anyone nearby. He raised his open hands and signaled Tim to stay where he was.

Doug walked past him and down his little path toward his shed. He opened the door and pulled out the deer carcass. He threw it over the railing on his porch and grabbed a small wooden chair. A fat boulder sat in his backyard. He put his wooden chair next to it and grabbed the deerskin. Sitting down and facing his house, he peeked at its rims and corners. He saw no movements on either side. Hutch and Mata must have left to begin their search. Doug raised his hand and beckoned Tim to his spot.

Tim looked back and forth and hopped over some bushes. His feet were caught, and he slapped his frame right onto the grass.

"Oh jeez, you okay?" Doug jumped up and ran over to lift Tim.

"I'm fine. I just didn't sleep a whole lot. Probably need some shut-eye or something." He shook his head. "I'm good." Tim let go of the blanket and rubbed his shoulder.

"Hey, that's a nice thick carpet. I don't see any blood or bruises."

Tim looked at himself. "Yeah, I guess I'm okay." He took a few steps and stood next to the deer carcass.

Doug followed him and sat in the chair near the stone. "So, are you following them? You look a little dirty."

"I saw Hutch fix his glider last night," Tim said.

"Yeah, I thought he was going leave today. But he and Mata are looking for my wife and our kids."

"Wait, what?" Tim shook his head. "I thought he found them already."

"Why?" Doug shook his head too.

Tim looked down. "I went to a party with Hutch last night. He fought someone. Later, he fixed his glider in a spot I thought it was in, but I had never seen before. Then he met that dude, and it looked like the old guy was mentally connecting with people."

"Slow down." Doug raised his open hand toward Tim. "Hutch is a fighter?"

"Sit down ." Tim sat on the porch and motioned toward the chair Doug was near to.

Hutch and Mata made it through the field and stopped when they reached the creek. The big guy turned north toward the hill range and turned back to see Mata looking south and downhill. Turning back to Hutch, Mata said, "Head north. They're fishing. The creek will lead us to their spot." He pointed in the direction Hutch looked.

Hutch shook his head. "North of here, I haven't seen any lakes yet

...but I haven't seen it all. I'll follow the creek to see if there's a pond in the hills."

"Perhaps there is one where the current goes." Mata turned and began walking with his head down. It was evident that he was searching for footprints.

Hutch turned and made his way toward the bridge. In his head, he heard, *Let me know if you find them.* Mata's voice made his spine ripple for a moment. He kept walking and thought to himself, *I hope I find them before you.*

Mata crept slowly and tried to consume the state of the surrounding environment. Light breezes brought scents of rotting corn stock roots, tractor diesel fuel, and tree pollens. The odors were not ambrosial. Towns and machinery produced scents that Mata had left behind long ago. The calming sounds and natural scents of the forest were missed. Keeping his mind on finding the boys, he took a deep breath. No scents of peanut butter or worms met Mata's nostrils. He expected those scents if children were camping and fishing.

Walking slowly downhill with the current of the creek, he kept his eyes open and let them creep up into the hills. Mata looked as if he were walking in slow motion. He listened, remaining aware of the sounds of ripples in the current.

After pacing downstream for an hour, a small lake crept into his view. Fat, green bushes surrounded it. The reflection off the water came into his view from about ten feet away. He sat down immediately. Shutting his eyes, Mata opened his ears and listened to his surroundings. A light breeze slapped the bush leaves onto one other. A few trickles from the creek hit the lake lightly as it poured in. Mata reopened his gaze and looked straight at the lake.

The sound of a light plop caught his ears. A tiny ripple opened in the center of the pond. Nothing followed. Keeping his knees on the ground, he leaned forward to catch a movement in the water. His face was pressed against the bush in front of him.

A tiny V ripped into the crown of the pond. It came quick and slipped back into stillness. Mata held his breath for a few moments.

He couldn't tell if it was from a fishing line he couldn't see or from a minnow. Another rip repeated in the pond. He switched his gaze into the direction the V continued pointing toward. The bushes rimmed the pond but separated at a tiny opening. A flat trail was held behind the gap. He hadn't seen it before. The trees behind the bushes had shaded the pathway.

Mata crouched low beneath the upper rim of the bush patch. He paced down into and through the creek, up onto the other bank. Slowly climbing and crouching to remain unseen, he kept moving around the rim of the creek. Not quickening his pace, he listened again. He heard birds and far away cars, but nothing else. As he curled around the lake and got near to the trees, he looked at the ground for footprints. There was nothing there. Closing his eyes, he breathed in through his nose. No scents of fish or campfires reached his nostrils.

Creeping around the bushes, Mata saw a tiny footpath up the hill and into the trees. He rose up, standing upright. The lake looked the same. A sound of the creek's continuation grabbed his ear. He could see the brink of a tiny waterfall beyond the crest of the pond. There were no fresh footprints and no used fire rings. Looking back up the path, he turned and followed the trail.

He paced toward the trail. But before he reached it, a man in a camp chair caught his eye. Mata turned to him as the man held a thin fishing pole that had a metal loop at its tip. The line ran through the loop and into the water. Sandy yellow and rippled, the fishing pole looked as if it was an old bamboo stalk. A plastic blue line holder sat in the man's lap. Mata watched him reach down to open his tiny cooler.

The man turned his head and saw Mata staring at his fishing rod. "I've got another beer if you need something," the fisher said.

Mata smiled but said nothing. The man smiled and tipped his cap at Mata. He sniffed and pulled his unpolished aviator glasses off his face. He sneezed into a tiny towel and then used it to polish his lenses. He put the lenses back on and scratched the towel on his old slumping neck skin.

He reached back down to his cooler and saw Mata still standing nearby, "You sure you don't want one? I've got a cup." The old man cracked open his can and turned back to look at the fishing line while he took a sip.

Mata took a step toward him and said, "Have you seen a woman and her two sons?"

"I saw some in the park this mornin'. But *all* those kids go the park on this kinda mornin'. It's Saturday." The man raised his beer can and looked into the sky as if saying the word "Saturday" was saying "cheers" to God.

"You haven't seen anyone hike on this path?" Mata pointed behind his shoulder into the trees.

"I have. Some were with kids."

"Did any look like a middle-aged woman and two kids?"

"Seems like we're the same age. Ain't it a bit too late for us to be lookin' fer women and children?" The fisherman giggled and turned back toward the pond.

His chair raised an inch off the ground and floated swiftly six feet forward and hovered over the pond. He couldn't turn back. The chair faced the center of the pond just as before. He didn't hear a voice nearby, but within his head he heard, *Tell me who you've seen. Please describe them in detail.*

He didn't know who to talk to. Breathing faster, he pushed his hands down on his camp chair armrests and raised his butt off the bottom. He turned and saw Mata's hand pointed right at him.

"What do you want?" he said out loud.

In his head he heard, *Who have you seen today? Tell me . . . or show me.*

The old man rested his butt back into his chair and didn't speak. He closed his eyes and remembered the faces he had seen that morning. Mata closed his eyes too and drew his hand slowly back toward himself. The chair drifted bit-by-bit back toward the soil and floated four inches above. When Mata quickly passed through the recent memory of the old man, he lowered him four inches until his feet touched down and his chair sat on the soil.

The man hadn't seen Rose or the kids. Mata turned away from the trail and began hiking back toward the direction he came from. He felt as if he was driving a semitruck in the dark. His mind was speeding as his body dragged but an inch behind him.

52

Tim and Doug hiked up the side of the creek, wearing green and brown garments and caps. They were attempting to camouflage themselves, but they didn't have any army clothes. Doug wore a thin backpack filled with water. A long, thick plastic straw sprouted out of the top of the backpack and affixed to its shoulder strap. Every time they stopped walking, Tim reached over, grabbed the straw, and took a sip off of Doug's shoulder.

"Do you really have to keep doing that? I only have so much. And I mean . . . you're sucking a lot . . . of water."

Tim let go and backed away. "Sorry, I just . . . I'm tired, I think. I didn't even drink last night."

They reached the bridge and saw Pete at the top. He leaned on the bridge barrier while pointing his face at the sun. It looked like he was blissfully catching sunrays with his eyes closed.

"PEEEETE," Doug whisper-screamed toward him.

Pete turned down toward the loud whisper and smiled. "Oh, hi, guys!" He waved and slowly hiked down the bank. He was wearing an orange shirt with *Tang* written on it.

Doug turned to Tim. "Why did you need him?"

"He saw everything that I saw last night."

Pete smiled and reached out for the straw on Doug's shoulder. He popped it into his mouth and took a long sip as Doug rolled his eyes and stared at Tim with an attitude.

"Oh, *he* drank at the party," Tim added, as he pointed at Pete.

"Puh-puh parched," said Pete as he grabbed his belly. "Thanks for that." He wiped his mouth with his sleeve. "You guys ready to find your plane?" he pointed at Tim, then turned and pointed at Doug, ". . . and your *fam*?"

Glider

Doug rolled his eyes again and looked at Pete.

"Yes, Tim wanted your help. He trusts you," said Doug. "And I trust you both, based on what you saw last night."

"Yeah," said Pete. "I saw someone kick Hutch in the face. *And* the guy's heel went straight through Hutch's nose."

He poorly repeated the motion, punching through the air in front of Tim's face.

Tim backed away quickly and looked at Doug. "It looked better than that."

"I bet." Doug smiled. "So, the plane is right here?" He pointed just in front of them.

They looked under the bridge, but the only thing they saw was the damp soil surrounding the creek.

Tim took a step forward and said, "Watch this."

He shook his hands, preparing to touch the invisible glider. He raised his right hand and waved it directly in front. When his hand touched the glider, they heard a metallic *clang*.

Doug looked forward and didn't see the plane. But he saw Tim's hand resting directly in the air. Hearing the sound of him hitting metal, Doug watched Tim's eyes open wider.

"He didn't make it physically invisible, just visually." Tim smiled and turned toward Doug. "Touch it."

Doug moved forward and calmly pointed his finger and slowly reached out. When he touched the frame, the image of the plane opened into his eyes. It was almost as if a memory flashed back into his brain. It felt like he had forgotten its existence, but it had always been there. He took a step away.

"That is so weird," Doug said. His stomach churned.

"Cool," responded Pete. He reached out and whacked his knuckles onto the same area the others had touched. "Weird," he said as he sat down. Then he closed his eyes and happily burped out loud.

Doug shook his head and looked at Tim.

Tim smiled at Doug. "So, can we move this into the trees?"

Doug and Pete looked at him and didn't seem to understand.

"Hutch has been hiding this from us. Why? We've been offering him help the entire time, right?"

"Not me," said Pete.

"We drove him home last night," said Tim.

"Oh, right."

"He's been living in my house for the past week," said Doug, as he sat down on a rock near the creek. He took a deep breath and looked back at the glider. "And he looked worried today, didn't he?"

Tim shook his head.

"If he didn't want anyone else to see this plane . . . I don't blame him, but yeah, he and the new guy are looking for my wife and our kids." Doug looked down for a moment. Then he raised his leer, looking like he made up his mind. He shot up off the rock and walked toward the plane. Laying a smack on the side of the glider, he looked at Tim. "So you said we should hide this?"

53

Greg sat with his legs crossed and his eyes closed. A light breeze floated across his neck. He breathed in slowly, smelling the air tumbling through the field and across the pond.

Rose said to Greg, "There should be only two men walking through the field. Find them."

When he closed his eyes, his visible spectrum stretched over the mountain ridge and scanned through the fields like a goose gliding over a valley. His gaze expanded rapidly. It was as if the goose exploded into a flock and all their perspectives were included. The spread of vision felt natural. As his perspective multiplied, he found two men walking north, but separated by miles.

He took in a breath quickly. "I found them." He opened his eyes and stood straight up.

She put a hand on his back and said, "It's okay. Take a breath."

Greg slowly turned his head and saw Virg sitting with his eyes closed and his legs crossed.

"What are you seeing?" asked Greg.

"I'm looking through Mata's eyes," he said. "He's looking toward the bridge. That one we put the plane under."

"Does he feel your presence?" Rose asked.

Virg slowly shook his head. "I'm breathing slowly, and it doesn't feel like he notices. He hasn't said anything or sent any messages my way." He sat still with his eyes closed.

Greg shook his head, trying to forget the fear he felt the previous evening—being torn from sleep by Mata's voice. "I mean, nothing like last night." Then he looked back at Rose. "I saw five men in the field."

"Hutch and Mata? Who else?" she asked.

"My dad, his baseball friend—Pete, and Doug . . . uh, *your* dad, Virg." Greg turned back to his friend.

"Mmmm, mnnn," Virg barely shook his head to the side. "The old guy doesn't see anyone under the bridge. I don't see any shadows or even the plane." He kept his eyes shut but moved his face toward Greg. "Where'd you see the dads?"

"It looked like they were in the trees. Like, just behind the spot we were lying on before the glider crashed," Greg said.

Virg's eyes were closed, but his eyebrows rose for a moment. "He's turning his head."

Looking through Mata's eyes, Virg saw one of the old man's wrinkly cheeks rise a few times. The nose's rim disappeared in Virg's gaze as the left cheek rose for a few sniffs.

"Where to? Is he looking for—?" Greg said.

Virg cut him off. "He's looking up the hill . . . into the woods."

Rose grabbed Greg's shoulder and said calmly, "Contact Tim. I'll contact Doug."

He turned and looked at her. "What are we gonna tell them to do?"

Rose sat down and crossed her legs. Closing her eyes and clasping her hands together, she responded, "They should hide."

Pete swung his arms, turned his torso, and let go of another branch. The leafy limb flew over a bush and landed lightly on a pile of branches. A big stack of fallen boughs had been stacked on top of the glider. Before that, they had slowly hiked the glider up the big hill and placed it about thirty yards into the woods.

Pete let out a big breath, sounding tired. "I think I'm done, boys. My mouth is feeling dry." As he turned back to look at the other men, he saw them standing up straight and staring through the trees.

The two men didn't move a muscle.

Pete didn't notice. He walked toward Doug.

"I'm gonna steal a little sip, if ya don't mind." He reached over

Doug's shoulder to grab the rubber straw on the backpack. Pete put the straw into his mouth and looked at Doug's face. His mouth was open, and his eyes were wide and still.

"Whoa," said Pete, "you okay?" He looked over at Tim. His wide and unmoving eyes were exactly like Doug's.

Turning back to Doug, Pete saw the man blink and regain his focus.

"Let's get outta here," Doug said as his pupils contracted.

Tim looked at Pete. "Hey, we've got to climb some trees and hide. There's a guy not far away."

Pete raised his shoulders. "Okay, does he wanna help us?"

Doug put his hand on Pete's shoulder. "We've gotta get out of here now . . ." his head swiveled a bit ". . . and hide."

"How do you know?" Pete raised his arms.

The two men didn't respond but turned their heads to look at each other. The scenario seemed too complicated to explain. They turned their eyes back to Pete and looked like they couldn't explain.

"Cool. Life-saving psycho-kinetic stuff?"

His two friends nodded. Tim took a step forward as he grabbed Pete's arm. "Let's get outta here. You'll thank me."

Tim and Doug began to run past the covered glider. They hopped through bushes and deeper into the forest. Pete followed as quickly as he could while catching all the bush branches with his face.

"Where we goin'?" said Pete.

Tim turned back. "We'll get deeper into the woods, find a thick tree, climb up, and hide ourselves as best we can."

Pete looked down and shook his head. "I'm already tired. Who'd you say was comin'?"

Doug stopped jogging and turned toward Pete, "A guy you don't want to meet."

Pete raised his eyebrow about to ask a question.

Doug, staring at him, said, "Trust me."

Mata hiked along the creek until he saw the bridge. He was about 100 yards away, but he didn't smell the scent of campfire smoke that was held in the old glider's wooden frame. He was used to that smell. Also, he knew where the glider had been hidden. Turning his head around, Mata caught a different scent. Someone around here had been drinking. His nose plucked the pore excretion of alcohol from the air. Someone imbibed the night before. They smelled dark and salty.

Closing his eyes, Mata's nostrils pulled his focus toward the hill covered in trees. He opened his eyes and let the scent drag him across the creek. Taking his time, Mata gazed across the grounds. As he reached the hillside, he saw a line of trampled grass.

A light breeze passed through the trees and rolled down the hillside. A sweeping scent met his nose. The tall grass at the top of the hill passed a smoky scent down to his nostrils. *Hutch's glider?* He asked himself. Pacing up the hill, he reached the peak. Calmly touching the smoky foxtail grasses with his arm, he pushed by and made his way into the woods. He was almost enjoying the hunt.

As Mata passed by the rim of trees, the scent of the hangover vanished. The breeze died down. He pulled in a breath as he shut his eyes. Oak-moss and pine scents floated past. Opening his eyes, he scanned across the grounds as he made his way deeper into the trees. After five minutes of gentle hiking, the smoky scent held by the glider's frame hit him again, heavily. Turning his head back, Mata noticed a thick pile of branches. A small reflection on the glider's rim caught his eye.

"Are you close by?" Mata asked.

He smiled and looked around. No sounds or scents crawled toward him. As his eyes began to roll up toward the branches above, a sound crept into his ears.

We're up the creek. Want to fish with us?

Mata's head whipped to his right. He gazed toward the creek's origin. A small chain of mountains looked to have a gaping valley between them. The further ridges were a touch darker and not as detailed in his vision. It looked like the creek was coming from a big valley just beyond the nearby hills.

He closed his eyes and silently responded, *Invitation?*

We're at the natural groundwater basin. Just past the highest peak to your right. Northeast.

Mata smiled a bit and squinted. His gaze found the tallest peak on the hillside. It looked to be, maybe, five miles away.

I'll see you soon, he responded, without moving his lips. His body turned toward the mountains as he began a hike toward the rim of the woods.

As Mata began pacing down the hill and into the open fields, Pete wiped the sweat off his forehead. His wrist smelled like the scent of an old, salty cup of booze. Tim pulled his gaze from looking down at Pete, turning up toward Doug. The three men were hugging the trunk of a tree. Standing on boughs of the tree and covered by branches below, the men were about fifty feet off the ground.

Doug looked straight down and raised his index finger to his lips. Both men beneath him stared straight up. It looked like they were asking, *"Can we go down yet?"* He moved his finger away from his face and pumped it a few times in the air. Silently saying, *One minute, one minute.*

Virg smiled while holding his eyes closed. "He didn't find them. Close, though. He found the glider."

"How far away is he?" asked Rose.

"Close to where *we* started. He's not rushing."

Greg turned toward Rose. "Hutch is close."

Virg still held his eyes closed, looking through Mata's. Another widening of the nostrils made Mata stop his pacing. He turned a bit to his left and kept hiking.

"Man, he really puffs those nostrils. Can he smell *everything?*" said Virg.

From about thirty yards away, a voice responded, "Mata wanted to make it easier to find what he's looking for. He's been working on that for a long time."

Hutch took a few steps down the hill as his eyes slowly searched from left to right. "You've learned how to make yourself invisible."

Virg's eyes opened, and he looked up the hill. Greg and Rose whipped around to look in the same direction.

Rose whispered to the two boys, "He can't see us. Stay quiet."

She barely made any noise. Reaching out, she grabbed Greg's hand and laid her palm on her son's shoulder. They both turned and followed her. Even though she was invisible to Hutch, she bent over and snuck away to circle the pond. Greg snuck right behind her.

When Virg stood up, he turned back toward Hutch and stared at him. Staring at the big man, Virg noticed a tense eyebrow ridge on the big man's face. Was Hutch afraid of something? The boy felt his stomach turn, and then he curled his index finger and touched his palm. He dragged the index from his thumb's joint to the tip. Virg appeared in Hutch's view.

The searcher turned his head toward Virg, and they both stopped moving.

"Are you okay?" asked Virg.

"I'm worried," responded Hutch.

"If Mata finds us, what's he gonna do?"

"Usually, he tries to help . . ." Hutch's voice stopped. He cleared his throat. ". . . It's different now."

"He used to help? To make our skills sharper?"

Hutch looked down at the grass. "But it's been different recently."

"Why are you trying to find us if you know that?"

Rose came out of nowhere, appearing just behind Hutch. Virg's gaze shifted directly onto her. She lowered a short log and lifted it quickly above her shoulder and behind her head. With a swift whip, she connected it to the back of Hutch's skull. The hit blacked him out as he rolled down the grass a few times. His body lay still behind a patch of weeds. Silence. The mother and her son stared at each other.

"He wants to find us for Mata," said Rose.

Virg turned and ran toward Hutch as he lay facedown on the ground. There was no blood on his head. It looked like Rose just hit him hard enough to remove his consciousness.

"I think he wanted to help us," said Virg to his mom. "He looked regretful."

"That's not what I saw," she said. "I don't trust him like I did before."

She looked around and saw Virg's backpack with a top handle and two straps on it. "Can you cut those straps off your backpack? We need something to tie his hands and feet together."

Virg's eyes widened. "Wow, Mom. That's badass. Are you used to doing this?" He looked a little doubtful.

"He hasn't been honest with me. The ball's in our court, and I'm not playing anymore. *I'm* the coach." She looked back at Virg grabbing the backpack and using a Swiss Army knife to release the straps. "He followed us this far," she added.

"The big guy looked confused, kinda. Or uncomfortable . . ." Virg stopped talking as he thought about the situation. He finished cutting the straps off his backpack and said, "Is he afraid of Mata?" tossing the straps toward his mother.

Rose began to slowly knot the straps around Hutch's wrists and ankles. "Honestly, I don't know." She raised her eyes to meet her son's. "But I am."

54

The three musketeers waited in the trees for about ten minutes. Doug checked his watch until it seemed that Mata wasn't coming back. He snapped his fingers together and looked down to find the other two guys looking straight up, back at him.

Doug said, "Let's climb down. I think he's gone."

"Thank God. My knees are aching. And I really have to pee," responded Pete.

He made it to the ground first and ran only three steps before he unzipped his fly. He let out a very satisfying groan and didn't finish until after Doug and Tim both reached the ground. The two dads started walking toward the glider. It looked as if Mata hadn't noticed it or touched it.

"You think he saw it?" Tim asked Doug.

"I have no idea, but he definitely didn't try to uncover it."

"He knew about us."

"I think he knows about *them*." Doug widened his eyes, facing the path Mata had walked toward.

"Yeah, why else would he leave? We weren't perfectly hidden," added Tim.

"Rose contacted me. You heard Greg's voice, right?"

Tim nodded.

"Maybe they did the same with him." Doug raised his shoulders.

Tim looked back under the branch pile and kept his eyes on the glider. Then he had an idea. "Should we try to distract him from finding our kids."

"We don't know where they are . . . Wait, she wrote that they're going fishing on the note she left for me," said Doug. "She loves that natural pond in the valley between the hills."

"Well, what if we use the glider? We can find them, right?"

Doug shook his head. "I have no idea. I've never flown before."

"And there's only one seat in that thing." Tim sat down and crossed his legs.

They both got quiet for a moment. Pete took a few steps past them and tapped the rear rudder on the glider.

"I've piloted crappier ones than this in Vietnam. Want me to take it for a little trip? You can fly these pretty low." He smiled and added, "... Low enough to see who's makin' beer in their own garages." Pete smiled and raised his eyebrows.

"It's not safe. Plus, you don't have any family that's currently being hunted," said Tim.

Pete crossed his arms and tried to look professional.

"What is *actually* 'not safe,'" he showed the quote with his fingers, "is flying a plane or a glider with *NO EXPERIENCE*." He bowed as if he were a royal duke, offering the kings his skills and service.

Doug and Tim both sighed and looked at each other. They had no argument. Tim turned his head back. He met Pete's eyes, and they both smiled.

"Don't have any fun up there," said Tim.

"When have I ever *not* had fun?" Pete raised his arms and happily smiled.

Nothing else was said. Pete turned toward the glider and began to pull branches off the top. The other two men rose and made their way close to Pete to help him.

When they finished removing the sticks and leaves from the glider, the three men picked it up and moved it back to the rim of the hill. They carried it slowly through the forest and placed it down at the edge of the hill, facing the creek. Doug and Pete removed the wings tied to the glider's body as Tim collected his tools. The two without the tools held the wings up as Tim matched the cusps and screwed them back on. Tim popped the wheels out from the fuselage and laid them straight down as Pete and Doug lifted the body.

Taking their time and focusing on their project, they helped one another and said almost nothing. As it came together, it felt like Pete's trip was about to happen. The two dads became a bit uneasy as Pete's flight got closer and closer to takeoff.

Tim inspected the bottom of the glider and then rose to his feet.

"It looks pretty good. There doesn't really seem to be anything wrong with it." He rested his forearm on a wing.

"Is the mini-engine still alive?" Pete lightly swung the propeller blade for half a spin.

Tim lifted the glass door on the cockpit and reached down to touch the dashboard. He flicked the switch and nodded at Pete. One propeller blade was pointing at ten o'clock. Pete laid his hands on the blade's tip and threw it down. The engine caught the rhythm as the propeller blade flowed in a circle with its twin. It flew around like a functional propeller for about five seconds. Doug smiled as Tim flicked it off while his hand was still in the cockpit.

"Well, it still works," said Doug. He removed his water pack and handed it to Pete. "You want to take some sips with you?"

Pete waved his hand. "That's okay. I won't have any room. The cockpit looks pretty tiny. Thanks, though."

Doug walked straight toward Pete and wrapped his arms around him. He squeezed tight. Then Pete lifted one hand and patted Doug's back.

"Thank you." Doug stepped away. "You're a good man."

"Naw, I'm a *skilled* man." Pete smiled. "I'll be fine."

He turned back to the glider and raised his foot and looked confused. "How the hell do I . . . ?" He couldn't find an easy way to get into the glider.

Tim got down on his knee and clasped his hands together. Pete let out a laugh and then stepped on Tim's hands. He grabbed the open cockpit and launched his other foot into it. He slowly turned around, then crinkled his face as he tried to fit into the seat properly. Finally, he sat and looked pretty comfy.

"Whelp, it's been nice knowin' ya guys. I think I'm moving to Key

West. I ain't been there in a while. First free ride I've ever had," said Pete. He laughed and then turned his head like he thought of something. "Do you guys have a walkie or a satellite communicator?"

"Well, good thing you didn't take my water pack. I have two Garmins." Doug opened a pocket in the satchel and pulled out two small walkies. He handed one to Pete.

"Charged?"

"They're always sitting in a charge nest in my garage. Feelin' lucky that I remembered these."

Pete held a walkie and turned the dial to *On*. "Channel?" he asked.

"Don't fiddle with that knob. We camp. They're connected already." Doug turned his on and punched a button. "Copy?"

They all heard it through the walkie-talkie in Doug's hand.

"You bet I do," responded Pete.

Doug said, "And if you can, just distract that guy who visited us. Let us know how our kids look if he's not paying attention. Maybe you can find us and tell us what's going on."

"I'll be your announcer! I've always wanted to do that for the Phils." Pete lowered his hand for a high five.

Doug put his hand in Pete's. "Enjoy the game."

Tim walked in front of the glider, held the propeller, and looked at Pete. Doug helped him close the cockpit lid. When Pete flicked the engine on, he raised his thumb at Tim. After flicking the propeller, Tim ran around the cockpit and grabbed the left wing. Doug waited at the right wing. They waited until Pete gave two thumbs-up, one on each side of the aircraft canopy.

Doug and Tim began to jog, pushing the glider to the edge of the hillside. When they reached the little cliff, they both felt like it wasn't going fast enough. They were right. The front wheel rolled down swiftly and hit the ground hard. They kept pushing and began to run. For a moment, both men holding the wings kept their hands on it as the nose flew straight down on the hillside. After two seconds, the glider rolled too fast for them to hold. They let go.

It kept rolling down toward the creek as Tim and Doug came to a stop. Keeping their eyes on the glider, they felt a breeze roll up the ridge from the valley below. At the same moment, Pete pulled the rudder, shifting the wings. The little winglets flung down toward the hill.

The two men saw the glider rip away from the ground swiftly. It held the speed consistently and flew straight across the land until it reached another lowering of the ground. The valley opened up again toward a lower section and when Pete crossed it, he raised the throttle again. Within twenty seconds, the glider almost disappeared as it lifted higher and higher. When the silent ship reached a small chain of clouds, it pumped right through and disappeared. After a few moments, the men on the ground saw the propeller aim toward the mountain chain—the same direction as Mata.

Tim turned toward Doug. "Did you think that was gonna happen?"

"Nope, not at all."

The walkie in Doug's pocket buzzed and let out, "10-1."

Doug looked confused.

Tim rolled his eyes and then smiled. "That means that he has to pee. Basic talkie lingo."

Doug punched the button on the walkie. "I'd have to pee right now too if I were flying that thing. Great job."

"10-4," responded Pete. "Eyes open for your fams, over."

"Copy that," said Doug.

55

Waking up slowly, Hutch didn't open his eyes. He felt the swelling and tightness on the back of his neck. Squeezing his eyelids, he smelled the dirt and felt his wrists were tied together. Lying down, he felt his ankles were tied up as well. Not moving, he just let his ears tell him where he was and who was nearby. He heard a light splash in a pond and the trill of a woodpecker.

A sound he recognized reached his ear. Was it close by? It reverberated around the lake. He knew it was Rose's voice.

"That's a nice casting. You're getting better."

Are they fishing? Hutch thought to himself.

He tried to send a thought to her. *Are you here?*

Out loud, Rose responded, "You're awake. C'mon, boys. Let's go check out the spy."

Connecting with Hutch directly, she sent, *I didn't hear what you said, but I felt the energy. We made mental helmets. You know how to do that?*

"I do," said Hutch. He opened his eyes and again felt the tightness of his neck muscles. "Did you hit me?"

From about fifteen yards away, she heard him. "Yes. I don't like being followed. Have you ever been followed before?"

"I'm not trying to follow you. I'm trying to find you and let you know that I think you're in danger," Hutch said, as he began to try to pull his wrists apart.

Rose got nearer, but didn't respond. Then she crouched down to look into Hutch's eyes.

"We felt like we were *going to be* followed. Then you followed us. You *are* the danger. Am I wrong?"

"I wanted to help you ... to hide or do something that would not let Mata take them." Hutch moved his head toward the kids.

"Where's he planning to take us?" Greg came around Rose's shoulder.

"He doesn't take people unless they agree to study with him."

"He's not gonna steal us?" asked Virg.

"He hasn't stolen anyone. But he's not going to ask your parents. He only wants your interest ... and agreement." Hutch looked into Greg's eyes and then turned to look at Virg.

"What is he offering?" asked Virg.

"He wants to know if you're satisfied with your life or if you want something more."

"He can help us with this?" asked Greg. He looked down at his hands for a moment. "Like you kinda did?"

"You're different than most kids ... most people. Sometimes, you have to be my age to *want* to work at something. When you're a kid, it's easier to change your life."

Doug turned toward Rose and made a painful expression. "Can you untie me? I have to touch my neck. Gosh, my head hurts."

"*You* have already changed their lives. They don't feel safe at this moment," responded Rose.

Hutch curled his legs and said to the boys, "Your life always changes when this skill shows up. You're lucky this happened so early. As a kid, you have time to work on your skills. Besides, I haven't really taught you anything. You guys have gotten better on your own."

Greg and Virg looked at each other, then looked back at Hutch.

"... but I don't know if Mata can help you anymore. Things have been different, lately." Hutch closed his eyes again and stayed still.

He opened his eyes and turned his gaze toward Rose. "She's right."

Hutch turned back toward the kids. "You can trust her, but I don't know if you can trust Mata. Besides, I think that he'll find you."

"What about a tryout? Can we show him what we can do and leave if it doesn't work out?" Virg raised his shoulders.

"People have died at his camp, right? He pushes people," said Greg.

Hutch almost whispered, "He wants to see your limits. Your potential."

"Is this about him or them?" Rose pointed at the kids.

"It used to be about them. Everyone like them," responded Hutch.

"Has it been happening for a long time?" she asked.

"It hasn't seemed like a long time, but . . ." Hutch closed his eyes and rested his head back down on the dirt, "he's been writing what he calls a 'historic manual' or dictionary or something. Can you please take these off now? I want to help." Hutch wrestled with his tied-up ankles and wrists.

Rose moved closer to him. "He's writing a book? Who's it about? Regardless, what the heck is going on at that camp?"

"What if we don't have any limits?" said Greg.

"I feel like we've been teaching ourselves way more than you have." Virg raised his shoulders looking at Hutch.

"We've been seeing much more than you told us about," added Greg. "I've looked through your eyes."

"I was looking through Mata's eyes right before you arrived," said Virg.

Hutch's head whipped over to look into Virg's eyes. "If that's true, I'd bet he knows where you are right now. And he'll be trying to find you."

Rose kneeled down, grabbed Hutch's chin, and took his attention back. "What's the manual about?"

Hutch looked at Rose and rested his head on the grass again. He closed his eyes. "It's about all the possible gifts we can have. It's about how to create, find, and improve your skills. He needs more examples and wants to help those who discover their skills. It might make their gifts more accepted. His book could be a way-of-life manual."

"But if you're worried about him, does he include the negative examples? Mistakes he's made?" asked Rose.

"I haven't read it."

"So, you're guessing." Rose threw her hands in the air and turned away from Hutch, pacing back and forth.

Greg took a step forward. He reached down and put his hand on Hutch's shin. He collected a fistful of Hutch's pants and raised them until they reached just above his kneecap. He looked at the skin and saw the scar he had seen in Hutch's memory.

"I saw your memory. That little girl *did* stab you. You hid it from me somehow. Why should I trust you?"

"It's amazing that you can see other people's memories already," said Hutch. He smiled.

Greg stood up quickly and backed away. He turned to look into Rose's eyes. "Let's get out of here."

She looked into Greg's eyes and turned to face Hutch. "We've got nowhere else to go," said Rose. "Also, if Mata's on his way, we might need backup."

She grabbed the knife from Virg's backpack and crouched behind Hutch.

"You want to help us, right?" she held the knife to Hutch's neck.

"I want to keep you safe," said Hutch, looking into her eyes. "You were such a good teacher back then—probably a better one than me. These kids are more advanced than any I've met. I want to help."

Rose's breath trembled for a moment. She grabbed the strap on Hutch's wrists and pulled his hands away from his back. She lifted him lightly off the ground and pulled the knife through the strap. He rolled a bit and put his hands on the ground. The knife went between his ankles as Rose lifted the strap. It popped open.

Hutch stayed down and sat with his knees up. His arms wrapped around his knees, and he stretched his back to a curve that pushed his stomach onto his thighs. Pushing his head up and back, he let out a big breath and lightly cracked his spine.

"Ahhhh," he moaned as the crack made the others flinch. Then he grabbed the back of his head and petted the back of his neck. "Man, I don't remember that hit, but I feel it now."

Rose walked down to the lake and dipped a cloth in it. She twisted it and let go of the water on her way back up the hill. Placing it flat on the back of Hutch's neck, she said, "So, you've saved people's lives before, I assume. Got any ideas?"

Glider

The glider was silently rolling through the sky around the cloud level. Pete was flying through wide berths, fixating on panels of the fields and forests. Looking for those little guys, he made his way over the ridge for a fourth time. Passing by the valley, he turned port as he reached the further ridge. When he turned, his view through the cockpit window opened wide. He saw a nice large lake below.

Before he leveled out, he focused on the hill beside the lake. For an instant, a little color of copper caught his eye. The sun hit it. He looked back quickly, as a head of red hair caught his eye. A collection of green plants surrounded her. *Must be Rose*, he thought. He looked back up at the panel for a moment and then shot his glance back down. A shine bounced off some form of metal near the same spot. Was that a canteen or a tent?

I found 'em, thought Pete. He leveled out the glider and pulled back on the handlebars for a moment. He punched the walkie button and said, "I see where the fam is hiding."

The static on Pete's walkie stayed solid for a few moments and then he heard, "Thanks, Pete. Are they okay?"

"All I see is camping and fishing gear around them."

"Have you seen the other guy?"

"Not yet," responded Pete, "but I found 'em. I'll make another pass."

He knew that he had to fly in a wide circle to get a better look. Swiftly floating over the mountain range, he looked back down at the fields he initially passed. A heavy shadow kept moving through the fields, rolling across the corn roots. The moving animal looked like a small bear. But it wasn't rambling; it was just hovering across the field. Its long shadow didn't move. It just followed him without moving. Pete's gaze shifted and saw a little figure moving quickly without shifting its weight.

"Is that thing flying?" he asked out loud.

Pressing the walkie, Pete said, "Can that old dude fly?"

He waited a few moments. Then he heard Tim's voice. "Say again."

"I think I'm seeing somebody fly." Pete released the button.

The static lasted for about five seconds on his walkie.

"Ummm, is someone flying? . . . Like, up where you are?" Doug responded.

"No, but that thing I saw, he has a shadow that's not connected to him. I think he's hovering toward your family." He stopped for a minute. ". . . Over."

About a foot above the ground, the man held his hand open. His palm angled down at the sliced cornfield beneath his feet. He was looking at the tracks of the kids and their followers. His fingers pointed forward, and he floated in that direction. Aimed behind him, his feet never touched the dust or the shadow that followed.

He wasn't pushing his pace. Moving at a jogging speed, he kept his eyes down—right on the track of the trail. Mata's nostrils kept flashing wide open as he followed the same scent.

When he reached the base of the mountain chain, he slowed his pace a bit. Footmarks progressed across the mountain wall at a low angle. It looked as though the boys had avoided the vertical steepness directly ahead. Mata raised his eyes toward the peak, and then rolled them down the hillside. To his left, he saw a dirt path surrounded by tall pampas grass on either side. A light breeze made the plumy and white flowers sway at the tips. Just beyond, the trail rose slowly and continued over a lower rim of the hill.

He sucked in a whiff of the surrounding scents. The corn behind him took his attention, and then some notes of pine rolled into his nostrils for a moment. He turned his head and continued on the path as he caught a smell of peanut powder from a bag of nuts. His lips broke into a smile, exposing the warm color of his teeth.

Turning his fingers toward the trail, his body swiftly floated up the hill. He stopped for a moment and let his feet rest down onto the trail. Closing his eyes, he touched his skull just above his ear and turned his face toward the peak of the mountain. For a moment, his mind opened wide. Almost peering through the mountain directly, images of the lake and the small family flew through his introspection. The ginger red of Rose's hair flicked past Mata's view. He lifted his eyelids.

I'm close, he thought, sharing with anyone around. No one had heard his projected thought. All he heard was silence. No response came back to him from the boys. A squirrel scurried by him and hopped onto a tree. He looked back at the trail and then opened his hand toward the ground. Mata's body rose from the silted footpath, and he flew up the side of the mountain.

56

Pete had made another short haul around the hills and let the dads know where their kids were. He saw Rose and Hutch for a moment, and then they disappeared. The two boys were still standing next to the lake.

Pete pressed his walkie button. "I saw 'em, but the adults . . . I don't know where they went. Over."

Tim looked at Doug. "You think they know that a guy is floating toward them?"

Doug shook his shoulders. "Who knows? They probably do."

"Let's head over and help . . . if we can," said Tim.

"Let's save Pete first. It's better if we have another person to bring with us."

Tim wiggled his mustache for a moment to think. "Yeah. Bring him down."

Doug pressed the button on his walkie. "Pete, is there a safe place to land?"

"Well, I might try to hit a road or something . . . uh, it's not really fun to just roll into a cornfield," he responded.

Tim and Doug looked at each other and then turned to the road. They both hustled down the hill and made their way over the bridge. Harvested fields surrounded a flat spot on the road. However, it wasn't that long. The bridge ended the east side and trees and mailboxes were about forty yards down the road on either side. The landing spot west of the bridge didn't look very long.

"You think he could land here?" Tim looked at the guardrails on the bridge. They were about six feet off the ground.

"It looks tight," said Doug.

"He's good at this, right?"

"Who knows?" Doug shrugged. "He got off the ground. He can get back down . . . right?"

Tim looked back up into the sky. The glider was floating above.

Doug noticed Tim's worried look. He pressed the button on the walkie and said, "Just west of the bridge, there's a clear spot on the road, but it doesn't look that long."

There was silence on the radio for a few moments.

"Hokeydoke," Pete said through the walkie. "Looks kinda short, but it's better than kinda rocky."

He curled the glider around and began his descent. Doug ran down the hill toward Pete's descent to cover any traffic near the bridge. Tim ran down the hill too. He rushed past Doug and stood on the road, waving his arms. Tim stopped just around the area he hoped Pete was aiming to land on.

Pete began to lower the lever as he aimed the vehicle at the bridge. As he began to descend, his knees began to wobble. The elevation meter on the dashboard was falling fast. It looked like he'd touch the road just behind Tim, but the landing didn't look long enough. Keeping the glider angled toward the road, he whipped down fast and connected. His back wheels touched the ground once and his front wheel popped off the road once before it returned. Pete pumped his emergency brake, and the glider screeched loud as one back tire ripped and kept sliding across the road. As it squealed, the glider tore four mailboxes out of the ground as it grinded past them. The angle of the road raised as Pete rolled up toward the post office. Luckily, the glider stopped about an inch from a pine tree.

Tim and Doug ran toward the glider. A car was rolling down the road toward the cockpit. It stopped just as Tim and Doug reached the glider. The width of its wings closed off both lanes on the road. Pete popped open the cockpit window and stood up.

"Ooof, my butt is stiff," he said.

"Let's get ya down and roll this thing off the road." Doug raised his hand to Pete and helped him get out of the glider.

As he exited the little cockpit, Pete made a bunch of uncomfortable noises as his joints cracked. The driver who stopped opened his car door and got out. He stood next to the car, and his mouth dropped wide open.

Tim turned to the guy and said, "Yeah, we've been seeing crazy stuff too. Give us just a minute if ya don't mind."

"I've never seen a plane land right in front of me. I thought I was driving on a runway for a moment," said the driver.

"Just give us a minute," said Doug. "Sorry about the pit stop."

The three men gripped the wings and the cockpit, just like they did before the takeoff. Raising it up, they turned back onto the road and walked it down the middle until they reached the field. Turning toward the corn stumps, they kept moving it until it was off the road. They rested it down in the field and turned back toward the guy who was still standing and looking amazed. He had followed them a bit.

Pete waved at the man and said, "Thanks for not crashing into us! I tried to do the same with you."

The driver barely smiled and waved at Pete. He jogged back and hopped into his car. Slowly, he drifted by the men. The driver stared at the glider and picked up his speed as he drove past it.

Tim was checking the status of the wings and the wheels. "No dents in the wings. Those mailboxes must've been pretty light." Tim kept walking around the glider. "There's one wheel that popped, but I'm not surprised."

He turned toward Pete. "Holy crap, man," he smiled, "you really did it. You flew it, it's not on fire, and you didn't die."

"Yeah. What were you expecting?" Pete smiled.

Doug and Tim hugged him at the same time.

Virg and Greg stood by the lake with their fishing lines in the water. The sun reflected off the lake and warmed their faces. Virg squeezed the rod as his mind rolled around the plan. It wasn't really about fishing.

Glider

They were waiting for Mata to arrive. Hutch and Rose made themselves invisible and waited up on the hill to see what Mata would do. They planned to protect the children and contain Mata, somehow, when he arrived.

Virg didn't speak; he just shared his thoughts with Greg. *Are we supposed to be scared of this new Mata guy?*

Greg didn't turn to look at him but responded as he kept his eyes on the water. *Well, Hutch seems afraid of him . . . and Hutch is a BIG guy.*

You saw Hutch fight at that party, and he seemed like a karate champion or something, right? Virg thought.

Greg pulled his fishing line in and whipped it back into the pond. He let the memory pass. *I dunno. It feels like we can protect ourselves, to me. We figured out how to use telekinesis. We can make ourselves invisible. We're talking right now without actually* speaking, *ya know?*

The two boys looked at each other and smiled.

Virg touched Greg's shoulder. When he turned, Virg thought, *Thank you. You're a good friend.*

Virg wrapped his arms around Greg, and they hugged.

Greg said out loud, "I'm gonna catch a fish first!" He whipped his reel quickly as Virg did the same. Nothing was caught. The silence returned.

They left their lines in the lake and waited. Sitting back down with their lines in the water, they didn't move. No one would have known if they kept having a conversation. It was silent and easily flowing from one mind to the other. Calming sounds of robins, toads, and bees lightly filled the air around them. Time passed by as the sun rolled across the sky. Separated clouds wheeled past the sun every few minutes.

The boys forgot about their mission while Mata floated down the hill with no sound. As he approached the boys, he let his body lower until he touched the ground. The boys sat next to each other with their lines in the lake. Mata took steps toward them.

He got closer and asked, "Can I show you the best way to fish? You may not need the rods."

Both boys turned and dropped their rods on the ground as they stood up. Mata raised his hands to show the boys that he didn't intend to touch them. He kept walking toward the lake as the boys moved out of his way. They watched him lower one hand and crouch down toward the rim of the lake.

"To find them, close your eyes. Put your hand into the water. Touch the stones in the basin and feel the vibrations."

He kept his eyes shut and lowered his hand into the water.

Wrapping his fingers around a stone, he said, "Now, raise your hand off the stones and feel the movements within the standing water."

He whipped his hand up and out of the water. Mata opened his eyes. As he did, the lake burst. Greg and Virg saw a myriad of different fish floating above the water. They all dripped, and it sounded like a tiny storm passed right in front of them.

"Tell me which one you like." Mata kept his hand pointed at the lake and turned his eyes to the boys.

Virg widened his eyes across the field of floating catch. It looked as if all the coins in a wishing well had been pulled out and hovered above the rim. They all wiggled about three feet above the water. A two-foot-long trout had a freckled purple tummy with deep green shading. It twitched hard and grabbed Virg's attention. Mata saw the kid's focus and let floating fish fall straight back into the lake.

It almost sounded like the beginning of an Olympic swimming race. The splash bounced up and slapped down, leaving bubbles across water. The lake looked like the top of a lemon meringue pie.

"You like this one, do you?" Mata and Virg kept their eyes on the long trout.

"... It looks pretty big," said Virg.

"Hungry?" Mata kept his hand up, pointing at the fish and looked at Greg.

"Yeah, *I'm* hungry. Almost always," said Greg.

Mata looked back at the long trout. Turning his hand from the lake toward land, the trout whipped away from the center of the lake and stopped two feet in front of him. When it reached them, its shook its rear fin. Raising his left hand to match his right, he closed his eyes.

Virg and Greg watched as the fish began to vibrate. When Mata moved his hands farther apart, the bones in the fish started to snap and slip out of the scales. Both boys took a step away. Mata raised his wrinkled eyelids as a popping sound came from the fish's muscles. It was all held in a sphere floating over the grass in front of them. As he opened his eyes and raised his middle finger, the bones laid themselves in the grass.

"There's no blood," said Virg. "Wicked."

"How'd you do that?" asked Greg.

"You'll have more questions in a moment." Mata raised his gaze above the boys and found a stump. It was sitting about five feet from their tent. He pointed his left hand at it and snapped his fingers.

The boys turned around as a sound caught their ears. A fire burst from the top of the stump behind them.

"Fire!" shouted Virg.

He turned toward the lake and then looked for a bucket. Then he realized that there were no buckets or anything to collect water in. Virg turned back to look at the fire.

"We can control it," Mata said. He moved his hands from the lake toward the lit-up stump. The trout followed from one side to the other. Before the carcass reached the flame, Mata flicked his pinky finger as a vein burst in the fish. The blood was removed, and it floated up above the trout's body. He circled his hands to move the blood pool beneath the muscles. Conducting just an inch forward, the fish followed Mata's hands. Cooking above the flames, the blood disintegrated. He turned his hands and pulled the pieces apart, then floated them to the rims of the flame. This movement lowered the cooking temperature before they were ready to eat. As he held the three pieces in place, he turned toward the boys.

"Are you hungry?" he asked.

"I wasn't, but that smells pretty good." Greg stood up and took a step toward the fire to inspect.

"Greg," said Mata, "stay where you are."

Greg stopped and looked back at the old man.

"Can you raise your hand and bring that piece to yourself?"

"Which one?" asked Greg.

Mata twitched his fingers and one thick-flaked piece of fish began to slowly spiral in the air. Greg understood. He raised his hand toward the fish and stopped the slow turning in the air. Pulling his hand back, the cooked piece dripped a touch of moisture on the grass. It floated toward Greg, and he held it in front of his head. He turned to look at Mata.

"It's cooked, right? You're not poisoning us or anything? I feel like I have to ask."

Mata smiled and lifted his hand toward the floating piece in front of Greg. He twitched his finger and a tiny section ripped itself from the body. Whipping his finger toward himself, the piece quickly shot into his mouth. He chewed, closed his eyes to show his enjoyment, and swallowed.

"Tastes pretty good to me. Let me know if it's up to par with your cooking," said Mata.

Greg turned back to look at the piece of fish. He raised his other hand and twisted and pulled his hands apart in the air. The floating piece matched his motions. A tiny scrap was ripped from the top corner, and Greg combed his fingertips toward his mouth.

The pinky-orange piece reached his tongue, and he bit down.

"Wow, it's tender," said Greg. "Virg, snag a piece."

Virg had already lifted his hand and began to pull a piece of fish from the fire. As the section reached him, he rippled his hands back and forth and began to break the meat into pieces. He held his hands in one position and began to blow back and forth to cool down the steaming pieces. Flipping his fingers one by one, Virg shot little pieces into his mouth and chewed quickly.

"Dang. Dis dish ish purty gurd," Virg got out as he chewed.

Mata smiled and let out a breath, showing his satisfaction.

"You both are quite natural," Mata said. He curled his hand and let his fingertips roll toward his palm. The meat remaining over the fire lightly spun around in the air as he pulled it near to him. He connected his fingertips and slowly pulled them open. The filet ripped to pieces, and he began to lure them into his gullet.

Virg finished the fish. "So, this was pretty good . . . umm . . . You have a camp for people like us? And your name's Mata?"

The man sat down on the grass and crossed his legs. He leaned forward and coughed lightly. "Yes, my name is Mata. I help run a community of people like you. Many call it a camp because it's in a forest. It's a society. I invite people with skills like yours."

Greg sat down across from Mata. "I've seen some of the things that happen at your camp. It looks dangerous."

"What have you seen?" asked Mata.

"I've dreamt things, and it feels like I'm watching someone else's memories," responded Greg.

Mata stared into the kid's eyes. "Gregory, memories and dreams are not the same. You can receive information through dreams, but your own perspective of those may not be the reality."

Greg looked down at the grass and let his mind wander. Was he just imagining all of this? No.

"I saw Hutch's memory of a little kid stabbing him in the leg." Greg took a breath. "But he removed the scar when I looked."

"Maybe he didn't want to show how dangerous it was to explore your possibilities." Mata looked deeper into Greg's eyes while leaning forward. "Or maybe he didn't want to show you how dangerous it is for him to teach people like you."

He turned his eyes to Virg and then glanced up the hill.

"I smell Hutch." He looked back down at Virg. "And your mother."

"They think that you're dangerous," Virg whispered.

"I am. I don't think that limits are healthy for someone like you. Do you want to see what you can do?" Mata raised his shoulders. "Do you feel like you waste your time in school when you have these skills and you're not focusing on them?"

Greg jumped in. "We taught ourselves telekinesis in the cafeteria garden."

Virg kept his eyes on Mata. "But is it dangerous?"

Mata turned to Virg. "I can't promise to keep you safe. I only have a few skills—same as you. But I will be there for you if you try to open your potential. I encourage your progression."

"Can I fly?" asked Virg.

Mata rested his hand on the ground. He pushed against it, and his body naturally rose a few inches off the grass. He kept his hand flat, but removed it from the earth. His legs remained crossed, and he raised his back into a straight position. He was floating a few inches off the ground.

"This, you can learn." Mata smiled.

Hutch and Rose appeared out of nowhere behind Mata. Her arms were extended, and a ball of light surrounded Hutch. Sitting in a lotus position with his eyes closed, Hutch's hands lay on his knees. Then he tossed a pebble beneath the floating man.

Hutch closed his eyes, and the boys saw him take a deep breath with his jaw wide open. A low groan, so low that it seemed too deep for it to be Hutch's actual voice, shot out of his mouth. The tone of voice began to grind, and he raised his hands slightly. As it did, the pebble floated up an inch and quickly whipped around in a circle.

The boys watched the stone heat itself and morph into an orange color. As it whipped even faster, the color shifted into red and then a bright yellow.

Virg turned his eyes up to meet Mata's. It seemed like the old man knew what was happening. The elder let his eyes wrinkle up as he smiled back at Virg. It looked like the man knew what was happening but didn't feel worried or surprised.

Hutch stopped groaning and sucked in a breath. The vibration around the stone stopped. The pebble shifted into a light blue. Hutch raised his hands another inch, and the steam, escaping the stone, swung around in an open cone. Wrapping the bubble Rose held around Mata, the cone squeezed around it.

Mata raised his hand and turned to Rose. "Your boys are far different from the rest. Can you raise them to the peak of their potential? At this age, they can perform almost anything they try."

"Potential? Depends on my values. Do you focus on magic performances or thoughts about their well-being?" she responded.

He turned back to the kids and lowered his hand. The light from the stone pinched the ball he was held in, and he disappeared as the stone let out a wisp of smoke.

Rose lowered her hands, and Hutch opened his eyes. The boys looked past the smoke at the adults. They looked tired.

Hutch and Rose looked at the kids and smiled, but the boys didn't smile back.

57

Rose and the kids had packed the tents and fishing rods. The people who sent Mata back to the forest began walking back home, climbing over the mountain.

"I know you have questions," said Rose.

"Why are we so afraid of him?" asked Greg.

Hutch took the reins. "He has let people die, Greg. We don't want that for you."

"It seems like you don't really want to *teach* me, either. Am I right?"

"That's not it at all." Hutch let out a breath that sounded frustrated. "The best teachers for us are ourselves."

"What does that even mean?" Virg seemed short-tempered. He threw up his hands.

Hutch turned to Virg. "If you're a teacher, experiments are important. Experience is important. Just like observation and protection."

"So, we're students?" asked Greg.

Hutch sounded calm. "He wants you to teach yourself. I let you do that too. Like him, I think it's helpful to be your own teacher, but you're not ready to be one yet."

"Why not? You keep mentioning our age. Aren't we at the right age to experiment?" asked Greg.

Rose spoke. "Yes, but not old enough for protection. What do you know about protecting the person next to you?" she shook her head toward Virg. "There should be things you focus on before experimenting."

"We've been teaching ourselves for a week. I'm not even the same person I was seven days ago." Greg threw his hands up at his sides and looked down. "I can't even think the same way. Stuff just jumps into my brain."

Virg added, "And we've taught ourselves at school. 'Experimenting' is really the only option, so far."

"Patience," said Rose. "That is the best option you have. One week doing this has not given you everything you need to know."

Rose and Hutch were walking in front of the boys. A silence hit them as they stopped turning around to check on the kids. It seemed like they both had worries of their own. As they reached the peak, they turned onto the long path that rimmed around and down across the hillside.

As they made their way down, the four of them took a peek over the field and the next hill. They spotted two guys walking across the field wearing camouflage. The third guy they saw was what drew their eye. A hot orange shirt on Pete's torso was viewable from over a mile away.

Rose stopped walking, closed her eyes, and mentally contacted Doug. *We're okay. You can see us up on the hill in front of you. We sent that guy packing.*

She waved her arm back and forth above her head. They saw the three hikers in the field stop moving. A moment later, Doug made the same waving gesture as Rose and pointed at them with his other hand. The guy in the orange shirt stopped moving and put his hands on his knees and leaned forward. Hutch let out a little laugh when they saw Pete fall down. The orange belly fell back as Pete lay down and spread his limbs onto the field. He stayed just like that for a while.

Lying in the field and feeling exhausted, Pete closed his eyes for about twenty minutes. A few crunchy sounds woke him up. He opened his eyes again and turned his head. Rose and her party were trudging through the field, looking right at him.

"I'm glad you're getting some rest," she said. "Doug told me about your flight. Thanks for trying to find us." She smiled and crouched down to pat Pete's chest. She got up and walked over to Doug for a hug.

Pete blinked again and wiped his eyes with his wrist. Then he stretched his legs, adding, "Oh yeah. No problem."

"You used my glider, right?" asked Hutch.

Pete opened his eyes as Hutch crouched down next him, taking Rose's place.

"Uh . . . Was that your glider?" asked Pete. He wished he were still asleep.

"Any repairs necessary?" asked Hutch.

"Looks pretty good. Maybe a wheel or something . . .?" Pete let his mind rush to find a reason. "I gave you a ride home last night, right?"

Hutch smiled. "If it's just a tire, that's no biggie." He extended his hand and lifted Pete off the ground into a standing position. "You care a lot about these people, huh?"

Pete raised his shoulder. "Who doesn't?"

58

When they left the fields and hiked back on the side of the road, Greg, who ended the line of hikers, looked back at the hillside. His eyes rolled up the hill, where his adventure had begun. Staring into the trees, he saw two little eyes between the tall grasses. It was that little dark grey fox. He saw its orange-rimmed ears whip forward and open in his direction. It wasn't late afternoon yet, but that fox looked wide awake. Greg smiled for a moment and turned back toward the group.

At the Murphys' house, the furniture on the porch looked quite comfy. The hikers had spent so much energy that they all wanted to lie down. The couches and chairs looked like they offered them naps for the rest of the day. All plopping down on the cushions at the same time, they looked at one other.

Doug began the conversation. "Well, that guy," he took a deep breath, "he was pretty weird, huh? He left without you, right, Hutch?"

The big guy lifted his hand to massage the back of his neck. "Yeah, he's gone."

Greg jumped in. "He left without us."

"That's kind of the point," said Rose.

"Thanks for protecting these guys," said Tim to Hutch. "And I'm sorry about your glider."

Hutch nodded, showing that it was okay.

"So, why didn't you go back with him?" Doug asked. "You're working with him. Am I wrong?"

"Why couldn't *we* go back with him?" Virg looked upset.

"We're trying to keep you guys safe," said Rose.

"It's not safe to be independent?" Virg sounded angry. "That guy showed us how to find food and cook for ourselves. That's not something that *you've* taught us."

Rose kept her composure, looking back at her son. "I've taught you lots of things, Virgil. But you're still in school. There's a lot more for you to learn at this point in your life. Cooking and camping are important and interesting, but you need structure. You need a rhythm. You're still a human being."

"I'm a kid whose life completely changed in the past week. If you think I'm cool with just learning cursive and playing kickball, you're not feeling what I'm feeling. I've learned how to teach myself all sorts of things." Virg stood up and looked at Greg. "We've been better teachers than you."

He started walking out of the yard toward the alley. Then he turned and looked at Rose. "Mata's been a better teacher than you . . . in five minutes."

Grabbing the fence, he pulled it open and nodded at Greg. His friend stood up and followed him toward the alleyway.

"Hey, get back here." Rose stood up and followed them.

"I don't want structure," said Virg.

Doug looked at Hutch and said, "Well, your boss is a better teacher than you, huh?"

"He's not bad," responded Hutch.

"I'm imagining that it's dangerous if they take lessons from your boss, right?" said Tim.

Hutch looked at Tim. "It'd be very different."

Rose followed the boys around the fence and onto the alley. They had turned away from her and were walking toward the park.

Calmly, she started. "Listen, Virgil, I love you. Please don't run off. We want to keep you safe. Stay with us. We'll give you some time alone, I promise. Just relax and rest."

Virg stopped and turned around, looking at his mom. She looked worried. She looked afraid. For a moment, he felt sorry for her. Greg took some steps back toward Virg's mom. He gave her a hug and looked up at her.

"Can I just grab a baseball and some gloves from the garage?" Greg smiled at her. "We just need a little time alone. A toss in the park is cool with you?" He took a step back and shrugged his shoulders. "It's still Saturday."

Rose smiled and took a step back. She reached up to take a tear out of her eye before she let it roll down her cheek. Looking at Virg, she asked, "Can I get one from you too?"

He walked over and hugged her. As their eyes met, Rose smiled. Virg gave her a little squeeze and let go. She didn't see a reaction from him. When Virg led the other boy up the alley, Rose couldn't look away. Watching them hike up the alley, she waited until they walked past the bushes and turned onto the road's rim.

The boys ambled down the road with no plan and looked tired. Their steps dragged across the sandy dirt beside the road. Barely raising their knees, they left dragged footprints along the road. Their keisters and hamstrings were still recovering from the hikes around the lake.

"So, they're afraid of Mata," said Virg.

Greg turned to him.

Virg continued, "... but he seemed pretty calm, right?"

Shrugging his shoulders, Greg said, "I mean, he looks *old*. But people who get that old are either totally calm or upset about *everything*, right?" He lifted both hands and wiggled them up and down, weighing each option.

Virg raised his shoulders. "I mean, he seemed pretty chill. Plus, the guy showed us how to do tons of stuff in, like, one minute."

"Well, your mom showed us how to communicate and hide our thoughts last night," said Greg. He tugged a little leather knot on his baseball glove.

Dragging his feet with each step, it looked like Virg wasn't interested in defending his mom. He punctuated with each step, "But. She's. My. Mom." Standing up straight and skipping to his side, he said, "I want to fish with my hand and cook on a fire I just made." Virg put his hand to his head and used his other hand to mimic Mata. Moving his hand, he imagined that he dragged a fish out of the road and cooked it over a neighbor's front yard. "She didn't teach us that," he added.

Greg stopped walking. "It still feels like Hutch can't really answer our questions. And I think that he won't, even after what happened today. Your mom did, a bit, but she doesn't want to share everything with us." Greg turned and began to walk into the baseball field's parking lot. "You think Mata can? He probably has more experience."

Virg waited a moment to answer. "You think the oldie would've woken us up last Sunday?"

"If he did . . ." Greg stopped for a moment. "Would he have shared as many memories as Hutch did? Did pilot man plan to do that?"

"He told us that he made a mistake. Also, the first thing we saw him do was a mistake. He landed in a cornfield." Virg took a step out of the parking lot and walked over to the dugout on the baseball field.

Greg followed him, and they both sat down on the bench, out of the sun. He turned to Virg. "I want to go to school."

Virg looked perplexed. "It's Saturday."

Greg smirked. "Mata's school. We'll be the teachers. That's what everyone has said to us over the past week. We should be our own teachers."

Reaching his hand out, Virg looked at Greg. "Let's find out how to get up there."

"Maine?" asked Greg, as he put his hand down onto Virg's.

"I've been teaching myself for a week. So have you. Field trip on three . . . one." Virg lowered his hand.

"Two," said Greg with a chuckle.

"Three."

"Field trip," they said together. Virg got up off the bench, spun the baseball up, and let it fall into his glove. He jogged out onto the first-base line.

Greg got up and followed him. "You got a notebook still?"

"Always," said Virg. He rotated his butt and touched the tiny notebook in his back pocket. A little clasp of a pen hung from the pocket's rim.

"Toss first. Notes second, right?" asked Greg.

"Bunt!" Virg yelled as he ran backward toward the home plate. He threw the ball down on the ground toward Greg.

Running into the field, past first base, Greg lowered his hands and snatched the ball. He turned and fired it back at Virg. It smacked into the kid's palm and made Virg's face crinkle.

In a deep announcer voice, Virg yelled, "Ouchies. That hit the pitcher right in his palm. That's gotta hurt! Also, that stinky first baseman didn't even try to get the batter out at his base. What a stinky teeeeeeam!" He raised his arms and made an open-mouthed crinkled sound, mocking a huge audience.

Both boys let out a laugh and kept firing pitches at each other. For a moment, they didn't worry about or notice the animal keeping its eyes on them.

"You remember how they transported the old guy outta here, right?" Virg asked Greg.

"It looked like they let him float a little, then dropped a spinning stone, and pumped him outta here," Greg said as he threw the ball back.

"In theory, does the stone matter?" Virg caught the ball and chucked it back.

"Ugh, I dunno," Greg responded. The ball hit his mitt. "I'd guess you could use any kind of rock. We saw that little sucker spin, I remember. The really important part was how Hutch sounded. His voice sounded like a deep canyon echo . . . I think."

Having been following the boys silently from the hillside, the fox was lying low in the creek bed, between the field and the forest. It kept its eyes on the two boys as if it could hear their conversation.

"I'll try it! It's groan time!" Virg yelled. He dropped down into a squat. Above his head, he smacked his hand against his glove. He looked like a king crab with mismatched pincers. A thin, prepubescent groan began spouting from Virg.

Greg tossed the baseball up into the air, raised his other hand, and held it spinning in the air. He closed his eyes and thought about Mata. Not knowing where the blue-eyed fisherman was, Greg just kept the image of the old man's face in his mind.

Virg looked at the ball and raised his hand. As he did, it began to spin so fast that smoke raised off the top. A moment passed, then a blast of fire pounded in every direction from it. The flames spun into an upside-down cone above the ball.

Ending his howl, Virg watched the ball turn into a deep red. The flame didn't stop changing. Greg took a step back, and the floating ball shifted to purple. Not even a second later, the ball and flame rippled into blue.

"Greg!" Virg looked at his friend and pulled his baseball glove off his hand.

With his hand steady and still pointing at the ball, Greg shook his head in disbelief.

"You know where it's going?" said Virg.

"Nope, but I can see his face." Greg shook his shoulders.

"Whose face?" asked Virg.

"I remember where Hutch walked with that little girl. I see it."

Virg looked amazed. "Let's try!"

He lifted his knee, pulled his weight back, and chucked the baseball glove at the twirling flame. Spiraling up and over the first-base line, the glove dropped down and into the flame. It held there for a moment, finished its spin, and disappeared into a plume of smoke above.

"Strike one!" Virg let out with a laugh. He jumped up and down twice in his excitement.

The two boys looked at each other and then looked back at the flame.

"I'm keeping this open," said Greg as he lowered his hand and kept the ball hovering a few inches from the ground.

"You *do* know where it's going, right?" said Virg.

"Yeah, I can feel it's going in the right direction." Greg nodded and closed his eyes. An image passed in his consciousness. Within his vision, he saw the place where the kid ripped that tree apart. The place where Hutch got stabbed in the thigh. Greg knew that was close to Mata. "I see it," he said.

Virg smiled and began running toward the ball. "I trust you," he screamed. He jumped up into the air over the ball.

As his feet came down toward the blue cone of flames, his body spun around for a millisecond. He kept falling down as his body separated into smoke clouds and swiftly disappeared.

Greg couldn't believe what he saw. "How are we doing this?" he said. He laughed at himself and his disbelief for a moment. Then he shook his head and slowly took four steps back and supposed that he'd do the same thing that Virg did. He clapped his hands, rubbed them together, and crouched down.

The moment he did, he saw a movement at the corner of his left eye. He didn't want to explain what he was doing and didn't care if anyone saw him transported to somewhere else. He took two running steps forward; the thing he didn't look at was almost right beside him. He pumped another step on the ground and lifted his leg for a fourth step. Jumping beside him, he saw the grey and orange fox leaping at the same time. Before he could stop himself, the fox's shoulder connected with his hip. They whipped around in a circle together just above the flame.

To Greg, it looked as though they went up, not down. The sensation of floating for a moment made him feel like a cloud in the sky. He felt as if his body and mind were separated into molecules. As the smoke separated and disappeared on the baseball field, his vision became only a deep black color. The balance in Greg's body shifted, like he had turned upside down. His blood rushed to his head for a moment. Before he could even think about where he was, he opened his eyes.

59

Lying on his back, Greg was staring directly up into a thick rim of tree branches. He felt a soft pad of weeds and some thick roots beneath his shoulders. Pushing up to peek around, a person behind him grabbed his armpits and helped lift him until he was standing.

"You invited a fox?" Virg whispered into Greg's ear. He pointed over Greg's shoulder at the fox. It lay with its front paws crossed at the base of a tree. Greg shook his head for a moment.

"I saw it appear right next to you," said Virg. "It got up first."

When the fox saw Greg stand and look at her, she moved her nose toward the big hole in the ground. Greg turned his focus and realized that they had arrived at the place he imagined.

"That's where the girl tore the tree from the ground. This is the place," said Greg.

He turned his focus back to the fox. The black nose of the animal took in a few scents. It stood up and began to pace in a direction. Turning back to them, it shook its nose twice in the same direction.

Virg took a step back. "Dude, does it know where we want to go? I mean, I've never seen a dog invite people in a direction."

"Who are you?" said Greg.

The fox lowered its nose a bit. It looked at them through its eyebrows like a boss staring at its crewmembers impatiently. Then it waved its nose in the same direction again.

The two boys looked at each other and couldn't think of anything to say. Following a fox never really seemed like an option to them. Looking back at the boys and seeing their incomprehension, the fox backed up a few steps and hid behind a sycamore's trunk. For a moment, a soft sound of bones knocking together and a pour of juice onto the dirt rimmed around the forest. The boys both took a step back and held their breath.

"Did that thing just die?" Virg held onto Greg's arm.

They both lost their breath when a human stepped out from behind the tree. Her grey and auburn mane fell down onto her matched overcoat. The jacket was still covered in the fox fur. She looked at them, raised her arm in the direction she suggested, and said, "This way, guys."

"Mom?" Greg said, as he stepped toward her.

"Sue, that's you?" Virg grabbed his bangs, pulled them back and couldn't let go of his head. It looked like his brain had exploded, and he had to hold it together.

"How?" added Greg.

"It's been about a week since you figured out about yourself. I didn't really get a good time to talk to you about this." Sue shrugged her shoulders.

"But we've seen you . . . the fox, like, following us and stuff," said Virg.

"Yeah, you guys were experimenting. Looked like you needed someone to be there for you, just in case you needed some help."

Greg responded, "You know we're in Maine right now, right?"

"I heard you say it," Sue nodded. "Did you hear what I told you all in the backyard a few nights ago? The night when Hutch was grilling."

The two boys looked at each other and had no idea what she was talking about. They both looked back at her with their mouths open.

"I know an oyster farmer not too far from here. I can smell them from here." She raised her nose and pulled in a breath, "I could smell them even while you were still waking up from that transportation," she said to Greg.

"But what about Mata? Do you know where he is?" said Greg.

"I think he can smell as well as I can," she responded.

Virg let go of his hair and slapped his leg. "Oh, man, you're so right. I saw him sniffing a number of times in the fields. That's how he found us?"

"He'll find us again?" asked Greg.

Sue opened her arms. "He might. Want some food before he shows up?" She waved her hands toward herself.

Greg ran over to her and hugged her. She squeezed him tight, then let go and whipped her face in a different direction. A scent pulled her nose toward the pond. Sue began walking toward a lightly salty freshwater pond on the coastline. She waved to the boys to follow her.

After a ten-minute walk, they began to hear the wash and roll of waves in the river. Once they saw it, they followed it downstream to find an extended lake. All of a sudden, the scent of salt popped into Virg and Greg at the same time. A moment later, they both saw a vast collection of water with trees and a dirt beach rimming it. On the far side of the lake, the circle of the forest led to a small opening. They peered through the opening and saw big waves rolling into a small opening. They were looking at the rim of the horizon over the Atlantic.

Letting their eyes inspect the rim of the pond, an oyster farm shack drew their eyes. It had a little dock, a long ranch building, and a stack of oyster cages just sitting on the grass. The rest of the cages were floating just an inch above the rim of the water. They saw it all stacked in a big rectangle. It almost looked like a farm made of floating Legos. All the cages were equally separated and in perfectly straight lines.

Sue pointed at the ranch house. "That's where your uncle works."

"Bryan?" asked Greg. He remembered his uncle's name, but hadn't seen him since his third birthday. He remembered the guy's voice, but not his face.

"Kit? Is that you?" said a man on their left around the lake's rim.

The tone of the voice was exactly what Greg remembered. He whipped his head and saw the orange hair and beard on his uncle's face.

"Uncle Bryan!" Greg shouted.

"Kit! Your kid got huge!" said the man, as he dropped a screwdriver back into his little wooden dinghy. He walked toward them and broke into a smile.

He opened his arms, and Sue walked over to hug him. It'd been years since they saw each other. They held each other for a moment and turned back to the boys. *He's getting older every day*, she thought, looking at her son.

She pointed at the little messy-haired boy beside Greg. "This is Virg, Greg's best friend." He raised his hand, and Bryan smiled and waved at him.

"You know your nephew . . ." began Sue.

Greg ran into Bryan's waist and hugged him.

"Ooooh, I remember you. Do remember when you slapped me right in the eye?" Bryan pointed at his left eye. "I almost lost it that day . . . but it was a good birthday. You didn't like oysters back then." He reached back out and gave Greg another hug.

"Can we stay with you for just a bit?" Sue asked.

"Of course, Kit." Bryan began stepping toward his farmhouse. "What are you kids doing up here today—" He stopped and looked at them all. "And how did you get here?"

Virg jumped in and threw up a hand. "Hang on, why is her name 'Kit'?"

"Well, she figured out how to find stuff . . . in the forest . . . kind of better than us." Bryan realized he'd said too much. He looked back at Sue and stopped speaking.

"It's okay. They saw me turn from a fox back into a human," she said to her brother.

He let out a deep laugh and smiled back to the kids. "Okay, so you know why we call her 'Kit.' She can turn into a fox."

Greg and Virg heard that said out loud for the first time. They stopped walking and realized that she had always had this power. Even her brother knew about it. The two adults didn't see the boys stop and take in the idea.

"Why didn't you tell us?" said Greg.

"You think *we* can do that?" asked Virg.

"Hang on," said Sue. She raised her hands at the boys and turned back to her brother. "We got here because Greg and Virgil figured out that they are the sons of two women with powers that very few people have."

"It's always the moms who can do way more than you think they can," said Greg.

"Totally different than dads," said Virg. He and Greg met eyes and laughed, covering their mouths—trying to hold it in.

Sue continued, pointing at Virg and Greg, "They were visited by a weird old teacher and got inspired, but he was kicked out by Virg's mom and her friend. The old guy wasn't invited and seemed dangerous. Rose worked with him a while ago, but she quit. Greg found out where the teacher was from. Here," she waved at the ground beneath them. "And they got here fast." She rolled her hands around a few times, trying to find a name for it, "by transporting . . . in an old, weird way. He's probably not far from here."

"Wait, *who* is from here?" asked Bryan.

"His name is Mata," said Sue.

Bryan looked at her a moment and then smiled before he said, "Mata? Does he really Mah-tuh that much?" Bryan let out a deep laugh and then looked around at the others. Silence surrounded his punch line. "Mah-tuh? Matter? Does he really matter that much?" He still got no response from them. They looked confused. "Okay, fine." He looked down at the kids and changed the subject. "This teacher matters so much that you needed to come up to Maine to visit him?"

Virg piped up. "I mean, this guy wants us to grow. The two people we were with this whole last week were just trying to hold us back. They barely taught us anything."

"Well, Rose taught us how to keep ourselves safe," noted Greg.

"That sounds pretty helpful," said Bryan.

Virg looked out at the lake. He aimed his arm at a floating oyster cage. Without saying anything, he closed his eyes with the image in his mind. Raising two fingers, a cage was lifted out of the water. It's ropes hung down on either side, still connected to the other cages. Virg could see the specifics of the cage through his link to it. Feeling it through his fingers, it was almost as if he were an inch away. He inspected it and pulled up the latches keeping it closed. Raising the top hatch, he pulled three oysters from the opening. Lowering, locking, and returning the cage to the lake, he kept the shells floating and dripping.

Pulling his hand toward himself, the three oysters flew quickly toward Virg and stopped inches from his hand. With his other hand, he lifted two twigs off the ground and let them hover under the oyster shells. Snapping two fingers onto his palm, a fire burst from the twigs. The shells dried off on the bottom. When they did, Virg snapped the shells open and twirled them upside down. The smoke from the twigs was being caught in the curvature of the shells.

His audience held their silence as he finished the trick. Virg flipped them back over and lifted his pinky finger. The oysters were pulled up from the shell until their little connectors popped clean off.

Bryan, seeing someone float things through the air and prepare an oyster without touching it, sat down on the ground to calm down. He didn't even check to see what he was sitting on. Never having seen anything like this in his life, he took a deep breath.

Virg opened his eyes. "Learning this kind-of-thing in five minutes was pretty helpful too."

He spread his fingers and the little meats hovered toward his treat receivers.

Bryan reached out to grab the oyster with his index finger and his thumb. He pulled it from the air and tossed it in his mouth. He bit twice and swallowed.

"Wow. I might ask you to stay around. Need a little intern gig?" he asked.

Virg looked at him. "I want more lessons from that guy who's around here somewhere."

60

Doug began walking up the alleyway. His wife had asked him to check on the boys before sunset. It was late afternoon. Doug had put his sunglasses and baseball cap on before he hit the approaching sunlight on the horizon. He felt that it was nice to get out of the house and go for a park visit. Also, Rose was right—the kids had been gone for some time.

As Virg's father passed by a few porches, some of his neighbors were hanging out and sipping on some cocktails.

"Hey, how's it goin'?" he said quietly as he connected eyes with them.

The two people were sitting in wooden rocking chairs, wobbling back and forth. They both just waved and took a sip together, watching their neighbor go from one place to another. It seemed like this was their weekend action flick.

Doug kept walking and getting nearer to the park. He turned up the drive and paced slowly into the parking lot. As he turned and climbed the little hill, he smelled something that reminded him of camping. *Mmmmm,* he thought, *smells like leather and firewood.*

He walked down the field toward the home plate. A little ring of black dirt sat a few feet in front of the base. Sitting in the ring of ash was a burnt baseball. The string binding the ball was missing and the rims still stuck to the cork center. Doug leaned over and snatched the ball from the ground. It wasn't hot, but it had been on fire.

Looking behind himself, he inspected the first-base line. Random footsteps were all over that one line. Turning his head and noticing their footprints, he also saw something that looked like dog paws. He kept following the steps and realized that there were no steps that exited the field. It looked like they all just ran to the plate . . . and disappeared.

He began backing away and turned quickly. Doug started jogging back down the hill and across the parking lot. When he hit the entry road, he looked across the street—trying to lock eyes with those neighbors.

Reaching the road, he turned his eyes to his left and jumped back. A car let out a big honk and whizzed by him. He looked at the car and then turned to look back in the direction of his neighbors. The two sippers looked a bit worried.

Standing and grabbing his porch rim, the old man said, "Hey, you okay?"

Doug raised his hand and waved. "I'm okay." He looked both ways and jogged over the road to the porch. He asked the neighbors, "Did you see two kids go into the park today?"

The lady behind the man, sitting in her rocking chair, said, "He didn't. He's been sleeping during the Eagles game."

Doug looked over at her and took a step toward the staircase onto their porch.

She continued. "I saw them walking into the park when I was out here watering my flowers."

"Did you see a dog with them?" asked Doug.

"No," she said and shook her head.

"Well, I saw—" Doug started.

She spoke over him. "But I heard a little firework up there." She pointed at the field. "And you should tell them that I don't like that sound. Our little guinea pigs don't like 'em either. They start screaming when they hear a little boom."

"You heard fireworks?" Doug said.

"I heard somethin'. Sounded like a pop. Like those noisemaker rocks." She pretended to throw something down on the porch floor and then took another sip from her glass.

Doug didn't respond. He had no idea what had happened, but he knew that he had to tell Rose.

"Thanks for your help. Have a good Sunday." He backed away and began to run back toward his home. Rose needed to hear this as soon as possible.

As he ran toward the alley, he heard behind him, "Come by again if ya wanna meet the guinea pigs."

He turned back for a moment and waved. Then he kept running as quickly as he could down the alley.

Rose stared at Doug, and then turned to look at Hutch with weary eyes. She took a deep breath and let it out. Nothing was said.

Hutch took a step toward her. "Should we try to find them?"

She screamed, "Now!" and smacked her hand down on the kitchen table.

He raised his hands out in front for protection. "I think I know where they went." Hutch took a step back and sat down.

"Oh, you do?" Rose sarcastically responded. "I think that we should get to the camp before them."

Hutch shook his head. "I don't know if they went to the camp. They haven't seen it. But I'd bet that they're close."

"Greg saw what you thought about, right?" Rose looked at him.

Hutch corrected Rose. "No, just my memories."

She nodded, then had a thought. "We're not taking your glider, are we?"

"I hope not," said Doug with a worried look on his face.

"It'll only fit one of us." Hutch shook his head. "And I can't leave it here."

Doug nodded, and thought about Pete. "The last pilot was hungover." He thought about Pete's size ". . . probably pretty often, and he barely fit."

"Glad he got home in time for his nap." Rose shrugged her shoulders and turned to Hutch. "How long does it take you to fly back to Maine?"

"Maybe a couple hours? Three-ish? That's a guess. Depends on which direction the wind is blowing in." Hutch shrugged.

"I helped you send your boss back," she said. "Now you have to help me get to him."

"You'll get there before me." Hutch lowered his eyebrows.

"That's the only option we have." She shook her head and sat down, staring at the floor.

Hutch and Rose just stared at the floor for a few moments.

"You two want some dinner before you take another trip?" Doug went over to the stove, took a pot off the wall, and laid it on a burner. He reached into the cabinet and took two soup cans from the shelf.

The two magicians looked at Doug and said, "Thanks."

Rose looked back at Hutch and said, "You're sending me to the camp. Then you can meet me there." She got up and walked over to her front door. On the wall beside it hung a little flower-painted box that held their new mail and a little notebook in it. She pulled the notebook, sat down at the table beside Hutch, and grabbed a pen.

Seizing his hand, she put a pen in it and said, "First off: map that camp for me. I'll know where to go if you don't make it there in time." She poked him in his chest with her finger. "Got it?"

61

Mata opened his eyes. Catching a scent on the breeze, a memory was pulled from his brain. It smelled familiar, but he was unsure. Then he remembered it. Earlier in the same day, he had smelled the corn roots and diesel fuel when he was in the field. He thought about the shoes of those kids. The dust and crumbs on their shoes, maybe the boys too, were somewhere nearby.

The nearest town, about twelve miles south, wasn't what he smelled. They seemed a bit closer. Sitting with his legs crossed, he closed his eyes again and then uncrossed his legs. Pushing his hand on the moss beneath him, he rose to a stand. Turning toward the current of the breeze, he slowly and continuously pulled the odors from the air. It was as if he tasted things nearby. A hint of smoked salt reached his nostrils. It was almost as thin as a single molecule. He took a step forward and hoped that the breeze would continue. The burnt bark almost smelled like a swamp maple tree.

He asked himself, "*The coast?*"

Taking a step backward, he opened his eyes, looking in the direction of the scent. Then he turned away and focused on the camp lodge. Hopping up the steps, his pace began to quicken. Mata opened the door and looked past the kitchen, back into the office. He saw a stack of his maps midlevel on the bookcase. Ripping the local Maine map from the shelf, he slapped it down on his desk. On the map, he looked in the direction of where the breeze came from. He dragged his index finger down the southeast river. From his spot up in the hills, the river ran straight down and opened up in a little circular bay. The tiny opening to the ocean made him ask another question to himself.

"What else did I smell?"

He thought about the coast and the combination of fresh water and salt water. *That was an oyster that I smelled*, he thought. Mata's wide smile uncovered his yellow teeth. "They got their invite."

62

Rolling the glider up the hill, Rose and Hutch were holding onto the wings and making torturous noises. Huffing and puffing, Hutch was pushing the side that held the flat tire. Step by step, Rose had to wait for him to reach the same level as her wing so as not to roll the whole craft straight onto him. When they reached the top of the hill, they both let go and rested their hands on their knees. Rose got down into a squat to breathe deeply. She heard Hutch let out a few low-toned curse words.

Rose looked at Hutch, saying, "Oh, I'm glad you sound so ready for your flight." She let out a few chuckles.

Hutch was sitting in the grass and turned to look at her under the frame of the glider. They met eyes. He saw her sarcastic expression and then he felt a little chuckle roll into his gut.

"Thanks for helping me get this up to the top," he said.

"Let's take a minute." Rose was still leaning over, holding her knees. "Take a breather. I don't want to get sent to the wrong place." She turned around and sat down in the same direction as Hutch.

They looked over the cornfield and past the bridge. A calming breeze rolled up the hill. Rose's hair raised up above her shoulders for a moment. She closed her eyes and took a deep breath, enjoying a moment of relief.

"You think that Mata will have already found them by the time we arrive?" she asked, turning to Hutch.

He turned toward Rose. "I'd bet that *they* already found *him*."

"Maybe . . ." she said, as her focus was taken by something moving down on the road.

Someone was walking down the street, toward the bridge. It looked like Tim. He left the road for a moment and started to walk down toward the creek.

Rose stood up and waved her hands above her head. "Hey, Tim!"

He looked up the hill and saw them with the glider.

Getting closer, he began to hike up the hill. He said, "Oh, thank goodness I found you before you left. I talked to Doug, and he said that you were up here and about to leave. I was there when the kids left your place to hit the park. He said that when they were on the diamond, they left again . . . and went, like, far away!"

"Yeah, we're going to try to find the kids. You left us before we found out that *they really* left us," said Rose.

Tim shook his head. "I ran back to your place to see you and Doug." He rested his hands on his knees when he reached the top of the hill, just like Rose. "Sue left me a note too. She wrote that she'd be back, but she was going for a walk in the park. She wasn't there. Neither were the kids." He was silent for a moment. "You think that they took her with them?"

Hutch and Rose looked at each other. She turned back toward Tim. "I don't see why they would. She doesn't know anything about us, right?"

Tim cocked his head to the left. "You mean your weird magical stuff? I don't think so. I never brought it up."

"Did they say, 'we're goin' to Maine' in the park and invite her?" Hutch asked in a sarcastic voice.

Rose and Tim whipped their gaze at each other. Their eyes opened wide at the same time. "Maine," they echoed.

Rose turned toward Hutch. "Her brother lives there. She told you that when we had her over at dinner—first time you cooked that deer. Her brother is an oyster farmer."

Hutch rested his forehead in his hands. Tim looked at the ground and paced around in a circle while Rose stood up and said, "Calm down, Tim."

"What if she's with them? Is she safe?" Rose asked Hutch.

"If she's with a farmer, she's safe. Mata likes those kinds of people," said Hutch. But he didn't look confident. It seemed like he was just trying to calm the others down a bit.

Rose turned back toward Tim. "I'll look for her. She's probably safe if she's with our sons. They know how to protect someone else." She reached out and grabbed Tim's shoulders. "I taught them."

Tim looked into her eyes, then shook his head. "I've gotta go with you. What if she's not safe? What if that weird guy will experiment on her, like she's some kind of a mouse?"

Hutched jumped in. "I don't think he does that kind of stuff."

Turning toward Hutch, Tim's voice got higher. "Why should I trust you? You're not a camp teacher. You're a liar!"

"Hey," Rose kept her hands on Tim's shoulder and shook him to focus on her. "We can protect her."

"*I* can," said Tim, looking at her. "Take me with you."

"I don't know about that," said Hutch.

"We can protect *him* too," she said to Hutch. "And he might be a good decoy."

Hutch raised his eyebrows for a moment. He unknotted his bandana from around his neck, unrolled it on his hip, and rubbed it around his neck and his ear. Finally, he shrugged his shoulders and said, "Okay."

Tim looked at Rose. "So, what should I do?"

"We'll find out once we get there," answered Rose.

She turned to look at Hutch, adding, "Chuck that stone. We're ready."

Hutch stood up. He pulled a pebble off the ground, just in front of his two future shipments. He held it in front of his eyes, polished it with his thumb, and then put it down near Rose and Tim. When he let out a low groan, almost from his chest, the stone spun and floated off the ground. And a pathway opened above it.

The blue cloud surrounding the gateway made Tim's eyes open wide. He took a step back. Rose turned to look at him. She grabbed his hand and looked back at Hutch. The big guy stopped, raised his glance, and shook his head.

"C'mon, Tim. Let's find our fam." Rose squeezed his hand and pulled him with her as she took a step toward the opening. Tim moved with her and disappeared when she did.

When they vanished, Hutch let the portal close. He looked at his glider for a moment, and then looked down the hill at the road that led to the post office. He took two steps down the hill, making his way toward the phone. Then he stopped. He turned back toward the glider and went back to it. Opening the windshield, he flicked the engine on and then went back to swing the blade. It whipped around and kept its spin continuously.

"We've got time," he said to himself.

Hutch climbed into the cockpit and closed the hatch, as well as his eyes. He touched his temple and raised the popped rear tire from the ground. Imagining a hand holding the belly of the glider, he pushed the aircraft toward the cliff of the hill. As the plane began to roll, Hutch kept his eyes shut. About ten yards before the glider hit the creek, he imagined the hand under his craft shifted up to the front. The tip of his glider rose up and off the hill. One second later, the body and tail followed. It soared a yard above the other side of the creek and continued up and into the sky. Left behind was the cornfield, the bridge, and the Murphys' house. Doug saw the glider for a moment, as he hoped he would. He was sitting in his backyard, reclined in a porch chair with Hutch's deerskin resting on the boulder behind him.

"Best of luck," yelled Doug. He watched from his backyard as Hutch's glider climbed toward the clouds.

63

Inside the oyster house, Bryan sat at the end of his breakfast nook.

"So, you guys didn't know that she could shift?" He nodded at his sister, Sue.

"I don't know why she didn't tell us . . ." Greg looked at his mom.

Sue responded with a relaxed poise, "You didn't find out until I showed you. Before that, I was just protecting you both." She nodded toward Virg. "Now, I'm doing the same."

"Can we do this too?" asked Virg as he pointed at her fur coat.

"Maybe. But I don't know how to teach you."

"Who taught you?" asked Greg.

Sue shook her head. "No one."

"How'd you find out you could do it?"

Bryan answered before Sue did. "She imagined it one night while she was sleeping."

Sue corrected him. "I had a dream."

Greg and Virg looked at each other. Greg asked, "What did you dream?"

"I was dreaming about our mother." She looked at Bryan, then turned back to Greg. "You've never met your grandmother. She passed away before I turned twenty."

"How?" asked Virg.

Bryan answered, "Well, she was coming down with a cold. No one really knew what it was, but it didn't seem like it was going to kill her or anything."

"She died from a cold?" said Greg.

"No," said Sue. "When she got sick, she lay in her bed for a few days. When she woke up from her nap, she told us that she was having conversations with her mother while she slept."

"I asked what she was dreaming about," said Bryan.

"She said, 'I'll tell you sometime,' and we didn't push her . . ." added Sue. She looked down at her feet—deciding what to share or to keep away from the kids.

Bryan took over. "After that, she left one night. We didn't see her leave, but we heard her say, 'I'm feeling better. I just need some fresh air.' We were in our bedrooms, but she didn't come in. She just said it out loud from the living room. After that, we heard the door close. We fell back asleep, thinking that she was feeling better. But she didn't return."

"Your grandma returned that night," Sue told Greg, "not through the door, but in my dreams that night. She told me what her mother had given to her, a fur coat. In my dream, she placed it on my shoulders and told me that this was part of me now. I dreamed that she walked me through the forest and that it felt different than usual. We were both walking, but lower to the ground. I realized that she and I were foxes, sharing the scents in the breeze and nudging each other as we walked."

Bryan jumped in again. "What did she tell you about *her* mom . . . our grandmother?"

Sue continued, "She said that her mother did the same for her. It's now time for me to be able to shift back and forth. It's time for me to be able to protect the family."

"She killed herself?" Virg said with a horrifying look on his face.

"No," said Sue. "She stayed a fox. It was her time to pass it on."

"She passed on 'the shift,'" said Bryan. "No one believed us."

"Well, we only told Mom's sister. But our aunt didn't believe it."

"So we stopped telling people. We just told them that she died," added Bryan.

Virg asked, "But she didn't die?"

Sue smiled. "She was still alive. I could talk to her and visit her whenever I wanted, but she was a fox. She didn't hang around us very often. She didn't need us anymore. Hunting, playing, sleeping, she could do those on her own."

Greg asked, "But why did she give that 'shifting' ability to you?"

Sue looked back at him. "She told me that our family still needed a protector. She said that Grandma referenced the future, and told my mom that it was my turn."

"Why don't we ever get informed about this stuff?" said Virg. "That's like one of the coolest things I've ever heard. You're a protector? That sounds like a video game!"

"Who are you supposed to protect?" asked Greg.

Sue looked at him and nodded. "You, Greg."

"Did they see what is going to happen?" Greg added.

"No . . . Well, I don't think so. But they felt that you would need a protector," Sue answered.

Greg felt Bryan's hand rest on his shoulder. When he gave Greg a little squeeze, the feeling reminded him of Hutch's hand. It felt big and callused.

A moment later, the four of them turned their heads toward the door. They heard a bump on the outdoor wood porch near the door. Without saying anything, they all assumed it was Mata.

Bryan stood up and pointed at Sue.

She mouthed, without speaking, "I'll follow." Bryan then shifted his finger toward his back door. She took one step away, following his lead. Turning the knob silently, she opened the door just a crack. The boys turned to look at her. Virg's mouth hung open as they watched her crouch down, touch the floor, and pull her jacket up over her head. In about one second, the shift from human to fox was almost instantaneous. The jacket rolled forward and misted into the air as the fox appeared behind it.

Greg sucked in a quick breath as the fox turned away from them and silently stepped outside, down the stoop, and into the grass. Looking back at the front door, just like the kids, Bryan stepped ahead and opened it.

Pulling the knob, the door opened into the shack. "Good afternoon, sir. Are you looking for oysters?" asked Bryan to the man standing at the doorway.

Mata's long grey pelt was lit from behind. There were no lights on in the cabin, but the people inside knew who they were looking at.

"Hello, sir. We have some visitors, don't we?" Mata shifted his gaze from Bryan to the boys. "I expected them, but they came to see you first." Mata took a step inside.

"I'm Bryan," he said, as he extended his hand toward the thin, wrinkly fingers of his guest.

Mata didn't look at him but latched his hand with Bryan's and kept his eyes on Greg and Virg. He didn't pass by Bryan, but the boys felt that the old man wanted to get near to them.

His gaze turned back to Bryan. "May I try one of your oysters? I could smell them out near the estuary."

"Of course. Care for a lemon or some sauce to pair with it?" Bryan let go of Mata's hand, opened his fridge, and looked around at his mild hot sauces.

"No, but I would love to see the boys pick one for me. Would that be all right with you, Bryan?" Mata stepped back out the door, then took another step to keep the doorway open. He extended his arm down the stairs and toward the wooden pier.

Bryan turned back to him with a lemon in his hand. "That's okay with me. Virg picked three a little while ago. Smoked 'em up and served us. Pretty good," he said. Then waited a moment and asked, "I'm sorry. What's your name?"

"It's Mata," said the man politely. "I live not far away as a camp teacher." He turned his gaze back to the kids. "Gregory, an oyster. Would you care to try?"

Greg stood up from the table, but looked apprehensive. He didn't want to leave the shack.

Mata walked toward him, stopped in front, and extended his hand. "It's good to see you both again. No need to show me your skills, but I'm curious."

Greg reached out and shook Mata's papery-skinned hand. It felt like it was dry and full of narrow bones. It was almost like Greg agreed to follow him without saying anything.

"Thank you," said Mata, "I've heard a lot about you two, but I haven't actually seen your performances yet. You and Virgil have taught yourselves quite a lot, so far, correct?" Mata squatted downward to look up at the boys. He waited for them to nod their heads.

When they did, he smiled and nodded his too. "I have a place nearby. If you want to spend some time there, you can show me what you've found—what you can do."

"Do you answer questions?" asked Greg.

"If I know the answer, I can," said Mata.

"A week ago, we learned that we're different. If we visit you, can you show us how to live on our own? I think we have enough skills to have a different life."

Mata looked into Greg's eyes. "It's different already, isn't it?" He stood up and made his way back to the door. He extended his arm toward the lake. "Come. I'm getting hungry. Care to find an oyster for me?" After beckoning with a wave to the kids, he turned toward Bryan and added, "Lemon? Is that what you would choose to pair with them?"

Bryan turned toward the kids. "You guys want some lemon with the oysters? If you stay here, I've got some good sauces too." He looked a little worried.

"Sure," said Virg. He got up and walked through the open door.

Greg met Bryan's eyes and nodded. The kid walked past Mata and through the door, following Virg.

Mata looked at Bryan. "Thank you," he said, and then turned toward the kids. He walked through the door without touching it and swept his hand, shutting the door behind himself.

64

Rose and Tim found themselves on a scout reservation. The space around them was open. A ring of flattop stones surrounded a campfire pit as natural benches. Just behind them was a wide single-story house. Dark brown shingles lined the sides of the long cabin. It looked as if it held an office, a mess hall, and an indoor campsite. Through tiny windows, they saw a little bookshelf, a long table with a battery-powered ceiling fan, and some sheets hanging from a bunk bed.

Tim turned his head toward the cabin and began to peek into the windows. He didn't find anyone in the cabin. But he tried to hide himself from anyone who could have been on the other side.

Looking around the grounds, Rose noticed a little footpath with no weeds or roots covering the natural trail. She was drawn to the edge of it. It looked like camp members left footprints across the path. About fifty yards away, she saw a little stone-stacked tube with a wooden lift above it.

"They've got a well," Rose hollered toward Tim.

He was peeking through a window. "He's got quite the office."

Turning around off the path, Rose jogged around the fire pit. When she reached the cabin, she looked through the window with Tim. She saw Mata's cabinets and thought about inspecting the office. How different was this new area, compared to the camp she had worked at years ago.

"Let's take a peek," she said, as she began walking toward the door.

Tim saw her step onto the porch. "Hey!" he said, "Are we allowed to go inside?"

"I'm a previous employee. So, yeah. Also, your son saw some weird stuff in his dreams," said Rose. "Let's see if there's anything we should be worried about."

Tim nodded and followed her. Rose opened the door and made her way through the office and the kitchen. Nothing that she saw held her attention. She kept walking until she saw the bedroom. There were two bunk beds with sheets and pillows. Three of the mattresses held the sheets tucked in. One looked as if it had been slept in the night before. She didn't know what to think, but she took a step back.

Tim said something but sounded far away. Rose turned around and walked back through the kitchen and into the office. A bookcase was moved. It was as if it was a doorway on a hinge.

"Tim?" said Rose, trying to find him.

"Down here," she heard coming from somewhere past the bookshelf. She walked around it and looked at a staircase that went down.

Following a link of Christmas lights pinned to the ceiling, she reached the bottom of the staircase. It looked like a regular concrete basement. Tim was standing right next to something that looked like a stand-up tanning tube.

Standing with his head angled to the side and a hand pulling on his mustache, he said, "Umm, does this guy need to be tanning . . . uh, secretly? Why is this hidden behind a bookshelf?"

"I've never seen anything like this," said Rose. She walked next to Tim. "I mean, I've never seen this in a basement . . . I've seen it in a tanning salon." She grabbed a handle on the upper half of the tube.

Letting go and taking a step back, she looked over Tim's shoulder and found a pair of goggles hanging on the wall. "Just what I was looking for," she said. "You wear goggles if you get into a tanning bed." She turned to look at Tim, "Don't ask me why I know that."

He raised his hands, visually uttering, "No questions, Your Honor."

Reaching around Tim, she took the goggles off the wall and put them over her eyes. "Whoa," she reacted. She couldn't see through the frames. The lenses were painted over with a deep black color.

"I could see through the shaded goggles when I did this." She pulled them off and stuck them onto Tim's face.

"No one sees anything when they put these on," said Tim with the goggles over his eyes.

Rose looked past him. She glanced into the tanning tube and saw handles on the ceiling. As she let her mind wander, she imagined that Greg and Virg would just be tanning, rather than studying, if they lived in this cabin.

"Hey, if you tan in here, don't you need those crazy lamps?" Tim was hunched over and touching the inside of the tanning bed. His fingers were feeling the open half-circles running from the bottom to the top around the empty tube.

"Yeah, you need tanning lamps if you want to get a tan," said Rose.

She heard herself say that and realized the strange difference. "No one is tanning in these."

Tim backed out and looked at her. "Do you have to change the lights after every tan session?"

"No. I'd bet that they're using this for testing their skills," she said. "Get in," Rose added as she put her hand on Tim's shoulder.

She tossed the goggles at him too. He caught them, holding them on his chest as he took a step up and into the tanning bed.

"Hey, do I wear these too? I don't wanna tan," said Tim.

"You won't. I just want to test something. You're safe," she said as she held the door. Pushing the door closed, she noticed the strange thickness of the door. It looked like it had a few layers added onto the original frame. She shut the hatch and turned the lever to lock it.

"Tim," she said out loud, "can you hear me?"

She waited and looked at her watch. She waited ten seconds and then pulled the lever back and pulled the hatch open.

"Did you hear me?" Tim said with the goggles on.

"Nope. And that's what I thought would happen," she added. "It's an isolated capsule. I think this helps keep people from distractions if they want to explore their thoughts or ideas about how to get better at their craft."

Tim pulled the goggles from his face. "Or it's for detention. I don't want to be in here anymore. Let's go back upstairs." He gave the goggles back to Rose.

She didn't move and stared into the vessel without a focus. "... You might be right." Then she let her gaze roll up and down the interior of the vessel. Something weird caught her eye. Noticing some little thin lines outside the empty light cups, she reached in and touched the lines. They rimmed around with corners at their ends to make little rectangles.

Rose held her finger in the center of one little panel and pushed it. It popped back toward her and stayed connected at a side hinge. Within the panel laid a little microphone. She tapped another and found a little speaker.

"It's not for tanning. It's for ... research?" she said.

"Let's get outta here. If the Mata guy isn't here yet, I'd bet that he'd be back soon. Should we be stickin' around in someone else's basement and wait for them to show up?" asked Tim.

Standing up straight, Rose turned to look at him. "I'm glad you said that. I'd be inspecting this thing for hours. And I might never figure out how he's using it."

She walked past Tim and started climbing the basement stairs. Tim hurried behind her and followed. As they reached the first floor, they went around the back of the bookcase. Tim pushed the shelving back to attach it to the wall behind them.

"Let's get out of here and find a spot to see when he comes back. Maybe he'll lead us to our kids," said Rose.

"... Unless he's already got them somewhere in this building, and we haven't seen them yet," responded Tim.

Rose walked through Mata's office and stopped for a moment. Turning back toward his desk, she pointed at it and shifted her gaze up at Tim.

"You think there's a journal or a spreadsheet in this thing? I want to see what that thing downstairs is used for. Don't you?" she asked.

"Um, I kinda wanna get outta here. This place is a little spooky."

"Oh, grow up," said Rose. She walked in front of him and opened the two lower drawers on the desk. "Look in that one," she pointed at the one on her right. "I'll peel through this one and try to find something."

Tim followed her instructions. He crouched down beside her and began sifting through the files. Slowly combing each folder open, he looked at the title of each document. They just looked like directions around the campus, specifying what each area was used for. He got through those and hit a journal that held all the necessary updates and processes of their water well and the electrical system. He pulled it up and out of the drawer. It showed him the layout of the cabin.

"Wow, this place is pretty big. We didn't even see the entire basement," said Tim. "Looks like it's bigger than the cabin."

He kept inspecting the pages of the facility maps. It looked like they had a weird solar panel at the corner of a runway. There was a picture of a little airplane on it too. He recognized the glider that Hutch had flown. A little illustration matched his memory of the glider.

"They have a runway," said Tim.

"They've gotta have one," responded Sue. "That big guy has got to land somewhere."

"True," said Tim as he looked back into the files.

Rose backed away from the drawer and stood up as she pulled three thin leather books with her. "Hey, this looks like a journal. I see the dates. These are recent."

Tim stood up as he looked at what she was holding. Suddenly, she slapped a leather book into his chest.

"Take a peek at this. I'll look through the other ones," said Rose.

"Copy that," responded Tim.

He sat down and opened the leather-bound book. Dates were written on the top-left corner of every page. Below, it listed a name and then jots of actions, responses, and analysis.

12/20/2019

Natalia (eight years)

12:00 p.m.: Hutch in command. Field trip down open path to patch of old degrading trees. Testing of telekinesis.

Success: Tree elevated. Tree ripped molecularly. Tree thrown in every direction. Hutch protected tested member—created shield upon explosion.

Memory test: Connected, transferred, shared. Patient remembers after (fourth share).

Status: Kept in cell. Memory erased. Future tests unplanned.

Unforeseen: Hutch stabbed above left knee. Item used: shred of ripped tree root.

Tim turned to look at Rose. He couldn't even say anything. Resting his finger on "Memory test," he shoved the book toward Rose. She looked back at him.

"I'm seeing the same thing. These are his journals," she responded.

"Should we take them with us?" asked Tim.

"We can't. I don't want him to know that we're here." She looked down at her watch. "Also, we've gotta get out of here. I don't want him to know that we're looking through his stuff either." She stood up and put the journals back into the drawer. Pushing it closed, she looked behind herself—searching for any apparent changes they had made in the room.

"Close that door behind you," she said, "and shut that drawer," pointing to the desk.

"But what if he tests the kids? What does that do? In the journal, he listed that a test on an eight-year-old was the fourth one he'd done. Is that bad?" said Tim, looking frightened.

"I don't know, but let's not let it happen." She watched Tim close the bookcase door and push in the drawer. When he looked back at her, she added, "Follow me."

She walked down the steps and past the fire pit. She looked around and walked up a little hill. Pushing her way past some bushes, she put herself behind a chain of them. Then she turned back toward Tim, who was following.

"We'll find them; just be patient. When Mata shows up, go knock on his door and ask him where the kids are," she said.

"Me? Is it normal for him to have regular people knock on his door?" asked Tim.

"Probably not. In fact, I'm sure no one ever knocks on his door," said Rose.

She looked at Tim, crouching next to her. He was looking down at his hands and cowering upon the thoughts of his near future. She reached out to touch his shoulder.

Giving him a little loving squeeze, she said, "Hutch is on his way. I'll be here. If anything happens, and I don't know if anything will, I'll protect you. But you, as a distraction, can be very helpful." She smiled and kissed his cheek.

Tim smiled at her and said, "I'll do it. What's the rest of the plan? Hearing that makes me feel better."

Bryan wanted to keep his eye on the kids. He turned the knob and followed the gifted ones down toward the lake. *Don't close the door on me*, thought Bryan. He took a few steps down onto the dirt trail that led to the dock. Seeing the kids and their teacher pulling stones and little fish from the water, he turned to look back into the woods.

Sue, I hope you're keeping an eye on these kids, Bryan thought. He didn't see a fox anywhere in the bushes. He turned back toward Mata when he heard, "Tell me, boys, did your parents follow you here? How was it that you arrived?"

Virg turned toward him. "We wanted to come to see you. Greg figured out how to create the portal . . . or whatever you used."

"You watched your mother and Hutch create one for me," said Mata.

"We did," confirmed Greg.

"Did they do the same? Did they follow you?" the old man asked.

"I don't think so, but I'm not sure. We just saw them do it when they sent you back here. We haven't seen them since we left," said Virg.

Mata turned to look at Bryan. "Have you seen them?"

Bryan shook his head slowly.

"Do they know that we're gone?" Virg said as he turned toward Greg.

Greg turned his head away from the lake, back into the forest. The sun was below the tip of the trees. The light was slipping away. "I bet they will soon."

"Can I ask if you'd like to visit the camp?" Mata looked at the kids and then turned back to Bryan.

Bryan didn't know how to react. There was nothing he could do. Suddenly, he just blurted, "You can stay with me if you want to. I have extra beds."

Mata turned his eyes back to the kids. "Is that why you came here?"

"No," said Virg.

Greg looked at Bryan. "No."

He smiled and felt like he should say goodbye to his uncle. Walking toward Bryan, Greg looked past him as he took a few steps. Beyond his uncle, he saw a slight shimmer of eyes in a bush behind the tree line. He wondered if Mata had seen them too. Sharing a hug with Bryan, Greg rested his head on the big man's chest. Bryan squeezed him softly but with feelings of love and protection. To Greg, it felt like Bryan wasn't going to let go. He didn't mind.

Changing his focus from Bryan's chest up to his eyes, he leaned his head back just a bit. Seeing the fear in the man's eyes, Greg squeezed for a moment and mouthed to him, "*We'll be okay.*"

The fisherman smiled and slowly opened his arms but left his hand on Greg's shoulder momentarily.

Greg turned back to Mata. "We'll come with you. When do we leave?"

"When you're ready." The old man's gaze shifted from Greg to Bryan.

Bryan didn't smile or speak. He just kept his eyes on the old man.

"I can offer you a ride, boys. Does that sound okay?" Mata asked.

Greg and Virg looked at each other. They looked confused. Virg looked back at Mata and shrugged his shoulders. The bearded man held his hand open at Virg and raised it slightly. Virg whipped his arms out to his sides for balance as he was lifted off the ground.

"Cool," he said as he rose.

Greg watched it happen and then said, "Okay."

Raising his other palm and pointing at Greg, Mata lifted the kid's feet above the ground.

The boys smiled at each other after they watched Mata begin to float. The old man's shoulders and head stayed in the same spot. He lifted his heels and floated at the same level as the boys.

Turning toward Bryan, he said, "Thank you. Perhaps we'll see you again."

Before Greg's uncle could respond, Mata flew away from Bryan out over the lake. The boys did the same thing, matching him. The floating people stared at him for a few seconds, then turned and flew straight up the river. Bryan took a step toward the lake, and then, out of the corner of his eye, he saw a fox quickly sprout from the wild weeds. Sue jumped over roots and past the trees. She was following the kids, but was she going to lose them?

He took another step toward her and saw her reach a speed he never imagined possible. There were no sounds of the bushes and brambles being hit with her feet. She kept running, but it was almost as if she wasn't even touching the ground.

65

The sinking sun was making the horizon warm and rose-colored. A shade of golden weeds rested on top of the lower line of rosy hue. Within the trees, only a bit of muted natural light remained at the campsite. Rose was hiding herself in the bushes, about fifty yards from the cabin. Tim sat on a flat stone, looking at the fire pit. His gaze faced cool coals; his body was pointed toward the cabin.

Rumbling and dribbling behind the cabin, the river kept rolling. That sound almost made Tim fall asleep. With light vanishing and the sound of a calmly repeated current, he took a few moments just to enjoy his surroundings. He closed his eyes for a moment and held them shut.

Before all the light disappeared, Tim opened his eyes. When he did, he saw a dark figure float over the river. The ill-lit ghost connected his feet to the ground beside the cabin. Tim stood straight up and took a step back. Two smaller dark spirits touch the grass beside the river.

"Greg . . ." said Tim.

He took a few steps toward the twilight floaters. The tallest shadowed creature raised his hand above his head. A bright light flashed from his palm. Tim put a hand over his eyes, as his pupils couldn't squeeze quick enough.

"Oooph . . ." Tim said out loud as the shine from Mata's hand blinded him. "It's Tim! I'm Tim. Do you have a military flashlight? That thing is bright."

Tim pulled his hand away from his face but didn't open his eyes.

"Hey, Dad," Tim heard as some rustling footsteps followed. "How'd you get here?" Greg said as he reached his father and gave him a little hug. "You're not, umm, transporting yourself like us, are you?"

"I have no idea. I didn't transport myself. Well, I don't think so. But I don't know who *did* transport me," Tim said. "I was looking for you two over in the park but didn't find you. All of a sudden, I ended up in the woods. I found a cabin and thought, 'Someone will probably show up.' Glad you're both here."

His response made Greg furrow a brow. "You don't know how you got here?" He turned to look at Virg. "Did we create a hole that's still open?"

Mata closed his hand, removing the light beam aimed at Tim. He took a few steps down the hill toward the fire pit, slowed his pace, and extended his hand toward Tim. "Welcome," he said.

"Thanks," said Tim as he grabbed Mata's hand. "I don't know if the portal is open or what. I didn't even see a portal. Maybe there's some kind of glitch."

"You got here before the boys did. When I found them, they were not close by. You took the same portal, did you? How did you find this place?" asked Mata.

Virg answered for him. "Well, if the portal was still open, maybe it shifted. We got a better idea of where this place was once you showed up. You pointed up the river. I thought about a place like this." He rolled his hand around in a little circle.

Mata turned toward Tim. "The sun is going down. Care to see the place? You're welcome to stay this evening."

Tim shivered for a moment. It was dark enough that no one saw him move. "Okay, I can do that. I don't know how to get home."

"No, you don't," said Mata.

The three Pennsylvanians followed Mata onto his stoop and entered the cabin. Rose was still crouched behind a row of bushes. Watching them enter, she saw where they were going as a few interior lamps flicked on inside the shack. About ten yards to her right, she heard the sound of little twigs crunching and a small breath. Turning, thinking she'd see a squirrel, she saw a beautiful grey fox with an orange ring around her neck.

The fox turned its head toward Rose. Strangely, the corners of the mouth of the fox rose up toward its ears. *Is she smiling at me?* Rose asked herself in her mind. She raised her knee and pulled it away from the fox.

Closing one eye, the fox let her smile fall back into a regular position. Rose whispered to the fox, "Did you just wink at me?"

She put her knee back down and rested her hands on the ground, nearer to the fox. Leaning forward, Rose said, "Who are you?"

Near the Maine campsite, up on a hill sat a long-razed forest patch extending about a hundred yards. It was only about thirty feet wide. If you were flying a 757 airplane across the little empty patch, it wouldn't even pull your gaze. It was close to a spring river with the same small openings between the trees. The runway that Hutch was used to landing on was near an Appalachian cliff rim, close to a large river valley. It wasn't high up, but the river valley beside it provided an easy liftoff for the glider. The shadows of the trees softened the looks of the open grounds. Hutch knew precisely where he would land. He'd done it many times. For Maine locals, seeing a glider in the sky was like seeing a boat on a river—give a wave and don't worry about their destination.

He lowered his glider toward the landing strip as he reached the split between the forested trees. The sky held a soft robin's egg blue just before Hutch descended below the tops of the trees. The light almost vanished completely as he touched down and pumped his brakes. Popping the windshield and hopping out of the glider, he adjusted his eyes to the evening light. His pupils widened as he enjoyed the scent of the pine and fresh water. The sound of the crickets and owls made him feel at home.

Once he could see in the darkness, he exited the glider and closed the windshield. Hutch pulled his handkerchief from his pocket and pressed it to his forehead. Wiping it across and around his neck, he turned and began hiking toward the campsite. Following the river, he eventually saw a few little lights coming from the cabin. Through the windows, lights threw little sheens across the stone benches and the fire pit.

Hutch stopped walking for a moment and thought about Rose. He closed his eyes and thought about contacting her. *Rose, are you here? Is Tim with you?*

There was no response, so Hutch opened his eyes and took a few more steps toward the campsite. After about thirty seconds, he heard a sound on his right. He stopped and turned away from the light. He waited. After another fifteen seconds, the sounds of footsteps grew. It sounded like two people were walking toward him, not just one. Crouching down and attempting to hide, Hutch still looked like a giant boulder resting next to a river.

"I didn't want to scare you," Rose said before Hutch could see her. She came out from behind a bush, holding the branches back.

Hutch saw a woman in a fur coat step through the bush and stop.

"But you've met this fox before," said Rose. "It seems she knows more than you think."

"A fox?" asked Hutch. He looked confused.

"I met you on your first day in PA," said Sue. "You've had a mission, haven't you?"

"I met you at the party, though. Later in the week," he responded.

"Before that. On the hill, at sundown, you told me you were just visiting," Sue said.

Hutch looked into her eyes and then noticed her dark grey fur coat with an orange ring around her neck. He took in a quick breath, and his pupils dilated. Her eyes looked the same as the ones he saw on the fox's face.

"Ah, you remember me, huh?" said Sue.

Rose smiled. "She's told me a lot about you. What she's noticed."

Hutch ignored her. "You can turn into a fox? How?"

"Inherited," said Sue as she smiled. "Do I get tested now?"

Hutch looked at her but didn't respond.

"You and Mata test them all, right?" asked Sue.

"I told her what I've seen, Hutch. Mata has journals in his desk," said Rose.

Hutch shook his head and said, "I tried to tell you about this."

"Did you?" asked Rose.

"When I got to Pennsylvania, I was looking for you. Mata said that it was time to contact you. You'd been gone for a long time, but he wanted to look at what you've done since you left. He's trying to find people who can help him understand why we're like this," said Hutch.

"And he's not trying to find out why he is acting this way? He's searching for people and then taking their lives from them . . . just for research." Rose threw her hands up into the air.

Hutch grabbed her wrists. "He's *trying* to help."

"He's *killing* people," responded Rose.

"Not all the way," said Hutch.

"What does that mean?" said Rose as she shook her wrists away from Hutch's hands.

"He's getting them to release their spirits," Sue said, stepping toward him.

Hutch looked at her. "He's letting their spirits leave if they want to . . . if they want to see what's on the other side . . . what's possible. If they do, and they don't return, he freezes their bodies."

Rose's eyes went wide. "And that's what's under the ground? Tim and I saw the map. You have frozen children under your cabin?"

"Only people who've agreed to see what's possible on the other side. They want to see what they can achieve," said Hutch. "He researches and records their exit from their bodies. He didn't always do it this way but finds more information upon their release. They still contact him about their vessel and their updates." He paused for a moment and looked away from them. ". . . It used to be a choice. Now, he coaxes people into leaving their bodies. He makes it feel like an option."

Rose turned toward the cabin. Without saying anything, she began to run. Flying past tree trunks and hopping around bushes, she got closer to the house. Before she got too close, she noticed a blur of the light within the windows. Slowing down, she stopped moving and raised her hand. Reaching out, she touched a nearly invisible shell. The light behind it looked scrambled.

"Goddammit!" she screamed. She slammed her fist against the barrier created in front of her.

66

Tim sat in the basement of Mata's cabin. Sitting on a stitched blanket on a wooden trunk, Tim thought it smelled like an old people's home and a diaper. Just in front of him, the boys sat looking at Mata's computer screen.

"Here," Mata touched the screen near its upper right corner, "you can see what we're recording if you take a journey."

Sitting in a green plastic chair beside Mata, Virg asked, "What does it look like?"

"I can show you," said Mata. "These are just your vitals." He pointed at the screen. "It shows how you're doing in *this* world while you're on your journey to the next."

"Where does it take us?" asked Virg.

"I don't know where it is. But I can show you where people have gone. They find who they are, and what they can do. The recordings are remarkable," said Mata. "Want to see one?"

"Yes," said Greg.

"Does this thing kill people?" asked Virg.

Mata turned to look at him. "No. This doesn't kill people. But some have chosen to leave this world when they visit the other one."

Tim stood up. "Where are they?"

"Who?"

"The people who have chosen to leave," Tim said.

"They left."

Tim took a step closer to him. "I'm not asking about their souls. Where are their bodies?"

"Oh, I thought you meant the people who went home." Mata chuckled. "There have been many people who have left this camp. They felt like they weren't learning anything. I tried my best, but not everyone has as much potential as these two."

He turned to the boys and looked back at Tim. "Everyone like them can explore the other world, but not everyone opens it and changes it. Some just visit, leave, and go home. These boys have potential, because they've taught themselves all their skills so far. They have imaginations and interests."

Tim fired back, "Yeah, but I saw your journal."

Mata moved slightly, stiffening his lower back and touching his beard.

"I saw that you wrote down, after a person's 'Memory Test,' that their memory was erased. What the heck is the reason for that?" Tim continued.

The old man took a moment and removed his hand from his bristles. "Some people ask me if they can have a memory removed. It's possible. I agree to whatever these people want."

Mata thought about asking Tim where he found the journal, but Greg pulled his chair forward.

"I want to know what I'm capable of. I want to see what I saw when we explored with Virg's mom," said Greg.

"Where did she take you?" said Mata as he turned to face Greg.

"In their backyard, she had us lie down and share our memories with one another," said Greg. "I can probably do it easily with your machine. Does that work? Is that what you want?"

"Whatever *you* want, that's what *I* want," said Mata.

He grabbed a suction valve and began to attach it to Greg's temple. The kid took it from his hand before it reached his head. He raised his finger to his temple, held the valve, and closed his eyes.

Tim looked at the computer screen as it began to flood the panel with statistics and pages of paragraphs almost immediately. Keeping his focus on Mata, Tim noticed the old man's eyes crinkle at their corners. His lips peeled into a smile—looking like he was enjoying the skills of Tim's son.

"Hang on," said Mata. He put his palm on Greg's knee. "Take a break. It's easier to research if you use this."

Mata stood up and opened the door to the vessel he had created. With his hand on the door, he explained the reason for using it. He showed the panels and pointed at his computer screen.

"This vessel helps to hold it all together. See those pages dangling from the printer and all these numbers that are flooding the screen?" He saw the boys nod their heads, and then he pointed at the vessel. "This will help us collect the information in order and also let me keep contact with you while you travel."

Virg looked confused. "Where do we go when we're in there?"

"Anywhere your heart desires," Mata smiled at him. "You can let me help you steer or you can enjoy your freedom. Explore. Share what you're seeing. Perhaps you can teach *me* a thing or two." He turned to look at Greg. "What do you want to see?"

"We want to learn . . ." Greg stopped for a moment, not knowing what he wanted. "When you showed us how to feed ourselves, you raised all those fish from the pond. That's when we wanted to visit you. What else can you show us? We want to live like you do."

". . . On our own, not going to school," injected Virg.

Mata looked at Virg. "Life *is* a school. Learn whatever you can. No matter what it is, it might help you." He reached back and grabbed a sheet of paper from the printing box. Taking a few moments to look at it, he said, "It's difficult to read. These are mostly just jumbled words." He flipped a few pages and looked a bit confused.

Then his smile lit up. "You lifted a . . . watermelon at your school. Then you fed the plants." He set down the pages on the floor. "Okay, let's learn what you are capable of."

Tim smiled. "You're gardening? At school?"

Greg looked back at him and said, "Pretty cool, huh?"

Tim let out a laugh. Then the silence returned. His son took a breath and stood up. Taking a few steps away from Mata, Greg turned to look into the vessel. He put his hand on the side of the open door.

Greg looked confused. "Okay, how does this work?"

Mata grabbed the armrests of his chair and pushed himself up. He

Glider

paced over to Greg and explained the machine. He showed handles to hold onto, black goggles to help him focus on his memories, and the door that would keep him within a silent chamber.

Mata lightly glued the machine's sensors to Greg's temples, and then the kid stepped into the cage.

"This will help you search your mind. You can show me what you've done, what you're capable of, and what you want," said Mata.

"I'm ready," said Greg. He turned away from Mata, grabbed the handles, and then pulled the goggles down over his eyes.

Mata closed the door behind him, and Greg heard a little snap . . . then nothing.

67

Rose turned back toward Sue and then looked back at the sphere. She jumped straight into it, with her shoulder aimed at the wall. Landing hard and slipping right off, she sat in the grassy mulch for a moment. She closed her eyes and imagined her hands could find a weak spot in it. Raising her hands, open to the globe, she rolled them in circles, trying to find an opening and stretch it wider. She kept moving her hands, but found nothing.

Hutch and Sue walked toward her while she searched.

Hearing the two behind her, she kept her eyes on the shield, but spoke to Hutch. "Any way you've ever opened this? Have you ever been held out of it? Help me."

"I can try to talk with him, but I don't know if he can hear me," said Hutch softly.

"Do it—now," said Rose. She seemed like she was about to explode.

Hutch shook his head and looked at Sue. She saw his eyes confirm that he had no way of helping.

"I know people who have no walls," said Sue.

Rose whipped her eyes back at Sue.

"My mother and my grandmother. They never leave, they just change." Sue took a few steps back away from Hutch and Rose, looking up into the sky.

Rose saw a little sparkle hit the corner of Sue's eye. A moment later, it almost looked like a spirit was lifted out of her face and shoulders. It didn't fly away and disappear; it pulled her up onto her toes, but stayed attached. The shape of the spirit looked just like the fox she had been. It was still attached to Sue, but it looked like her body was sharing her head and shoulders with it. It was almost like she had two heads that held the same space.

Sue looked straight up into the sky. Rose turned her head to see what she was looking at. It wasn't obvious. There were tons of stars and almost no light pollution in the forest. Nearly every star was sparkling over the treetops. Then Sue closed her eyes, as did the fox at the same time. The three stars in the belt of Orion almost flamed a bit brighter.

Rose took one step backward. "The Hunter's constellation," she said to herself. "Whom are you contacting?" she asked Sue.

Her head and the fox's face turned toward Rose at the same time. Sue opened her eyes and answered, "My family."

68

Standing blindly in the vessel, Greg couldn't hear a thing. Suddenly, a little sound gurgled from the speakers next to him.

The buzz became a voice. "When you're ready, just think about your memories . . . what's happened so far. My machine will copy. Then we'll figure out where to go from there." A click followed as Mata had let go of the button.

Greg thought about his memories of when Hutch arrived. He remembered riding his bike with Virg—finding their mental connection. His mind wandered to their practices and explorations. He remembered the painting splatter on the bush next to the bus and the hummingbird that drank from the invisible flower. All the experiences of his dreams and the past week flowed through him.

As his thoughts reached the memory of entering the cabin with Virg, he heard a sound within the vessel. The sound of a big pop was followed by creaks. That drew Greg's focus. A moment later, his legs felt like they were going numb. It shot up into his lower back. He didn't feel his body's motion as he fell toward the side of the cage. His hands got numb before he even hit the floor. As his head descended, he heard a little needle retracting into an open tile on the wall.

Greg closed his eyes. As he did, it felt like he had just reopened them. His body felt like it was just floating upward. Before he knew what was happening, he saw the outer panels of the vessel. It was like his spirit was floating upward. For a short moment, he saw his father stand up and turn toward Mata. Virg was sitting behind the old man. Then he hopped up off his chair.

Continuing upward, Greg felt himself flow through the first floor and over the roof. When he blinked, he saw the top of the forest below.

As he blinked again, the rim of the planet was visible. He turned his head back in the direction he was flowing toward. Three bright stars made him close his eyes. They were too bright.

Once he opened his eyes, he was somewhere he'd never imagined.

"Is he okay?" said Virg.

The machine stopped pumping info onto the screen. Sounds of its reception ended and the lines went flat.

Tim focused on the screen. "You're not getting any more info. Is he done?"

"I'm not sure. This doesn't typically happen," responded Mata. He didn't move. To Tim, it didn't look as though Mata was worried.

Virg sat back down and touched his finger to his temple. He reached out to his mom in pure silence. *Mom, can you hear me?* No response. He waited a few moments before, *Mom*—He didn't finish.

He jumped off his chair and quickly shot over to the vessel. Virg ripped the door open and saw Greg lying with his head and shoulder rested on the wall. His legs were bent.

"Hey, Tim, he needs our help!" said Virg. He pulled the goggles up and over Greg's eyes. His friend looked like he was dead. Greg's eyes remained open, but the color of his brown eyes had a layer of grey over the entire globe.

Mata took a step up and out of his chair. Tim stood behind him, looking at the screen. When Mata took a step forward, Tim turned to Virg's chair, ripped it off the floor, and whipped it against Mata's temple as hard as he could.

The old man didn't see it coming and fell straight onto the floor.

She didn't know what to do. Rose had been waiting for Sue to say something, but she could see that the woman was on a trip. Sue was lightly turning her shoulders back and forth and looked like she was hitting bumps in the road as she popped up and down on her toes.

Rose kept her eyes on Sue, but a little noise of evaporation made her turn her head back toward the cabin. There was no film in the air now blocking her view. She had been standing right next to the thing that kept her away from the kids. Extending her hand to where she had been ramming her fist, she felt nothing. When she realized the shield was gone, she sprinted straight toward the cabin.

Hutch was looking at Sue, but noticed Rose running quickly toward his home. He looked down to the ground and picked up a rock. Before Rose got to the stairs, Hutch wound up and whipped the stone straight at his friend. It spun and connected hard with Rose's skull. Her body kept taking steps, but then it fell straight down on the ground. Once she hit the dirt, Rose didn't move.

"Payback," said Hutch. He let a little smile come out.

He turned back to look at Sue and took a step toward her. Suddenly, he felt a rock hit his shoulder. It didn't hurt, but he looked down at the ground where the rock fell. He picked it up and looked in the direction of where the shell came from. It was an oyster. Another one came spinning toward him and connected directly between his eyes. A few little drops of blood began to flow from his forehead. Closing his eyes, he lost consciousness and fell straight down onto the dirt on his back.

Bryan stood up from behind a bush about twenty yards away from Hutch.

"Payback," said Bryan. He reached back and rezipped his fanny pack.

Walking toward his sister, he didn't say anything. He turned Hutch over onto his stomach and unzipped his fanny pack. Then he reached in and pulled out a few of his oyster cage zip ties. Reaching down, Bryan began to tie Hutch's hands together. Looking over toward Rose, he got back up and jogged over to her. He rolled her over and pulled her up into his arms.

Wiping the crumbled leaves and dirt from her face, he started talking to her softly. "Rose? You okay?"

She heard him . . . barely, but began opening her eyes. Not able to speak just yet, she lifted her hand up and touched the back of her head. She pulled it back and didn't see any blood on her hand. Then she turned her eyes up to Bryan.

"Hi, Bryan," she said slowly. "What's going on? Am I at your farm?"

"You just got hit in the head with a rock. Hutch threw it at you. Just stay calm. No need to get up yet," said Bryan.

She turned back and forth, taking in where she was.

He saw her panic. "It's okay. It looks like Sue is calling for backup."

After a moment, Rose touched her head again and looked like she was getting back to where she was.

"Where's Hutch?" she asked.

"I just tied him up after knocking him out." He smiled at Rose.

She let out a laugh. "Good. I did that to him yesterday. Just felt right."

Bryan let out a deep laugh.

Suddenly, the door to the cabin burst open, and Tim stepped onto the porch.

"I think we need some help," he said staring at Bryan.

His eyes turned toward Sue. For the first time, he saw two beings sharing one body. Facing him, he saw her standing on her tiptoes. She was looking up into the sky, but it wasn't just her. In thin and visible lines, he saw a fox within her. The fox was standing up in the same position. Its mouth and nose followed hers and extended beyond. The little furred ears rose from her skull. A tail came out from behind her and extended backward. It looked as if it was keeping her balanced.

"I knew it . . ." he said, "but—" he didn't finish.

Bryan said to Rose, "Are you okay?"

"I'll be fine," she said. "He needs help," she said as she looked onto the porch at Tim.

"Okay," said Bryan. He looked up at Tim.

She rubbed his arm for a moment. "It's good to see you, Bryan. Thank you."

He smiled at her, then rose to his feet and hopped up the stairs, following Tim into the cabin.

Rose sat up and crossed her legs, rubbing the welt on the back of her head.

Sue's two faces pointed upward, but she wasn't moving. She just aimed her focus toward the darkened sky. It was as if her noses pointed toward Orion's Belt. Her spirit was flowing through the thin black abyss, but those Three Sisters were quite far away. With her consciousness flying almost as fast as light speed, she held her gaze toward the stars. Part of her *was* moving—quite fast through the space between the earth and Orion's stars. She felt almost nothing, even though her spirit was rocketing faster than a spaceship. Before she reached the constellation, she felt a presence nearby. Looking around herself, she saw a tiny comet. It wasn't touching the atmosphere, but it had a little crispy tail on its end.

Keeping her focus on the belt of stars, she aimed her shoulders toward the comet. As she got closer, she saw the face of her son. She stopped thinking about the stars, her family, and her mission. Her mind focused only on seeing Greg. He was on the same trip as her. She thought, *He has a direct connection to them too.*

Sue opened her eyes and felt the consciousness hit her body at warp speed. The image of the fox surrounding her disappeared, and she fell down onto the wood chips. Immediately, she looked up into the sky.

Greg couldn't hear her, but she said, "I was looking for them ... but so are you. You'll find them." She let a smile hit her. "I knew you could do it."

Tim and Bryan ran past the bookcase and climbed down the stairs. They reached the lab and saw Mata lying down, unconscious.

Virg was sitting in the vessel with his finger on his temple. "Mom, you're okay," he said out loud. His eyes were still closed.

On the floor in front of Virg, Mata pushed himself up onto his knees with one arm. The kid didn't see him. He was focused on connecting with his mom.

The old man raised his gaze and looked directly at Tim and Bryan. They both took a step back—showing their fear. They saw the weak man shiver as he pushed up off the floor and rose to his feet. Lifting his hand up toward the two men, he closed his fist and whipped it up and away. In one swift moment, Tim and Bryan slammed into one another and got lifted up the stairs and thrown back into Mata's office.

Both bodies whipped straight into a wooden wall. The two men fell onto the floor and exhaled. A second later, the bookcase whipped itself closed.

"Shit," groaned Tim.

Rose entered the office and looked down at the two guys on the floor. "What just happened?"

"He woke up," muttered Bryan as he rubbed his back while lying on his side.

Rose touched her temple. "Virgil, I'm upstairs. I'm coming your way."

Virg was sitting on the floor with his eyes closed. He touched his temple as Rose heard, "I'm glad you're h—"

The voice stopped. Rose didn't hear him finish. She opened her eyes and saw the same vibrating see-through barrier she saw before.

Virg didn't hear his mom finish her response. He opened his eyes, seeing Mata crouched down and building a circular shield rim from the ceiling to the ground. Next, Virg watched the old man turn toward the vessel. Virg stood up quickly looked at the vessel, then ran toward it again. He had left Greg's unconscious body after his dad had knocked Mata out.

"Stop. He's mine," said Mata, raising his open hand toward Virg.

The look on the old man's face gave the boy a shudder. The man was crouched down and his face held a vicious snarl, showing his yellowed teeth. Virg took a step back and touched the back of his neck. He felt the sweat. All of a sudden, he had an idea. Virg's hand whipped up from his neck and over his head. Then he ripped it down and touched his chest. An unseeable ripple darted around his head. He turned and ran straight over to the vessel.

Hopping through the open door, Virg saw Greg still lying down with his eyes closed He wrapped his arms around his friend and drew the door closed with his mind. As he held his friend, Virg thought about the evening in the forest when he and Greg had thrown rocks at each other. They were laughing as the stones whipped right through their bodies. Virg smiled as he held his friend.

The door of the vessel whipped open. Virg looked into the angry eyes of the old man. Mata's hands were rested on his sides. Holding onto Greg, Virg saw the host raise his arm and whip it down toward him and his friend.

Nothing happened.

Stepping forward, Mata touched his temple and closed his eyes. Virg felt nothing. Opening his eyes, Mata looked frustrated. He took steps toward the boys and reached out to grab Greg's shirt. The old man's hand went straight through Greg and past Virg. He stubbed his fingers on the wall behind the two boys. Mata looked at his hand and then met Virg's eyes with his own.

He took a few steps back and out of the vessel, smiling at the boys. "You've learned well." Mata took a few steps back into the room. He sat down, crossed his legs, and closed his eyes.

Mata turned his attention to his pupil. Turning his head straight up, he cracked a tiny hole into the shield he had built.

His voice shot directly toward Hutch's mind. "Are you near yet?"

Lying on his side with his head in the grass, Hutch didn't budge. His arms and feet were tied together behind his back, but he began to wake up. He opened his eyes and saw pure darkness surrounding him. Smelling the wood chips and hearing the grasshoppers chirping, he turned his head toward a bit of light. Seeing the cabin, he remembered where he was.

Hutch closed his eyes and tried to contact Mata. *I'm* . . . He didn't know what to say. . . . *Where are you?* he thought.

Mata responded. *Your students are with me in the basement. They've learned quite a lot.*

I'm tied together, and I don't know where they—was all Mata heard.

Sue was standing right above Hutch. She saw his eyes open and then whipped her heel against the back of his head.

In the basement, Virg watched Mata pull his hand back down from the ceiling. The old man's thick beard turned toward a small shelf. He whipped his hand toward himself in a slight circular motion. Virg saw a little notebook and a pen meet the man's thin fingers. Mata turned his eyes away from the computer and began scribbling into the book.

"What are you learning?" asked Virg.

Mata looked into his eyes. "Touch his chest."

Virg looked down at the unconscious friend in his arms. He pulled his hand back from Greg's armpit and touched his chest.

"Feel a heartbeat?" asked Mata.

Virg hugged Greg and felt the heartbeat touch his hand.

"Yeah," said Virg.

Mata scribbled on the notebook.

"What are you writing?" asked Virg with a touch of anger.

Looking up from the notebook, Mata responded, "I'm writing about who survives. How do they do it?"

"Survives what? Your test that kills them?" shouted Virg.

"Each student makes their own choices. I want to see why and how. Greg's response was going fast. I gave him a sedative," said Mata.

"But why?"

"I need time to process the boy's memories. He's being held for research." He looked back down at his journal.

"You're not going to teach us?" Virg asked. Mata didn't look at him.

Virg's eyebrows crawled down, and his lips pressed together. He raised his hand from Greg's heart and pointed it at Mata. The rage inside of Virg forced him to squeeze his hand closed. It looked as if he was trying to choke the old man. Mata felt nothing. But the journal in his hands began to mush its pages together as his pen split into pieces. The pages were ripped and stained with the pen's ink as Virg squeezed his fist together.

The young hand, pointed at Mata, spun a little half circle. The journal's wet pages were ripped into tiny pieces. Virg quickly opened his hand, like he had with the watermelon. The flecks of ink and paper pieces burst apart and flew into Mata's eyes. The little explosion sent inked crumbs of pages up and under his wrinkly eyelids.

The old man screamed in pain and touched his face. As he did, Virg saw the rippling rim on the ceiling disappear.

Virg touched his temple and sent, *Mom, can you hear me?*

Greg floated toward a chain of stars and saw something in the corner of his eye. He didn't change his focus. Aiming his face at three bright stars, he asked, "Where am I going?"

Then he saw something nearby but couldn't tell what it was. *Who's up here?* he thought.

The floating object off to his left disappeared, and he felt his speed heighten. He blinked his eyes twice. Then he stopped midair. He saw nothing. No lights, no stars.

He closed his eyes and then heard, *You're here already?*

The sound wasn't from any specific place. It just bubbled through his ears from within.

The same voice sounded warm and sweet. *We felt a little ripple when you took off.*

Greg didn't recognize the voice, but it sounded a little like his mother. He didn't know where to look, but a little movement caught his attention. It almost looked as if the sound were coming from a black hole or a dark cloud. The humming ripple came into Greg's vision from nowhere. It was one of the stars he'd been floating toward. Still appearing millions of miles away, the star looked bigger in scale—about as tall and wide as Greg.

Feeling as if the star matched his size, Greg opened his arms wide just to compare himself to it. When he did, a little black hole popped open at the center of the star. Slowly, Greg saw the hole widen and thin out. It separated itself into microscopic lines. They almost disappeared into nothing, but Greg saw shapes it was making as the lines stayed attached to one another. In front of his eyes, the rims of the hole composed two faces in the same space. It looked like a woman and a fox were holding the same space.

Greg could see the light from the star coming straight through the nearly invisible pair of bodies floating in front of him. He almost felt like he was imagining the hybrid creature. Then skin tone filled the face of the human as the grey and orange colors slipped out to the tips of fur on the fox's face. They were different, but they blinked at the same time. It was like they were connected.

The same person? Greg asked silently.

In his head, he heard, *Same spirit.*

The woman and the fox both winked at him.

Greg thought, *Am I dead?*

Not yet, he heard. *You'd be nowhere if you were dead. This is the place where we rest.*

So, I'm alive?

You are alive here, and you're alive somewhere else, the woman and fox responded.

A moment passed. Greg heard nothing, not even a neutral midtone.

I didn't know you were ready. Did your mother tell you to visit? asked the binary.

Greg let a moment pass and then asked, *Who are you?*

The two faces smiled. The old woman's eyes wrinkled at the outer tips as the grey fox showed its teeth. She didn't make a noise, but moved her lips.

"I'm your grandmother," was what Greg thought he saw.

He heard nothing. There were no surfaces to bounce the sound. But he saw her speak those words. He wanted to suck in a breath, but then he realized that he wasn't breathing. He was floating in a universe, communicating with a spirit he was related to.

Smiling and showing his appreciation, he thought, *I saw Mom turn into a fox today.*

It's for protection. You can as well, thought the grandmother.

I have to protect my friend, thought Greg. *Maybe myself too.* He looked down beneath his body and saw almost nothing, just an endless sea of darkness. He turned his head back up toward his grandmother. *What's your name?* he asked.

Dot, she thought. He heard it.

Greg wanted to hug her, but he didn't move. He looked through her at the star for a moment.

How do I do it? he thought. *Mom never taught me. I just saw her do it.*

You smell everything—the rocks, the bugs, the old oil on a garaged antique—better than anyone else, right? asked the spirit.

You bet I do, thought Greg. *Is that a requirement?*

It shows me that you're ready, thought the grandmother.

How do you know? What if I'm not ready? asked Greg.

I don't know what will happen. Perhaps you'll disappear, thought the spirit. She turned back and the two sets of eyes met Greg's.

Will I get lost? Will I disappear? thought the boy.

Here, you must find out what you are, she thought to him.

But I don't know who I am.

If you know, you'll feel it. If you guess . . .

Greg finished her statement, *. . . incorrectly, then I can't return.*

You can, thought Dot, *but you won't return as who . . . or what you were.*

That statement made Greg feel lost. He closed his eyes.

You'll be both, he heard in his head. *Think about what you've been and what you can be.*

Greg looked back at Dot. *I believe in you*, was what he saw her lips say, but he didn't hear anything.

Follow me, he heard. His grandmother smiled and turned back toward the star. The colors on both of her faces disappeared as she turned. She began floating toward it. He could still see her in those rippling and reflecting lines that showed the borders of her body frames.

Follow me, Greg heard again in his head.

He leaned forward and began to float toward the old animal. She aimed directly at the star and moved toward it, but it didn't get any bigger. As they sped up, Greg noticed a little black hole in the middle of the star. The hole barely blocked the beams from the star, and then it spread wide incredibly fast. It passed Greg's peripheral vision and changed color. It went from pure darkness to a dark shade of grey.

Run! Greg heard in his head.

He whipped his legs back and forth. As he began, the color of the hole expanded vertically and whipped around his full eyesight within a millisecond. The color surrounding him split into shades of blue above and green below. He saw his grandmother, Dot, in front of him. She was running so fast. But she was only a fox. Her gait was swift and flowing like a natural hunter. He didn't even see her change.

She slowed herself down for one moment and reached Greg's side. The fox turned to him and thought, *How does it feel?*

How does what feel? he thought.

Around them, the blue colors above had grown soft-white splits and became the upper rim of the sky. Below, the green color broke into pieces and included yellow and brown shades between. It felt like they were flying to a familiar place.

I don't feel anything, thought Greg.

Remember how it feels, he heard. *It should feel natural.*

I feel fast, he thought.

Remember that, Dot responded.

He felt like he was flying, which he was, but he also felt like he was controlling the speed with his own body. He'd never moved so swiftly before. It felt natural.

Greg didn't look at his grandmother for a moment. His focus flowed down toward his hands. The hands he saw were almost almond-shaped. They were covered in fur, and whipping back and forth in such a strong rhythm. He smiled and turned his head back to his grandmother.

How did I learn this? thought Greg.

This isn't a skill. This is who you are, he heard.

When she smiled at him, he felt the blades of grass beneath him. He almost floated between his strikes on the ground.

Remember how it feels, he heard. *That's all you need.*

What if I need you? Can I howl? he thought.

Foxes can't howl, she thought. *Look at the stars. I'll be there.*

Thank you, thought Greg.

The fox disappeared beside him. The fade was almost instant, but Greg saw his grandmother's face appear for a moment, then vanish.

I'll see you again, he heard.

When Greg closed his eyes, he heard the sound of a rippling drain. It reminded him of lying in Virg's backyard with his mom. He coughed and opened his eyes. Around him was Virg's arm. Greg heard and saw Mata holding his face and screaming. He turned up to see Virg with his eyes closed.

69

Rose heard her son's voice. She jumped up and flung open the basement door. Hopping down the stairs, she hit the concrete floor and turned to see Mata holding his face. He drew his hands away and grabbed his cloak. Pulling it up and into his eyes, he rubbed it back and forth for a moment and opened them to see Rose at the foot of the stairs. Mata turned to see both boys with their eyes wide open.

Seeing Mata focusing on the kids, Rose whipped her hands toward him and circled her fingertips around his body. A visible barrier began to circle him as he continued touching his eyes. She saw him trying to wipe off the ink and paper stuck to his face.

"You're back," said Mata to Greg. "What did you find?"

Greg rolled forward a bit. He felt Virg's arm around his chest. Placing his hand on Virg's arm, he turned to look at his friend.

"I'm good," he told Virg.

"Thank goodness," said Virg. He smiled and let go.

Pulling the suction cords from his face and neck, Greg stood up. He held them and looked at Mata. "You have records from my experience, right?"

The weary-looking man looked at Greg and shook his head.

Greg turned his focus to Rose. "You don't have to," he said, pointing at her circling hand—finishing the rim around Mata.

"Oh yes, I do," she said.

Greg raised his open hand at Rose and then looked back at Mata. "You want to know where I went. You want to find out what my possibilities are ... what I can do?"

"That's what I want," said Mata.

"And that's *all* you want?" asked Greg.

"I want to see where you went. You came back on your own. How?"

Greg looked back at Virg's mom. "I'll show him."

She kept her hands pointed at Mata. "Show him what?"

Without speaking out loud, Greg answered Rose, *Something he's never done before.*

"Want to come with me?" Greg asked Mata.

The old man nodded. "Yes."

"Your body won't come with us, just your spirit. But I can show you," said Greg.

"I understand." Mata nodded.

Greg laid his hands on the ground in front of him. When he closed his eyes, his spine made a sound. A deep-pitched snap came from his lower back. His ribs looked as if they were ripping themselves apart. His hindquarters rose into a higher angle and curled as a tail reached out from his tailbone. His head went down as if he were looking at his stomach. Pulling his face back up into the vision of his spectators, his nose had projected out, and his teeth grew longer. Two seconds passed. Almost immediately, the alterations blurred into a total transformation. It sounded as if someone had kicked a heavy bag of dice, and it settled itself. The fur flowed out of his skin as the formation of his body altered completely.

Greg stood on four legs. The outer corners of his eyes touched a line of orange mane. Rolling from his eyes onto his shoulders, the bright pelt of orange flowed into his dark grey coat.

"Are you ready?" asked Greg.

Rose turned her eyes away from Mata and toward Greg. She let her hands fall to her sides. The ring around Mata gently whispered away.

"Almost," said Mata.

He raised his arm at Rose. She was lifted from the ground and slammed against the basement wall behind her. Mata swiveled his hand quickly. As he did, Rose's wrist snapped and angled down toward the ground. She let out a deep scream. Virg screamed, "Mom," as he stood up. She reached toward her broken wrist and tried to hold the bones together as they were.

Greg looked straight at Mata and leaped toward him. With his mouth open, he ripped through Mata's chest and snapped down his jaws on Mata's spirit. The aged man's body fell unconscious to the floor. However, invisibly to the Rose and Virg, his spirit rose from his body as the fox held his sternum in its teeth. In the basement, it looked like the fox's body had passed out on Mata's stomach.

As the two spirits left and their bodies fell down into unconsciousness, Rose fell off the wall back onto the floor. She winced as she hit the cement and closed her eyes hard—sucking in a deep breath.

Virg ran toward her and asked, "What happened?"

"He broke my wrist," she said, ". . . to protect himself. I hope that Greg knows what he's doing."

"He looks like he does," said Virg. "Do you think there are painkillers in this place? I'll run up and grab a pill for you," he said. He turned and ran up the stairs. ". . . if I can find one."

Rose shook her head, but let her son hurry away. She looked down at her wrist and took in another deep breath. It felt like the bones were shattered into dust. Raising her gaze, she watched the grey fox lie unconscious on the wrinkled man's body. Mata's face looked like a Rorschach psychological test. The inkblots spread across his eyes and faded onto his forehead and nose. She looked back down at Greg.

"I hope you know what you're doing," she said, looking at the fox. Then she took in the fact that he could turn into an animal. He found out how to do all of this in a week. "Perhaps you do. You know more than me."

She began to feel the blood flowing into her wrist. The pain came on fast. She closed her eyes and lay down on the floor.

70

Greg's jaws held onto Mata's spirit until they passed through the atmosphere of the planet. Their speed increased and almost felt like a dream to Mata. He looked at the fox and their eyes met. Greg released his jaws from the man's spirit and opened some space between them.

Moving his lips, Mata shortly realized that there was no verbal way to communicate. He heard nothing. As he closed his eyes, he shot through the empty space. Reaching out to Greg mentally, he asked, *Where are we going?*

We're going to meet someone, responded Greg.

Is this where my students have gone?

I don't know.

Who did you find? We're going to meet someone, are we not? asked Mata.

Yes, thought Greg—*my family.*

Mata smiled. *I've found who I've been looking for.*

Greg didn't say anything.

Mata continued . . . *Someone whose family has power, knowledge, and history. Endless existence.*

Greg hadn't thought about it before. He met his grandmother. But was she dead? He'd never met her on Earth before. She told him that *he* wasn't dead. But he didn't even consider if the woman had passed or still lived. It all happened so fast that he didn't even consider it. He thought that he was taking Mata to a place that the man couldn't return from. Perhaps he was wrong. Maybe this was just what his teacher had been looking for.

Where did your students go when they disappeared? asked Greg.

Similar to you, a few of my students have left and then returned. Mata's head went up as he looked into the angle they were headed. He continued, *When they did return, I would ask what they saw. Some were dishonest or didn't describe what I saw on their memory report. One said that he met his family . . . But no one returned with a skill such as yours.* Mata's eyes came back down to look at Greg. *You're a shape-shifter. I've never known anyone like you before.*

Neither have I, thought Greg.

Is your family just like you? Can they teach me?

I'm just like them. Maybe I'll teach you.

Mata smiled.

The two kept barreling toward Orion's Belt. A consistent silence almost made their eardrums ring a single note. It was almost a note that they imagined. They both needed something.

Mata looked down at Greg. *How did you become a fox?*

My grandmother showed me how.

How did she show you?

Greg thought for a moment. Then he shared with Mata, *She asked me what I felt—then asked me to follow it.*

Mata nodded at the fox. He slowly closed his eyes and then turned his face up toward the stars. Greg did the same. When they both shut their eyes, they both felt the deep pull of their gravity. The speed increased profoundly. Both men felt it and opened their eyes at the same time. When they did, they only saw pure darkness. Greg felt his pupils dilate. Then they pulled back in when a bright light revealed a star that felt close.

The fresh fox turned to the old man beside him. He saw Mata open his mouth. The old man looked afraid for a moment, then the corners of his mouth pulled back. Greg saw the bottom tips of Mata's beard float in various directions. The ancient man looked as if he was being given a gift. He looked so thankful. With the floating beard and widened eyes, Mata looked like he was excited—just like a squirrel seeing a free chicken finger.

Greg turned his eyes back to the star. The hybrid faces of Dot rose from a dark point in the middle of the belt's beacon. It looked the same as it did before. Her presence was felt more than seen for a moment.

The two guests thought they saw lines being released from the black freckle on the star. The rim of her skulls began to ripple and appear almost invisibly.

My spirit, shared Greg.

The two faces of Dot appeared slowly in front of the men.

Nice to see you, the two men heard.

You're a shape-shifter, thought Mata. *How do you do that?*

Dot didn't respond. She turned her gaze to her grandson.

He wants what we have. He's been trying to follow others, but no one has led him this far, thought Greg.

She kept her eyes on Greg. It looked like she was trying to read his expression. Then she slowly turned her gaze toward Mata.

What are you? Mata heard in his head. Dot curled her head to the side just a bit. She looked like a fox waiting for a movement or an action it could read.

Mata didn't respond. He was rolling his mind around the question.

To help specify the question, Dot asked him, *Do you want to return as who you were?*

No. I want more. I want to be something else too, shared Mata.

Dot looked at the little fox for a moment. Then she turned her focus back to the man.

What do you like to eat? the two men heard.

To eat? thought Mata.

Dot looked curious. *I don't know your family. Not everyone is like us.* She turned her chin toward Greg, but kept her eyes on Mata.

Closing his eyes, Mata pulled a breath in through his nose. He found no scents. Then he just imagined a pleasing taste in his mouth. Simple, natural, and satisfying, his home in the forest rolled back into his memory.

Walnuts, he thought. *It's been a long time since I've had one. I never find them in Maine.*

Can you smell them? Dot thought.

I remember the smell, shared Mata.

Dot and the fox closed their eyes.

In front of Mata, a walnut appeared. He looked at the hybrid woman for a signal. *Is this a test?* he thought.

Mata reached out, grabbed it, and ripped the shell from the nut. As he pried open the shell, his hands began to turn brown and sharp. He bit into the nutmeat as a long and puffy tail whipped down from his backside. It popped back up and smacked his back. The fresh squirrel looked back and forth at the foxes and quickly shoved the walnut meat into his mouth.

He found what he'd been looking for, thought Dot into Greg's consciousness.

The two faces of Dot grew more expansive and filled with their natural colors. She became more visible and floated toward Mata's tiny, furry body.

It's time, Greg heard.

He watched his grandmother's mouth snag Mata's scruff coat behind his neck. Dot and the squirrel began to float away from him. He turned his body and extended his nose toward them. Closing his eyes, Greg felt his body swiftly slip down toward his human body on Earth.

71

Tim held Rose's arm and hand while Virg lightly wrapped it in some thick paper he found. She was sitting on the floor with her back against the basement wall. Her son had found rubber bands in the upstairs office and lightly bound them around the paper on her arm. The two men faced her, but she was looking between their shoulders at the unconscious bodies behind them.

All of a sudden, Mata's body began to twitch. Rose saw the movement. It made her widen her nostrils and pull in a deep breath.

"Virgil, he's coming back," said Rose as she raised her other hand toward Mata.

Her son spun around in the direction she pointed. Virg saw the grey beard shake quickly. All of a sudden, a sound made Virg step back. It sounded like a split of Mata's lower spine. The crack and disintegration sound repeated itself. Tim held Rose's broken wrist but turned toward the strange sounds.

The three of them watched and heard the transformation of Mata's body. As his bones snapped and the air in his body whistled out of him, the unconscious old man shrank in front of them. His disintegration let the fox's ribs and face lower down onto the floor beside him.

Mata's shoes lay empty as his legs were pulled up and through his clothing. His head was pulled down toward his chest and got sucked into his robe.

As the man disappeared, Virg turned to Rose and asked, "Mom, what's happening?"

Rose kept her eyes on the movement and barely shook her head, as if saying, "Who knows?"

Suddenly, the sounds ended. The movement stopped. But it looked like there was something small left under Mata's robe. Then they saw a movement. Something tiny was scurrying under the robe. Near Mata's shoes, a little squirrel popped out from under his pant leg. It turned its head back and forth and stopped when it saw the fox. It stopped and didn't move, as if the stillness made it invisible.

Then Greg opened one of his eyes. The squirrel turned away and immediately looked for an exit. It saw the stairs and quickly shot itself toward them.

No one could move fast enough to catch it. It hopped up to the floor above and jumped through the open door.

All of a sudden, the people in the basement heard a snap. It sounded like something in the office whipped against Mata's desk.

"I got it!" they heard coming from upstairs.

Next, Bryan stepped down the stairs holding a fishing net's handle with his other hand pinching the top of the opening.

"I found this in his tool room. Thought I'd get him with this." He looked down at the squirrel twitching in the net. "Is this him? I didn't think he'd be so tiny."

Virg stood up and scrunched his nose, looking at the squirrel.

"That's him," said Greg.

Virg turned to look at him and saw his friend wearing a little fur coat. He ran toward Greg and hugged him. Virg pulled in a breath and smelled the scent of the fur.

Looking over Virg's shoulder, Greg asked his dad, "Where's Mom? Is she okay?"

Tim looked at Rose and watched her close her eyes and hold onto her wrist. Pulling his hands away, he turned and climbed the stairs quickly. Rose reached out to Sue, mentally.

Hi, honey, you okay out there?

When his dad ran up the stairs, Greg looked straight at Rose. He saw the purple skin surrounding her wrist and the swelling that puffed it out.

"Oh, I'm so sorry," he said. "I had no idea . . ."

"It's okay," responded Rose almost in a whisper. She couldn't push her breath. Rose just needed to keep herself calm to deal with the pain. "You did good," she let out, and then smiled briefly at him. She closed her eyes again.

Greg's clothing was lying in the vessel he had jumped out of. He went straight in to grab them. To change, he closed the door quickly and threw them back on. Picking up the fur coat from the floor, he thought, *This is me*. He felt the fur with his hands. Then it combed through his vessels softly as it vanished in his hands.

Upstairs, Tim got to the porch of the cabin and couldn't see through the darkness.

"I'm good! I've got Hutch tied up. He's unconscious," Sue shouted toward the cabin. She had heard the message that Rose sent.

Tim ran back to the stairs and shouted down to the basement, "She's good. Hutch is tied up."

Virg saw the pain his mom was feeling through her facial expressions. She was trying to breathe deeply, and her nostrils were getting really wide when she sucked in a breath. Greg opened the door to the vessel, stepped out, and saw Virg's face.

Virg turned to Greg. "Let's help get her upstairs."

Greg nodded. He and Virg helped lift her up from the floor. She could walk, but Virg kept his arm around her torso just to keep her balanced. Greg walked up the stairs behind them, just in case they tripped.

Slow and tired, the wanderers walked out onto the porch together. Bryan was still pinching the net closed as the little squirrel shivered. They were lit from behind on the porch.

Sue saw them and shouted, "Over here."

The crew paced slowly through the dark path until their pupils dilated. The moon and the stars were still spilling light through the trees. Greg saw his mother and ran over to hug her. She squeezed him and kissed the top of his head. Looking over Greg's shoulder, she saw Rose holding her wrist.

"Are you okay?" Sue asked.

"I'll be okay," Rose said as she crouched near Hutch. She looked up at Sue. "But he won't."

Rose rested her broken wrist on her thigh, then reached out with her other hand to pinch Hutch's ear. She pulled it enough to wake him up.

"Hi, friend. Remember when you knocked me out?"

Hutch opened his eyes and winced as his ear was getting pulled. When Rose let go, he looked around and couldn't see anything. Slowly, his pupils widened in the darkness. One at a time, he noticed each member of the two families surrounding him. He didn't see Mata. Suddenly, a man he didn't recognize took a step toward his feet. The stranger, lit from the side by the cabin's lights, was holding a metal wand with a circular rim with a net. At the bottom, a little squirrel was wrapped in the net.

"What happened?" asked Hutch.

"Our sons protected us," said Rose. "Your boss didn't." Rose pointed her finger at the squirrel in the net.

Hutch looked at the squirrel, then rested his head in the dirt, and looked up into the sky.

"I shouldn't have listened to you," said Rose. "When you landed in PA, you told me he had changed. You weren't happy here." She paused for a moment. "But you came to us because Mata asked you to."

Hutch didn't look at Rose but responded, "I did."

"When you and I had people come to the camp, we'd help them. They'd learn about themselves. It hasn't been that way for a long time, right?"

"Not long. But yes, it changed. I wanted to help people. But I saw Mata lose it, and . . . I wanted to help him."

"You weren't helping him get better. You were helping his obsession," said Rose. Then she winced and sat back on the ground as she grabbed her wrist.

"Mom, we've gotta get you to a hospital," said Virg. He was staring at the swelling and the deep purple surrounding her wrist.

Tim touched her shoulder lightly. "Let's do what we did to get here."

Rose opened her eyes and looked at Hutch. "He can't help us."

"I can," said Greg. "How do you think we got here?" he said, looking at Virg.

Looking at Sue, Rose said, "Leave him tied up." Turning her gaze to Hutch, she added, "Don't follow us."

"Follow me," Hutch heard. The man at his feet looked down at him. "I can see that you're strong. Know anything about oysters?"

Hutch looked at Bryan. "You need help?"

"Well, I'm gonna need a squirrel babysitter. I've got a wooden box with a screen on it. Ya wanna help grab some twigs and leaves?" Bryan raised the net that held the squirrel.

Hutch didn't respond.

"I mean, I could use a hand at the farm too," added Bryan.

A smile crept onto Hutch's face. "Okay."

Taking their focus from the conversation, everyone turned toward Rose when they heard her groan again. She sucked a heavy breath through her teeth.

Virg heard his mother's pain. He reached down to grab a stone. Throwing it up toward the trees, he closed his eyes. Virg remembered his backyard and hummed into a groan as the stone stopped rising and began to tumble down. He raised his hand, and the rock stopped falling. It started to spin and light up with a light blue color. The cool tone reflected off of the nearby faces. Virg lowered his hand toward the ground as a cone opened from the top of it. He stopped his movement when the stone was an inch from the dirt.

He opened his eyes and looked at Rose. "Let's go."

She turned her head toward Bryan. "You're good?"

"I'm not worried," said the uncle.

Rose looked at Tim. He looked at Sue, and they both reached down to grab her armpits and raise her into a stance. They helped her enter the blue cone and followed.

Virg looked at Bryan. "Can we come back?"

"I hope so. I want you to write down your oyster recipe. Yours is better than mine," said Bryan.

"Will do," said Virg.

Bryan turned his eyes to Greg.

"Thank you," said Greg. He hugged his uncle, backed away, and stepped into the cone.

Virg smiled at Bryan and took a step. He disappeared. The light from the stone softened, then went out.

Bryan looked back down at Hutch. "Want me to snip that cable on your wrists?"

Hutch closed his eyes again. "Nah. I can do it. Just leave me be for a little while."

"Okay," said Bryan. He shrugged his shoulders for a moment. "Suit yourself. Me and nut-addict will see you tomorrow. If you don't show up, I'll cut ya out of those cuffs after your nap."

Bryan put the handle of the net on his shoulder, then shifted the pinch from hand to hand and pulled out his compass. He took a look, turned, and followed the arrow back east.

72

Doug took Rose to the hospital once she got back. The doctors reset her wrist bones and cast her arm. It was late, so they offered her a room for the night. Rose fell asleep almost instantly. Doug sat on the chair beside her bed and crashed into a long snore.

From his backyard, Virg followed the Murphys back to their house and got ready for bed with Greg. The boys felt lucky that Sue had brought them ice cream sandwiches. Eventually, they were forced to brush their teeth. The boys finished and came back downstairs to say good night.

When Tim saw them, he turned off his TV. Then he turned to them and said, "You guys don't have to go to school tomorrow . . . or Monday. But see how you feel when you wake up. I can take you in late on Monday if you're up for it."

The boys thanked him and then looked at Sue. Greg walked toward her and opened his arms for a hug.

He looked up at her with a smile and said, "Mom, you lied to me. I didn't know we were animals."

"I didn't lie. But omission is natural if you can't even grasp the concept," said Sue.

"Yeah, I wouldn't have understood . . . or believed you," said Virg.

Sue and her son chuckled at his statement as they hugged.

"Let's go get some sleep, all right?" said Sue.

The family walked up the stairs together and parted ways. In Greg's room, he hopped into his bed as Virg crouched down and lay on the trundle. The boys didn't turn the lights out. Looking at one another, they both took a deep breath and finally let it out.

Virg asked, "Are you ready to go back to school?"

Chuckling briefly, Greg said, "Probs not. But I'm ready to focus on something else."

"Found what you're looking for?"

Greg thought for a moment. Then let out, "I mean, since the night Hutch visited us, I've wanted to know what I saw in my head. But really ... I wanted to know who I was. Now, I do. I know who I am and *what* I am."

"Yeah, you smell better these days, right? You've always wanted to file those whiffs."

Greg didn't laugh. His mind was wandering.

"Virg, I never figured out what happened to Mata's previous students ... or experiments," said Greg.

"They got outta there, right?" suggested Virg.

"I'm guessing that they did," said Greg. "I guess we'll see."

He reached up and pulled the chain hanging from his lamp. It went dark, and the boys closed their eyes.

Rose woke up in her hospital bed. Her brow was dripping sweat. She raised her left hand and felt the weight of the cast. Putting it back down, she grabbed her sheets with her right hand and wiped the sweat off her face.

Her husband lay in his chair with his mouth open. Softly, a grumbling snore was sputtering from his mouth. A little plastic light on the wall lit his face. She smiled to herself. The door to her room was open. She heard a few quiet voices out in the hallway. It sounded like nurses were speaking with one another about their plans. She looked at the darkened TV screen and saw a dark, mirrored image of herself.

Hutch said something that crept back into her head.

In her head, she heard herself say it again: *You have frozen children under your cabin?*

Hutch had responded, *Only people who've agreed to see what's possible on the other side ... What they can achieve.*

Rose shivered while she was sitting up. The pain in her wrist made her lie back down on her hospital bed. She closed her eyes and thought about reaching out to Sue. Remembering that Sue couldn't respond mentally, she thought about the kids. *They didn't hear Hutch say it*, she thought to herself.

She remembered Hutch facing her, saying, "*He's letting their spirit leave if they want to . . . if they want to see what's on the other side . . . what's possible. If they do, and they don't return, he freezes their bodies.*"

Her heart was beating fast. She could feel the blood flowing through her wrist back and forth. It hurt. She opened her eyes and tried to breathe slowly.

The boys aren't ready, she thought. Looking down at her wrist, she thought, *I'm not ready*.

The man was lying on the dirt. His hands were still tied behind his back. Even though he had been trying to pull off the zip ties, the plastic ribbons still felt tight. Hutch was squeezing his fists hard, pushing the tendons on his wrists against the zip ties repeatedly. He took breaks, and then he squeezed his hands a few times.

He stopped for a moment. Taking a breath, Hutch coned his hands—pushing his pinky palm toward the base of his thumb. Slowly, he dragged the skin on his hand across the sharp plastic rim and out of the zip tie. Some of his skin had been ripped off, but he didn't mind. Hutch pulled the knot out on his neck bandana and tied it around one of his hands.

Walking toward the river, he looked up at the sky. He knew exactly where he was headed. Crouching down and cupping his left hand near the river, he let the stream rush over and clean his wound. Leaning down closer to the water, Hutch opened his mouth and filled his cheeks with a stream of cold water. Standing back up, he swished the water back and forth over his teeth. He swallowed and turned to look down the river.

Turning back toward the cabin, he looked at the front door. It was still open. He walked onto the porch and stopped moving when he reached the door frame. There were no lights on inside the old scout shack. Calmly, his hand reached in and grabbed the doorknob. For a moment, he almost pulled it shut.

Hutch raised his gaze into Mata's office. He stepped inside the cabin and made his way toward the bookcase, where he pulled the spine of a book from the cabinet. When he did, the doorway to the basement opened. Stepping down the stairs, Hutch flicked his hand open and faced up. He twitched his other hand over it and a light blue ball appeared hovering in his hand. The light helped him see where he was headed.

Walking through the basement, he passed the vessel, the computer, and the pages lying disheveled across the floor. Then he stopped at the far wall. Hutch looked under Mata's small desk. Searching with his hand, he stopped letting his fingers crawl when they met a little button. He punched it once. A moment later, a gear squeaked. Then the desk slowly lowered itself down into the floor. A horizontal doorway opened across the bottom of the wall.

Hutch bowed down to walk through the open, low rectangle in the wall. He reached his foot out to rest on the top shelf of the desk. He took another step up and into the room that had just opened.

It was dark in the room. Hutch raised his lit palm and looked down at the far side of the room. There was a metal receptacle box hanging on the wall. He walked over, opened the door, and looked at the buttons and their coverings. None of the button levers pointed to the "off" section.

The man looked down at the wires connected to the box. He followed their routes and turned his lit palm toward the open room. All six wires led to seven-foot-long ice chests. They hummed lightly. The humming freezer sounds were barely noticeable. He smiled and made his way back. He returned past the desk, up the stairs, and into the office.

When he caught a breeze from outside, Hutch closed the door behind himself. Turning around, he paced back down the porch stairs and toward the river. Then he stopped and lay down in the grass. The sound of the river's movements—pops and ripples—across the stones calmed his mind.

He stood up and followed the river down toward the oyster farm.

Hutch said to himself, "I'll see you soon, boss."

Printed in the USA
CPSIA information can be obtained
at www.ICGtesting.com
JSHW022327031224
74722JS00004B/6